FALLEN CREST HIGH

THE 1ST IN THE FALLEN CREST SERIES

NYT & USA Bestselling Author
TIJAN

Interior Formatting by Elaine York/Allusion Graphics, LLC/
Publishing & Book Formatting
www.allusiongraphics.com

CHAPTER ONE

It was a Friday night, two in the morning, and my two best friends were shrieking in drunken laughter behind me. I sighed as I pulled into the gas station. My little Corolla had been chugging near empty for the last few miles. And I'll admit that I'd been worried we would've broken down on the side of the road, not for my car's sake, for my sake. I didn't know if I could've handled walking with Lydia and Jessica. And on cue, Lydia rammed her elbow in the back of my head.

"Oh, Sam!" Muffled laughter. "I'm sorry. I didn't mean—" She dissolved in laughter once more.

Jessica wrapped her hands around the passenger seat and leaned forward. "Can we go to another party?"

"Puh-leaze?"

"No." I unclipped my seat belt and started to get out.

They scrambled out, or tried. Lydia tripped and was nearly clocked by my side mirror. Jessica tumbled after and leaned her weight on Lydia's shoulders so she wouldn't fall while she sidestepped over her.

What a friend.

"Why not? It's our last Friday night before school. Come on, Sam!"

Lydia stood and straightened out her skirt and top. When her boobs were back in place and the skirt barely covered her ass, she turned her pleading eyes on me too. "It'll be fun. Come on! I know where a public party is."

Jessica whirled to her. "Oh! That sounds awesome."

They bounced together. Both wore flowing skirts, tight tops, and brown curls that flung everywhere. When one hit me in the face, I swatted it away.

"I'm taking you guys home. You're both drunk."

"Come on, you're such a loser tonight," Lydia moaned.

Jessica frowned and flipped her hair over her shoulder. "Yeah, you are. What's going on with you?"

"Did you and Jeffrey have a fight?" Lydia's eyebrows wiggled up and down. She peeled over in laughter once more.

I gave them my polite fuck off smile and each rolled their eyes. Then Lydia lifted her nose and got a whiff of gas station pizza. Her stomach growled and off they went. As I watched them skip together, holding hands, and giggling over the fact they were drunk, I leaned back against my car.

While the gas was guzzling into my car, I heard Jessica's question again. Was something wrong with me? And I sighed. Only my whole world had changed that afternoon. I could see my mother's face when I had left Jessica's house and went home for the afternoon. We'd all been so happy to go out that night. Even me. Yes, Jeffrey was usually an ass, but a small part of me had wondered if tonight was going to be the night we slept together. He'd been my boyfriend for three years now. He was nice, well, he was a douche at times, but he still seemed to like me. And I liked him too, but while my mother had been happy jumping from bed to bed before she got knocked up with me, I didn't want to end up like that. So I had taken everything slow with Jeff, but when I got home to get ready for the party that night, little butterflies were in my stomach.

They died and burned in flames when I opened my front door. Boxes upon boxes were lined inside and in the middle of them sat my mother. A bottle of wine was half empty beside her as she sat in her silk bathrobe. Tears coated her face, but when she saw me a bright smile was forced out.

"Hey, honey." Hiccup. "How are you?"

I let the door go and it slammed shut behind me. "What happened?"

"Oh." She gave me a dismissive wave. "Nothing. You don't need to worry about a thing."

"Worry about what?"

"We're going to be fine."

I hadn't moved. My purse still hung from my arm. "Mom, what happened?" Boxes were everywhere, even in the kitchen. I saw two empty wine bottles in the sink.

"You and me, honey. We're going to be just fine."

"Where's dad?"

Her hands froze. She'd been taping up a box, but she sucked in her breath and held still.

"Mom?"

She finished the rest of her wine and she almost fell backwards from the effort. When she set the bottle aside, I asked again, "Mom, what's going on?"

She started sobbing. "Oh honey. I'm so sorry about this. I really am."

"Mom! What's going on?"

"Ifellinlovewithsomeoneelsean dwe'releavingyourfather." She hiccupped again and swiped at some of her tears.

"What?"

She took a deep breath. "I...we're leaving your father."

My insides screamed at her. My hands curled into fists and I wanted to launch myself at her. I wanted to pound the hell out of her, but I didn't do any of that. Instead, I collapsed on one of the couches and I listened to everything she said. She'd fallen in love with someone else. She wanted to be with him. She told dad, he kicked us out, and tomorrow we were going to move in with this boyfriend of hers.

"Who?"

"Huh?" She lifted tear-stained eyes to me.

"Who?"

A soft sob and she whispered, "James Kade."

"James Kade?"

She nodded and wiped her arm over her face. "He has two boys your age, honey. You might know them."

Know them? Everyone knew them. Mason and Logan Kade. While they were rich, their dad owned five of the factories that our town thrived on, they chose to go to public school. Everyone knew the Kade brothers. They could've gone to the private school, where most of the rich kids went, or where I went because my dad was the football coach, but they'd shaken everything up when they chose public school.

And now I was going to be living with them?

As I watched my mom, who sobbed as if she'd been the one cheated on, something shriveled up inside of me. I would never be like my mother. Never. And sorry, Jeff, but that meant he wasn't going to be getting laid by me for a very very long time.

However, after I had spent most of the afternoon and evening packing my things, he wasn't excited to hear my change of plans when Lydia and Jessica waited for me to go to the party that night. In fact, he'd been a jerk. Not surprising. A few choice curse words, a few beers guzzled, and he wiped his mouth clean of me.

"I'll get someone better, bitch. You're not the only hot chick here." And off he went. His jeans rode low, a beer in hand, and his hair gelled into badass spikes.

I rolled my eyes and went in search for my friends.

Heaven help me, but Jeff would be back. I was at the point where I wasn't sure if I cared or not.

An Escalade wheeled into the slot beside mine. At first I didn't pay attention, lost in my world-ending daydreams, but when someone shouted all my attention snapped back to reality.

Four boys spilled out of the vehicle and two passed by me.

I sucked in my breath.

"Fuck that, man. Let's go to Molly's instead," one boy laughed as he hung on his friend. He threw his head back and laughed on a carefree note. His brown curls danced and he seemed invigorated. "You'll get pussy there. Promise."

He laughed another maniacal laugh before the two disappeared inside.

My hands clenched the gas nozzle tightly and I couldn't take my eyes off of him.

Logan Kade, my soon-to-be-roommate. While I watched through the window, he laughed at something his friend said. Lydia and Jessica saw who was in the other aisle and quickly went to flirt with them. The friend looked interested, but Logan skimmed a bored eye over them and went back for something more inside the store.

I hadn't seen the Kade brothers up close, not in a long time, but I'd heard plenty about them. Logan was a junior, like me. Mason was a year older. Both were good looking and Mason was rumored to be six foot one with a muscular build. He played defensive lineman for a reason on his football team. Logan had the leaner build, but he was an inch shorter.

I snorted to myself. I couldn't believe I even knew these details. As I cursed my friends inside for their gossiping ways, I glanced back at the Escalade and froze once more. Two green eyes stared back at me.

Mason had been filling up his vehicle and watching me the whole time.

I swallowed painfully and was barely aware that my gas was done. I couldn't look away from him.

Logan was handsome. There was no doubt about that, but he had nothing against his older brother. Now I understood why so many gossiped and whispered about the Kade brothers. The hairs on the back of my neck stood straight up and my eyes were locked with his in some sort of battle.

I couldn't look away. I just knew that.

His friend rounded the vehicle and leaned beside him. Both watched me and I saw the grin come to his friend. He crossed his feet and looked like he was at the movies, popcorn and all.

Then he said something and Mason smirked at me.

"Mase, dude. Candy flavored condoms." Logan leapt across the lot and did a small dance when he handed a box to his brother.

I knew I shouldn't have been watching, but I couldn't stop myself. I was riveted by both brothers. Logan was bobbing his head in rhythm with the music that blared from the gas station's speakers while Mason hadn't taken his eyes from mine.

That's when I knew without a doubt that he knew who I was.

I sucked in my breath and my knees trembled for a moment. What'd I do? Did I do something? Then I remembered my mom sitting in between all those boxes, tears down her face, and an empty bottle of wine beside her.

Fuck them. And fuck their dad.

My mom wasn't a saint. I knew that for sure, but she'd been with my dad for the last seventeen years. Now she cheated? Now she decided we should move in with her new boyfriend and his family?

Fuck them all.

My eyes hardened. Mason's narrowed. And I sneered at him before I went inside to pay. When I came back out, Lydia and Jessica were still in the bathroom; Mason passed me to pay inside. He wore a black leather jacket over a black shirt and jeans. His black hair was cut short and his eyes held mine in some form of trance as he passed by me. His jacket rubbed against me, he passed so close, and we both turned to watch the other.

My heart faltered for a moment.

The same hatred I felt for him was in his eyes.

Fuck him.

I lifted my lip to sneer at him and I knew he read the message because he narrowed his eyes, but shouldered inside the store.

I sighed and went to my car to wait. Logan and their friends were inside the Escalade, laughing about something. Then the door pinged its exit and I stiffened. I knew who'd be coming again.

I looked, I couldn't help it, and met Mason's gaze as he neared me. He paused close to my car and looked like he was going to stop.

I lifted my head up, ready for whatever he was going to lay on me, but two cars screeched to a halt not far from us.

His eyes snapped up. "What the hell?"

"Hey losers!" a guy yelled and cursed at them as he ran from the car with something smoking in his hand.

"Oh hell!"

"Mason!"

Logan and their friends were out of the car in an instant. Mason rushed past me and I stood there, shocked, as all four dragged the guys from the other cars. Logan grabbed the smoking thing from the guy's hand and gave it to his brother. Mason took it and threw it in the first car. And the rest of the doors were flung open. Guys from that car poured out. Then another smoking thing was produced and Logan flung it into the other car.

Their two friends were still punching some of the other guys. Mason and Logan started punching the rest. It wasn't long before the cars were filling up with smoke and I got the first whiff of fire.

"Oh no," I muttered to myself and dashed to the store. After I flung open the door, I screamed, "Lydia, Jessica, get out here now!"

They rushed from the back section and stared, dumbfounded at me. "Sam, what's going on?"

I latched onto Lydia's arm and dragged her out with me. "We're leaving. Now."

Jessica followed behind, but braked in the middle of the lot. Her eyes were wide as she took in the sight before her.

I shoved Lydia inside the car and twisted around. "Get lost! The cars are going to explode."

Mason and Logan's friends heard me and stopped. They grabbed Logan first, but all of them dragged Mason away from the guy he was punching. Fury lit up his face, but when Logan said something in his ear, he turned and leapt for his Escalade. As he climbed inside, his eyes met mine for a second.

I shrugged and shoved Jessica behind Lydia inside mine. Then I hurried into my car and we were out of there in a flash.

Everything happened so fast.

Lydia and Jessica were bowled over in the back. "I can't believe that happened!"

"What did happen?"

"Logan Kade is so hot."

Jessica snorted. "Logan is? Didn't you see Mason? I'd do him in a heartbeat."

Lydia moaned. "Let me go to bed with my dreams right now. Why can't they go to our school?"

Jessica grinned again. "I heard it's because public school is tougher. They didn't want a pansy school."

Lydia fanned herself. "Whatever. I don't care. I'm transferring."

Then Jessica grew serious. "You think that'll be on the news?"

Lydia lifted her shoulders. "All I know is, how are we supposed to go home now? Sam, please, please, please can we go to another party? I bet I know where they're going."

I dropped them off at the party and left for home.

CHAPTER TWO

My weekend was spent packing and moving. The Kade house wasn't a house at all. It was a mansion, one that had pillars on their front patio. A fountain was in the foyer with a spiral staircase behind. Then there was the kitchen. It looked like it could've been built for a restaurant, with a chef that went with it. His name was Mousteff and he had a twitchy mustache and meaty hands. My mom introduced us, but it was with a hand waving in the air as if she was the first lady giving a tour. When we moved beyond the kitchen I glanced back. Moustefff was sharpening a meat cleaver. He winked before I turned the corner.

As for the actual moving, James Kade paid for a moving company, but he and his sons still helped with some things. Mason and Logan moved past me, grabbed boxes, and took them inside. I didn't look at them. They didn't look at me. And not once did anybody say a thing. The only two who talked were my mother and James. He was a tall, slender man with graying white hair. There was a kindness in his blue eyes, but he never met my gaze, not even when he walked behind my mother with a hand at the small of her back.

"Analise," he murmured in her ear. "I have friends who've invited us out for drinks tonight."

She gave him a bright smile and whirled around, her hands raised in a clap. "Oh, that'd be wonderful. I'm excited to meet some of your friends."

"Mitchell and Malaya Smith. He owns Smith Telephones, the local company."

As they turned a corner, I heard my mother ask in a breathless voice, "Do you think Malaya would be interested in meeting for tea one afternoon? I'd love to meet some of the other ladies."

I snorted to myself, like my mother would be welcomed among that club. Then my phone vibrated in my pocket. Lydia wanted to go to a party that night. Jessica sent me another text not long after. Then Jeff sent me one an hour later with an apology for his behavior.

I ignored them all and slid down the wall in my room. It was covered with boxes, a bed that five people could've slept in, and two couches on the far side. I had my own apartment. Maybe I wouldn't have to see anybody any longer.

Here's hoping.

I ventured out once during that night. My stomach had started to cramp so I figured I needed something to calm it down. As I tried to find my way to the kitchen a large television boomed from inside some room. The local news was on and I heard the news anchor report on a local car bombing incident.

"Two cars were on fire outside a gas station in the town of Fallen Crest. Each of them was owned by two teenage boys who attend Roussou High School. This incident is believed to be one of many in a long list of vandalisms between two schools, Fallen Crest Public High School and Roussou High School. Their football teams are arch enemies. An upcoming game is scheduled between the two and officials fear this is only the beginning of what seems to be an ongoing rivalry between the two schools. Sidney?"

Logan stood up from a couch and turned off the television. As he turned, he saw me in the hallway. I skirted ahead, but not before I noticed another head on the couch beside him. When I found the hallway for the kitchen, I glanced back. Mason and Logan both walked the opposite way, dressed in low riding jeans and tee shirts.

That was my only human interaction for the rest of the night; even Mousteff was gone. When Sunday dawned bright and early, I rolled over and checked my phone. Lydia and Jessica had called throughout the night. Jeff tried a few times, but he stopped texting at five that morning. My phone rang again and I saw it was nine in the morning. I figured Jessica and Lydia never went home if they were still trying so I turned it off, then yawned as I sat up.

I headed home that afternoon to make sure we'd gotten everything we'd need, or my mom would need. I knew she'd send me back and forth for any little item and it would've been the end of the world until she'd gotten it. Not that I would've minded, but her timing was never at decent hours.

When I had checked the upstairs and entered the kitchen, I heard the front door open.

"Dad?"

He paused in the doorway. He wore his coach's jacket for the football team, red and black. "Hey, honey…"

I gestured around. "I'm just making sure we didn't forget anything."

He grimaced. "You mean if Analise forgot anything."

"Yeah…"

He winced again and I bit my lip.

"Uh, dad…You weren't around this weekend."

"Yeah." He ran a hand over his face. "Your mother thought that would be for the best, if I cleared out. She didn't want any awkward run-ins."

"Oh."

His smile was painful. "Do you like your new home?"

"My new home?" I frowned. "This is still my home."

He looked away.

"Isn't it?"

His jaw clenched. "Your mother feels it's best if you stay with her, permanently."

"But…what? You're still my dad."

"I'll get to see you at school, honey."

"Dad!"

"I should get going. We're starting our Sunday practices. FC Public is going to be tough this Friday. We play them, you know, your new…"

I narrowed my eyes and spat out, "My new what? Roommates? My mom's boyfriend's sons? They aren't anything to me."

"Yes, well, it never hurt to make friends, Samantha."

I flinched at the sound of my full name. It was only used when I had disappointed him, once in seventeen years.

"I'll see you at school, honey." He moved past, and then hesitated for a moment. His hand patted my shoulder before he left. When the door shut, I released a ragged breath and sagged in a chair.

My life was screwed.

When I returned to the mausoleum, my mom was in the back patio area. I had to pass by to get to the stairs that were right next to my room. She saw me and called out, "Hi, honey. What'd you do today?"

James sat with her, but when I stepped outside he stood. "You can have my seat, Samantha."

I knew my mouth twisted into a scowl, but he waved a hand to the chair and gave me a polite smile before he disappeared inside.

Analise beamed at me. "Sit, sit. Let's chat."

I sat and glared.

She pushed a cup to me. "James didn't touch his coffee. You can have it. I know you like those coffee drinks."

It went ignored. "I went home today."

"Honey, this is your new home." She frowned and glanced towards the ocean. A divider wall sectioned off their backyard, but a small trail led from behind a door in the divider to the beach. "Isn't it beautiful here?"

"I saw dad."

She picked up her cup. "I just love tea."

"Since when?"

"Oh, Samantha. You're too funny sometimes. I've always liked tea."

"You've been a caffeine addict since I was little."

"Yes, well, I'm trying to wean myself from that. Tea is much better for you."

"And is James better for you too?"

She turned and set the cup down.

"Is he, mom?"

"So you saw your father?" Her voice hardened. "He wasn't supposed to be there."

"At his own house?"

"I asked him to stay away. I knew you'd go back today to make sure we had remembered everything."

"You didn't want me to see him?"

"It's for the best, Samantha."

"For who? You? He's my father."

She patted my arm once and leaned back, tea back in hand. "You'll see him at school. Your tuition is still going to be paid."

"Why wouldn't it?"

"We're getting a divorce, honey. You do know that certain things in life change during these times."

"Yeah," I bit out. "Like families."

The corner of her mouth curved down and she set the tea down. Her hands were gentle as she placed it back on the cup holder. "I am your family, Samantha. It'll always be you and me, but now I have James. You should get to know Mason and Logan. They're very nice boys."

"And you've gotten to know them?"

"I have." She watched me. "A few times."

"When?" My stomach churned inside. My hands clasped onto the back of my seat.

"Over the last year, I've had dinner with them."

"Over the last year?"

"I did tell you that I left your father. We've been struggling for a long time, Sam. I know you noticed, though you never say anything. You should talk more, honey. It's healthier for you."

"You cheated on dad for a year?"

She sighed. "I didn't cheat—"

"You said a year. You've been cheating on dad for a year?" I leaned forward in the chair. "Did dad know?"

She rolled her eyes. "Like your father was a saint. It takes two to keep a marriage. David hasn't been around for years. You might want to ask him why he's been so absent too. Or didn't you notice?"

"He coaches a football team. He's gone a lot."

"Football season doesn't last a year, honey. You might want to wake up if you're going to start casting blame." Her voice was like whiplash.

I shoved back the chair. "It takes long hours, sometimes two practices a night. They're already starting their Sunday practices. They have training that lasts all year, mom. It's a private school. Their football program is a big deal there. I know all the hours it takes. Jeff's been on the team for three years."

She sighed again. "You and that Jeffrey boy, he isn't good for you either, Sam. His father's a mechanic and his mother works as a cashier at the grocery store. There isn't a future with him."

I reared back. "I'm not marrying him."

"I know you, Samantha. You've been dating him since before you were freshmen. And even I noticed that he cheats on you."

A cruel smile came to me. "You're right, mom. You would notice. Cheaters can always tell when they've met another cheater. Congrats on being in that special club."

I sailed inside, but stopped short. Mason and Logan both sat at a table. They watched me. I watched them and then I darted upstairs. It didn't take me long to change clothes and grab my iPod. When I went back downstairs, they were gone. It didn't matter. Nothing mattered.

I hit the driveway running and kept going. Running had always been an escape for me and it still was. I didn't return until it'd grown dark and my body could barely stay upright. When I walked back inside, the whole place was silent. Eerie. My footsteps echoed in the hallways.

When I went past the dining room, my mom spoke from the table, "You've taken up running again?"

I took out my headphones and stood there. Sweat dripped off of me and I wondered if she'd make some comment how I dirtied the floor.

She sighed to herself and stood. "I guess I shouldn't be surprised."

I mopped some of the sweat off my face.

"I had dinner with James and the boys. They asked about you, but I told them you were upset with me. And do me a favor, Sam, eat something tonight? I don't want to start worrying that your eating disorder is back."

When she went down a hall, I saluted her back and then extended my middle finger. Then I rolled my eyes and went to my room. After I showered, I sat down and turned my phone on. It beeped continuously. Jessica and Lydia were at a bonfire. There was no word from Jeff. Then I shut it back off and crawled in bed.

My first day of the school year was going to be exhausting. I knew the whole year would be. The weekend had just started it off with a bang.

CHAPTER THREE

It was the first day back and I was a junior this year. Before last weekend happened, I'd been ecstatic for the year. We were juniors, one year away from being seniors. Then IT happened and I had no idea how the day would go.

My dad was their varsity football coach. He was beloved by many rich fathers and even a few mothers. The guys respected him. And my mother had left him high and dry. As I walked towards my locker, I wasn't sure what reception I'd get. If people would sympathize with me or label me a whore, like mother like daughter and so on. But when a few of the football captains rushed past me without a second glance, I wondered if no one knew...

Then Jeffrey fell against the locker beside me. His hair was filled with mousse and he gave me a crooked grin.

Oh, those dimples, how they used to work on me.

He grunted. "You no showed all weekend. What's up with that?"

"After that great farewell you gave me on Friday?" I reached inside for my books. "I have no idea what you mean."

He rolled his eyes. "Come on, Sam. I texted you a ton and I apologized. You didn't text me back at all."

I shrugged.

"Jess and Lydia were hurt. They thought you'd show."

I shrugged again.

He sighed, "What's with the act, huh? What's wrong with you?"

My eyes snapped to his. "What are you talking about?"

"You've been weird since Friday. It's like someone died in your family or something. What's going on?"

"How was the party and bonfire?"

He sighed again. "Whatever. They were fine."

"Did you find another hot chick there?"

His jaw stiffened. "You're playing that card?"

"I'm playing a card? Why don't you tell which one it is because I'm not aware of the hand you've dealt me."

He pushed off from the locker, rolled his eyes, and strutted away.

I didn't do anything. I didn't curse, sigh, or feel like crying. What I did do was roll back my shoulders and put my bag in the locker. Another day, another adventure. I took two steps towards my English class before Jessica and Lydia bounded up to me, literally.

We all wore uniforms, but their skirts barely covered the bottom of their ass cheeks. A lot of girls had the same. My friends had their shirts unbuttoned to show off their cleavage, complete with the red and black lacy bras each of them wore.

"Hey…"

Lydia readjusted her shirt so more of her right boob showed. "You totally were absent this entire weekend. What's up with that?"

Jessica nodded with a solemn look on her. "We were worried about you."

"Really?" I arched my eyebrow up.

They both nodded, and then someone walked past us and down the hallway. Their expressions changed immediately. They went from seriousness to exuberance.

Jessica clamped onto my arm and leaned forward. "Ashley DeCortts and Adam Quinn broke up this weekend."

Lydia nodded. "We heard that Ashley slept with one of the Kade brothers. Adam found out and dumped her. It was real and public, at Kara's bonfire last night. I was front and center."

"She was."

"You were?"

"I was. It was awesome. Adam was all grrr and 'I thought we meant something to you,' and she was all, 'I did, but a girl can only do what a girl can do.' It was awesome. Totally. I wish that happened at every bonfire."

"You should've been there."

"Yeah," I deadpanned. "I should've been."

"So where were you?" Jessica asked, but both of their faces turned to blank masks as they stared at me.

"What?"

"Where were you? We went to your house, but no one was there. Lincoln said that your dad was at some conference over the weekend. Did you go with?"

"I had family commitments this weekend." I lifted my shoulders. "I wasn't supposed to say anything."

Lydia leaned closer. "It's football confidential?"

"Yeah."

Jessica frowned. "Really?"

"Really. My dad would get mad. I wasn't even supposed to say anything."

"Oh." Lydia looked at Jessica. "They do play Public this week. He might've gone to a conference for more pointers. That team is good, really good."

I clenched my jaw and my fingers tightened around my books. "What are you talking about?"

"Mason Kade." Lydia gave me a 'duh' look. "He's the star of that team. I heard Adam Quinn talking to Mark Decraw that he thought Kade can go pro some day. I'm not sure about Logan, but they were mainly focused on Mason. I think he's scared of him. He's the one that tackles, right? He can sack Adam the whole game, right?"

Jessica and I frowned at her.

Lydia rolled her eyes. "That's what I heard anyway, that Adam's scared of Mason Kade."

My fingers clenched tighter around the books and my knuckles went white. I was so sick of hearing about the Kade brothers, either of them. And I tried to remember if it'd always been like this, but I had never cared.

I was grateful when my class started and I tried to avoid Lydia and Jess the rest of the day. Bonus, no one else seemed interested in me. I didn't pick up any extra buzz about my dad so I was safe to bet that he hadn't spilled the beans. Everybody was more interested in the Double A break up, Ashley and Adam.

The week passed uneventfully. Lydia informed me on Wednesday that the Double A team was still broken up and Adam had been spotted by Nancy Burgess's locker that morning. Jessica made a disgusted sound and stomped away. I thought I heard a few curse words, but wasn't sure. Probably.

And I met Jeff for pizza that night. He liked the buffet, I liked the salad bar.

"You need a ride home?" he asked as we went back to the parking lot.

"Nope. I drove, remember?"

A look passed over him. "Yeah, about that—why did you drive? I usually pick you up."

I shrugged as we came to my car. "I'm going to Lydia's after this. It makes sense."

"Oh. Okay…" His frown never left and then he leaned in for a kiss.

I breathed out as our lips touched and felt his hand cup my cheek. His lips were soft and he didn't apply pressure. As his thumb stroked my cheek, I let out a soft moan.

Jeff smiled and rested his forehead against mine. "That was nice, huh?"

"We've been doing this for three years. It should feel nice."

He chuckled and kissed me again. This time he was more insistent, harder. I leaned back against my car and Jeff pressed against me. His hand tilted my head up and his kiss grew more demanding. When his tongue swept in, I pulled away.

"What?"

"What do you mean 'what'?" I pushed him back. "I don't want to make out on the street."

He rolled his eyes. "What do you expect? Is this why you drove here, so you wouldn't have to kiss me?"

"What are you talking about?"

"Come on, Sam. We used to be hot and heavy, but the last couple months you're ice cold."

"I didn't think you cared. You've been so distracted lately." I bit my tongue.

His mouth clamped shut. "What are you talking about?"

I took in the storm in his eyes, how his jaw was clenched and the stiffness of his shoulders. And something gave way in me. This wasn't a fight I wanted right now. At least, this wasn't the fight that I wanted.

I glanced away. "Nothing. It doesn't matter."

He touched the back of my elbow. "Hey, what doesn't matter?"

I didn't look back, but some tension left me at the softness of his voice.

"You think I'm cheating on you?"

I met his gaze now. "It's nothing, Jeff. I've got a lot on my mind."

"Like what?"

"Like how I need to get going. My mom's been on a rampage about family time. The longer I'm at Lydia's the later I'll be. You know what she's like."

He still frowned, but nodded. "Yeah, okay. You want me to pick you up for school tomorrow?"

"I'm good. I've got a car."

"That's not the point, Sam."

"I know." I didn't care.

He sighed and turned away. "You're kinda being a bitch, you know."

As I watched him go, I stood there. I knew I was being a bitch, that wasn't the problem. Then I sighed when my phone vibrated. Lydia wanted me to hurry so I got in the car and drove over.

When I got there, she was bouncing like a rabbit on meth. She squealed as she pulled me to her room. "Jessica told me today that Adam Quinn asked about you!"

My insides snapped to attention. "What?"

"Yeah." She grinned and nodded her head up and down. "Can you believe it?"

I watched as some drool slipped down her chin. "Why would he ask about me?"

"Who cares! He did. Aren't you excited?"

"What did he say?"

"Are you kidding me? I think he asked how you were doing. You want a soda?"

"You've had enough for both of us."

"Huh?" She stopped bouncing and stared at me.

"Nothing."

Then she grabbed my arm again. "Get excited, Samantha. You can dump Jeff, finally."

"Dump him? Why?"

She snorted and threw herself backward on the bed. As she landed with her arms spread out, she rolled her eyes. "Like you really care about the guy. When was the last time you went out with him?"

"Tonight. We just had dinner."

She stopped short and jerked upright. "Really?"

"Yeah." I sat at her desk. "Why?"

"You and Jeff had dinner tonight? As in right before you came here?"

"What's with the twenty questions? Yes. I had dinner. With my boyfriend. Who I have been dating for three years."

"Oh." Her mouth shut, though her eyes were still wide.

"I get interrogated for this?" I stood up and started for the door.

"Don't go!" she called out and caught my arm. Then she sat me down with a serious expression on her face. "So if Adam Quinn asked you out, you'd say...?"

"No. I have a boyfriend." I frowned. "What's going on with you? You're acting like Jeff and I broke up."

She lifted her shoulders weakly. "Well...you two don't act together."

"That's crap. What's really going on? You always ask me about Jeff, if I've seen him at the parties or whatever." I folded my arms over my chest.

Then I stared her down. Hard.

Lydia swallowed. "I, just, I, nothing. Adam Quinn would make a way better boyfriend than Jeff. He was faithful to Ashley when they were together. She wasn't, but that's beside the point. Come on, you can't turn Adam Quinn down because of Jeff."

"Uh, yeah I can."

"Jeff cheats on you every weekend." She jumped to her feet.

"So I've heard." I grabbed my bag and headed out the door.

"Wait, Sam. Don't go like this. I'm sorry."

"For what?" I whirled around to her.

She stopped an inch from running into me and her mouth opened, closed, and then opened again. Her eyes looked to the ceiling. "Uh, for...hoping you'll dump Jeff because he's a scumbag?"

"Thanks, Lydia." I headed for my car. When I shut the door behind me, she had stopped following. I saw she had the phone to her ear so I turned mine off. Jess would be calling in a minute, after she'd heard the whole story from Lydia first.

I didn't care. As I drove away, I sat back. I really didn't care, about any of it. And I knew in the back of my mind, far far in the back of my mind, that this wasn't the healthiest feeling. But then again, I didn't care.

When I walked inside, it was dark. No one was around, but a plate was left on the kitchen table with a sandwich wrapped in saran wrap. My name was posted next to it, but I bypassed it and headed upstairs for my running gear. Five minutes later and I was back out the door. This time, I only stayed away an hour. However, sweat still ran down me as I went into the kitchen for a glass of water.

I sat at the kitchen table to finish it because I knew I'd need a refill before I headed upstairs to shower and crawl in bed for the night.

I was almost done when the door burst open and laughter filled the room. The smell of perfume and booze followed behind. I slumped further down in my chair and watched when Mason came into the kitchen. He turned for the fridge and stuck his head inside. Logan came next with a blonde wrapped around his arm. Her top barely hung on her and it exposed the side of her breast.

He laughed and pressed her back against a counter. As his head sunk to her neck, Mason glanced up and stopped. He saw me in the darkness.

Neither of us said a thing. Neither of us looked away.

The girl shrieked when Logan nuzzled further down her top.

Then he drew back, grinning. "Mase, man, you think I should bang her here? You think Momma-Wannabe would be upset? My stuff next to her teacups? Oh, a sandwich." He unwrapped the one left for me and ate it in three bites. When he was done, he gulped down a glass of water Mason held out for him and then turned back for the girl.

She started laughing again, followed by a quick moan.

Mason leaned against the sink. He never broke eye contact with me and he folded his arms over his chest. "You can do her wherever you want."

Logan tickled the underside of her breast and the girl giggled. Then she looked up, panting. Her eyes roamed up and down Mason as she asked in a husky voice, "You want in, Mason? You can have me too."

Logan burst out laughing, and then clamped a hand on her arm. "I think not. I don't share like that. You're mine for the night, girl."

When he dragged her away, she reached out and trailed a finger across the top of Mason's bicep. As they went up the stairs, she was still squealing and it wasn't long before he told her to shut up or

Momma Wannabe might wake up and no one would get laid that night. Then it was quiet in the kitchen.

I hadn't moved a muscle, but I did now. I pushed back the chair, crossed to the fridge and refilled my glass. The hair on the back of my neck stood up. With stiff movements, I turned, ignored the scalding burn from his gaze, and headed upstairs. As I got to my room, I shut the door behind me and let loose a long breath of relief.

I was surprised to find my fingers were frozen around my glass. It took a few moments before I was able to loosen them back up.

CHAPTER FOUR

Friday night came and went. I stayed in, but Fallen Crest Public won against Fallen Crest Academy by a landslide, 32 to seven. I knew my dad would be heartbroken, but I still felt as if he had kicked me out of the house. My sympathy scale was in the negatives. The only high point was that Jessica and Lydia were both so hyped about the parties; they forgot to harass me into going. Jeff did the same, though I knew he was always sore after a loss. Even if he didn't play since he's second string, I knew he'd be grumpier than normal.

Apparently, my new roommates were the highlights of the game. Mason sacked Adam seventy percent of the time and Logan ran in for three of the touchdowns. I got all that from Lydia's text messages.

"Honey, are you going out tonight?" My mom found me the next afternoon. She came into my room and took a seat on one of the couches with a cup of tea in her hand.

I was in the bathroom and had just gotten out of the shower. When I saw her curl her legs underneath and tuck them away, as if she were sitting with the Queen of England, I snorted in disbelief. Then I let loose the towel I had wrapped around me and walked into the room.

"Samantha!" she gasped and glanced at the door. It'd been left open.

I stood and perused my closet. Ignoring the shiver that ran over my naked body, I pulled out a pair of black skinny jeans with a black tank top.

"Honey, I wish you'd put some clothes on."

I pulled out a black lacy bra and a pair of black thongs.

She sighed behind me. "I suppose this is you trying to get back at me, hmmm?" She took a sip. "I should expect this. Malaya said this is what teenagers do when they've been displaced from their homes, especially girls. I can only wonder what else you have in store for me."

I threw the thong to the side and pulled the jeans on. Then I glanced in the mirror. Analise's mouth twisted in a frown, but she took another sip.

"Are you sleeping with that Jeffrey? Is this why you're dressing like some…"

I turned around, slowly. "Like what, mother?"

Her lips shut for a moment and then she exhaled, "Like a whore."

One of my eyebrows shot up. "You think I'm a whore?"

She set the tea cup aside and smoothed out her skirt. "I think you're dressing like one because you want to get back at me. You never used to dress like that."

"Yeah, well, I used to have a family." I ducked my head and pulled the top on. When it fit like a glove, just above my jeans, I leaned forward to inspect my face in the mirror. I wasn't anything great, long black hair, thin with a runner's build, and eyes that were bleak.

"Samantha, honey, I worry about you. You're so beautiful and I know that other boys can tell."

I looked back at her. "What are you talking about?"

"Jeffrey." Her hand raised in a helpless motion. "I worry that you're wasting your high school years on him. He is clearly not good for you. Look at you; you're thin as a rail."

My mouth twisted.

"He obviously cheats on you. Even your friends have told me this."

"You've talked to Jessica and Lydia?"

"Of course, I have. They're your friends."

"When?"

"What?"

"When did you talk to them?"

"Oh, I don't know, maybe a month ago."

As a breath of relief left me, I turned back to the mirror and did up my hair in some braid. Jessica taught me how to do it so I tried. It didn't look the same, but it'd do. It was swept up and some strands fell free. I knew Lydia would croon in approval. Then I toed on my sandals.

"Where are you going, Samantha?"

I'd been prepared to walk out and ignore whatever else she was going to say, hell, I would've enjoyed it, but her soft voice made me stop. I cursed inside as I turned. "I'm going to some party with Lydia and Jessica."

"Oh."

I wanted to roll my eyes. I wanted so badly. "Why?" I didn't.

"I think Mason and Logan are going to a friend's get together. Maybe you could go with them? You can't keep ignoring them."

Her idea of a 'get together' was their idea of a 200+ house party. I wasn't sure if my mom chose to be dense or if this came from the new relationship.

"Sure, mom. I'll get right on that."

She sighed, "Honey, at least try for me, please. It's important to me if you get along with them."

I stopped what I was doing and watched her in the mirror. If I hadn't known her all my life, I would've wavered at the broken look on her face. It was like she'd lost her puppy. Then I cursed myself. I knew I was wavering anyway.

"I'll see if Jess and Lydia know about any Public parties. I'm sure Mason and Logan will be there."

She brightened and flashed me a smile before she picked up her tea again. "It means a lot to me, honey." Then she pressed a kiss to my forehead and sashayed out of my room with her skirt swinging around her hips.

I'd been sucker punched by my own mother. She'd gotten me to fold.

Then I looked in the mirror again and changed everything. The black was thrown to the side and instead I pulled on a pair of pink skintight pants with a flesh-colored sparkly top that molded to my body. I grinned as I turned and headed out. My mom would've had a heart attack if she'd seen the new outfit.

Instead, I was content with Jessica and Lydia's reactions.

Jessica frowned and twisted her shirt in her hands. Lydia's eyes popped out and her mouth kept opening and closing like a fish. Finally she remarked, "You look good, Sam."

"Hot damn," one guy remarked as he and his friends moved past.

Another one gave me a wolf whistle while a third asked if he could feel me up. The last one asked if I'd go to dinner, but I grinned until I felt a pair of hands snake around my waist. I was pulled back against a body and a pair of lips started on my neck. I heard the chuckle and relaxed, slightly.

Jeff whispered in my ear, "Can we please go somewhere? You walked in that door and I got hard."

"Sweet nothings. That's what I look forward to from you." I patted his cheek and walked away.

He groaned behind, but followed. His hand curved around my waist and he pulled me close again. "Seriously, Sam. I've got an itch that I really want you to scratch."

At that moment, a guy burst through the crowd and landed beside us, against the counter. He glanced over with glazed eyes, but threw his head back and started howling. Some guys' answered and Jeff's hand tightened on my arm. When it increased and became painful I started to say something, but the crowd parted at that moment.

My words died in my throat.

Mason and Logan walked through the crowd with a few of their friends beside them. They strode forward as if they owned the party, which it felt like they did. It was a Public party. Jeff and I were next to the drinks so they stopped close. Logan skimmed an eye over us and grinned, but turned and grabbed a bottle. He started pouring drinks while Mason took one that was offered from someone. His eyes were locked with mine.

After a moment, Jeff nudged me. "You know Kade?"

"No," I clipped out and shoved through the crowd.

The group howled again as Jeff followed behind.

Lydia found us in a back room later on. She gripped a cup in her hand with a drunken haze over her eyes. "Did you see them?"

Jeff groaned. He had a hand curled around my waist and he'd been kissing my neck for the last hour. He pulled away and fell back against the couch now.

"Them?"

"Mason and Logan Kade."

My frown was quick. I couldn't block it.

Jeff noticed. "You sure you don't know them?"

"I don't need to know them to not like them."

Lydia swooned, "Mason is so gorgeous. Maybe I should tell them I was at the gas station that night. I bet he'd talk to me then. Maybe I will." She looked hopeful as she scanned the room.

"Pretty sure he went upstairs half an hour ago with some blonde," Jeff clipped out.

She frowned. "Oh."

"Where's Jessica?"

The excitement burst forth again as Lydia turned back. "She's in the back playing pool with Logan Kade."

"Really?"

Jeff shifted beside me on the couch. "I'm going to get something to drink. Sam?"

I held out my cup, but he left without it.

As I frowned after him, Lydia took his seat. "She's not playing with just him, but a bunch of others. I'm sure he doesn't even notice her, but maybe. Maybe they'll start to date. Could you imagine that? Being Logan Kade's girlfriend?"

"He's not that great, Lydia."

She frowned. Some of the drunken haze tried to clear up. "What do you mean? Have you talked to him?" Then she nodded to herself. "That'd make sense. You were out there. You saw the whole thing. Did they threaten you? You've never said a word about the car bombs. People don't know that you witnessed the whole thing. I bet they told you to shut up about it, didn't they?"

I gripped her arm tight.

She kept on, "Can you imagine being threatened by them? I'd have a hard time trying not to jump in their arms. Mason's so dreamy…"

Some people near us started to pay attention to the conversation. I saw their glances and as she rambled on, I felt more and more attention. My hand squeezed harder. "Lydia."

"Huh?" She tried again to focus on me.

"Shut up." I had a death grip on her now.

She gave me a silly smile. "Or did you get it on with them? I wouldn't blame you, especially with Jeff. Who cares about him, right?"

I snapped and stood up. "Would you give it a rest? They're not that great and my love life, if it is one or not, isn't your business."

When I whirled to stalk out of the room, I stopped short. Logan stood in the doorway with a cup in hand and a pool stick in the other. Some of his friends were around, but Jessica had a hand on his arm. She frowned when she saw me, but glanced up to Logan with a small smile on her lips.

Logan narrowed his eyes with his mouth in a firm line. I watched how his hands gripped the cup tighter. And then I stormed out. I didn't care if I pissed him off or not. Hell, I would've enjoyed that.

I tried to head for the front door, but there were so many people. I kept getting lost and so I headed up the stairs. It was empty and it was somewhere I could gather my sanity again. However, as I pushed into a bedroom, I hadn't expected to find Jeff in the bed with another girl.

He glanced over his shoulder with a scowl, but his eyes went wide. The girl twisted out from underneath him and tried to pull down her black tube top. Lipstick was smeared over both of their faces.

I gutted out in a laugh, "Are you kidding me?"

"Sam, wait." He scrambled off the bed. I turned to bolt, but he caught my arm in the hallway. "Wait. Please."

"I'm not even surprised." I spoke in a calm voice. My heart was racing. I knew my face must've been red because I felt my blood boiling. My arms, legs, knees, everything trembled and shook, but my voice sounded like I had asked if it was raining.

He paused and watched me.

"Isn't this the cliché ending to us?"

"Ending?" His Adam's apple moved up and down.

"Yeah," I laughed outright now and swept a hand towards the bedroom. "You were making out with another girl."

He narrowed his eyes and pulled up his pants.

A door opened behind him. It was quiet, so quiet that if I hadn't seen it, I wouldn't have sensed his presence. Mason came out with a skinny blonde on his arm. She looked unable to stand, but I saw his hand grip underneath her legs and he lifted her against him. She hung on around his neck and leaned a head against his chest with a contented smile on her face. He narrowed his eyes when he saw me.

Then Jeff broke the spell. "I know it looks bad."

"Looks bad?" I spat out. "Are you dense?"

"Yeah, well, you had me going so hard all night." He gestured at me. "Look at you, Sam. You're hot, hella hot. And I get nothing. I've been your boyfriend for three years. It's taken me a damn year and half to see your tits."

My eyes turned to a glare.

He ran a hand through his haphazard hair. "I'll change, Sam. I've gotta. I love you."

"You don't love me." I said it quietly.

"Three years. That's gotta mean something. Please, Sam."

"You don't love me."

He looked ready to argue, then something flashed over his face, and a snarl came out instead. "Why don't you get off your high horse? Fine, we're done. I'm not even going to kiss your ass. It hasn't done me a damn thing in the three years we've been dating or the two it took me to get you. I can be half the nice guy I am to you and I've got no problem getting panties to drop."

I geared myself.

He spat out, "You're just some high class bitch that ain't high class, Sam."

Mason lifted his head. His eyes remained narrowed to slits, but no other reaction came from him. His face was a blank mask.

I tore my eyes from his and found my soon to be ex boyfriend's in a glower. "Don't you want to know who I've been with? You don't have any inkling?"

"I know that you've been cheating on me. Even my mother knew."

"That makes you look like a fool." A cruel smirk came to him. He stuck his hands in his pockets and a prideful look came over him.

"Maybe. Or maybe I didn't give a crap."

He grew quiet. "Yeah, you're screwed up, Sam. I've never known another girl who'd stay with a guy if he cheated the whole time."

My heart skipped a beat. The whole time?

He laughed again. The sound sent shivers up my spine. "You've got no clue who with, do you? You've got piss poor taste in friends."

"Friends?" I wrung out. My eyes gleamed with an ugly feeling.

He was so smug. "Jess has been giving it to me for two years now."

"Jess."

"And Lydia knew. She's known the whole time. She's helped us cover it up too."

"Lydia knew?" I parroted like a fool.

Jeff chuckled and shook his head. "I'd be up here with her now if she wasn't so obsessed with Kade. Ever since the car bombing, it's all either of them talk about. I told her to get straight. The Kade brothers are going down. They set fire to those cars. The cops have to know—"

Mason started to step forward.

I cried out, "Shut up. You don't know a thing about it!"

Jeff frowned.

"I was there. I was outside and you don't know anything. Jessica and Lydia were inside. They didn't see a thing. They were wasted that night."

Mason moved back a step. The girl on his arm looked up with concern, but settled back against his chest a moment later.

"It don't matter. They'll get what's coming to them." His mouth curled up in an ugly smile.

I slapped him. When it was done, his head snapped back and he stared at me, his eyes wide. The air had grown thick, tense. I found it hard to breathe. Then I turned and left. This time I found the front door and I drove off. The hand I slapped him with shook even after I got home and crawled in bed. I tucked it under me and tried to go to sleep.

I never fell asleep that night.

CHAPTER FIVE

When the morning came, I rolled out of bed and went for a run. I didn't last long, four or five miles, but I slowed to a walk and I didn't return home till noon. When I did, I was surprised to find a bunch of cars parked in the driveway and on the road. Then I rounded to the back patio and saw a ton of people by the pool area. The door in the divider wall was open and more people were on the beach.

The Kades were having a party. Joy.

Then I checked my phone after I had showered and ate a few crackers. Lydia and Jessica both wanted to know where I'd gone from the party and why I hadn't said goodbye. I turned my phone back off. There was no one else I cared about who would call.

As I headed to the kitchen, Mousteff was there in his chef's white apron and he wore a hat too. He brandished a cutting knife and gestured to the table in front of him.

"Sit," he grunted.

I sat.

He sliced up some meat and put it between two pieces of homemade bread. A parsley and tomato were placed on the side before he set the plate in front of me. A knife and fork were plunked beside it, along with a glass of water.

"Eat," he grunted again.

An apple was cut up next. He put the bowl beside me, turned his back, and left. I didn't see him for the rest of the day.

Later in the afternoon, I headed back to the kitchen for some water. When I went past the patio, I peeked out again and saw the group hadn't left. A bonfire had been lit on the beach and most of the people were around that now. Loud bass blared through the windows. It got louder when a door opened and closed.

I didn't glance up, but Mason stepped next to me. He reached around me and pulled out a pitcher. When he moved back to pull out a glass, I let out my breath. I hadn't known I'd been holding it.

I didn't turn around. No way.

Suddenly the door flew open again. Logan's voice carried through as he howled and ran through the house. Then a car door was slammed shut in the front of the house. When I looked over I saw Mason watching through the kitchen window. A small smile was on his face. He looked softer, just a bit.

My stomach kicked a notch.

I spread a hand against it and frowned. What the hell was I doing?

Then the front door was thrown open and we heard Logan holler, "Finally! Dude!"

Male laughter responded. When Mason left the kitchen window, I took his place and saw Logan trying to dry hump some guy. I didn't recognize him, but they had so many friends. He was tall, over six feet and his jet black hair matched with Mason's. The two almost looked like twins. While he went out to greet the new arrival, both gave each other a hug with a smile on their faces. It was so genuine, that I clenched my hands around my glass and turned away.

I didn't come out of my room for the rest of the day. When I did, it was past ten in the evening. The party was still full force outside by the beach. No one was beside the pool and I was surprised by that. Then I checked my phone and regretted it. Lydia sent me a text: **Jeff said you guys broke up. CALL ME!**

I turned it off and put on a movie.

My body was tired so I did nothing on Sunday, except for the little homework I already had. I heard my mom's voice once when I ventured downstairs, but Mousteff told me, "Mr. and Other are gone for day. Cooking in cities is better than cooking at home. No one cares. You eat." And he dumped a bowl of soup in front of me with some crackers on the side. When he went back to the kitchen I heard him muttering to himself.

It was late when I heard Mason and Logan in the hallway. A third male's voice was with them so I assumed that it was the guy from before.

"Nah, man. That's her room. You're parked in the east wing." Logan's voice carried down the hall.

Two doors shut after that and it was silent for the rest of the night.

When I left for school, Mousteff stuck his hand out as I passed by. He held a brown bag to me and barked, "Eat. Lunch."

I took it and there was more muttering as I left. I couldn't hold back a small grin, but it was gone when Lydia and Jessica caught me at my locker.

"What happened with Jeff?" Lydia sounded breathless.

Jessica frowned and readjusted her hold on her books. "You never reply to my calls anymore. You're not a very good friend."

I slammed my locker shut. "Get away from me you whores."

Lydia gasped, "Me?"

Jessica got red in the face and hurried away.

I watched her go, but when Lydia stayed I snapped, "You covered for them. A disloyal bitch is the same as any other disloyal bitch. Shove off, Lydia. I don't want anything to do with you."

She hung her head, but glanced up quickly. Her feet shuffled in place and she said in a hush before she scampered away, "Adam Quinn is going to ask you out. Everybody's talking about it."

I closed my eyes, not something I wanted to deal with.

When I went to my last class, my lab partner kept glancing at me. After the twelfth time, I sat back. "You got something to say?"

She looked around and then pulled back her red curls from her face. It didn't matter. The frizzy hair clung to her skin. She didn't seem to mind. Her excitement couldn't be contained when she leaned forward. Her pudgy elbow rammed mine off the table. "You and Jeff Sallaway broke up, right?"

I nodded and crossed my arms over my chest.

"Is it true that Adam Quinn asked you out?"

I lifted an eyebrow.

A high-pitched squeal left her. It sounded like laughter. "He was asking your friends about you this weekend."

"They're not my friends."

"Oh." Her eyes kept darting around. "So are you gonna say yes?"

"Who are you?"

"My name's Becky Sallaway."

My mouth quirked up. "You're Jeff's cousin?"

She shifted in her seat. "Only through marriage. My mom married his dad's brother. Are you going to go out with Adam Quinn?"

"Why are you asking me? Did Jeff ask you to?"

Her mouth gaped open a second before her pasty white cheeks matched the color of her hair. "That pipsqueak? He's a loser. Not like Adam Quinn."

And she wasn't one? I rolled my eyes. "Why do you care so much?"

She shrugged. "Maybe I want to be friends."

"Friends are overrated."

"Not if you've got good ones."

"And you're going to be a good one?"

"Better than those two. Jessica Larsen's been jealous of you since sixth grade when Forrest Adams thought you were cute and Lydia Thompson doesn't have the backbone to be a good friend. She always does what Jessica tells her. Everyone knows that. I've always wondered why you didn't know that."

I sighed. "He hasn't asked, but the word is that he's going to."

"Are you going to say yes?"

The bell rang and I scooted my chair back. "Why don't you say yes for me?"

She hurried to catch up as I started to shoulder my way out the door and to my locker. The day had been long and I was in need of a good tiring run.

Panting, she tried to mop back her hair again. "Do you really want me to? I'll go find him right now."

"Sure."

When she stopped and headed one way, I kept going. The girl was a freak. But then a different freak planted herself in my path.

I groaned on the inside while I couldn't hold back a snarl. "Jill."

She tilted her chin up and her blue eyes flashed. As she flipped her bleach blonde hair over her shoulder, she responded, "Samantha."

I started to move around.

She blocked me.

"What do you want?"

"I'm dating Jeff."

Nothing surprised me anymore. "That was quick. You two been scooting and booting for a while?" Then I gave her a smile. "Are you my homewrecker?"

She narrowed her eyes. "Jeff asked me out last night. I've decided to date him."

"And you're going to make him change?"

The bottom of her uniform top started to ride up her waist. She reached down to pull it down, but stopped. A satisfied grin came to her and she let it up even further. One of her hands moved to the bottom of her skirt. She pulled it down an inch so her hipbones showed, along with the black thong she wore.

"Look at you," I purred. "You wanna be Britney Spears? Wear the pigtails tomorrow. I'm sure Jeff would love it."

She moved closer. "Only when I give him head."

"That's the spirit."

Her smug smile slipped a bit. I knew she was a cheerleader, she'd forgotten that.

"You do know he cheated on me with my best friend for two years, right?"

"He won't with me."

I laughed. "He won't cheat with you or he won't cheat on you? I'm sure both will happen."

"Jessica Larsen won't be sleeping with him anymore. She only did it to get back at you and from what I've heard; she's close to getting Logan Kade to date her."

"Yeah." I threw my head back and laughed. "You'll be luckier thinking Jeff won't cheat on you."

"He's wanted me for years." She pulled the other side of her skirt down as well, readjusted her hold on her books, and arched her back slightly. Her breasts were on display as people went past; the guys had stopped a while ago and were watching. I heard the whispers and knew this'd be all over school, probably already was.

"And you're the Mecca for his dating daydreams?" I caught sight of Becky on the sidelines. Her cheeks were inflamed and she pointed to the corner. When I looked over, I saw a confused Adam Quinn against the wall with some of his football teammates. He pushed some of his blonde hair out of his eyes and scratched his forehead.

Then Ashley DeCortts pushed through the crowd. She sidled next to Jill and touched her on the arm. "What are you doing, Jill?"

"I'm making my stand." Her eyes drilled into me.

I rolled my eyes and snorted. "Are you kidding me? You can have Jeff. I don't want him back." Then I thought about it again. "I haven't wanted Jeff for a couple years now."

Someone gasped. Someone laughed. And I turned to leave, but I stopped when I saw him right behind me. A look of hurt was evident when he met my gaze for a second.

My jaw hardened and I pushed through the crowd.

When I saw the men's locker room door was open and no one was inside, I went without thinking. My dad's office was in the back and his door was open. I paused in the doorway. I'd rarely come to his office because of where it was, but I took a deep breath. I was there now.

The small bathroom that attached to his office had the door closed. The toilet flushed and a moment later he came out, drying his hands.

He froze for a brief moment. "Samantha."

"Hi." I glanced over my shoulder. Male voices carried through the room and I heard them coming closer so I closed the door and sat in one of his chairs.

"What are you doing here?"

I hugged my books on my lap. "I haven't seen you since we moved out."

"Yeah...I know." He sounded tired as he sat behind his desk. His body was tense and his finger started to tap on his chair. I watched as it continued to tap, a habit I knew he did whenever he was nervous.

"How are you?"

A small grin appeared. "I'm okay. I'm the one who's supposed to ask you how you are."

One of my shoulders shrugged. "I'm not the one who's getting a divorce."

"Yeah, there's that."

"Jeff and I broke up."

"Oh?"

"He was cheating on me."

My dad's face remained void of any reaction.

My hands twisted together in front of my books and I looked down at my lap. "With Jessica. You remember her, right?"

There was silence.

I ploughed on, "For two years and Lydia knew. She helped them lie about it."

I waited and then after a minute, he asked in a quiet voice, "Why are you telling me this, Samantha?"

"What do you mean?" I looked up now. I needed something; I was looking for it in him. I didn't know quite what, though.

"I'm sorry that Jeffrey cheated on you. That's a horrible thing to find out."

"Like you and mom?" I swallowed thickly.

He froze again. His finger stopped tapping. And then a deep breath left him and he hung his head a moment. When he looked up again, I reeled back. The pain was so clear, so evident in his eyes. I was speechless for a moment.

He choked out, "I can't keep lying to you, Samantha."

Lying? "Dad?"

He closed his eyes and looked away. "I'm not your father."

I laughed.

"I mean it, Sam. I'm not your biological father." He caught my gaze again.

He was serious. I saw it in them and a flare of pain stabbed me in the gut. I almost bowled over, but my fingers caught my chair's sides and dug in. My books fell to the floor, one of them thumped on top of my toe. I didn't feel it. I was caught in his eyes and I felt seared by them and by his words.

Something cracked. I lifted my hand and saw blood trickling down from underneath my nails.

"Sam, let go of the chair."

"What?" I jerked my chin upright. I couldn't see him. He had blurred and there was two of him. They were starting to swim around.

"Let go."

I opened my mouth. No sound came out.

Then he got up and rounded my chair. He forcibly lifted my other hand and there was more blood from that one. Two of my nails were gone.

He cursed under his breath and left.

My head slammed to my lap and I gasped for breath. No way. There was no way…

Footsteps were heard coming back and hands lifted me in the air. There were more faces now, but I didn't pay them attention.

"Put her on the trainer's couch. Quinn, get the nurse."

I was placed on my back and both of my hands were lifted in the air. I felt some cool liquid poured on them as they poked and prodded. I looked at the ceiling. The white tiles above me looked like they were mocking me.

"Sam. I'm sorry." His voice was muffled close to me. His hand brushed some of my hair from my forehead. "She made me keep that secret all your life. I should've told you a long time ago. Analise didn't want—"

The footsteps were coming back. They were louder this time. My head rolled to the side and I saw a nurse and another man hurrying to me, they looked like they were moving through the air. Some guys were behind them.

"Get 'em all out, Quinn," my dad barked.

I frowned. Not my dad. David.

"What, honey?" He bent low to me.

"You're just David now."

He frowned and closed his eyes. He seemed to struggle with something and then when he opened them, they looked bleak. He looked how I did now. "Yes, Samantha. I guess I am."

CHAPTER SIX

Becky sat next to me where the sidewalk dipped to the parking lot. I'd been there after the school's nurse had tended to my hands and after my da—David took the football team to the field for practice. That'd been around four. It was six now.

"I don't understand why you won't let me drive you home," Becky grumbled.

I stared straight ahead.

"You want something to eat? Let's get something to eat. I'll drive."

I jerked my head in a nod and stood up. When we got to her car, I winced as I tried to open the door. Becky hissed and moved me out of the way. She opened the door for me, and then climbed on her side. As she started the car, she muttered, "And you expect to be able to drive home like that? You can't even open a door. You're crazy."

I grinned. "I thought you were going to be a good friend."

"I am and I'm telling the truth. You're crazy."

That shut me up.

Her voice took on a giddy note. "Did you see how Adam was hovering over you? It was so romantic."

I hadn't. I'd been distracted.

"You guys are going to make a great couple. I can already tell."

"How?"

"What?"

"How can you tell? You don't even know me."

"Well... Okay, I'm being honest here, but you weren't all fabulous before. I mean, I've always known who you are. We're lab partners, seriously, but I didn't care. But something changed with you this year. I have no idea what, but it's like you don't care anymore." When we pulled into a coffee shop, she laughed. "Then you showed up at that party in that outfit. It sounds stupid, I know, but there's just something about you, like you're a mystery or something. Everyone knew Jeff wanted you hardcore that night. And everyone knows he's been cheating on you. Then you showed up today and you told off those pathetic excuses for friends."

"Are you obsessed with me?" My hands were starting to throb. I sucked in a breath when I tried to flex one hand, but stopped right away. What the hell had I done?

She laughed another one of those high-pitched squeals and flipped the red curls over again.

I cringed.

"Um, no. Are you crazy? I mean, you are, but are you?" Her laugh weakened. She turned to face me in the car. "I've known Adam all my life. He's my neighbor and he's a good guy. He's one of *the* good guys. I was thrilled when he broke up with Ashley."

"So why don't you date him?"

Her cheeks got red again and her hands started to fidget in her lap before she tugged her skirt further over her knees. She mumbled something then.

"What?"

When she looked back up, her whole face was red. "I'm not good enough for him. I'm fat. I know it. Everyone knows it. Your friends used to call me hippo every day until—they still do."

I frowned.

"Anyways, I'm happy that he likes you. Last year I wouldn't think you had any balls. I mean, look at who you were. You had two sleazy best friends and an even sleazier boyfriend. They were all sleazy together behind your back. Some people thought you were stupid or had special needs or something."

"Thanks," I said dryly.

She brightened. "Now you're awesome. Jill Flatten tried to decimate you and you got away from her, easy as pie. No one does that. And you made her look stupid too."

"Is that hard to do?"

"Ashley DeCortts is afraid of her. That says something."

I grinned. "Are you going to buy me dinner now? All this flattery, then you drove me, now's the food part? What's next? A movie and a drink?"

She went back to tugging her skirt down again.

"Relax." I caught one of her hands, but grimaced from the contact. My hands were going to be in rare form for a while. I swallowed the pain down. "I'm sorry I'm not as excited about Adam Quinn. I don't know him. I've never cared to know him either."

She turned to the window and mumbled under her breath, "He's only the best guy in school. That's all who he is."

"I think you should try for him."

A corner of her mouth twitched up. "He doesn't like me like that. He's interested in you."

"Okay, well, we'll have to wait and see, hmmm?" I elbowed my door. "Can you help me out over here?"

"Oh." She scrambled around the car and opened my door. As we walked inside, she started to bounce up and down. "I picked up an application here for a job. I'm hoping to work here. I think it'd be awesome. Everyone cool comes here, you know."

"When'd you turn your application in?"

"A month ago."

"Have they called for an interview?"

Her smile dimmed when we approached the counter. "The girl said they were fully staffed, but they'd call when they had some openings."

A Help Wanted sign hung underneath the cash register.

"Can I help you?" A brightly smiling petite girl waited for our orders.

I shook my head. "No."

"What? I like this place." Becky hurried after me towards the door.

"You tore into me how I let people walk over me last year. If we're friends, then take my advice. Don't let this place walk over you." I pushed open the door and started to step out, but a wall slammed into me from the side.

I cried out and blinked past tears from the sudden pain. It speared through me, but hands caught my shoulders and set me to the side.

"Oh….hi…" Becky had become a third grade little girl.

I sucked in my breath through my teeth and tried to numb down the pain. It felt like fire as it bolted up my arms and through my legs. I couldn't see for a moment when more tears kept threatening to spill out.

A voice asked, "What happened to her hands?"

Becky shuffled around on the sidewalk. I could hear her blushing. "She had an accident."

"Did she scratch some girl's eyeballs out or something?" The same voice laughed and another male voice joined in.

"I dunno. She won't tell me." Becky's voice had grown soft, even weak.

Enough of my tears had cleared and I was able to see who was in front of us.

My heart stopped. Of course. My luck.

Mason was in front with Logan beside him and their friend on his other side. Logan had been the one asking. Their friend still snickered. And Mason watched me with impenetrable eyes.

I scowled.

Then the friend asked, "Can she drive home with those?"

Becky had been watching the sidewalk, but her head whipped up. "No. I know. I've been trying to reason with her so I could drive her home, but she won't let me—"

I shook off Mason's hand. He'd been holding my elbow and I surged away. "I'm fine."

"Sam, wait." Becky jogged to catch up.

I bypassed her car.

"I drove you here."

"I'm fine," I repeated through gritted teeth and when I rounded a corner, I started to run. Forget my iPod or running shoes; I was grateful that I'd worn sneakers to school that day. I'd just run home.

And I did, or I tried. At mile ten, I slowed to a walk. My legs hurt from the different sneakers and my back hurt from my bag. When a car slowed beside me, I snarled when I looked over. I was ready for anybody, but David stopped beside me.

The fight left me in that instant.

He reached over and unlocked the passenger door and I climbed in, though my body was stiff.

He blasted the air conditioner and started off again. Then he turned the radio off and leaned back. His voice was weary. "I saw your car still in the lot and I wondered how you'd get home."

I let out a breath. I had nothing to say.

"Then I remembered what you said about Jeff and Jessica and Lydia. Do people know you're staying with the Kades?"

I shook my head. My throat was too thick to talk.

"Yeah, I imagined that." He watched the road and his voice grew distant. "You were always so stubborn and proud. I used to worry about your pride, even when you were three. I always told Analise that it'd either make you or break you. I'm not sure which it is."

I closed my eyes.

The car turned at an intersection. "I know you might have questions for me, but I'm not sure they're questions that I can answer. Analise always wanted me to keep quiet so I did. I loved her. And now…"

"You raised me all my life."

He stopped the car somewhere and held my gaze.

My heart thumped, it was so loud in my ears.

He looked emotionless, but then he turned away and pressed a hand to his mouth. "I did." He was choked up. "I did, Sammy." And he took a deep breath. "Listen, if you'd like I can give you a ride to school tomorrow. I know you won't ask anyone and you don't have your car right now."

I realized we were a block from the Kade mansion.

"I will be here at seven tomorrow morning, on the dot. You don't need to call or anything. Actually, don't call. I'll be waiting for you."

I jerked my head in a nod. He reached across me and opened my door. As I got out and used my elbow to shut it, he called out, "See you tomorrow, Samantha. Get some sleep tonight."

Like that was going to happen.

He sped away and I walked up the mansion's driveway. There was only one car parked in front, my mom's new convertible she'd gotten the week we moved in. My heart started to pound again when I went inside. And then I heard her voice. It grew louder until I found her in a library-like room with her back to me. She had a phone pressed to her ear.

"Yes, honey. I know that." Pause. "Oh, I'm sure they'll be fine. Samantha's adjusting just fine—well—no." She sighed. "I'm sure he's not that bad of a boy. Mason seems very sure of himself. No, I know. Yes….okay, honey. I'd like that a lot too." She listened to the other end for a minute. "Everything will work out wonderfully. I promise you."

Then she laughed. The sound peeled through the room and it jarred me. I jumped back and tried to block the pain from the movement.

"Okay. Yes. I love you too. Bye."

I opened my eyes in time to see her turn around. Her eyes widened a fraction of an inch. "Honey, I didn't know you were there. How are you?"

I waited.

She gasped.

She saw my hands.

"What did you do?"

When she came over and started to reach for one of them, I jerked away. "I'm fine. It's nothing."

"Were you in a fight?"

I fought against the urge to puke. All accusations, all questions I had went down my throat then. I didn't want to hear her lies. I wasn't sure if I could stomach more fake promises coming out of her mouth either.

"I was trying to open this door, it was stuck, and someone banged it shut from the other side. They didn't see my hands."

"That's it?" my mother asked flatly.

"What do you mean?"

"Nothing." She shook her head and plastered on a smile. "The boys are coming home soon. They had practice that ran late, but James and I wanted to have a family dinner. What do you think?"

"It'll suck."

She sailed past me. "Do you think they'd like meatloaf? They seem like the kind to like meat, maybe pasta? Chicken and pasta? The chef went home, I asked him to go. I wanted to cook this dinner by myself."

I scowled and followed her down the hallway.

She turned into the kitchen. "You want to help, honey? You could make your famous green bean dish. You always made that for Jeffrey."

"Can I invite him?"

Her laughter bounced off the walls. "Oh, honey. You're so funny. You must get that from your dad. David could be funny at times."

As she went into the kitchen, I went to my room. My skin felt like it was stretching off of me. My feet wouldn't stop moving. Dinner or no dinner, I had to get out of there or I'd be bouncing off the walls too.

When I had changed into my running shoes with my iPod on my arm, I hit the sidewalk. As I ran down the driveway, Mason's black Escalade pulled in. Logan's yellow one came behind, but I didn't look at either of them and started running.

I'd have to go back. I knew that. I couldn't keep running from my mom or what she'd done to our lives, but for now this was how I was going to deal with the storm that was happening inside of me.

At that point, I didn't care when I went back home. It could be long past midnight before I returned, preferably when everyone was asleep. I'd slip in, sleep, and sneak back out. I took a deep breath and pumped my arms higher in the air. This was going to be my life, until everything would crash underneath our feet.

It was only a matter of time.

CHAPTER SEVEN

It was late when I hobbled inside. At this point with my bloody hands, the weak legs, and how much I've been running, it was time to admit that I needed to cut back. Making myself numb might not have been the healthiest way to handle recent changes in my life, but I wasn't sure if I dared any other option. Talking had never been my strong suit.

As I passed a room, the light switched on.

I could feel Analise's anger from where I was and I hadn't looked yet.

So I did.

Her face was white, eyes strained, mouth pinched, and her arms were folded over her chest. My mother never folded her arms, it was deemed unladylike and too confrontational. Then her foot started to tap on the floor.

Guess I pissed her off.

"Do you know what time it is?" she clipped out.

No clock was in sight. I shrugged.

"It's one in the morning. One in the morning, Samantha." Her leg moved off the other and both feet were now on the floor. They stopped tapping.

She still remained on her chair.

I tilted my chin up. "Do you know what's happened to my life?"

She made a disgusted sound and hissed at the same time. "Are we back to this? You knew my marriage wasn't working out. You should be happy for me, Samantha."

"Happy?" My voice cooled. "It happened a week ago."

"Would you rather I were in an unhappy marriage?"

"How could I tell? You were fake all the time."

Her eyes threatened to bulge out and she sucked in a dramatic breath. When she talked, it was forcibly controlled, "What are you talking about?"

"You're the fakest person I know. Why are you really pissed off? Is it because I missed your precious *family* dinner?"

"I'm fake?" She started to stand up.

My eyes went flat. "So much that I can't stand being fake. I'm real all the time. Congratulations. I have no friends because of it."

"I'm fake?"

"This is news to you?" I laughed as she drew closer.

There was a stillness to my mother. Her anger was so vivid, but I was past caring. My body ached. My hands hurt. And I was tired, so tired of everything.

She stopped in front of me.

I met her gaze and my hands formed into fists. "What do you want? Tell me what you want me to say so I can go to sleep."

Her voice grew soft. "You missed dinner tonight."

"We're back to this?" I mocked her. "Your precious dinner?"

"It was an important dinner."

"I highly doubt it." I started to leave, but she caught my arm.

She hissed, "I am talking to you."

"Not anymore. I'm moving out as soon as I'm eighteen. That's all you need to hear from me."

"What?" she gasped.

"Reality check, . This is your life. This is your boyfriend. I don't want any part of it. I want to be home with dad again. I want to move in with him."

"You. Will. Not. Live. With. Him." She had to take breaths to calm down. Her arms started to tremble, her chin was rattled. Her eyes clung to mine in a beseeching manner, torn between pleading and commanding.

"Why not?" I tested her. "He *is* my father, right?"

Her mouth shut in a firm line.

"Doesn't he have some right to see me? Don't I have a right to see him? Why is it always your way? You didn't give me any choice. You said we're moving and we did, just like that. We moved because you said so. Well I don't want to be here. I don't want to be a part of your boyfriend's family. This is your thing, not mine."

"You are my daughter."

"Am I? Are you sure? How many nights have we eaten together since the move?"

"I wanted—"

"It would've been once, tonight. And that's because it's what you wanted, not me. You've stopped being my second we moved in here. The only role you fulfill is his girlfriend as the wannabe wife of James Kade."

Analise went white around her mouth. Her arms jerked up in balls, but she forced them back down. Her arms shook and her hands started to tremble. She choked out, "You will respect me—"

"Where's my respect? As your daughter, don't I get respect?"

"I am your mother—"

"I wish you weren't—"

She slapped me. The force of her palm pushed me back a few steps and I cradled my cheek as I whirled back to her. She stood there, ashen in the face and with her hand still in the air. The palm was spread out and she looked from her hand to me in disbelief.

The pain was numbing. And a part of me wanted more, but I said, "If you slap me again, I'll hit you back."

"Samantha..." She darted towards me.

I jerked away and retreated to a far wall.

"I..." Her eyes kept spinning around the room, from me to her, to her hand, and back to her feet. "I..." Then her face cleared and she looked back up. She spoke in a calmed voice, too calm. "The dinner tonight was important to me."

I narrowed my eyes.

She swallowed and hung her head again. "I wanted you there."

"You want to know where I was?" I didn't wait for her answer. "Running. I've gone running almost every day since we got here. I run until my body can't take anymore and then I go to sleep and I get up, go to school, and I can't wait until I can do it all again. I don't want to feel anything, mom, because sooner or later, we're going to be out of here. Have you thought about that? What happens when he breaks up with you?"

"We're getting married."

I hesitated for a beat. "And I repeat, what happens when he breaks up with you?"

"Didn't you hear me? James proposed to me. We announced it tonight at dinner."

"Oh," I bit out. "Well, then I'm so sorry your daughter wasn't there to represent your side of the family. He had his two sons, right? Their friend too?"

Her eyes narrowed again and she was still, so still.

I laughed, mocking. "And you looked at your side of the table and there was my empty chair. You were humiliated, weren't you?"

"Yes." Her teeth were gritted together.

"I'm humiliated every day we're here. I'm humiliated you left dad for this—"

"You will watch your words."

"I won't. Why should I? You don't watch yours." I pressed a fist into the side of my face. My hand had grown numb and I laughed. It rumbled from the bottom of my stomach and gurgled out. The sound sent chills down my own spine. "I love you. I'm divorcing you." A pause. I glanced up and held her eyes. "Your father loves you."

Her eyes went wide and she paled again. This time she was as white as a sheet.

I let out a deep breath, one to calm me, but the storm started to take over. "Your father will always love you. I'll always love you. I'll protect you. I'll put you first in my life." My mouth twisted into an ugly smile. "It was all lies, wasn't it, Analise?"

"You know," she breathed out. She looked horrified.

"Why are you marrying him? You just want to find a new daddy for me? David couldn't keep lying to me anymore?"

"That wasn't….this isn't…Oh, Samantha…" A sob came from her.

"Stop it," I snapped out.

Her mouth clenched shut and she watched me. A tear came to her eye.

"You don't get to feel bad for yourself." My whole body started to shake. "I wish I'd never been born from yo—"

She swung her hand wide and it smacked against my cheek. This time it hit across my nose and as my head was thrown to the side, I tasted blood. I glanced up, felt my insides churning, and fisted my hand. I threw my whole body behind.

I watched her in slow motion. She looked from my face to my hand and her mouth formed a small o. Her eyes widened, but then something caught me. I was hauled backwards in the air and against something. I tried kicking free, but an arm held on tight around my waist.

"Samantha!"

"Let me go." I kept kicking, until I heard laughter from behind.

"You could help," a male voice reverberated from behind my ear.

"I think you got it under control."

I was swung around and I saw Logan, James, and the friend in the doorway. Logan wiped a hand over his face as he continued to laugh. The friend was fighting back a smile and James gave me an emotionless expression.

I doubled my struggle.

Mason's arms tightened around me.

"Let me go. I won't hit her."

He grunted and dropped me.

I swung around and he watched me with caution.

Then I swiveled on my heel and went to bed. Not a word was spoken behind me and when I left the next day, Mousteff gave me a sheepish smile as he handed out his brown bag. I took it as I passed and met my da—David a block away. He was quiet when I got in the car, but I felt his attention. His eyes raked over my face, but he didn't say a word. I breathed out in thanks when we pulled into the parking lot. I hurried from the car before he got out of his side and I was in the school early enough so no one was in the hallways.

The rest of the day passed in a similar fashion.

Jessica and Lydia kept their distance. Jill Flatten sneered as she passed by once. Her arm was curled around Jeff's. He avoided my gaze and stared straight ahead. Then there was Becky. She gushed about the Kade brothers and how they had talked to her. She asked once about my hands and I lifted them. It was funny. I'd forgotten about their pain until she asked, but then she started to gush about Adam Quinn in the next breath.

Apparently, he told her that he did want to ask me out.

My hands had started to hurt again, but I listened to her story and tried to block the pain out. I asked her when he said he wanted to ask me out. She looked the other way while one of her shoulders jerked up in a shrug.

Adam Quinn never said a word.

Over the next week, things were at a bypass at home. Analise avoided me. I avoided her. And the boys seemed to have disappeared.

It was perfect.

When I got to school on Thursday, the rumors started.

I was a whore.

Jeff dumped me because I had herpes.

Lydia and Jessica were my friends because my mother bribed them.

My own dad hated me, he barely talked to me.

Then I cornered Becky at her car one day and demanded to know where the rumors had come from.

She squealed as she got red in the face, "Lydia."

My eyebrow rose up.

"And Jessica."

I waited.

"And Jill Flatten. She really hates you."

"I knew it."

Then Becky said in a small voice, "And Ashley DeCortts."

"Wait—what? Why does she hate me?"

"Because Adam likes you."

I rolled my eyes. The guy didn't give a damn. When would she drop this obsession of hers?

"What else could go wrong?" I muttered under my breath.

The back door burst open at that moment and the football team jogged across the parking lot on the way to the field. Their spikes clattered against the tar and the sound was soon deafening.

"Hi," Becky squeaked with a small wave.

I turned to see that Adam Quinn had fallen to a walk as he drew close. He stopped with his helmet in one hand and a water bottle in the other. Up close, I saw why so many girls wanted to love him. Striking blue eyes, golden curls with streaks from the sun, and a square jaw that would've sent romantics swooning. Hell, they already did.

He towered over us with shoulder pads that made his already muscular shoulders larger. His chest tapered down to a slender waist and he grinned at Becky. His eyes scanned to me. "You need a ride home, Becky?"

"No." She sounded breathless. "My mom let me use her car this week."

"Good old Nancy." His grin brightened. "Am I still invited for chili and cornbread this weekend?"

Becky's foot started to push a rock back and forth on the ground.

She didn't look up. "Yeah, of course. I know Eddie might come home this weekend."

"That's great. I've missed your brother." He cast me another questioning look.

I sighed and held out my hand. "I'm Samantha."

His hand enveloped mine. They were rough, slightly calloused, probably from throwing the football, but they weren't so rough to the touch. I could see why he dated Ashley DeCortts, the girl that seemed to reign over the cheerleaders. I suppose she daydreamed about the Ken Barbie he reminded me of, how he must've been the prince to her damsel in distress fairytale.

"I know. Adam Quinn."

"I know."

We grinned at each other.

"How're your hands?"

A faint scowl came to me. I remembered that he'd been there. "Oh, they're…" I lifted them up and shrugged. "I guess they're okay. They'll heal."

"You can drive home today?"

"What?"

"I saw your car here that night. Then I saw coach take off. I figured maybe you didn't have a ride or something."

"Oh, yeah. No, I'm fine. I've been driving all week."

"That's good."

"Yeah."

Becky continued to hang her head and I arched an eyebrow.

"So," he watched her too. "Are you guys going to the beach party tomorrow night?"

Her head snapped up and her cheeks were in flames.

Not surprised.

Then she mumbled out, "I' dlove to, butIdon't know whereit's at."

"There's a party?" I asked with a frown at my redheaded friend.

"Yeah." His teeth were blinding. "You could both go with me?"

Becky whirled to me. Her eyes were fervent with hope.

"I…" I wanted to say no, but a stricken look came to her eyes. I crumbled. "Sure. You can pick us up at Becky's."

"Great."

"Great."

Becky breathed out, "Great!"

"I'll—uh—I'll see you then, I guess?"

I nodded. "See you then."

He jogged after the team, but glanced back with a small wave before he got onto the field.

Becky whooshed out, "I can't believe I'm going to a party with Adam Quinn."

My shoulder nudged her. "Maybe there's hope for you after all."

"What do you mean?"

"Here's your big chance." I gave her a duh look. "He's going to be drinking. You're going to be drinking. I can drive us home…"

Then she squeaked again and clamped her mouth shut. Her cheeks got big and her whole body was soon red, even her hands and fingers.

I laughed. "Now you just have to figure out what you're going to wear."

As I headed to my car, I heard her groan behind me. Somehow, things didn't seem so bad when I had a friend to distract me. Too bad it wouldn't keep. I wanted something to keep.

CHAPTER EIGHT

Becky was bouncing off the wall when I got to her house the next afternoon. I was dressed in a see-through white summer dress that tied behind my neck. My black bikini was visible underneath and I had on simple black flip flops. While I was going for comfort, Becky wanted sexy.

She let out a dramatic groan and collapsed on her bed when I went to her room. One of her arms had been pulled through a black tube top, or that's what it looked like. A blinding rainbow colored bikini top had been pushed up. When she rolled over, she cried out, "I can't fit into anything."

"What are you talking about?"

"I have nothing, nothing! I'm so fat, Sam."

I frowned and grabbed her hand to pull her up. When she looked at me, I shrugged. "What do you want me to say? If you're trying to be a model, you need to lose weight. I think you're fine just how you are."

"Thanks a lot," she grumbled.

"I thought friends were honest." I flashed a grin.

She stood back up and struggled to pull the rest of her tube top over her left boob. Then she started to hop around. "Yeah, but it'd be easier to take if you didn't look how you did."

I scowled and crossed my arms over my chest.

She paused mid-hop. "That's a compliment."

"Oh." I loosened my arms. "My mom's always on me about my weight."

"You could gain some. You want mine?"

I chuckled and watched as she continued to hop around, sometimes skip around the room. After an hour, when Becky stopped to pant with beads of sweat on her forehead, I gestured to a dress in her closet. "Why don't you just wear that?"

"Ugh." She let out another drawn-out groan. "That makes me look like a tan marshmallow."

"It does not. You wore it to the first day of school. I thought you looked nice."

Her eyebrows arched high. "I didn't know you knew who I was back then?"

I shrugged. "I didn't, but I still thought you looked nice."

"Your besty Jessica called me fatso that day."

I rolled my eyes. "If she went out of her way to call you a name that meant you looked good. And I bet some guy she wanted to flirt with was looking at you instead."

"You think?"

"I know so."

"It's my last option anyway. I need to lose weight, or buy new clothes and I refuse to buy new clothes." She grimaced. "My bank account won't allow it and I can't live down the fact that I'm a size larger since last year."

"You could go running with me."

She shot me a dark look. "I'm not that desperate. I'll try walking first."

When she pulled on the black dress, it fit her. It was snug in places it was supposed to be and loose in places that she was embarrassed about. After a few twirls in the mirror, I gave her the thumbs up and waited until she finished her make-up.

I called to her in the bathroom, "This is a beach party, right?"

"Hmmm mmm." Her voice was muffled from the bathroom.

"So why are you putting make-up on?"

Then she came into the room. "Because it's waterproof and because Adam's taking us."

I frowned at that logic. "He's picking us up?"

"Yeah, in thirty minutes."

"Why'd you have me come over two hours earlier?"

She posed with an arm on her hip and rolled her eyes. "Are you serious? You're my girlfriend. Aren't we supposed to get ready together?"

"I'm ready."

"Yeah, well, I needed the moral support. And besides," she flashed me a smile and a wink. "My mom has wine. I thought we could raid her cabinet."

"Oh." I surged upright on the bed. "Why didn't you say so in the beginning?"

Becky giggled as she led me downstairs and we both had a glass. We'd had our second when her phone vibrated and she continued to giggle as she knocked over her mother's lamp. "Adam's outside."

When she stood, her knees buckled and I caught her arm. "Are you okay?"

She gave me a weak wave. "Oh, no worries. This has more to do with Adam than the wine, but I didn't eat all day. Oops." She giggled again and her face was lobster red.

When we got outside, the silliness was gone and her limbs became rigid. Her back was stiff, her chin down, and she walked like a robot. Adam gave her a small frown, but shook his head slightly. When we climbed in, he asked, "Are you guys ready?"

Becky giggled into her lap.

I sighed from the back. "What party is this?"

"It's a Public party. Is that okay?"

Her head popped back up. "They're only the best kind."

Adam chuckled and rested an arm on the back of their front seat. His fingers scraped her shoulder before they fell against the headrest. I saw her almost faint.

"I guess so. More people, right?"

"And the Kades."

My scowl was back.

Adam mimicked my reaction.

Becky was clueless as she bobbed her head up and down. "I heard it's their party. They're actually inviting people at our school."

"Wait, what?" I shot forward and clasped onto their seat.

"Yeah." She was a grinning idiot. "They're usually so exclusive. I mean, I heard no one's allowed in their house, but I guess they live on the beach. It's in front of their home."

Every tendon in me wanted to snap. By the time we got to my house, the tension suffocated me and was weighing me down. Becky hot-footed it out of the car, but my legs couldn't move.

A party. At my house. By my soon-to-be-stepbrothers.

Adam had grown silent too as he glanced back. "You okay?"

Becky shoved her head next to his. "Yeah, you look pale, really pale."

"I'm fine." My voice was calm, but my body trembled. My knees buckled an inch when I got out of the car, but Adam caught me and held me upright. I flashed him a smile in thanks and then turned to see Becky's grin falter a bit.

My stomach dropped. That wasn't good.

A crowd of people had congregated at the bottom of the driveway, but they started to head around the hill and down to the beach. I let out a small breath in relief. I remembered their other party. No one had entered the house then and I hoped no one would this time.

When we bypassed the gate around the pool, Becky grabbed one of the bars. "Look at that. They have their own pool and a hot tub." Her eyes were wide as she took the rest in, the sand volleyball and basketball courts.

Adam touched her shoulder. "I think they have a bonfire started down here."

"Oh, wow…" Becky was lost in stardust as she followed the line downwards.

I breathed another sigh of relief when I saw the divider door was still closed, not to mention locked.

Then we were on the beach and there were three bonfires. A keg had been hidden in some bushes towards the back of the beach with coolers placed all over. When people quickly congregated to them, I figured they had alcohol inside.

"Oh, look!" Becky pointed to the farthest bonfire.

Logan and their friend were there with others grilling over the fire. Soon music blared from speakers placed by the pool.

Adam suggested we sit around one of the smaller bonfires and after we snagged some lawn chairs, Becky jumped back up. She was all smiles. "I'm going to get something more to drink. You guys want?"

She hot-footed it away before we could answer and Adam looked over with a hesitant smile. "More?"

"We got into her mom's wine."

"Ah, I see. Nancy. She does love her Moscato."

I grinned. "My mom's decided she loves tea, not the coffee she's been drinking since I was born, but tea now."

The small smile disappeared. "Yeah, uh…I heard your dad that night…" He seemed to be choosing his words.

"No one knows. Please don't say anything."

He nodded quickly. "I won't. I wouldn't—I mean—I know what that's like, to have your personal life on display, you know?"

I nodded. "Yeah…"

"So," he sat forward and leaned closer. "You and Sallaway, huh? You two were together for a while."

"We were."

His eyes seemed to be watching me intently. "And you don't think there's any chance…?"

It took a moment before I realized what he was asking and my eyes went wide. "He cheated on me for two years with my best friend. Some girls might tolerate that, but I have self-esteem."

His shoulders loosened and he grinned. "That's good, I mean, you deserve better."

"Any girl deserves better."

"You're right. No one deserves a cheater."

From the dark look on his face, something relaxed inside of me. He understood. "I heard DeCortts cheated on you?"

He looked startled for a moment and then cleared his throat. "Yeah, uh, she did."

I lifted a shoulder. "It was all over school."

"I know, I just…hearing it from a stranger is different, you know…"

"I was informed the two of you were the 'hottest couple ever'." I thought those were Lydia's exact words.

He stiffened in his chair. "I guess so. She's—she threw herself at one of the Kades, of all people." He laughed and gestured around.

"Which one?"

"Logan, I think." He frowned, and then shook his head. "It doesn't matter. She said he turned her down, but I still knew what she'd done. I heard the whole thing at some stupid party. Then Peter told me she'd been sleeping around for the last six months."

"Peter Glasburg?" His best friend.

Adam nodded. "Yeah, I don't know who with, but I trust him. Peter doesn't say much and if he said it, then it's worse than he let on."

I grew silent and turned to watch for Becky. She'd been gone a while, but I couldn't squash an inkling of jealousy. He had a friend who looked out for him and that friend wasn't the one to sleep with his girlfriend. My mouth clamped shut and my chest grew tight as something burned inside of me.

But then Mason and Logan's friend walked towards us from the beach. He had gone past at some point and he was now going back to the other bonfire. A couple of beers were in his hands and as he started to bypass us, he stopped, backed up, and frowned at us.

Adam lifted a hand. "Hey, man."

The friend shot him a look and glanced at my hands. The gauze I had used to wrap my fingers was gone. I scowled up at him, waiting for what he was going to say, but then he held out a beer to me.

"Thanks." The word felt awkward on my lips.

He rolled his eyes and kept going.

Adam twisted around to watch him. "Do you know him?"

I shrugged.

"That was…odd. Do you know who that was?"

Again, I shrugged.

"That was Nate Monson. He's best friends with Mason Kade. He moved away last year, but I guess he comes back to visit." Adam continued to look at me strangely. "I have never seen him do something like that. That was weird."

"Do something like what?"

His eyes seemed to be inspecting me. "Be nice to a random girl that he or his buddies aren't sleeping with."

I shifted in my seat. "I'm not sleeping with anybody, if that's what you're getting at."

His hands shot in the air in surrender. "I didn't mean that. I've just—do you know him?"

I sneered at him. "His name's Nate?"

"Yeah." Adam leaned forward and rested his elbows on his legs. "He's bad news, like really bad news. I heard him and Kade are not a good team together."

I snorted, "Which Kade?"

"Mason." He frowned at me. "What'd you mean by that?"

I fought the urge to roll my eyes and popped open the beer. "I just meant that the Kade brothers seem close, it'd made sense if he was friends with both."

"Oh." Adam leaned back again and stretched out his legs. "I don't know about that, but I heard when he and Mason Kade get together, it's not good."

"You're scared of them?"

"No, but they played football together against me last year. I'm happy that I only get sacked by Kade this year and not both.

Anyway, whatever. I'm sounding stupid, aren't I?" He gave me a grin.

I sipped the beer, but it tasted flat.

"Maybe I should go find Becky and get something to drink?" His blues sparked in good humor and another knot in my stomach unraveled.

When he left, I watched him go. My hands were curled into my chair and I jerked a hand up to finish my beer. Another was handed to me and I looked up. This one was from Logan. He had a sober look on his face, but he wasn't watching me. I shifted and saw that he was staring in the direction Adam had just gone.

When I took the cold can from him, it slipped from my hold. He caught it and sat in Adam's seat as he held it to me again.

I held my breath, but I didn't say a word. Something in me wouldn't allow it, but I opened the beer and put it in the chair's cup holder.

He stretched out his legs and lounged back for a moment.

Then he sighed.

I heard the small sound escape his lips and was confused. It was a sound that I'd make.

Laughter rang clear not far from us. I realized that Adam and I had picked seats farther away from the party. I didn't know if it was for privacy or because of the loud music, but I was suddenly aware of the looks we were getting now. Had Adam and I gotten the same interest?

"They went to the city this weekend." Logan's voice sounded rough.

I glanced over and he lifted his head up.

"Mase went to go see our mom tonight."

We had both been watching the crowd and when two figures separated themselves from the rest and were headed towards us, he grimaced before he stood.

He didn't look at me. I didn't look at him, but he held out a second beer. I took it and then he sauntered away. The party-boy air was back with him when Logan neared the crowd. Some girls eyed him with sultry poses and his friends made way for his arrival.

When Adam and Becky stopped by the chairs, neither sat nor said a word.

Then Becky said in a rush, "Was that Logan Kade?"

I gripped the beer tighter and kept my voice neutral. "I wanted to ask about Jessica, if he was going to date her or not."

Something flashed in her eyes and she clipped out, "I heard that he told her to get lost. She's back to rubbing herself all over my cousin again. I just walked past them."

My hand gripped the can tight and I chugged the rest of it.

Adam shot her a look.

Becky's mouth opened and hung there. "I mean…she's not good enough for Kade. That's what I think. And my cousin's a loser, a first class loser."

Adam grunted.

She bit her lip and pulled a chair over. "Are you okay, Sam?"

I finished the beer and put it away. It was the last bit of alcohol that I'd consume that night or heaven help me, I would do something I'd regret later. I almost hit my mom once, I wouldn't be held back a second time with Jessica.

CHAPTER NINE

The party went late, but not late enough. Becky was stumbling drunk by the time Adam parked his car outside the two houses. He had to help get her inside and then asked if I needed a ride home. After he asked, he gave me a rueful grin. "Sorry, you're sober, aren't you?"

"I only had those two beers."

"Yeah." He scratched his head and Becky's snores soon thundered down to where we stood in front of her door. He laughed and shook his head. "She's something else, isn't she?"

"She likes you." I watched him carefully.

He stood still for a second and closed his eyes a fraction.

It was enough. I knew where he stood. "Stop being nice to her. You won't hurt her so much then."

He nodded and ran a hand through his hair. "I know. I do. I like Becky, just not that way."

I shrugged and started towards my car. "She's not Ashley DeCortts, but I think that's a good thing."

"Hey." He hurried to walk beside me. "Do you—would you want to meet for dinner tonight?"

I opened my car door and turned around to look where Becky's room was. "That's my only friend right now."

"She's my friend too and I could be another friend."

My laugh was genuine. "That's what you say now, but when I don't put out it's going to be a different story." My eyes narrowed on his. "Because I won't, you know. I never had sex with Jeff and

I'm not going to start again with you. My first and only time was a mistake I will never make again."

"I know. That's okay. I respect you for that."

Another one of those knots unraveled in my stomach again. Why did it happen with him? And at, times when I felt he was being honest?

I tilted my head to the side and studied him. "Are you really this nice guy or is this an act?"

He grimaced. "I'm nice. I am, but I'm not being that nice to Becky."

"No, you're not."

"She's the only person that you talk to. I didn't know how else to approach you without looking like a complete loser."

I rolled my eyes, but couldn't shake the slight smile. "Try not going through the friend that likes you next time."

"Next time?" His hand caught my car door and held it open.

I looked at it, saw he wasn't going anywhere anytime soon, and stared him straight in the eyes. "What do you want, Adam Quinn?"

His eyes widened an inch, but he didn't miss a beat. "Dinner. Just dinner."

"And if I don't want dinner? If I want to bail? If I bring Becky with?"

His smile looked painful. "Then I think you're not being a good friend either."

"Maybe." I got inside and shut the door, but I rolled the window down. "Or maybe I don't believe in friends anymore."

He leaned down. "For what it's worth, Becky's the best friend you could get. Those other two were jokes."

I gave him a small wave and started home, but I muttered under my breath, "You don't say."

When I pulled into the driveway, I had to key in the code for the gate. It wasn't usually closed, but I figured the party was still in full gear. After I made sure my car was in the garage and the front gate had been closed again, I headed inside and towards the kitchen.

A peak of sunlight was starting outside and I saw it was five in the morning. When I'd gone to all-night parties with Jessica and Lydia it was a tradition to go for breakfast in the morning and on cue, my stomach rumbled. However, as I opened the fridge, the bright light filled the room and I screamed.

Mason stood behind me, leaning against the kitchen counter with one foot crossed idly over the other. He looked relaxed and carefree, but everything in me went on alert. The hairs on the back of my neck stood straight up and I knew he was anything besides relaxed.

When he didn't say anything, my insides clenched even further. So this is how we were going to be? Fine. I reached inside and pulled out some slices of meat. I was determined to ignore him or, at least, not let him bother me anymore than he already had. My stomach wanted a sandwich and I wasn't leaving the kitchen until I got one.

An arm reached around me and I jumped. My heart doubled in pace and I bumped against his chest as Mason reached for the water pitcher. He caught me from moving back into him with one hand on my arm. I held my breath as he held me in place. When his arm moved clear of me, I sagged in relief. Then my fingers deftly plucked out the tomatoes and a head of lettuce.

When I pulled out a cutting board and a knife to start on the lettuce, Mason placed a glass of water into my hands.

I stood there, dumbfounded, as he nudged me over with his hip. Then he picked up the knife and I watched in almost sick fascination as he started to cut the lettuce and tomatoes. A moment later, he pulled out cheese and arranged all of them with the meat between two slices of bread.

He put the sandwich on a plate and pushed it into my other hand.

I stood there, water in my left and the sandwich in my right. My mouth was open. I knew I needed to close it, but I couldn't.

He reached into a corner cabinet and pulled out some rum. After he mixed himself a drink, he sat at the kitchen table and kicked out a chair for me. I sat, but I didn't remember doing it.

He leaned back and sipped his drink. It was early in the morning so the sunrise peaked into the room more. The bass from the music was muffled through the windows and then the air conditioner kicked in. We could barely hear the party still going strong outside.

He raked a hand over his face. "They're going to be out there all weekend."

I didn't hide the grimace that came to my face.

"Logan said you went down there."

I gulped down half of my water. "You went to see your mom?"

He jerked a shoulder up. "It's not her fault my dad's a prick. I'd want to know."

"She didn't know?"

He gave me the first grin I'd ever received from him. It was soft and I knew it had more to do with his mom than me. "They divorced last year and haven't talked since. James probably didn't feel she was worthy of this information."

My eyes went wide. I couldn't stop them. When I realized I was staring, I shoved the sandwich in my mouth. Then chewed.

His eyes narrowed, a gleam of anger glittered in them. His mouth drew shut and his jaw tightened.

My stomach clenched again and something burst in my body. I shifted, uncomfortable, on the seat. I shouldn't be there. I shouldn't be hearing this, talking to him. It wasn't right. When a full blown alarm started to sound in my head, he shoved back his chair and stood.

He took my now-empty plate and glass to the sink. As he passed, he tapped my shoulder lightly. "You should come down. I think Nate got some jet skis." Then he was up the stairs and gone.

It was like he'd never been there. I still sat at the kitchen table.

I never went down to the beach. I didn't want to chance a run-in with Jessica, Lydia, or Jeff. I didn't care about the others, but a headache had started. It grew as the day progressed. When the evening came around, it had lessened dramatically. I felt a bit more human and checked my phone.

There was a text from Becky: **Adam likes you. You should go out with him**.

You like him.

I waited a minute. **He doesn't like me and I'd rather he were with you than someone else. No one's good enough for him**.

Oh Becky. I groaned, but replied: **Maybe**.

Good. I gave him your number.

And sure enough, I saw an unknown number had texted me: **This is Adam. Dinner?**

I stared at it. What the hell was I doing?

He sent another: **Please? I'm being a loser here**.

I smacked my forehead with my palm. **I'll meet you at Mastoni's, 830**.

It wasn't even thirty seconds before I got back: **See you then!**

Again, what the hell was I doing?

Mastoni's was a nice restaurant. I'd been there once with my parents, or my mom and my fake father. Analise wanted to dress up so we did. I wore a simple dress while hers was blaring red. David wore a dress shirt and khakis. It'd been good enough for me, not for her. As I walked inside the cool interior, heard the fountain gurgling, and saw all the foliage around, I remembered the fight that had happened that night.

It'd been my first two-hour run.

This time I wore jeans and a black top, nothing special. This wasn't going to be special. When I spotted Adam at the bar, he waved, and I saw he must've felt the same. He had on khaki cargo shorts and a blue polo. He looked good, but not the dressy that my mom had wanted so long ago.

I preferred this night already.

He held out a drink for me as he drew near. "Hey, I got this for you."

"You're twenty one?"

Perfect white teeth flashed me. "The manager's a friend of the family, plus, I used to work here a while ago."

Oh. I took the drink from him. Great.

"I already got a booth for us; it's kinda in the back if that's okay?"

It was. Privacy was always good, but it wasn't long before a group of girls took the booth beside ours. When we waited for our food to come, they sent flirty looks and smiles Adam's way. I was sure they talked louder for his benefit too.

When the food came, I heard one of the girls exclaim, "I didn't know Nate was in town."

"Oh yeah!" Another shrieked in laughter. "You didn't know? He's been here for a week."

"Whatever, Natalie."

A third offered up, "I heard they're going down the beach to Roussou tonight."

The girls grew quiet for a moment.

"What are they going to do?"

"What do you mean?"

"They always do something. When Nate and Mason team up, they always do something. Last year they stole some police cars and then they went on a bender."

"I heard that too. Mason's dad paid off the cops. They vandalized some of the bars. He must've paid the owners off too."

Then the first girl spoke up with authority in her voice, "Well, they're doing something tonight. They disappeared from the beach an hour ago."

"How do you know?"

"Duh. Summer texted me. She's still there."

"Hey." Adam's hand jolted me back to our booth. He gave me a gentle grin. "You okay?"

"Actually…" I looked down at my plate of pasta. "I'm not hungry."

His smile stretched a bit. "You're not bailing, are you?"

I gave him a weak one in return. "I think I am. I'm sorry. I...I have to do something."

When I got to the house, Mason's Escalade was just starting to leave. I raced towards it and waved my arms in the air. He braked and rolled down his window. "Yeah?"

Nate grinned at me from the passenger seat, but I felt he was laughing at me.

I was breathless from my hurry and panted, "You're going to Roussou? I know where the coach lives."

Mason frowned. "What are you doing?"

"I want to go with you?"

Logan howled from the back seat and a fourth guy started to laugh with him.

"No."

"Yes." I grabbed his window when he started to let the vehicle roll forward. "Let me come."

Nate elbowed him. "Let her come."

"What?" Logan popped his head forward. "No way. No way in hell, Mase."

Mason jerked a thumb towards the back. "Get in." He popped open the back trunk area and I crawled in. My heart was pounding. I knew my face was red, but as soon as I heaved the door shut the Escalade shot forward.

It was an hour drive down the beach. Logan grumbled and sent me a glare every now and then. The fourth friend ignored him and after a while, started to give me a few grins. He offered me a soda too. Mason and Nate talked with each other and Logan would lean forward to join in.

Something told me that Logan was trying to persuade them to drop me on the side of the road. When they didn't, I relaxed a little. I figured we were too far for them to do that and then we were in the town of Roussou. It was small, but it was rich. A lot of wealthy men owned stock in internet companies, which helped their football program be competitive against Fallen Crest High and it was the reason why an extra sense of rivalry sparked between the two schools. I remembered hearing a rumor that the Roussou team had heavily recruited Mason and Logan for their team.

They'd given them a resounding middle finger.

"Where's the coach's place?" Logan glared at me.

I jerked forward to recite the directions. It wasn't long before we were outside the three-story house I knew where David played poker on Saturday nights. And then I saw his car. My hands curled into small balls and everything inside of me went cold.

My chest started to heave up and down at a rapid pace. But I only saw my father's car, not my father's car. David's car.

"What the hell?" Logan cursed and shot me a look. "There're people here."

"Does it matter?" I asked idly as I spied some fireworks in the back with me. Then I heard a door open and loud voices came across the yard. I snagged a couple of them and a lighter before I started to get out of the car.

"Are you crazy? He's going to tell."

He wasn't. I got out, but left the door open. David had started down the sidewalk to where his car was parked, but he stopped when he saw me.

"Samantha?"

I lit the fireworks and strolled to his car.

"Samantha! Don't!"

I keyed in his code, opened his door, and threw them in.

"Oh my god!" He rushed past me, but I locked the door. It'd take him a moment before he could get it open.

The fireworks started to sizzle and they exploded in the next second.

David threw himself away from the car, shaking and cursing.

My face was blank. I didn't feel a thing. My hands didn't shake.

My back was straight. My shoulders were square and then I turned back for the Escalade.

"Samantha, what did you just do?" David reached for my elbow.

I whipped away and seethed, "Get away from me."

"Get in!" Mason cursed and pounded the side of his door.

I whirled and threw myself in the back as he started to pull away from the curb. I heaved the door shut. It was silent in the car for a moment and then Logan and his friend threw their heads back and howled in laughter. I curled into a ball and stayed there. I didn't care about the smirk on Nate's face or how Mason seemed to look through me in the rear view mirror. He could try, he'd only see emptiness. The guys stopped a few times, left, and returned to do the same thing. I didn't know what they were doing. I didn't care. I'd done what I wanted.

CHAPTER TEN

They dropped off the fourth friend and the rest of us traipsed into the house. Logan picked up a phone and ordered a pizza. Nate snagged a cooler of beer and brought it downstairs to the media room. I followed behind. I didn't know why, I just did. When Mason turned on the news, I curled into a ball in one of the leather recliners and after a while I tugged a blanket on top.

When the news came on and there was no word of my vandalism or whatever the guys had done, I uncurled my legs and headed to bed.

Mason followed me.

"What?" I went to brush my teeth in my bathroom.

He perched on my bed, studying me with an impenetrable gaze. He barely blinked. "That car thing should've been on the news. Cops would've been called."

"It wasn't." I moved back to the room after rinsing my mouth.

"You seemed sure of it."

"I was." I pulled off my top, then my bra.

He still didn't blink and he sounded bored. "How'd you know that guy?"

"He's the coach at my school." I pulled on a tight tank and then shimmied out of my pants. The light hadn't been turned on so the room was dark except for a small amount of light that shone through my windows from behind a clump of clouds.

"That was your dad."

I hesitated and held my breath. He looked like a statue, a god made of stone with the light's shadow on him. His eyes were intense as he seemed to stare through me, into me.

"Yeah," I spoke in a small voice.

He nodded. "I got it."

As he moved past, his hand brushed my leg and lingered on the curve of my thigh.

I closed my eyes as a stab of desire flared in me. This wasn't supposed to be. I hadn't expected this.

Then he moved past and out the door. My hands and legs were a bit shaky when I crawled under the sheets.

It was past midnight, but I lay in bed. My mind was reeling from the look on David's face. There was a haunted feel to him, then when he saw the firecrackers in my hand a look of disappointment came next. For a second, I'd been ashamed but then I remembered the lie he had been a part of and everything hardened, it all became clear again.

He deserved it. He deserved more.

That was your dad…I got it.

Mason's voice floated in there too. My chest tightened each time I heard it. His face was unreadable, he was always unreadable, but something softened when he spoke those words. Heat flared all over my body and I threw back the sheets. I gasped as the cool air hit my skin, but another need pulsated between my legs. I clamped them together and hoped it would pass. It was an annoyance and not something I needed right now.

The sound of my phone woke me the next morning. When I answered, Becky greeted me with a chirpy voice, "Morning! Whatchadointoday?"

"Huh?"

"Come over. My family's grilling this afternoon and Adam's family is coming too. It'll be fun."

I grimaced against how sunshiney her voice sounded. My head pounded. "Yeah, maybe."

"Oh, come on, Sam. What else are you going to do today? Homework? You can do it here."

"Why do I feel like there's no other option here?"

"Because there's not. Be here in an hour or I'm coming to get you."

I grinned at that threat. "It'll be more than an hour. I'm going to go for a run first."

"Okay. Just come. We start grilling after church."

The clock said it was nine. "When is that?"

"After noon."

"You told me to come in an hour, but you're going to church?"

"My mom goes to church. The rest of us stay home."

"Oh. Okay."

"Just come. Okay, Sammm?"

"Yeah, okay. Be there in a couple of hours."

"See ya!" There she went away, chirping, as she ended the call.

It didn't take me long to get ready for my run and when I headed downstairs, the guys were in the kitchen. Coffee had been made and each had their own mugs. Mason lounged against a counter while Nate had hopped up on the counter. As I came closer, Logan was skirting around the kitchen. He seemed to be bouncing around with too much energy, but he stopped when he saw me first.

"Should we take bets? An hour? Two?"

Mason narrowed his eyes over his coffee cup. "I say an hour."

Nate grunted and dropped to the floor. He busied himself inside the fridge.

Logan draped an arm over his brother's shoulders and grinned at me.

My back straightened. His smile seemed more of a leer and I heard the mocking tone in his voice.

"She did see her dad last night so I'm guessing two hours, maybe more? Sound right, wannabe sister?"

My mouth tightened and I grabbed a water bottle from the pantry. "Don't be stupid."

When I moved to the door, Logan was in front of me in a flash. He laughed at me. "Did I hit a nerve? Your claws are showing."

I shoved him out of the way. "What do you think?"

He opened his mouth for a retort, but I slammed the door shut behind me. I hadn't taken two steps away before I heard his high-pitched laughter on the other side. Mason barked something and it stopped.

I sighed, but tried to clear my mind. That was what running was for. My head needed to be clear. I needed to quiet the storm in me and after an hour, it was successfully subsided. Sweat dropped from me as I made my way back into the house and I hadn't made it to the stairs before I heard my mother's voice.

"Really, Samantha. Can you dry off a bit before coming inside after your runs?"

I gritted my teeth and wanted to go right back for another run.

She came from one of the side rooms dressed in a yellow dress and a white sunhat. Her make-up was done flawlessly with bright red lipstick. Pink lipstick had been her favorite until a month ago.

She stopped in front of me and her hands perched on her hips. "David called me last night. We came back earlier because of it. What were you thinking, honey?"

I knew my eyes were either heated or they looked dead. It was one or the other because both emotions twisted inside of me. "You're a calculated woman. Figure it out."

"Sam—" She started to follow when I went up the stairs, but James' voice pulled her back.

"Analise?" he called from the hallway.

She sighed with a dark frown, but went to him.

I hurried upstairs and got ready for Becky's. Thirty minutes later and I was back out the door. It was a welcoming feeling with the mansion in my rearview mirror and when I went inside of Becky's house, the two places contrasted sharply. One was homey and welcoming and the other had a stranger's coldness.

An older woman, probably in her mid-forties, welcomed me at the door. Her dark brown hair was pulled up in a ponytail and freckles covered her face. It made her look tanned and healthy as her eyes sparkled in warmth. "You must be Samantha. Rebecca has told me so much about you."

"Yeah…"

She gestured inside. "Come in, come in. I'm Laura, her mother."

"Sam!" Becky hollered from somewhere inside. "Tell her to come out here, mom."

Laura patted me on the back. "Make yourself at home. Pretend this is your home from now on. Everyone's in the backyard. I was grabbing some fruit platters on my way back."

"Do you want some help?" I watched as she started to lift two giant silver trays of meat and fruit.

"Oh, no. Go and have fun. We're not going to get these nice summer days for long."

"Hi, Sam!" Becky waved from a small pool in her backyard. The raft slipped from underneath her and she screamed as she fell into the water.

Adam shook his head and came over with a can of soda. He had a lopsided grin on and sunglasses in place, dressed in only red swim trunks. "She can never stay on those things on a sober day."

I took the can from him. "She's drinking?"

"Wine coolers, nothing hard."

"But." I saw Laura at a picnic table where the food had been compiled. Another older lady was with her. She had blonde hair and wore a similar dress like my mother's. Something told me this was Adam's mother. "Her parents are here."

He shrugged and gestured to two recliners by the pool. "They're pretty lax about it. My folks aren't. If my mom saw a beer in my hand, I'd be running killers at five in the morning for a month."

"She doesn't say anything to Becky's parents?"

"They have different parenting styles, but they're old friends. They respect each other."

"Oh." For some reason I felt weird as I sat beside him. Becky came over a moment later with a towel wrapped around her. She perched on the end of my seat and water dripped off of her.

"Did you hear about the Roussou players last night?"

Everything snapped to attention in me, but I drawled out, "What do you mean?"

She leaned forward with an eager grin. "I heard the Kades went there with their friends. They wrecked your dad's car at the Roussou's coach's house and slashed a bunch of their football players' tires. Can you believe that?"

Adam frowned.

"Did your dad say anything?"

I felt Adam watching me, but gave her a casual look. "Oh, no. He didn't say anything about it."

"That's probably because he won't press charges. Your dad's nice like that, but I would if it were my car. I can't believe they did that. I wish they played for our team. We'd go to state for sure."

Laura called out, "Rebecca, go and get your brothers from the basement."

She frowned and stood up. "My stupid little brothers." And off she went, muttering under her breath.

"You haven't told her?"

I shot him a look and remembered he knew about my situation. My shoulders stiffened and the chair became uncomfortable to sit on. "It's no one's business."

"She's your friend."

"She's been someone I talk to for the last week. That's all."

"Really?" His eyes mocked me.

"It's none of your business either."

"Except that Coach Strattan's my coach and he's the best coach I've ever met."

"You've only been on his team."

"I do football camps in the summer, Sam. He's the best coach I've met and that's including FC Public's coaches. They got lucky that the Kades didn't go to our school. They didn't develop their talent at all."

I studied him underneath my eyelashes. "You sound a little jealous?"

He grimaced and stood up. "The Kades are some talented sons of bitches, that's all I'm saying. Your dad would've made them better than they are, they might be more respectful too. All they are is rich a-holes right now."

"Sam, Adam." Becky waved us over to the food table. "We need to grab our food first before my little brothers and all their friends get out here. They're like bugs; their saliva will be crawling all over the food."

And after we sat at a far table with our plates; eight boys who looked like they were in seventh grade burst through the back door. They swarmed around the table. Becky was right. As the afternoon passed, the guys never left the food for long. They were different heights, but all were skinny except for one that looked on the pudgy side. When Becky got up and got us some more beverages, her brothers and their friends took over the pool too.

She sighed as she popped open a beer. "There goes my tanning today. Little rodents."

Adam laughed and stole the water she had nabbed. "Come off it. You love your brothers and you know it. You dote on Jake and Greg."

She scowled. "I'm going to make their lives hell. JAKE!"

A boy popped his head out of the water. "What?"

"If you don't get your little friends out of the pool, I'm going to tell mom and dad what's under your TV."

He froze and his eyes got wide.

Then Adam laughed and stood up. "Don't worry about her, Jake. She won't do that to you. Come on, Becks." He tugged her from the table. "Let's you and me take Sam to the movies."

A pink flush came over her cheeks, but she pretended to pull against his hold on her. "I wanted to tan today, Adam."

He laughed again and swatted her butt. "Go get cute. We can make a matinee and it'll be my treat."

I watched as she tried not to make it look like she was hurrying inside. Then I frowned when he sat back down. "You're not being nice again."

His eyebrows lifted slightly. "I thought I was being really nice."

"You're not and you know it. What's your game?"

He let out a deep breath and glanced at his lap. A moment later he peeked over and I followed his gaze. Two older men were in a heated conversation. Their hands were in the air and each had a can of beer. "I don't feel like being here. My dad just got here."

"Which one?"

"The tall guy. He got here from a meeting ten minutes ago."

From the way he said that and how he was scowling at him, I figured Adam knew something I couldn't discern. His dad was handsome. He was an older version of Adam and he was dressed in custom fitted shorts with a white shirt. He could've been a model for a summer GQ edition.

Becky's dad was the opposite. His white wife beater had stains from the grill and his beer belly hung over his board shorts. He had a slight worshipful look on his face as he debated something with Adam's dad.

"Did he really have a meeting?"

Adam's mother had grown silent next to Laura where they sat underneath a patio umbrella.

He sighed. "What do you think?"

Understanding dawned. "This is why I've kept quiet about my situation."

"Yeah, well, that's not going to happen to me. He'll never leave her."

I heard the bitterness and asked, "You want him to?"

"I want her to."

I fell quiet. I didn't know what to say.

Then Adam surprised me when he tapped my arm gently. "My mom works for James Kade, you know. She's the assistant to his junior assistant."

I shot him a dark look. "So?"

He shrugged. "So nothing. She talks about how nice he is to her."

Relief flooded me and my shoulders sagged forward. Then I gave him a wicked grin. "Oh, so are you saying you could be stepbrothers with Mason and Logan Kade."

He grinned. "Yeah, right. Wouldn't that be a joke?"

I didn't know what else to say and Adam fell into a quiet slump. We were both like that, dazing off into our thoughts when Becky rushed outside. She had changed into khaki shorts and a loose top. Her hair was pulled into a high ponytail and she had a small amount of make-up on. Her eyelashes were black and long. I'd never seen her dressed how she was, even when we went to the party.

She looked nice and I cast a look at Adam underneath my eyelids. Did he think so? But he stood up and shot forward to his car. Her shoulders dropped an inch and the corners of her mouth turned down, but then she flashed me a bright smile.

"Do I look okay?" She touched the ends of her hair and patted them into place. They already were, but she kept pressing them down.

"You look good." And I meant it.

She cast me a furtive glance. "Not like you. You look great, like always."

I frowned.

"How was your date?" She put the chirpy note back in her voice and fell in line beside me as we followed where Adam had gone to his car. He waited for us, not within hearing distance.

I hesitated. Now I wasn't being the nice friend.

"Come on." She nudged me with her shoulder. "I really want to know."

"Becky." I grabbed her arm and held her back. "You like him."

Her mouth twisted, but she gave me a smile after. "It doesn't matter. He doesn't like me, not like that."

"He could."

"No, he couldn't. He practically drools any time you enter a room. He's always had a thing for you."

"What are you talking about?"

"Even before last year, he was interested. You were dating Jeff, though, so he asked Ashley out."

"Are you serious?"

"Yeah, duh." She rolled her eyes, but frowned when she saw that I was biting my lip. "You didn't know? Really?"

I shook my head. "I didn't know that Jess had been sleeping with Jeff for two years. How was I supposed to know this?"

"Oh. Well." Her shoulders lifted and dropped in a dramatic way. "You got your chance now."

Except I didn't and I didn't want it. Then I remembered last night when Mason touched me, how his fingers lingered on my thigh. I shivered as the same desire swept through me again.

Not good. None of this was good.

"Are you two coming or what?" Adam called us over.

"Yeah!" Becky shouted back and dragged me after with a forced excited look in her eyes. She tried to sit in the back, but I made her sit in the front.

As we went to the theatre I slumped in the back of the car and was quiet on the drive over. Both tried to pull me into the conversation, but admitted defeat when we got closer to the mall. I listened to them talking when we got our tickets and took our seats.

Their conversation wasn't forced. There was no taunting, strained silences, or fakeness. They sounded like two friends who'd known each other all their lives and then I realized that they *had* known each other all their lives. They were neighbors. Their parents were friends.

I made the decision then that I'd try to be the friend for Becky that she seemed to be for everyone else.

I sighed. If only I knew how.

CHAPTER ELEVEN

"We get out of practice early tonight. Your da—David's got something, I guess." Adam dropped a shoulder against the locker beside mine when I arrived the next morning to school. He folded his arms and his backpack's straps cut into the muscles on his arms and chest.

That annoyed me for some reason and I opened my locker to stuff the bag lunch Mousteff had shoved at me that morning. He had muttered, like he always did, but this time I was certain I'd heard a few curse words. And I was certain they were directed at me, well, me or my mother. Then I relaxed as I considered that. He was probably pissed about my mom again. That made more sense.

Adam had been watching me with an odd look. "Are you okay?"

"I'm fine," I bit out. I forced myself to relax. Sometimes being mean right off the bat wasn't good. And Adam had started to be one of the two people still there for me after my debacle with Jeff/Lydia/Jessica.

And speaking of, as I turned to Adam, I saw my two ex best friends at Jill Flatten's locker across the hall. All three of them were watching me with frowns on their faces. When they saw me, Jill giggled and leaned closer to the two. She whispered something and both of them started laughing.

Jeff stopped beside them, saw me, saw the exchange, and kept going.

Adam chuckled. "I think he's finally learning."

I rolled my eyes and started towards my first class. When Adam

TIJAN

walked with me, I asked, "So what about you getting out of practice early?"

"I was thinking we could try that dinner again."

I saw Becky at her locker ahead. She dropped her bag. Books and papers fell out of it and she knelt beside and lurched to grab everything before people kicked her things away. A few laughed and did what she tried to prevent, but one other girl helped her gather her stuff.

I sighed. "I can't."

"Why not?" Then he saw where I'd been watching. He stopped me with a hand on my shoulder. "Becky and I are never going to date. We had a heart to heart last night after the movies."

"You did?"

"Yeah." He nodded. His eyes skirted over my face, scanning me constantly as if he were looking for something. "She's really okay with you and me..." He hesitated. "Getting to know one another?"

I smirked. "And do I get a say in this?"

"Well, yeah, of course." But his cheeks got red, just a bit, and he scratched the back of his head. "So do you want to have dinner tonight? I was thinking you could even eat the food this time."

I rolled my eyes. "Yeah, sure." I waited a beat. "Can I bring Becky?"

He froze and I moved ahead, laughing. Then he called after me, "You're not funny."

I shook my head and kept laughing. I was funny enough.

I had Lydia in my first two periods and she kept giving me weird looks. Jessica was in my third and fourth period. She refused to look at me. Then at lunch, when Becky dropped across from me and Adam went to sit with his football team, Jill joined their table along with Lydia and Jessica.

Becky looked over her shoulder and her eyes got wide. "I can't believe them."

"What?" I was cautious as I opened my bag lunch. Then I relaxed. Inside were an orange, a bag of chips, and a peanut butter

91

sandwich. I gave her my chips, tossed the sandwich in the trash, and started to peel the orange.

"Jill Flatten. She's all over Jeff at the table. And I can't believe she's friends with *your* friends."

"They're not my friends."

"They were," she retorted and sent them a glare. Lydia had looked, but ducked her head down. "It's like Jill Flatten wants your life."

I sat back and fought off a yawn.

"Aren't you bothered at all by her?"

I shrugged. "Truthfully, no. It's sort of the last thing on my mind these days."

She gave me an incredulous look. "What else is going on in your life?"

If only she knew… I lifted a careless shoulder. "Jill Flatten does not bother me." Mason and Logan on the other hand… My mother… I shuddered. My whole life had fallen apart. Finding one good friend like Becky erased all the other friend drama.

"She bothers me." She peeked over her shoulder at them.

I looked this time too and saw all three of them had been staring at us. Lydia squeaked and looked at her food. Jessica's head whipped away and Jill only narrowed her eyes, but she held my gaze.

I narrowed mine back and stood.

Becky gasped, "What are you doing?"

I was tempted to shrug her off. I didn't know, but something propelled me across the lunch room. I stopped before their table and heard a lot of conversations hush. The football team sat at the 'popular' table, but most of the really popular girls sat at the other end where Adam was with the other varsity starters. Jill, Lydia, and Jessica sat at the far end where Jeff was, along with the other second string guys. Jeff was third string, actually.

Becky bumped into my elbow, and then apologized under her breath. She was panting from her hurry.

"Sam!" Adam called over and waved at us.

I ignored him.

Becky took my arm and hissed in my ear, "We can sit by him."

I shrugged her off and glanced up. I didn't know what made me look, but my fake father had entered the lunch room. He was dressed in his coach's apparel, a professional looking running suit with Fallen Crest Academy printed on his left shoulder underneath our school's crest.

"Yes?" Jill snapped at me. She tried to sound bored, like I was annoying her, but I heard the apprehension underneath it.

At the sight of David, everything hardened in me again. I was growing used to that feeling and I looked back at her. There was an added edge to me when I stepped close to their table and placed a hand right in front of her.

"Sam?" Jeff leaned forward and whispered. "What are you doing?"

Jessica still refused to look at me. Lydia had both her hands over her face, but her fingers were spread. She watched from behind them and I saw that she was holding her breath.

"You're wasting our lunch time," Jill snapped. "What do you want, Sam? You're pathetic."

Then Adam was beside me and his hand held my elbow. He pulled me back against him and spoke into my ear. As his lips moved, they brushed against me and I shivered from the teasing touch. "Sit with me. Let this go. Trust me, it won't be worth it."

"Fine." I released everything in me when I surrendered with that word.

He nodded and started to pull me away. I saw the looks of relief on Jessica, Lydia, and Jeff's faces. Jill looked disappointed, but David stepped in front of me. He gave Adam a polite nod. "Do you mind if I have a word with Samantha?"

I stiffened in Adam's hold and he cast a concerned look at me. Then he reluctantly nodded. "Sure."

David gestured towards the hall and I followed at a slower pace. I glanced back and saw that Adam had pulled Becky to sit beside him, but she watched me. Her eyes were small and she was biting her lip.

Then the door was pushed open and we stepped out into the empty hallway.

David gestured ahead. "My office?"

I rolled my eyes. "Is this about your car?"

"My office?"

I heard the forced politeness and followed. Everything in me was cement. I didn't care, not one iota, but I followed anyway. I was more curious to what he had to say and then when we were in his office and he shut the door, I knew he meant business. He indicated the couch across from his desk.

I perched on the end.

He took his seat and folded his hands on the desk. He looked at them.

I waited.

No one spoke.

Then he cursed under his breath and looked up. His eyes were bleak again.

I frowned. I didn't care why he looked like that. It made no difference to me now…

He started, "Do you know how much trouble you could've been?"

"If you had called the cops?"

"Yes," he snapped out. "Samantha, this is not a joke."

"I'm not laughing."

"If anyone else would've seen and had called the cops, I wouldn't have been able to protect you. The cops have the right to press charges, even if the offended party doesn't want them to."

"So you're saying you don't want me charged?"

He sighed and leaned back in his chair. "I didn't call the cops for a reason."

"Why's that?" I was in shock at my own voice. I sounded so bored.

He bit out a few curses. The hostility of them drew me upright again and something stirred in me. It was like I was coming awake again.

He glared at me. "Of course, I don't want you hurt. Why would you think that? I raised you, Samantha."

"Even though I'm not your daughter."

His chest heaved up and down and he looked like he was fighting for control. His voice was strained a second later. "I loved you, all your life, like you were my daughter. And what happened to you wasn't your fault—"

I shot to my feet, though I hugged myself. "According to Analise, it was both of your faults."

"I loved her." He laughed to himself. The sound sent chills down my back. "Because I don't make millions or because I'm not handsome like him doesn't mean that I didn't love your mother. I loved her very much."

I blinked. And everything was gone in the next moment. My anger vanished. My sarcasm, my self-loathing, my hatred for him—all was gone. And I collapsed down on the couch again. My face was buried in my hands.

He continued in a distant voice, "I loved my marriage how it was..." His chair squeaked and his voice was clearer now. "Stop hanging out with the Kade boys."

I looked up.

He watched me intently, his eyes never wavered away. "They are not good for you. They are dangerous to you."

It all shut down again and I stood. "I thought you said to make friends?"

"I was hoping for the best then. Now I'm preparing for the worst." His face was clouded. "Stay away from them, as much as possible. Please, Samantha."

I gave him a wry look. "If only it were that simple." And then I opened the door and went through the boys' locker room. The bell rang as I got to the hallway and I took refuge in my last three periods.

No Becky. No Adam. No one who cared was in those classes.

I was able to breathe easier knowing that.

After my last period, I escaped easily.

When I got to the mansion, I was surprised to find Logan in the dining room. He had books and papers spread out over the table and he glanced up idly. When he saw it was me, his focused snapped to attention. He gave me a lopsided grin, but my back straightened.

I wasn't fooled.

"We're doing a charity thing with your school this weekend."

I shrugged and went to the kitchen.

"It's another football game."

My hand paused when I reached for a water bottle.

"Your dad's going to be there." He'd gotten up and leaned against a counter close to me. "What are you going to do?"

I shut the door and watched him. "What do you mean?"

"Who are you going to cheer for? Your loser school or your new soon-to-be stepbrothers?"

"And why would you assume I'd be there?"

He shrugged, but I caught his cocky grin. "It's for charity. Your whole school will be there."

"When is it?"

"Saturday night."

"Why not Friday night?"

He rolled his eyes and pushed off from the counter. I tensed when he reached around me and opened the fridge. His arm brushed against my shoulder and he pulled out a container of juice. "Because we have our normal game that night. We play Collins. You should come, cheer us on."

"I think not." I pulled away and remained at a safe distance.

His eyes seemed to laugh at me. "Whatever. You've gotta come to the charity thing."

"And why's that?"

"Because we're going to win." He made it sound like it was the most obvious thing to do.

"Why do you think I care?"

"Because…" He chewed on his words. "Because Mason and I are the best. Why wouldn't you come?"

"Because I don't care about that?"

"Well, you should." He sounded miffed, like I had hurt his feelings.

I lifted a careless shoulder in the air.

He narrowed his eyes. "You're a bit odd in the head, aren't you?"

I couldn't hold back my grin. "What do you mean?"

"Most girls would blast it on the internet that we're your new stepbrothers. You act like we're your dirty secret."

"I like my privacy."

He shook his head. "We've got a couple parties this weekend too, if you want to go?"

"I'm good with my friends."

His eyes narrowed and he opened his mouth, but Mason came around the corner that instant. Logan clamped his mouth shut, but he continued to give me a puzzling stare.

"Let's go." Mason punched Logan in the shoulder as he bypassed us.

I looked over and held Mason's gaze before he went through the front door.

A different shiver went over my body at the sight of him and something left me when the door closed behind him. I refused to think it was anything more than hate…right?

CHAPTER TWELVE

That night I met Adam for burgers and he surprised me by bringing Becky. Everyone was happy until Jeff and Jill Flatten came in for their date night. They chose a booth across the restaurant so it was semi-easy to ignore them. When they left, Jeff gave me a once over and Jill gave me a glare.

Sigh.

I could've been a part of that.

Or not.

I shuddered at the thought of being with Jeff again, not to mention the deceit from Lydia and Jessica.

And since Becky must've been psychic, she shot forward and slammed a hand down on the table. "I heard Lydia telling Melissa Baker that Jeff asked about you."

Adam sat back.

"What are you talking about?"

She jerked her head up and down. "Uh huh. And Nancy Morrow overheard it too. He asked Lydia and Jessica about you, at Jessica's locker." She spoke like it was a hush-hush controversy.

"Come on, Becky. Jeff's not stupid."

"Yeah, he is."

"He knows that he's made his bed."

"My cousin is a jerk-one douche bag. I bet you fifty bucks that he's going to start talking to you again by the end of the month. And Jill knows it too." She pointed at the door with a French fry. "That's why she's upped her game against you."

"Since they got together, she's been like that."

"Yeah, but it's worse. I think she hates you." She glanced at Adam from underneath her eyelids. "And I think Ashley DeCortts is scared of you."

"Does she hate me too?" I hadn't done anything to anyone. Why did anyone care about me?

"No." Becky gave me a small smile. "It's not in Ashley to hate someone." She looked at Adam. "Right?"

He placed two hands against the table and pushed his chair back. When he stood, he plucked the bill from the table and went to the register.

"I think that's his answer for 'I don't care and let's get out of here.'"

Becky groaned. "I think he's mad at me."

"Why?"

"Because he brought me on your date, because he thought you wouldn't go without me, and now I'm bringing up Ashley." She leaned across the table and whispered behind her hands, "He still loves her, Sam."

When he started back to us, I stood. "Becky, you're just being you. Don't worry about it. You've got nothing to feel bad about."

She jumped to her feet and smoothed her hands down the front of her pants while she gave me an unsteady smile.

Adam stood behind me and asked in a low voice, "Sam, do you need a ride to school tomorrow?"

Becky's eyes got wide. She squeaked, but slapped both her hands over her mouth and jerked away.

As she hurried out the door, I couldn't stop a laugh. "Why are you like that to her?"

The corner of his mouth lifted. "Because she's so interested in everyone else's business. I don't think that's good for her."

"Let her be. That's just her being her."

"Yeah." His voice was wry. "I heard what you said to her."

I shrugged a shoulder. "That's how I feel."

As we both turned for the door, his hand cupped the back of my elbow. "You never answered about that ride."

I shook my head and pushed open the glass door. The evening had cooled and I knew I'd need a sweater soon.

Becky was already in his car, but I knew she could see us.

"Samantha?"

"My whole name?" I teased him before I gently twisted my elbow out of his hold. "I can give myself a ride. Thanks for the offer. That was sweet."

He tugged on the back of my pants when I was about to step down for the car and held me back. His voice was close to my ear. "I could give Becky and you a ride tomorrow."

I could imagine their reactions when they pulled up to the Kade mansion. And I chuckled dryly when I removed his hold from my pants. "That's okay, Don Juan, but I think Becky would appreciate a ride."

He laughed, huskily, and brushed against the back of my neck. "Maybe I'll do that then."

I gave him a curious look as I opened the front door and he rounded the car for his, but as he slid behind the steering wheel, his face was clouded. A wall had been put in place and from the little I knew Adam, I knew I wouldn't get that wall back down for a while.

When he drove us back to Becky's house where my car was parked, the ride was quiet. Even Becky was silent and I knew this was the right thing to do. He kept trying, but it wouldn't happen. It shouldn't happen. And he should give Becky rides. They were neighbors. A part of me felt he might start to like her, if only he'd get over whatever fascination he had for me.

I was broken. I didn't need to break anyone else with me.

When Adam pulled into his family's driveway, he didn't say goodbye. He got out of his side, shut the door, and strolled inside his family's house.

Becky gave me a sad smile as we were slower to get out. "He's mad. What'd you do?"

"Nothing." That was the truth. "He'll get over it."

"Yeah."

I sighed. How had I gotten into more drama? "I'll see you tomorrow."

"See you." She waved as I went to my car and drove off.

When I got home and after I had gone for a run, it was late. The place was empty, not a shocker. It always seemed empty except for the random sandwich wrapped in saran wrap that Mousteff would leave in the refrigerator for me. After I showered, I headed downstairs to the media room with a glass of water. I found Mason on the couch with the sports channel on the television and I hesitated in the doorway.

"Sit."

I jumped at his command, but I did.

He lounged back on the couch with a beer on the table beside it. The television lights played across his face. It gave him a dark look, a somber one that added to the alarm I always felt around him. His eyes were on the screen and then they were on me. I tensed at the sudden change, at the intensity in them, but steeled myself. I was starting to think this was what he'd always be like, primed and alert.

"Logan and Nate went to some party."

"Oh." I winced at how timid I sounded.

He yawned and looked away.

I was released from his gaze and my body sagged from the relief of it. "What party?"

He jerked a shoulder up. "Don't care."

"Oh."

Then he smirked. "Your mom wants to take Logan and me to dinner Sunday."

I narrowed my eyes. All the nerves I felt around him hardened at the mention of her. "Why?"

He looked back at me. The same caution was in his gaze as I felt in my body. "I was going to ask you the same question."

Then it clicked. "That's why you didn't go to the party. You wanted to question me about her."

He didn't blink. "You'd do the same."

He was right and I nodded. "If you want to know my mom's agenda, I'm guessing it's because she wants to get to know you guys."

"She told you on the patio that afternoon she knew us well enough."

So they *had* heard. I'd been wondering.

I sat up straighter in my chair. "She was lying."

He didn't say anything.

My voice grew bolder. "My mom wants everyone to do what she wants and she said those things so I'd do what she wanted. I think she wants to take you guys out for dinner to try and charm you."

"It won't work."

He said it so bluntly, but I knew it was the truth. A shiver went down my spine as I held his gaze in that darkened room with an empty mansion around us. Mason Kade was not stupid, far from it, and I wondered if I'd known it the whole time, if perhaps that's why I stayed away. He watched behaviors, he didn't listen to words. I wondered if Logan was the same and something in my gut told me he was.

"It worked on your father."

"My dad has a weakness for weak women."

Again, there was no judgment. It was a fact and he said it as such. The truth of it held more power because of the lack of emotion with him.

My throat had gone dry. "You called my mother weak."

"Isn't she?"

His gaze was searing into mine.

My chest tightened. My throat clamped up. "I—uh—"

He snorted in disgust. "You think so too, but you can't say the words, not to me. That's alright. I understand. She's your blood."

Then he looked away and again, my whole body almost fell from the chair. It was as if he had pinned me in place and I was free from the hold.

My hands curled in on themselves and I couldn't stop my fingers from trembling. I tucked them between my legs and took a breath. I needed to gain control of myself again.

In that moment, I realized that he always had that affect on me. The ice façade I reined over myself was plucked away whenever his attention was on me. He reached over and took it away like I was a baby with candy.

"Does my mom know you don't like her?" It was a weird question, but I wanted to know how he thought. I wanted to understand him.

He grinned at me. The power of that look with his piercing eyes, perfect teeth, and square jaw had me pinned against my chair again. I couldn't breathe for a moment.

Then I heard him laugh. "Your mom doesn't care. She cares if we're going to make a stink or not."

I snorted. That sounded just like her. "And are you?"

He shrugged and went back to the television. "As long as she doesn't screw with me and Logan or with our mom then I don't care who my dad pounds."

"And if they get married? My mom's not stupid."

"Your mom's a shark."

"Your father is wealthy."

Then he laughed again and the genuineness of it struck me. "My dad has money, but my mom is wealthy."

My eyes widened a fraction. I would put money down my mom had no idea about that tidbit. It made things a lot clearer, why the boys didn't seem to care too much about the marriage.

"Do you care?"

I was struck by how he seemed to really want to know. I shook my head. "Why would I?"

"Because your mom's going to look a fool when she learns how rich my mom is."

I hadn't considered it, but he was right. Analise was ambitious and she'd grown more ambitious since leaving my—David. It would burn her ego, in some way, and then I realized why he was telling me this. I was the one who'd pay for it. Analise would take her anger out on me and I sucked in my breath. I was grateful for his slight warning, because it was one that I'd need to keep tucked in the back of my mind.

We heard a door open upstairs and Logan's near-hysterical laughter followed a second later.

Mason grinned to himself before he stood up and left with his beer in hand.

"Mason! Dude, there was a girl with boobs out to here. I couldn't believe it." Logan's voice carried down the stairs. His laughter wouldn't stop. "Nate bagged her."

Mason's and Nate's voices joined in at a low murmur.

I tuned them out and turned the television to a different channel. When a bunch of rich women came on the screen, I settled back. My mom would've loved that show; she would've loved to have been on that show. When they started fighting with each other, I closed my eyes and fell asleep.

CHAPTER THIRTEEN

Becky gushed about her ride with Adam the next morning when she found me at my locker. She gushed about the charity football game at lunch. The next day was a similar chain of events except Adam sat with us at our table. It didn't faze Becky from raving about Saturday's game. On Thursday a few of his friends joined him at our table and one seemed amused by Becky's passionate monologue about the Kade brothers, who was better, who was better looking, etc. He teased and prodded her along until Becky seemed like she was going to shout from the rooftop how hot Mason and Logan Kade were. At one point I thought she'd been about to proclaim they could beat our entire football team, only the two of them.

She caught herself, blushed, and her head went down.

The guys didn't hold back their laughter and she turned to me. I patted her arm when she sighed, "I sounded like an idiot, didn't I?"

Even Adam couldn't hold back his grin.

And then things turned awkward when Jeff stopped at the end of our table. He had a tray of food in one hand and his backpack over the other shoulder. He hitched it higher and gave me a small wave. "Hey, Sam."

I leaned back.

Adam leaned forward. "What are you doing, Sallaway?"

Jeff looked around the guys and ended on Becky. "Hey, cousin. How's your mom doing?"

She glared. "She's fine."

"That's cool." He bobbed his head up and down.

"Jeff!"

Jill strode towards us with stiff legs. Her chin was clenched and her eyes glittered in anger.

One of the guys whistled under his breath. "Catfight."

Jeff shot him a look, but turned towards his girlfriend with a wide smile.

I saw it slip a little.

"Hey, babe. What's up?"

She latched onto his arm and her smile froze in place. "Nothing. What are you doing over here?"

He jerked his arm towards me. "I wanted to say hi."

"Why?" Her eyes seared at me.

Becky's hand rested on my arm under the table. I suppose she wanted to support me, but I was entertained. I grinned back at Jill and her mouth twitched a bit.

He shrugged again and tried to remain cool. "Because I think it's stupid that we're not talking. Lydia and Jess too. They were best friends." He stole a look underneath lidded eyes at Adam and the guys.

My back straightened. He was lying.

Jill's fingers curled into his arm and Jeff froze under her grip. Then he frowned and flung her hand off. "Ouch! Crap, woman. That hurt."

"So, Adam," Jill turned towards him. Fake warmth oozed from her pores. "How do you think the game will go on Saturday?"

One of the guys scoffed, "We have a real game on Friday."

Another added, "No one cares about that one."

Adam shot both a look and straightened in his chair. "I think we'll be fine."

"Why is that?" She leaned forward to give him a view of the upper curves of her boobs. Cleavage heaven was on display.

Jeff was eagerly lapping up his view.

Becky yipped out, "You don't think the team will win?"

Jill settled back on her heels and turned ice eyes towards her. "They did get creamed last week by them."

"Yeah, but that was a real game. It counted."

Adam shot Becky a dark look.

She didn't see it and plodded on, "This game doesn't really count. I heard the Kade brothers might not even play. They didn't come for the charity event last year."

"They have to come." Jill's eyes were sharp. "That's why we chose the football team, so they'd come."

Jeff moved back. "You want them to come?"

"What? I mean, you're going to do fine, honey."

"I don't play in a real game."

"Yeah, but it's for charity." She pressed herself against him and cooed again. "I bet their third string plays too. Charity for everyone."

Becky's mouth closed with an audible snap. The guys were silent for a second and then burst out laughing. Even Adam wiped at something in his eyes. Jill's eyebrows shot up and her smile froze in place.

Jeff tore himself away. "So I'm the charity? Is that what you're saying?"

"No, honey. Jeff! That's not what I meant." She hollered and went after as he stalked out of the cafeteria.

One of the guys whistled. "Man, Sam. You didn't even say a word. How'd you get out of that?"

I offered up a shoulder. "Talent?"

Both of Adam's friends laughed while Becky's eyes went wide. "You didn't, did you? I thought Jill was going to leap at you with her nails."

Adam shook his head. "I think that's why Sam kept quiet."

"Yeah, that pissed off Decimator even more. Good thinking."

"It hadn't been my plan, but I'll take it. Decimator?"

The guy struck a cocky pose. "She decimates her way through guys. The Decimator."

"I agree with that. She is a decimator." Becky went back to eating as she nodded her agreement.

Adam gave me a half grin. "You okay?" He lowered his voice and inched closer across the table.

I shrugged, but I didn't say anything because I didn't have anything to say. I didn't care about Jeff and I hadn't for a long time.

Adam kept giving me concerned looks through the rest of the day and the day after, but it didn't matter. I didn't care anymore and Jeff picked up on that too after I walked past him and Jill in the hallway. I hadn't known they were there until I almost bowled them over. They were with Lydia and Jessica. After I muttered a quick apology, one that I'd give to anybody, I hurried on my way. It wasn't until I was about to turn the corner that I looked back and realized who I had run into.

Jill seemed upset, but Jessica and Lydia stared at me. They watched me.

Jeff's shoulder slumped and he had a downcast expression on his face. When his eyes met mine for a brief second, I saw an apology flash through his.

It was over. Really over and he knew it as well.

My step had a lighter bounce to it for the rest of the day. That lasted until the end of the day when Lydia cornered me later. She'd been waiting at my car. I slowed when I saw her, but what could I do? I wasn't stupid enough or crazy enough to try running home again.

"Hey." She shot up from my car and twisted her hands together. "How are you?"

"What do you want?"

Hurt flashed in her eyes, but she looked down. "Nothing, I just—how are you?"

I let my bag drop to the ground before I unlocked my door. "I'm fine. You?"

She gave me a tentative smile. "I think Justin Beardsley might ask me out."

I nodded. "Cool."

"So you and Adam, huh?" A strand of her hair was wound in her hand and she began to twirl it around. "That's exciting, really exciting. I tried telling Jessica we should be happy for you, but—"

"Why would she?" My tone was flat. "She slept with my boyfriend for two years to get back at me."

Lydia fell silent.

"She doesn't care, now or then."

"Yes, she does. I know she does." But she sounded as if she wanted to convince herself.

"Jessica doesn't care. At least she has the decency not to fake it anymore."

Lydia's mouth opened, but nothing came out.

And Becky bounced up to us at that moment. "How's it going?" I knew she spoke to me, but her glare was directed at Lydia.

Lydia's hands started to twist together again. "Hi, Becky."

"Hi, Lydia. What are you doing?"

"I'm just…saying hi to Sam." She sighed. "Is that okay?"

Becky jerked her shoulder up and frowned, but she looked away. "I guess. It's Sam's decision. I mean…you guys were friends after all…before me."

I rolled my eyes. "Are you serious?"

Both girls jumped at my tone.

I tried to gentle it. "Are you two pissing on each other for my friendship? I don't deal with that. You both should know that."

Lydia seemed frozen in place as she watched me, but Becky hung her head. "I know. I'm sorry."

"I have to get home." I started to reach for my car door again.

"Are you coming to the game tonight?" Becky rushed forward.

"Probably not. Why would I?"

"Because they're playing Roussou. There might be a bunch of action tonight, with the guys being in town after what we heard the Kades had done to their coach's house and some of the other guys."

I frowned at that. "I haven't heard anything."

"Oh." She seemed confused. "I thought I told you about that."

"Well, you didn't."

"Anyway, are you coming tonight?"

"No." I didn't hesitate.

Lydia looked away. Her eyes had been glued to me, like I was a television show for her. Now her whole body seemed to retreat away.

I frowned at her, but was distracted when Becky asked in an excited breath, "And tomorrow? You have to come. It's for charity." Her voice turned into a whine.

I sighed, but I already knew I'd go. Logan had been harassing me over the past week with the same question. Mason never asked, but Nate told me once that he wanted me to come. I hadn't a clue why.

"I don't know. Probably, okay?"

Again, Lydia seemed struck by something. She fell back a couple of steps before she caught herself.

I snapped at her, "What's your problem?"

She blinked rapidly a few times before she rasped out, "Uh, nothing. You're, just, you've changed."

"Yeah. Life does that to you." Then I swung my door open and got inside. I couldn't explain it, but both annoyed me. And when I was able to get home and go on my run, my mind finally started to clear after a couple of hours. It took that long before I calmed myself down. When I returned home, the evening's darkness had started to creep in.

My mother waited for me at the dining room table. She had a large glass of wine before her and every room was lit up around us. Her fingers kept tapping the table in a nervous manner—or, as I got a better look at Analise—in an irritated manner.

I didn't even wait for her to say anything. I dropped to a chair at the table and waited.

My headache had come back.

"I am taking the boys out for dinner on Sunday after church. If you are able to refrain from physical violence, I'd like for you to join us."

Her tone felt like whiplash against me.

I jerked away, but readied myself again. She couldn't hurt me unless I allowed her. "Why do you want me there?"

She gave a dramatic long-drawn out sigh and whirled the wine around inside the glass. "Because you are my daughter. Mason and Logan are going to be my stepsons, your stepbrothers. You don't think I think about this? I'm concerned for you, Samantha. I really am."

"Really?" My tone was dry, I couldn't keep it out.

She winced against it, but swallowed it down. Then she forced out her bright sunshiney fake act. "How are things at school? Have you seen David at all?"

"Once."

"Oh." She seemed to pull away from me, though she didn't move in her chair. Then she threw the rest of her wine down the back of her throat. "That's good that you still have him in your life. Have you ever considered going to public schooling? Mason and Logan seem to do very well there."

I rolled my eyes. They would've been fine anywhere they went.

"So you want me at this dinner thing?"

"You are my daughter."

"And you can refrain from slapping me?"

She winced, but I knew the movement cost her. A slight curse slipped from her lips and she tried to hide it.

"Mother?"

"What?" She lifted glazed eyes to me. "I think the dinner will be great. I could cook something, maybe? No, that didn't end well the last time. You're right. Dinner out is the best idea. I'm so happy you think so."

Yeah. Me too.

CHAPTER FOURTEEN

Becky called me bright and early the next morning. "Bad news bears, Sam."

I rolled over and sat up with a yawn. "It's seven in the morning. On a Saturday morning."

"I know. I just got home."

"So you decided to call and say good morning? You suck."

"No." Her voice was bright and chirpy. "I'm still drunk so it's probably not sinking in yet, but I can't go to the game tonight."

I groaned. There went my one friend to sit with.

"There was a party on the beach by Lydia's house and I'm getting back. Mom caught me this morning so I'm grounded now."

"You went to Lydia's party?" I should've asked, 'Lydia had a party? And you went to it?'

"Oh no. The party was by her house, I think some other girl threw it, but I dunno. Anyways, we had to wait till Adam was sober enough to drive. I kept drinking all night. Lydia's actually kind of funny."

"You were with Lydia? You two were pissing on each other."

She giggled. "Not literally, but she explained a few things to me and I feel for her...sort of...not really. Oh well. So I'm not going to the game tonight so that means you don't have to go either. I know I was the only reason you were going anyway."

I picked at some lint on my bedcover. "I might've gone to cheer for Adam too..."

"Aw." Her voice melted. "That's so sweet. I'll make sure to tell him. It'll mean a lot to him. He doesn't think you care about him at all."

"Are you kidding me?" I grumbled into the phone. "You're the one that likes him."

"Yeah, but he doesn't like me."

"You're a bit not right in the head, Becky."

"I know!" she chirped again, followed by a giggle. "He held my hand to the car."

"Were you falling down drunk?"

"That and the sand was really tricky to walk through."

"I'm sure it was." I lay back down on the bed and closed my eyes. Something was telling me this phone call wasn't going to let me go back to sleep anytime soon.

"So, what'd you do last night?"

I grinned into the phone. "Well, I didn't get drunk and hold hands with my crush all night long."

She giggled again. "I wish it was all night long. Maybe I could get drunk more? You think he'd do that every time?"

"No."

"Yeah, you're right." She sighed. "It'd be nice, though. I wish I could hold his hand all the time."

"Why don't you just ask him out?"

"Because he doesn't like me. How many times do I have to tell you?"

"Whatever." I gripped the phone tighter. "I think there's something there. Maybe he'd have to man up and make a decision already."

Silence.

I sighed.

There was more silence on the phone.

Then I asked, "Did I say something wrong?"

Her voice was timid. "It's not that easy for some of us."

"What do you mean by that?"

"Sometimes all we have is our imagination."

I frowned and cursed under my breath. "Your imagination? Your fairytale that's holding you back?"

She sucked in her breath.

I bit back another curse. I'd forgotten Becky was one of those girls. "I'm sorry."

"For what?" She sounded like she had started to cry.

I cursed myself and hit my forehead with my hand. "For not being sensitive."

"It's okay," she hiccupped.

"No, I really am sorry."

"I know." She hiccupped again. "It's okay. I know you didn't mean it."

I gritted my teeth, but said nothing. The problem was that I did mean it; I meant every word of it and more.

"So, since we're not going to the game, my mom said you could come over tonight. You want to come over here? I think we'll do dinner and movies."

"Um." How could I lie myself out of this one? "My mom said something about dinner too."

"She did?"

"Yeah." I sat up and scooted to the edge of the bed. "But I don't know. I'm not sure what I should do. I might still go and cheer for Adam tonight."

"You're going to go alone?" She sounded so small.

"Maybe. I don't know."

"I don't want you to be alone."

"Oh no. I'll be fine."

My door opened at that moment and Logan stuck his head inside. When he saw I was on the phone, he lifted a hand in a half-wave and frowned at me. I motioned for him to go away, but he only grinned and pushed the door open to come inside.

"Uh," I said in a hurry. "I have to go, Becky. I'll call you later."

"You're really going to the game still? Alone?"

"Oh yeah. I'll be fine."

Logan stood right behind me. I turned around and he breathed on my neck now. I tried to shove him away.

"Okay..."

"See you. I'll call you tonight." And I hung up, breathless. Then I whirled around. "What are you doing?"

He smirked at me.

"This is my room. This is my privacy. Get out."

He laughed. "You're just pissed because one of your friends might've heard me."

"Do you blame me?"

"Nah, guess not." And he threw himself backwards on my bed before he scooted back to sit against the wall. "So you're coming tonight? You're going to cheer on your future brothers?"

My lip curled up in disgust. "Don't say that word again."

"Brothers?" Logan's hyena laugh came out and he twisted to chortle into my pillow. "I cnn't beliff ith."

I sighed and rolled my eyes before I took hold of his arm and started to pull him up. "Come on. Get out. I want to go for a run."

He dodged my hand and chuckled when he went to the door. "You should run with Mason sometime."

"What?"

"You should run with Mason sometime."

"What do you mean by that?"

He lifted a shoulder in the air. "He runs too, most of it's at practice, but I bet he'd smoke you."

I quirked an eyebrow up. "You think so?"

He puffed out his chest. "I know so."

"I can run for hours."

"So can he."

Then I shook my head and turned away. "I'm not going to get into this with you."

"What? That Mason's better than you at running?" Logan rushed around and blocked my way to the bathroom. His cocksure smirk was back in place and he folded his arms over his chest. "Why don't the two of you throw down? I'd like to see that."

I shoved him aside. "I'm not going to race, either of you."

He taunted behind me, "Scared?"

I froze. My shoulders went up, my chin hardened, and the hairs on the back of my neck stood straight up. I turned around slowly. "What did you say?"

He looked too sure of himself. "You heard me."

Both of my eyebrows went up.

"I think you're scared."

"Come again?" I laughed out with a pout.

He took a step close. "I think you're scared of losing."

"I wouldn't lose."

He took another step closer and he was against my chest. He peered down, through his thick eyelashes. His breath wafted over my skin. "I think you're scared of everything."

Something snapped and I shoved him back again, this time he slammed against my bed frame.

My arms were stiff against my side and I clipped out, "I'm not afraid of anything."

He laughed as he pushed himself up from the bed frame. "Whatever you say to yourself at night."

"I mean it."

"Yeah, yeah." He dismissed me with a wave. "See you, sister. Have a good one tonight."

When he left and the door had closed behind him, I let out a shaking breath and realized my fingers were pressed into the palm of my hands. I pulled them out and saw the blood start immediately. They'd been pressed so tight, so hard. I hadn't felt a thing.

My jaw trembled when I went back to the bathroom, but I turned on the shower.

I wasn't afraid. I wasn't afraid of anything.

The football stadium light's lit up the field, bleachers, and two of the parking lots around it. As I approached my school's field, a different sense filled me. I wasn't a fan of the game, but I had come at times to support David. Now I came to support the enemy, or who I had considered the enemy.

Lydia, Jessica, and Jeff at times had sat beside me.

After I got a soda and a football program, I sat alone this time. My two ex best friends were higher on the bleachers and I knew Lydia's mouth had fallen at the sight of me. Jessica refused to look, like always. Jill was on the track in front in her cheerleader outfit. She paused in her stretching to glare at me.

I sat back and drank some soda. Then I saluted her with the thing.

Her nose wrinkled up and she turned her back when Ashley DeCortts approached her. Both girls glanced over their shoulders at me after a moment. I gave them a wide smile this time.

It wasn't long before the teams ran out on the field. The Academy side gave Adam a big cheer when he was introduced in the line-up, but when Mason and Logan were introduced, I swore the ground shook.

I had no idea. It was as if they were gods. I shook at my head at how weird it seemed to me.

When the ball kicked off, I tried to pay attention to Adam, Mason, and Logan's numbers. The one that was most obvious was Jeff's, 33. It blared up at me as he stood right in front of where I sat. He didn't play the whole time, but that was fine by me.

During halftime there were a lot of announcements and drawings for the charity raffles. Ashley and Jill giggled into the microphone at one point for some sell-off. I had no idea what they were talking about. Their cheerleader-esque language kept creeping into the microphone. I grew tired of trying to figure out what 'pep' actually meant to them, but it seemed to go over well with the crowd. There was a big cheer and Jessica's name was announced after.

Lydia screamed the loudest. Jessica stood in surprise, but it was fake. She had a small smirk on her face and I knew whatever had been done was all a scam. She had known the whole time she was going to win. As she passed by me and didn't seem to realize I sat there, I sat up straighter. Whatever she had won must've been important for her to forget the chill-factor any time she was in my vicinity.

I nudged the girl next to me. "What'd she win?"

"A date with Logan Kade."

I grabbed her arm when she started to turn for her friends. "What?"

Her lip curled up and she gave me a look in disdain. "Like I said, a date with the ever-so-great Logan Kade. Get your hand off me."

I let go, but scooted closer. "Was that a drawing or something?"

She shrugged and rolled her eyes. "I have no idea. Can I talk to my friends now?"

"Oh yeah. Whatever."

The girl's bitchiness didn't bother me. She was a sophomore. She had two more years to get stepped on and I knew it'd happen. It always happened.

Then she surprised me when she looked back at me. "Aren't you Samantha Strattan?"

"Yeah. Why?"

"Shouldn't you know about your new brother being auctioned off?"

Everything stopped for me. The hairs on my neck stood up. My claws came out. My tongue fell thick, but I gave her the most polite look I would muster in all my years and asked in a voice so professional my mother would've been proud, "What do you mean by that?"

The sophomore narrowed her eyes, but rolled them after. "My twin sister goes to public. Logan Kade said that you were his new sister. Is that, like, not true?"

My heart started to pound and my chest got heavy. I felt a heart attack coming on, but I still asked in that painfully polite voice, "What do you mean?"

She made some sound and I felt snobbery written all over it. Then she tugged down her frayed mini skirt and wrapped her athletic jacket tighter around her. "Whatever. He probably made it all up."

"Yeah," I said faintly as she turned back away. "Probably."

Oh god. Logan had spilled the beans. People would know. My world was going to end.

Adam would know.

Jessica would know.

Lydia would know.

And, I gulped. Becky would know.

There'd be no anonymity any more. Everyone would know. Most would care. And I groaned as I lowered my head to my lap. People would either love me or they'd hate me. My guess is that they'd all hate me.

Round two of hell, here we come.

And, of course, Lydia dropped into the chair beside me at that moment. "Hi!"

I jumped from how cheery she sounded.

Then she scooted close and lowered her voice. "We only have a few minutes. Jessica's over the moon. I'm sure she'll be with Jill and Ashley for a while. How are you?" Her hand clamped onto mine and she gave it a squeeze.

"I'm...fine..."

Her smile stretched wide. "Good. That's good. I talked to Becky last night. She's so funny. Why didn't you tell me how funny she could be?"

"Because...." Had Lydia grown two heads? I swore one was sane, but this one—not so much. "I have no idea."

She doubled over with laughter.

I scooted an inch away.

She scooted with me and pressed her leg up against me. "Come on, Sam. How are you really?" She whispered behind a hand. "I heard that Adam likes you, like really likes you. That's great, although I knew that'd happen." Her hand squeezed again. "Are you excited?"

"Um."

She rushed in, "You'll make a great couple. I just know it."

The sophomore bitch turned back with eyebrows high. "You're dating Adam Quinn?" She gave me a once-over.

I returned the favor and spoke in her same bored, stuck-up tone, "Why's that your business?"

She clamped her mouth shut and turned away. A bunch of her friends behind us scooted forward and I knew the whispers were about me.

I was starting to get used to it.

"She's coming," Lydia hissed and shot from the chair.

A second later Jessica walked past my seat and back to her old one. When she saw me, her smile froze for a second, but then she murmured, "Hello."

I almost fell of my seat.

If Jessica gave me the time of day that meant she was happy, really happy, and that left me with a sense of dread. From the little time I'd had to get to know the real Jessica, I knew she wasn't happy unless she got whatever she had set her sights on.

Logan.

Maybe she thought she had him in her clutches after all?

I spent the rest of the game weighing my options. Jessica, ex best friend who'd been screwing my boyfriend for two years to get back at me and now she's best friends with his new girlfriend. Jessica wanted Logan. I happened to know the guy...what to do?

When the game ended and Fallen Crest Public had trounced my school, once again, I stood with the rest and started to make my way

TIJAN

towards the parking lot. Lydia squealed my name as I was almost off the bleachers and gave me an excited wave with a thumbs-up sign.

I wasn't sure what she was thumbing-up, but I gave her a small wave back.

When I got to the parking lot, I had to stand back with a bunch of others as our team first ran through, followed by the next team.

And then two arms came from nowhere and lifted me off the ground. I was swung around before I was placed back on my feet.

I leaned back and saw Logan's smiling face. "We won! Did you have any doubt? Tell me you cheered for the winning team?"

Oh no... I looked around. Eyebrows were up. Hands were hiding mouths and heads were bent together. Then I saw Lydia and Jessica behind me. Both had frozen looks on them. Jessica was white as a ghost.

"Hey!" Logan embraced me again. "I scored three touch downs, of course Mason got all the blocks for me, but I scored. Aren't you going to congratulate me, sis?"

"What?" Jessica choked out.

Then a hand clamped on Logan's shoulder and he was pulled with the rest of his team. He turned back and yelled, "You're going out with us, Sammy. We're going to party tonight. No more loser parties for you!"

One of his teammate laughed and said something in his ear. Logan tipped his head back and his hyena laugh came out again.

Then I turned back around and felt the ground start to shake again.

Mason had stopped behind me. He had a quizzical look on his face and he reached a hand to scratch at the back of his head.

"Hi." I clutched a hand to my stomach and wondered why I was breathless all the sudden.

"Hey?" He looked where Lydia and Jessica stood. "Are they your friends?"

"No." I shook my head and moved closer to him.

He did too and we were almost touching, his pads to my shoulders. He bent his head so he could hear me. "They were my best friends."

"Got it." Then he gave me a small grimace. "Your mom mentioned that you were coming for dinner on Sunday?"

I jerked my head in a nod. I couldn't catch my breath.

"Good," he sighed.

I looked up in surprise.

He shrugged. "She's bearable when you're around." Then he frowned. "Did I hear Logan yell at you to party with us?"

"Yeah. He did."

"Good." He nodded. "We might have some actual fun." Then his hand touched my shoulder, lightly and briefly. "Wait for me after this. I'll give you a ride."

I was about to tell him that I had a car, but he had started to jog after his team. There was a line of girls who had been watching and all looked as he went past them.

Before their heads could snap back to me, I started to turn away. Lydia and Jessica were in front of me, both with fierce expressions on their faces.

I steered myself. This was not going to be good.

CHAPTER FIFTEEN

Lydia pushed herself forward and was an inch from my face. I felt her breath on me. "You know Mason Kade?" She had a sharp tone, but she was shoved aside as Jessica took her place.

Her eyes were narrowed, mouth tight, and I wondered if steam could come out of a person. She folded her arms over her chest and cooled her tone. "How do you know Logan?"

I glanced around. Jill and Ashley had stopped not far from us. Their cheerleading bags were both on the ground and I knew they heard every word. Each wore a different expression, one seemed wary and the other looked to share in Jessica's fury.

I sighed and stepped back. "I don't know what you're talking about."

Lydia sucked in her breath while Jessica's eye narrowed even more. "Logan hugged you and Mason talked to you. You can't lie about that."

I shrugged and grinned. "Guess they're playing some game with you, Jess, because I don't know them. Never have, never will, never want to."

"Are you serious?" Lydia frowned.

I rolled my eyes and tried to exude a bored attitude. "Not my problem."

"Samantha." Jessica planted herself in front of me when I tried to turn away. She put her hands on her hip. "You can't be lying about this."

"I don't know them." I paused. "And if I did, what business is it of yours?"

She seemed to hesitate now.

"Exactly." I shoved her aside and started for my car, but Nate intercepted me. He held out some keys and remarked, "Here are Mason's keys. Give me yours; I'll take your car home."

I didn't turn around, but I knew Jessica and Lydia had heard. I could feel their disbelief and anger rolling off of them. I sighed and held out my hand. "Whatever."

Nate grinned as he plucked my keys for Mason's. Then he glanced over my shoulder. "I take it those are the two who stabbed you in the back."

"Pretty much."

He frowned. "You haven't dealt with them yet?"

"Not yet."

I felt his eyes scanning my face when he asked, "Are you planning to?"

"Guess I have to now."

"Ah." He tipped his head back in understanding. "Cat's out of the bag, huh? Sorry about that."

"Logan's not. He shouted it to everyone."

He grinned at that. "Yeah, when he decides he likes someone he gets pretty excited about 'em." He folded his arms over his chest. "He doesn't like a lot of people."

I didn't look up when I asked, "And Mason?"

I heard his husky chuckle. "Logan wouldn't like you if Mason hadn't given the stamp of approval."

I looked up now, breathless again. "And when was that?"

He shrugged and looked past my shoulder again. "When he stopped you from hitting your mom. If he didn't give a damn about you, he would've watched you clobber her. Hell, I wanted to get snacks for the show. When Mason steps in, there's always a reason."

I nodded. "I'm starting to get that."

He clamped his hand on my shoulder. "Don't worry about this stuff, your friends and all. Logan's bound and determined to make you have fun tonight so I'd relax and let it happen."

I grinned. "Ah, what all rapists say to their intended victims."

Nate pulled back, narrowed his eyes, but barked out an abrupt laugh. "Yeah, I guess." Then he nodded in the direction of Jessica and Lydia. "You want me to play guard dog until you're in Mason's car?"

I spotted the black Escalade not far and shook my head. "Nah. I'm good." Then I chuckled to myself. "This is becoming a whole adventure."

"Guess you could look at it that way." He patted my shoulder again. "See you later."

"See you," I muttered under my breath as I watched him cut through Jessica and Lydia like a knife would go through butter. He didn't care who he rolled over and both jumped back, eyes wide in shock.

I shook my head and couldn't stop another chuckle as I swung towards Mason's car. "Samantha!" Jessica called after me, but I ignored her until I was close to his car. Then I turned back around, leaned against his hood, and crossed my legs. I wasn't about to hide inside.

They stood where I had left and watched me. Jill and Ashley joined them and all four didn't say a word as they stared.

I lifted my chin up.

We were at a stand-off, but it didn't last long. Adam came out of the locker room and started to walk to his car. He caught sight of the other girls, followed their gazes and saw me. He stopped in the middle of us before he shook his head and came over. When he drew near, he reached up and shook out some of his wet hair.

"Hey." He nodded across the parking lot. "What's with the brigade over there?"

I frowned. I hadn't considered Adam before. "It's nothing, just stupid stuff."

"This about Sallaway again?"

I barked out a laugh. "No, not this time."

"Oh." He gave me a small smile. "So you came without Becky, huh?"

"Yep. I sat with some snobby sophomore even. Good times."

He grinned. "I just got off the phone with her."

"The stuck-up sophomore?" I teased.

"Becky," he laughed. "She said something about a sleeping pill so now she can sneak out. Want to go with me? I was going to pick her up before some party the guys want to hit tonight."

"What party is that?"

He shrugged. "I'm not sure, but it's a Public one so I'm sure it'll be good. You want to come with?" Then his eyes widened a bit and a quick frown appeared. "Isn't this Mason Kade's car?"

"Um…" I stood from the car. "About that, I should call Becky. There are some things I need to tell her first…before she hears it from the wrong people."

He stepped back and a wall came over him. "So you *do* know the Kades."

I hesitated and lifted my shoulders. There wasn't much I could say, not when I owed Becky an explanation first. She was the only one who really deserved one, if anyone even did.

"Got it." He nodded his head in an abrupt jerking movement. "Maybe I'll see you at the party, huh?"

"Adam." He turned and started for his car at a fast walk. I called after him again, "Adam."

"Are you dating your team's quarterback?"

I turned back around. Mason stood behind me and I searched for any inflection in his question. There was none. He didn't seem to care. His hair was wet from a shower and he wore a plain black tee shirt over jeans.

I shrugged now. "Not really."

He grinned and took his keys from my hand. "I would've sacked him harder if I knew that." As he unlocked the car and we both got in, he asked, "You hungry?"

Not after that, but I lifted a shoulder. "I guess."

"Good." He flashed me a smile. "I'm starving."

As he peeled out of the parking lot, we went past where Lydia and Jessica remained in place. Their mouths hung open, along with Jill's. Ashley seemed calm. She even lifted her hand in a small wave.

I ignored it, but a sense of unease settled deep in my stomach. It wasn't good. None of this was good. If only Logan hadn't announced it and if Mason had ignored me in the parking lot, or if I had gotten out of their way—this all could've been avoided. I could've prevented it by going straight to my car and not dawdling, but I had...had I done it for a reason? For this reason? Did I want my secret out?

"You want anything?"

I jerked my head up and saw we were in a burger joint's parking lot. "Uh, no. I'm good."

"You sure?" Mason jerked his head towards his door. "Come on. Come in with me. You'll need all the substance you can get once Logan finds you at the party."

I opened my door and rounded the car. My palms were sweaty so I wiped them down the front of my pants. My stomach's nerves kicked up a notch when Mason held the door for me. He let it go when I stepped inside and led the way through the next door until we got inside. The air conditioner was still on inside and it gave me goose bumps.

A girl stood behind the register and her eyes got wide when she saw Mason. I recognized her from my school and then I remembered who she was. Her father was the manager and he wasn't very nice from what Lydia had told me a year ago.

She gave me a timid smile. "Hi, Sam."

I waved, but didn't respond. I couldn't remember the girl's name.

Mason ordered for both of us and when he pulled out his wallet, her father came from the back. He shook his head and held out his hand. "Not from a Kade. I'm Walter Dubrois. I'm the manager of Burger Play."

Mason shook his hand. "Thanks, sir."

"Tell your father I said hello and you can eat free here anytime."

"Thanks again."

The food was quickly bagged up, by Walter himself, and I couldn't hold back a laugh in disbelief when we got into Mason's Escalade.

"What?"

I gestured to the building. "Does that happen often?"

He grimaced as he unwrapped his burger. "Sometimes, usually by some douche bag who wants to kiss my dad's ass."

I shook my head. "You get free food; you can basically sleep with any girl you want. You have a very different life than the rest of us."

"What do you mean by that?" There was an edge to his voice.

I looked over and held his gaze. The butterflies were long gone now. A storm had started to roll in. "I always knew you guys were like gods, but man, I didn't realize it was like this."

He lifted his burger. "Free fast food?"

"No." I sighed and sat back. "Never mind."

He grinned and turned the radio on. "Nah, I get it, but it's not all so great."

"Right."

"It's not." He gave me a hard look. "People are snakes, you just have to figure out their different colors, but they're all the same. Everybody wants something."

I put my food aside and hugged myself. "Like my mom."

"Yeah, like her." His tone hardened as well.

"I probably shouldn't say anything, but I'm sorry she bulldozed her way into your lives."

He watched me for a full minute before he put his burger away. "She's the same type of snake my dad is. I kind of think they belong together."

I grinned. "They'll screw each other up."

"I give it a year before he cheats on your mom."

I searched him for any indication of sarcasm or sorrow or even if he was laughing at my mom. Nothing. He was a blank slate. There was no emotion in him.

"I've started to wonder how much she cheated on David," I confessed.

"She was sniffing around my dad for almost two years."

His words stabbed me and my gut recoiled. "She told me a year."

"She lied."

I nodded. "I'm starting to get that."

"She met us a year ago, but she was around my dad for a year before that. Logan and I saw her go into one of his hotel conference rooms. He had just left our mom and she asked us to pick something up at the hotel—she's half owner. We were waiting for the general manager when we saw dad with some new sleaze." He gave me a wry look. "No offense."

"None taken." She was my mom and I should've defended her, but it was past the point where I could muster the energy. There was nothing left in me. Then I asked him something else. "Why are you and Logan being nice to me?"

Something sparked in his eyes. "Why wouldn't we?"

It was my turn to give him a wry look. "Come on. You guys are a-holes. You don't care and I doubt the fact that I might be your stepsister has anything to do with it."

He grinned and leaned back. "You didn't say anything about the cars before and you torched your coach's car for us."

"I didn't do that for you."

He shrugged. "Doesn't matter. You kept your mouth shut about a lot of stuff, most would've been trying to get close to us and use us. You didn't give us the time of day." He flashed his perfect white teeth at me. "It's refreshing. Then the day you were about to cream your mom, I realized you really don't care who we are. You hate your mom almost as much as we hate our dad." He shrugged again. "I don't know, makes me kind of like you." He chuckled. "Logan's told everyone about his new stepsister. He's proud of you."

My phone went off and I checked the text. It was from Becky: **At Kilbourn and 8th. Where r u? Adam said u wanted to talk?**

"Where's the party we're going to?"

"Fisher's house is on Kilbourn, by the parkway. Why?"

I sighed and sent a text: **Be there soon.** Then I looked up. "Just curious."

His eyes lingered on my phone. "Was that the quarterback?"

"Nope. She's the quarterback's friend. She's my only friend right now." Though, that could change after tonight.

He reached over and clipped my seat belt in, and then he dumped my food back in my lap. "You really should eat. Logan's got a list of shots he wants to pour down your throat. This is his way of hazing you into the family."

I'd gone numb, but I unwrapped my sandwich and ate every last bit. I had no taste, no sense of swallowing, but I did and when I was done, we were at the party. I looked up at a huge house on an even bigger hill. Lights and people streamed out of it and as I watched, a group of guys and girls slid down the hill and sailed through the air into a small lake. Their shrieks and laughs pierced the Escalade's wall, but the loud bass quickly covered them up.

"Fun," I bit out.

CHAPTER SIXTEEN

When we got inside, everyone knew Mason was there. Guys appeared from nowhere for a hand slap, a nod, or any greeting from him. Girls tried to curl on his arm, but he shook them off with an ease that was impressive. He left each behind and they all seemed not to realize what had happened before he was already gone. Then he stepped into the kitchen and a herald of cheers sounded out.

Logan was in the middle of the kitchen with his hand around the keg's nozzle. When he saw his brother, he lifted it up and let it go. Beer soaked everyone in the room, but no one was upset. The girls shrieked in laughter and the guys raised their drinks in salute.

So this was their life.

They were celebrities in Fallen Crest and I was starting to realize the magnitude of it all.

Then Logan was in front of me and bent forward. I was picked up in the air in the next moment and flung over his shoulder. He smacked my butt and turned me around. Then he lifted a cup in the air. The room quieted.

"This is my new stepsister. Help me and Mase welcome her to the family." He gave me a smirk when I twisted around. "By getting her drunk!"

Another round of cheers went through the room and I heard an echoing chorus throughout the house, though I doubt they knew what they had cheered for.

I hit him in the head. "Put me down."

When I was on my feet, I saw that Mason was in the far corner of the kitchen. He had a drink in hand and as I watched a blonde wrap herself around his arm. He didn't shake her off.

A glass was being nudged into my hand and I saw that Logan was trying to give me a shot. "What?"

"Take it. I'll do a shot with you."

I pulled him close and yelled in his ear, "I don't really drink, Logan."

His hand curved around my back. "Just let loose, for tonight only." Then he pressed his mouth to my ear and I heard the seriousness in his voice. "I want you to have fun and I won't let anything happen to you. Promise. Everyone will look out for you since I told 'em you're family."

He pulled away and clinked his glass with mine. "Drink up, sis."

"I'm not your sister."

"If your mom has anything to say about it, you will be."

A flash of anger went through me, but not at him. I gripped the shot glass and drained it. Logan whistled his approval and filled it again. And the night went on like that.

Mason disappeared and Logan wouldn't let me out of his eyesight. An hour later, after he'd been pulled downstairs for a game of pool, I looked up and saw Jessica. She was in a corner by herself. I didn't know anyone else in the room, but it was full of people and they all knew Logan. Most of the guys were tall and muscular with athletic builds so I assumed they were on the football team with him.

I searched for Lydia or Jill, but couldn't see them. Then I nudged someone beside me. When he turned with his pool stick in hand, I asked, "Anyone from Academy come tonight?"

He gestured outside. "They're all out by the lake. Why?" He narrowed his eyes. "You an Academy kid?"

"Ethan!" Logan barked from across the table. "Your shot."

Ethan gave me another suspicious scan and left. As he bent over and started to line up a shot, I felt someone beside me and looked up.

I sighed. Who else?

"Hi, Sam," Jessica spoke in a quiet voice. She inched closer when someone scooted past her.

I felt Logan's gaze, but he didn't join us. Thank goodness.

Her shoulders dropped an inch and I wondered if she had wanted the opposite, then I felt stupid. Of course, she did. Why else would my ex best friend talk to me?

"What do you want, Jess?"

"I need a reason to say hi to you? I thought we were friends."

Someone fell against the wall next to me and I didn't have to look. I held my breath for a moment and was thankful when Logan remained quiet.

"You screwed my boyfriend for two years. You haven't said a word to me since I found out."

Her smile seemed strained at the corners and she edged back a step. "What are you talking about? I talked to you at the game tonight."

I pushed off from the wall. "You said hi to me, after you had won a date with Logan."

"What?" Logan stood too.

"Yeah, Logan." She surged forward and gave him a sultry smile. "I won the date with you."

"What date?"

She faltered. "The one for charity. There was a raffle."

"You serious?"

Ethan leaned back from the table. "Dude, that pep girl asked you last week if you'd do it."

"Oh—I thought she was asking me out. She was hot." Logan flashed a smirk and whistled under his breath.

Ethan clapped him on the shoulder. "What'd you think when you never went out?"

"Nah, we did. Last night."

Jessica's shoulders dropped as each statement was spoken between the two. Her head hung almost to the floor now.

I had no sympathy for her, none at all.

Logan must've noticed my gaze because he spoke up, "Did you pay a lot for that date?"

Her head bounced back up. "Some."

A hard look entered his eyes. "Are you going to screw me afterwards?"

She gulped, but responded in a timid voice, "Is that what you want?"

"You think I take girls out for nothing?"

Ethan watched the exchange and I felt his gaze rest on me for a moment. Wisely, he kept quiet.

"Maybe if you liked her?"

Logan barked out a laugh. It sounded harsh. "You paid for me. You think you're a girl that I like? There's very few who'd fall in that category."

Jessica glanced at me. "You seem to like Samantha."

His arm came around my shoulders and he pulled me close. "Well, if she wasn't spoken for...and if her mom wasn't doing my dad then maybe..."

"Her mom?"

My face got hot. "None of your business. Logan, shut up about that."

His smirk vanished. "Sorry." I shoved his arm off and started to brush past him, but he caught my arm. "I am sorry. I didn't think about your situation."

There was a scathing comment on the tip of my tongue, but I twisted my arm free and shoved through the crowd that had appeared. I gritted my teeth as I had to push through the hallways. The house was huge, but it seemed the entire two schools had shown up. It was standing room only and that was an exaggeration.

I headed for the lake and took a deep breath when I was able to break free from the house. The crowds outside were widely dispersed over the backyard and down the hill by the lake. Bonfire smell filled the air, mixed with a moist feel that was from the lake and slip-n-slide.

Two girls dashed past me giggling and two more boys followed in pursuit. All of them were soaked head to toe. One almost bowled me over, but he caught me and rushed out, "Sorry, little Kade."

My blood boiled and I snapped, "I'm not a Kade!"

But he was gone.

Dammit, Logan.

As I made my way further down the hill, I spotted Mason and Nate. They were beside a bonfire in a far corner and each nodded in greeting, but they didn't come over and neither gestured for me to go to them.

Fine by me.

I relaxed a little and kept on. Finally I heard a voice I recognized. Jeff.

"So you know the Kades?"

I turned around and braced myself, but there was no anger in his voice. After I searched his face, I didn't see any in his eyes either and relaxed again. "I guess."

He grinned. "You guess? You either know them or you don't. Man, Jessica crapped her pants tonight."

"Really?"

He nodded and twisted his fingers in his hair to pull it up. It was full of gel and stood straight up. It gave him a Mohawk look. Then he messed it up and flattened it again. "Jill's going crazy too. She doesn't know if she should kiss your rear or be a bigger bitch to you."

I glanced around. No one cared about our conversation. It was refreshing. "What do you think?"

He shrugged. "Whatever. Good for you."

I sighed. "Jeff, what are you doing?"

"What do you mean?" He stood straighter.

"Why are you talking to me now?"

He shrugged again and slid his hands into his back pockets. "I don't know. Guess it feels okay now, you know? I mean, I felt bad about what happened with us and then I was with Jill so quick. I didn't feel like I could apologize to you and then the other day…in the hallway…" He took a deep breath. "I know it's over."

I remembered and nodded. For some reason my throat felt closed off.

He gave me a bright smile. "And if you're going to be with Quinn, he's a nice guy usually, but you should know that he's not always."

I frowned. "What do you mean?"

He jerked an arm towards the docks and boats. "He's down there being an ass. I guess he's pissed about you and the Kades knowing each other."

Great. If Jeff was the one who warned me then it was bad, really bad. And as I got closer to a pontoon attached to the dock, I heard Adam's voice. He was drunk and when I stepped onto it and peered under the canopy I saw a girl in his lap and one of his hands between her legs. The other was stroking her knee.

I took a breath. Something told me to be prepared.

He murmured something in the girl's ear and she let out a throaty giggle. It grated against my ears, but when I heard another squeal, I looked closer. Becky was huddled in the seat behind them. Her knees were drawn against her chest and she was hugging them to her. When her eyes met mine for a second, she squealed again and ducked her head down.

"Well hey there, Sam!" Adam heralded. He threw an arm out. "Welcome to our lowly depths."

I rolled my eyes and sat stiff in a chair towards the front. I turned towards them. "I see you've been enjoying the party."

"Why shouldn't I?"

The girl in his lap squeaked and shifted under his hold.

He grinned and nipped at her shoulder.

I eyed the happy couple before I met Becky's gaze. The sadness in her was evident and when she wiped a tear away, I stood. "Can I talk to you, Becky?"

"Why talk to only her?" Adam stopped us. "You've been lying to me too. Or were you laughing at us behind our backs?"

"I wasn't laughing at anyone."

Becky stood, but hesitated behind him.

"Becky, please. I'd like to explain."

Her hands were clasped together and she looked down at them.

Adam deposited the girl to another chair and stood between us. He stepped closer to me and asked in a harsh tone, "You want to lie to her again? Hurt her some more?"

I frowned and looked up at him. "Are you trying to intimidate me? Are you really this hurt because I didn't tell you I knew the Kades?"

He bit out, "You played me for a fool."

Becky stepped around him and laid a hand on his arm. "He's just protecting me."

"From who?" I looked around. "Me? Because I didn't want people to know my parents are getting a divorce?"

Adam laughed and shook his head. "Yeah, right."

"You knew it was happening. You were there when I was in my dad's office. You helped tape my hands."

Becky looked at him. "Is that true?"

"Yeah, but I didn't know about the Kades."

My jaw hardened. "I know them, I'm not screwing them."

He didn't say anything.

And Becky looked at me. "You're not with Mason Kade? Lydia said you got in his car and…"

I rolled my eyes. "Oh, for god's sake. If Lydia said it, it must be true, right? I can't believe this. You're listening to my old best friend who knew my other best friend and boyfriend were sleeping together behind my back for two years. I'm sure she's the best source in the world to listen to."

She hesitated. "She said you seemed close."

"I saw you get in his car," Adam said in an accusing manner.

"I did, you're right. So, of course, that means I'm having sex with him. I've gotten in your car twice. Have I spread 'em for you too?"

He looked away. "It's not the same thing."

"Yes, it is. And, by the way, why do I have to explain anything to you? You've been my friend for what? Two weeks? You asked me out a couple times and I'm supposed to open my closet for you? How many dirty skeletons do you have that I don't know about?"

His mouth shut.

"Exactly." I swung towards Becky. "I'm sorry I didn't tell you I knew the Kades, but it's not something I want to talk about. It has to do with my parent's divorce, another thing I don't want spread around the school."

Both of them looked away.

I sighed. "Can I ask you both to keep this quiet?"

The girl who'd been on Adam's lap lifted her hand. "I won't say anything."

I snorted. "Thanks for that. Who are you?"

She gave me a bright smile and flicked her bleach blonde hair over her shoulder. "I'm Tanya. I know Logan so I definitely won't say anything."

I couldn't believe this girl. "You know Logan?"

"We went out last night."

Of all ironies. I glanced at Adam. "You got a keeper there."

He sighed and rolled his eyes. "I was pissed."

Then Becky reached out and squeezed my hand. "You know the Kades?" The excitement in her eyes made me pause. Then I grinned and shook my head. Becky never stayed down for long.

CHAPTER SEVENTEEN

It was five in the morning and I was drunk. Becky had passed out next to me on the pontoon while Adam took his pep girl home long ago. I lifted my red cup and tried to sip from it, but there wasn't anything in it. I tipped it over and not a drop fell out.

When had that happened?

"I was told Tanya was down here."

A leggy blonde stepped onto the pontoon and bent down to get a better look under the canopy. Becky snored and rolled over.

I squinted against the moonlight at this new stranger. She had long hair, slightly curled, that hung almost to her waist and she wore a classy v-neck sleeveless shirt over tight jeans. The high heels caught my attention. Their silver color matched her top perfectly.

I sighed. This girl was sober. I could tell. I was usually sober. Not tonight.

"So…is she here?" she asked further.

"Huh?"

"Tanya. Is she here? Was she here?" She rubbed at her arms as if she were cold.

I lifted my glass to her. "You could drink some beer and get warm."

"No thanks." She eyed my glass as her lip curled up. I was sure it was in disgust. "I don't drink."

"I don't either, but Logan didn't care about that tonight."

"Logan?" She tilted her head to the side. "Are you the new sister?"

"I'm not."

And I wasn't. I didn't think I'd ever consider myself in that role.

"Oh. Sorry. You said Logan before."

I narrowed my eyes at this girl again. She didn't say his name in the usual hopeful manner of most others. She said it as if she knew him, and knew him well. Still, I held my tongue. He'd already done enough damage for me to add more to it.

"A guy took her home."

She sighed and looked away. "I can't believe her. Another guy."

I frowned. "His name's Adam. He's a good guy."

"Doesn't matter at this point," she snapped and started to leave.

"You said Logan."

She stopped.

"Did you mean Logan Kade?"

"*You* said Logan's name before."

I nodded. "Do you know him?"

"Well enough." She yawned and glanced up at the house. "I should get going."

"How well?" I started to stand and climbed down from the pontoon.

She stopped a foot away on the dock and studied me. "Why?"

I shrugged.

"Look." She gave me a forced polite smile. "A lot of girls want to know Logan and a lot of girls have known Logan. If you're looking for a hookup, he's the guy for you, but if you're looking for a rich boyfriend—I'd look elsewhere. Logan's not that type, for anyone."

"You sound like you know him pretty well."

"I do." And she rolled her eyes. "I know him a little too well. We dated for two years, broke up a year ago."

"Really?" I surged forward a step, but held myself back. I didn't want to appear too eager. "What happened?"

"What else?" She laughed, but it sounded hollow. "He liked my friends and me...and I liked his brother."

My eyes went wide at that. Mason? "Did you date Mason too?"

She snorted and shook her head. "God, no. Like Mason Kade would ever be nice to any girl who wasn't his precious Marissa?"

Marissa?

"I can't believe I said any of this. I'm sorry. Thanks for telling me about Tanya and this Adam guy. You don't have his number, do you?"

I pulled out my phone and called him. She waited and hugged herself. When a breeze picked up and wafted over the lake to us, it swept her hair in the air and wrapped around her and I was glad I'd kept my hair pulled back in a low ponytail. Then I heard Adam's voicemail and ended the call.

"Sorry. It went to voice message and he would've picked up for me."

She studied me again. "You're good friends with this guy?"

"Not good like that." I grinned at her. Then I gestured towards the pontoon. "He's got a soft spot for Becky, she's his neighbor. He looks at her like a kid sister."

"Ah. I get it. Tanya likes those types."

"Tate?" Logan stood at the end of the dock. "What are you doing here?"

She gave him an exaggerated bright smile and said sarcastically, "I was hoping to see you, Logan."

He frowned and scratched at his head. "But you live in Forrest."

"Yes," she snapped at him. "I drove two hours on the slight hope you'd be at Ethan's house. In fact, I had no idea you'd be here. I got in my car and drove, just drove. My gut brought me here."

He looked at me. "You know Samantha?"

She snorted and gave me a withering look. "Yep, we're best friends. I gave her the whole scoop on you so if you haven't bagged her yet, she'll know how to make it good for you in bed."

He gave her a cocky grin.

She upped the withering glare to a hateful one at him before she looked back. "I thought you said you didn't know him."

I shrugged. "Who doesn't know Logan Kade?"

"Right." She shook her head. "Why did I come back here? That's right, my whorish cousin. That's why."

"I thought you said she was your best friend."

"One of and she's also a cousin." She swung her purse onto her arm and turned around with a hand poised on her hip. "Logan, do you know this Adam guy?"

He glanced over. "Quinn?"

I nodded.

"Sam knows him better."

"Logan!"

He rolled his eyes. "Fine. He's the quarterback for the Academy."

"Where does he live?"

I raised a hand. "He wouldn't take her to his house."

She kept her back turned to me. "Logan, where does he live? Tanya's not home."

Logan looked at me.

I sighed. "He lives on 8th and Saxton Ave. I don't know his house number, but it's got a red mailbox on it."

"Logan," she urged again.

"Oh my god," he groaned. "Sam, what does he drive?"

"A car. I don't know."

"Logan."

He spoke for her again. "You've been in his car, Sam. I've seen you. What kind of car is it?"

"Sam?" Becky stumbled out from under the canopy, rubbing at her eyes. "What's going on?"

"Hey." I rounded on her as a different thought occurred to me. "Adam drove you, didn't he?"

"Yeah…" She yawned widely.

And that meant—I whirled back around. "He's still here. He wouldn't leave her so they're probably inside."

Tate stepped around me and folded her arms over her chest.

She bent forward and peered into Becky's eyes. "He wouldn't leave you?"

She shook her head, confused. "Who are you?"

Her eyes flashed in annoyance. "Doesn't matter. I've heard what I need to. Thanks." And she brushed past all of us. As she swept past Logan, he stepped to the side so her shoulder wouldn't hit him and whistled under his breath as he watched her trudge up the hill. She flicked him off behind her back, but he only laughed.

"Hey." Becky stepped beside me and held onto my arm. She struggled to stay on her feet. "Could I get a ride home?"

"What about Adam?"

She grinned, but immediately covered her mouth with her hand and jerked to the side. After a couple minutes and after she had stopped vomiting, she stood back up. "He took off long ago."

"You said—"

"She was not being nice." Becky shrugged, but clasped onto my arm again.

I couldn't stop the smile from my face, but looked where Logan still stood. "Could we both get a ride home?"

He chuckled. "Yeah. Mason sent me down. He and Nate are waiting in the front, but we better hurry. If Tate finds out we lied, she'll be after our asses and I don't want to deal with that girl right now."

"You mean you're not up for an ex this morning?"

He groaned. "She told you that, huh?"

We both fell in step as I tried to help Becky stay upright. "And a bit more. Pretty sure she regrets it now."

"She could tell I like you and that threw her."

I looked at him sharply. "How do you know that?"

He shrugged. "I know her pretty well."

I wanted to know all about their relationship and what Mason had to do with it, but I held my tongue when we climbed into the back of his Escalade. Becky gave them both a sloppy grin and a slurred thank-you, but she crumbled into a heap on her chair as soon as she crawled up. I had to boost her butt over so Logan and I could get in too. When we pulled up to Becky's house, Nate came around the side and hoisted her over his shoulder. He followed me inside and we snuck her into her bedroom after I fumbled through her pockets for her keys.

When the four of us got to the mansion, it was nearing six in the morning. I wasn't tired at all. I was wide awake. The nagging questions of Tate/Logan's relationship and who Marissa was had me energized. I could've gone on a run.

And then I decided to do it.

As I went through the kitchen, a big black bag was in the foyer along with a hiking bag. Mason dumped a rolled up sleeping pad beside it a second later. He had changed into ratty green khaki shorts and a sleeveless black shirt. It was tattered along the edges and had two gaping holes in the back.

"Where are you going?"

It took me a second to realize he'd asked my question. I frowned at him. "I'm going on a run. Where are you going?"

He checked his watch. "It's after six. You were up all night."

I kicked at his bag and heard pots and pans rattle against each other. "Where are you going?"

Who's Marissa?

He grimaced for a moment and then flipped his black sunglasses over his eyes. I could no longer read him. "We're going camping."

"Camping?"

"Something we do." And he turned to leave again.

I was a bit miffed as I stood there. He'd been all buddy-buddy and now—nothing. Camping. That's it. No other explanation, but then again I had to remind myself—who was I kidding? These guys weren't my stepbrothers and I highly doubted their father would really marry my mother.

Everything hardened inside again.

The truth was that my mother and I'd be out within three months. That was my guess. When that happened, it'd be like none of this happened. No Logan. No Mason. No Nate. Nothing. And I'd have to deal with Lydia and Jessica once again.

With that thought, I felt another burst of adrenalin surge through me and I could barely hold it in as I jumped through the door and started running.

None of it matter. I mattered. I was the only one. I had to take care of myself.

Those thoughts kept flashing through my head as my feet pounded the pavement. I ran and then I ran some more. Sweat was dripping off of me and leaving trails wherever I went and I went everywhere. I soared past Adam and Becky's house once, and then ran past it again.

Then I found a park and sprinted over the bridge. Ducks and geese scattered for me and the water felt good as I darted through a small part of a pond.

When my legs started to hurt, I headed back. And as soon as I approached the front lawn, my body crumbled. I fell to a heap on the lawn and stayed there until my heart and chest slowed down.

I was barely aware of the sounds of a car pulling out of the garage until it slowed beside me.

"Samantha?"

A black Rolls Royce had stopped beside me and my mom peered over James who was in the driver's seat. She was dressed in a pink dress with a hat perched on top of her head.

I frowned as I sat up. Was I delusional? My mom looked like she was dressed for a role in a Southern movie. "Where are you guys going?"

"It's Sunday, honey. We're going to church." She frowned a little. "Would you like to come? We could go to the later service."

I couldn't hold back my full body grimace. "No. I'm okay."

"Did you go running this morning?"

I heard the strain in her voice, but ignored it when I tried to stand. My legs were still wobbly. "No. I just look like I did."

"Samantha."

I groaned. "What? Of course I did."

"Well. Okay. Go inside and drink lots of water. And please eat something, Samantha. You know how I worry."

James said something to her and my mom called out again, "Oh, honey. The boys went camping. They'll be gone most of the week so if you'd like to have any friends over, go ahead. Maybe Jessica and Lydia? Or even Jeff? Are you two still together?"

James said something else under his breath to her and my mom giggled. "Okay, honey. We have to go. Love you."

She waved as he pulled out of the driveway. And then it was just me. I had the mansion all to myself. I trudged through the place and into my shower. After that, I curled under my sheets and rolled over.

CHAPTER EIGHTEEN

The guys were gone for an entire week. I had no idea how they could do that, but they did. I shouldn't have been surprised. I avoided my mother during the week and only once spotted James. I'd been sitting in the study room, which looked like my school's library when he walked in.

The door shut behind him. I lifted my head from the book I'd been reading. We stared at each other.

He was dressed in a pinstripe black business suit and he had a black briefcase in hand. When I saw a small brown bag in his other hand, I hid a grin. Mousteff must've gotten to him too.

Then he took a deep breath. "I am aware your relationship with your mother is none of my business, but I would like to get to know you at some point. I love your mother very much and I do not plan on letting her go."

And then he left.

He came in as silently as he left and when I watched the door slide shut behind him, not a sound came from it.

Chills ran down my body and I pushed back from the table and went to where I'd once seen Mason pull some brandy from a counter. It was still there and I took a swig of it. Maybe daytime alcoholism would be my next venture?

I put the bottle away when my stomach started to churn. Then I heaved a deep breath. Nope, daytime alcoholism wouldn't mix with me and I went back to my room and for my running gear.

When I was running back, it had been dark for an hour and a set of headlights approached from behind. I was two blocks from the house and I veered to the side. Most cars swept past, some slowed for caution, but this one slowed so it followed behind me.

I kept going.

What else could I do?

I put on some more speed and soon I was sprinting. One block left.

The car's headlights engulfed me and my shadow sprang out in front of me. It seemed to be laughing at me, dancing vigorously. My heart was already pounding, but cold sweat formed on my forehead. It spread throughout my body and my teeth were soon chattering.

I stopped.

Half a block from my house.

I turned and stared at the car. It had stopped, now in front of me. Then I heard the window slide down and someone leaned out.

I yelled, "What do you want?"

There was laughter from inside.

My hands balled into fists and I started to jerk forward.

Mason's voice slid over me. "You're an idiot."

My breath spat from me before I could stop it. I grimaced when it landed on my leg, but I couldn't stop from laughing in relief. "I'm an idiot? You're the idiots."

Logan popped his head from the passenger side. "We could've been mass rapists, dude."

"Dude?" I shot him a look and walked to Mason's window on trembling legs. "I'm not your dude."

Logan eased back in and smirked at me. "Not yet."

Nate chuckled from the backseat as he watched the exchange.

"Hop in." Mason nodded to the back.

I gave him a silly grin, though I didn't care how silly it might've looked. "I'm a half block away. I think I can manage it."

He shrugged and flashed me a grin back. "Up to you." And then he sped off. My eyes widened as I spotted the puddle, but it was too late. He drove through it and I was drenched a second later.

TIJAN

"Ugh," I groaned and held my arms out.

Logan's hyena laugh sounded out until they turned into the driveway.

Then I gritted my teeth and sprang forward. When I sprinted around the corner, they had started to climb out and I spotted the hose their gardener left out by the house. Logan had set a few bags on the ground when he turned, but it was too late.

"Hey—" His shout was drowned out when I turned the hose on and aimed it at him. Before Nate could jump out of the way, I turned and got him too. As I looked for Mason, I was shoved to the ground and the hose was pulled out of my hands.

I looked up and he stood over me with the hose pointed towards the lawn. A wicked look was in his eyes and I opened my mouth to try and stop him, but the front door opened at that moment.

"Sam?"

I groaned and rolled to my feet.

Mason turned the water off and threw the hose back to the corner.

"Hi, guys…" She faltered as she frowned at me. "Sam, what are you doing on the ground?" Her eyes skirted from me to Mason.

I stood and brushed off my running shorts. "Nothing. I think I ran too much, tripped."

"Oh." Her eyes never left Mason.

He narrowed his and the same closed down look came over him.

I sighed on the inside. "Mom, I'm going inside."

"Wait, honey." She turned to Logan. "Since everyone's here, tomorrow is Saturday. I was wondering if we could have our dinner tomorrow night."

"What?" Logan dropped a bag from his fingers.

"The one we were supposed to have last Sunday was canceled since you guys wanted to go camping so I thought…" She threw her hands in the air with a bright smile. "How about tomorrow night?"

"I'm sure we'll be at a party tomorrow night."

"Oh." Her bright smile faded and she glanced at me.

I fought the urge to roll my eyes. I wanted so badly…

"How about you and me, Sam? What do you think? We can have a mother/daughter dinner like we used to."

I tried not to let her desperation get me, but I found myself crumbling.

Then Mason asked, "Doesn't your school's football team have their annual dinner tomorrow night?"

My head snapped up. My football team. My father. My not-father. And the old rage flared inside of me again.

My mom's eyes closed and she turned away.

I didn't care. I snapped, "I'm good without that, mom. I wouldn't want us to be fake and not talk about things."

"What?"

"Like how you hit me. Twice." My eyes were cold. Everything in me was cold again and I remembered the feeling of that first slap.

"Honey, I…" She stepped towards me with an extended hand.

Logan cleared his throat and gave us both a forced polite smile. "Don't mind us. We'll be showering and going back out. See you."

All three of them grabbed the rest of their bags and walked inside. When the door shut behind them, I flinched in reaction. But I hadn't started to calm my nerves before my mother stepped close.

"Samantha," she spoke in a soft voice. "We should talk about that night. We haven't really…did David ask you to go to their annual dinner?"

I wanted to snap so badly. She said it as if it were a personal attack to her, that the man who had raised me all my life might have the balls to invite me to a dinner? As if he had no right since he wasn't my biological father.

Anger was pumping through me.

"Sam?" She said it so quietly. She had turned into a timid mouse and my mother watched me with wide eyes, a begging question in her depths.

"What?" I growled.

"Are you going to that dinner with David? I know it's for the families too."

I sighed and turned away. "I don't know, mom. Maybe."

When I started to walk inside, she called after me, "It'd be okay, you know. I'd understand. I wouldn't want him to be alone…"

And the door shut on her words when I stepped inside. I let it slam harder than normal. When I hurried upstairs and to my room, Mason's door was kicked open and he appeared. He was shirtless and in jeans. His hair was wet and he held a toothbrush in his mouth, but he watched me approach.

I whistled under my breath. "You shower quick."

He grinned over a mouthful of toothpaste and disappeared inside. A second later, he came back out and wiped his mouth with a towel. Then he grinned, sans his toothpaste, and leaned against his doorway. When he crossed his arms, his muscles bulged out, but it wasn't a show. That was him.

I fought the urge not to flinch under his steady gaze. "What?"

"Come out with us tonight."

"I don't think so."

Logan's door opened down the hall and he stepped out, but he didn't say a word. He waited.

"Why not? It'd be fun."

I wavered. "Where are you going?"

He lifted an easy shoulder. "Probably just some bonfire, nothing big."

And I hoped that meant there'd be no Lydia, Jessica, or even Adam. The week had been tolerable, but I felt the weight of all of them. Lydia wanted to be my best friend again and Jessica seemed torn. After Logan's humiliation, she had stayed away, but I still caught the few friendly grins she'd sent my way. Becky loved it. She was eating all the attention up, including how Adam still seemed pissed. She enjoyed being the go-between with him and me.

"Hey," Mason prompted me again.

I frowned as I tried to remember what Becky had said they were doing tonight. It was probably a party. It always seemed to be a party. "Don't you guys have a football game tonight?"

"Not for us."

"What do you mean?"

He shrugged again and scratched at his chin. "We skipped all week. No way can coach put us in."

"And that doesn't bother you?"

"He won't kick us off." He frowned. "Why do you care about that?"

His question threw me backwards a step. Why did I? I shrugged and slid my hands into the back pockets of my running shorts. I was trying to look cool. My sweat had dried, but my nose twitched at the smell of it as it hung in the air.

"Look," I started. "I'm not up for another party. Besides, I think that Tate girl is out for my head."

Mason shot up from the doorway and the wall slammed over his face again. "Tate?"

Logan's eyes clasped shut behind him and his head went down. His shoulders dropped.

I sucked in my breath and my eyes widened. "Uh…I mean…"

"You met Tate?"

I nodded.

"At the last party?"

I nodded again.

"Why'd she be pissed with you?"

I shrugged and looked away.

"Sam." He grasped my shoulder and I squeaked. I threw a look at Logan, but quickly glanced away. Too late. Mason followed my gaze and saw his brother. "Tate's in town?"

Logan's head lifted and a haunted look was in his eyes. "Yeah."

"When?" Mason's voice was biting.

"She came last Saturday. She was looking for a chick that Sam's quarterback was banging."

Mason looked back at me. His eyes were cold. "What does she want with you?"

"Becky and I lied to her. She seems like the type to hold a grudge."

"What the hell, man?"

It took me a second to realize Mason wasn't referring to me. I looked up with his hand still on my shoulder and saw something pass between the two brothers. Logan backed up and gave him a tight smile. "What do you want?"

"You're still covering for her."

Though Mason's statement came out quiet, there was a dangerous feel to it. The hairs on the back of my neck stood upright and I was frozen in place. His hands gripped my shoulder tighter. A bruise would appear there, but it didn't hurt. I didn't feel a thing at that moment.

"Sam, honey?" My mom's voice came up from the stairway.

Everyone reacted.

Mason shoved me away. When I caught my balance and looked up both of their doors had been shut. I hurried into mine and locked it when my mother turned the knob. "Sam, can you please talk to me? I'd really like to talk to you about David. And James told me he had a word with you. I'd like to talk to you about him as well." She waited a moment. "Please, honey?"

I stood on the other side and held my breath. My heart was pounding, but it wasn't from my mother, for once. And then when I heard her walk away, I let out that deep breath and sagged against the door. My hands and legs shook when I made my way to the shower so I slid down the wall and let the water slam over me.

It was an hour later before I went downstairs in sweats and a tank. My hair was pulled back by a headband and my body felt strong from the latest run. When I went into the kitchen, I expected everyone else to be gone, but drew up short. Logan sat at the table in the dark. A glass was in front of him and a bottle of Brandy beside that.

He looked up at me and his lip curved upwards in a snarl. "Hey, thanks."

"For what?" I eyed him, but relaxed when he didn't stand up.

"Tate."

"Where's Mason and Nate?"

"Where do you think?" he bit out and raised his glass for a drink. He set it down hard.

"What?" I couldn't believe this. "Are you being punished? Did they go out without you?"

He sighed and looked away.

"Are you twelve now?" Where had the cocky smooth-talker gone? Or the vindictive guy who had humiliated Jessica for me?

His voice came out low. "There's a lot of history that you don't know about."

"Why are you telling me that?"

His eyes found me and the seriousness in them held my breath. "So that you can tread carefully from now on." He pushed up from the table now. "My advice: shut up about what you don't know." He brushed past me as I stood still and finished the rest of his Brandy before he put the empty glass away. The bottle was left on the counter.

He left a second later and his yellow Escalade tore from the driveway.

It took me a moment to realize that my heart wasn't pounding. My legs were strong. And a sense of calm settled over me. What that meant, I had no idea.

CHAPTER NINETEEN

My phone woke me the next morning and I groaned when I saw that it was past eleven. "Hello?"

"Hi!" Becky chirped at me.

I swore under my breath and buried my head under my pillow. "Whatdoyouwand?"

"What?"

"Hold on." I sat up and wiped at my face. I needed to wake up. I couldn't handle how alert she sounded at that moment. "Hi…"

"Did you just wake up?"

When I tried to straighten my legs, they cramped up and I bit back more curses. Pain throbbed in them and I knew it was from the running. How long had I gone last night?

"Sam!"

"What?" I readjusted the phone when I felt myself waken more. "Tell me you're not going to bed now."

"I'm not." She giggled. "But my folks are going to the Fallen Crest Country Club with Adam's family. My mom wanted me to invite you. We'd pay for your entry and everything else is on Adam's dad. He has some account with the club, I think."

"Since when do you guys go to the Country Club?"

"My parents aren't members, but we go with Adam's parents sometimes. They're members."

That sounded right.

And then a different thought formed. "Is my mom a member there?"

She giggled again. "Do you mean is James Kade a member?"

I groaned. I'd forgotten she knew, hell—everyone knew. Maybe. I could spread a rumor that I paid the Kade brothers to act like they knew me. People would eat that up in an instant. Things would all go back to how they should've been, with me being alone.

"I have lots of gossip to tell you about last night too." She sounded breathless in her excitement and I perked up. Whatever it was would be good, or I hoped. I could use some gossip that had nothing to do with me.

"Okay. What time do you want me over there?" I swung my legs over and stood. They were a bit wobbly, but I pushed past it and hurried into my bathroom. "Should I meet you at the club?"

"We could pick you up?"

"Becky."

"Okay, okay. Yeah, meet us at the club. We're going to leave soon so call me when you get to the parking lot."

"Sounds good."

"Oh and I think Adam's bringing Tanya."

"Who's Tanya?" Then I remembered. "Is her cousin going to be there too?"

"I hope not." Becky kept giggling. "See you there!"

"See you," I mumbled into the phone before I ended the call and set it down. I frowned at it for a moment. She sounded very perky and very excited. Becky like that, with Adam bringing a girl, couldn't mean anything good...could it? Was I being paranoid?

I rolled my eyes at my reflection and went to work. My hair was a ratted mess, but by the time I had dressed in black skinny pants and a loose white long-sleeve shirt, my hair was back to its normal self. Straight and a little dull. It was how I liked it. I tucked it behind my ears when I slipped on some heeled sandals and grabbed my purse. This was the country club; I'd need to dress a little bit of the rich part.

No one was in the house when I breezed out except Mousteff. He poked his head out, saw my appearance and wolf whistled. I flicked him the middle finger, but he laughed as he went back to the kitchen.

When I pulled into the parking lot, it was full of brand new BMWs, Rolls Royces, and whatever other rich cars there were. I thought I spied a Lamborghini too. And then I straightened out my top as I started towards the door. With a text sent to Becky, I figured she'd meet me in the front foyer, but when I got there I drew up short.

Two guys in black suits stared at me with no welcoming smile. Uh…

A different guy emerged from behind them with a headset attached to his ear. He was dressed in a white suit and he gave me a fake smile. "Your name, miss?"

"I'm here with friends." My hands itched to spread out my top again or readjust my pants. It was as if slugs had appeared over my body from how they were staring at me.

"Their names?" The guy was cold.

"Uh…" My mind blanked. "The Quinns. I'm friends with Adam Quinn."

"He already arrived with a guest." He gave me that same cold smile. "You'll have to leave."

"No, no, no." Becky rushed around them and linked elbows with mine. She was breathless when she hurried out, "My mom paid for her."

He didn't blink. "Her name, ma'am?"

Becky couldn't stop a giggle behind her hand. "Samantha Strattan."

"David Strattan?"

My head snapped up. "What?"

"Your name is listed underneath a member's name. He listed you as a guest." The polite chill from him emanated everywhere. His lips moved to form a smile, but it didn't fit with his features. "Your mother will be refunded her money."

He extended his hand for us to enter the club, but both of us were still surprised.

"You may go inside? Please."

We jumped forward at his slight bark. Then Becky bent over laughing when we rounded the corner. "Holy Hannah! I can't believe that happened. What is with that guy? I bet he'd never had an erection in his life."

I glanced over my shoulder and knew he could hear every word we said. "Nah. He bats for the other team."

Her laughter raised a notch and I pulled her away before he kicked us both out. I patted her on the arm. "I had no idea my dad was a member here."

Becky wiped at her mouth and I knew she was trying to stop laughing. "I know. Me neither."

When she seemed to have accepted my statement, I relaxed again. She might've known about the divorce, but she didn't know the other stuff. I hoped no one knew. Then we weaved our way through a fancy looking dining room with chandeliers and glass tables. I made sure not to bump into anything. If I broke even a fork, I was sure I couldn't afford to replace it. And Becky pulled me the last bit before I blinked back the sudden brightness. The sun was blinding when we went outside and I heard splashing, glasses clanking, and children's laughter. Conversation buzzed around us and when my vision grew clear again I saw the back patio was enormous. It was gorgeous with three waterfalls and two fountains.

She led me to a back patio where I recognized Laura and Becky's little brothers. Adam sat at a back table with the pep girl from last weekend's party. His smile slipped a little when he saw me, but by the time we got to the table it looked natural.

"Hey, Sam." He sounded normal when he welcomed me.

"Hi, Sam!" His friend beamed at me.

"Tanya." He nodded at her.

"I remembered. Hi, Tanya. Your cousin's not coming, is she?" I sat across from them in a similar wicker chair when Becky sat beside me and gestured for a waiter.

She laughed and pulled up her skinny legs in the chair. As she hugged them to her chest, she rested her head on them and smiled at Adam.

He shared the intimate look before he replied for her. "No, she's not."

Then Tanya lifted her head and looked over her knees. "Tate went home this morning after last night."

"Last night?" I stiffened and glanced sideways.

Becky gave me an excited look. "I have to tell you all about that."

Oh no.

A waiter appeared and placed a champagne flute of orange juice in front of me. A plate full of breakfast food was next with bacon, waffles, French toast, and sausage. A bowl of fruit was put to the side.

I caught the waiter's sleeve before he left. "Can I have coffee?"

"Of course, ma'am."

Ma'am. What's with the ma'am stuff?

"Sam!" Becky snapped her fingers in front of my face.

"What?" I jerked around.

Adam laughed and the sound of it calmed me a little. Somehow, somewhere I had started to care for him as a friend. Who would've thought? The idea of it made me grin, but I tuned into my other friend. She wanted center stage.

"…and then her cousin showed up last night."

"Wait. What are you talking about?" I glanced at Adam.

Becky rushed out, breathless, "Why aren't you listening to me? I just told you that Adam was with the Academy Elite last night."

"What are the Academy Elite?" I looked around. Was I the only one clueless?

Adam reached for his water. "It's her term for the top circle. Miranda Stewart had some people over last night."

Becky sneered at him. "It's not just my term. Everyone uses it." She turned to me and her eyes were beaming. "Anyway, so Miranda had the Academy Elite over. You know, her, Emily, Amelia, and Cassandra. They're the top four girls in school, right?"

"Sure."

"Then Adam was invited—"

"I brought Tanya last night." He lifted their entwined hands.

They were an item now?

Becky poked me in the arm. "And Peter was there, so was Mark Decraw."

I nodded. They were the other two captains of the football team. This was the Academy Elite?

"And then—"

I interrupted her. "Were you there?"

She closed her mouth and flashed me a look. "No, but I heard all this from Adam."

He wiggled his eyebrows and kissed Tanya's hand.

I frowned at the display of affection.

Becky clapped her hands in front of me again. "Seriously, Sam! Pay attention."

"Okay, okay."

"So Jeff and Jill showed up. Miranda let them stay for an hour, since Jill's on the cheerleading squad and Jeff's third string. But then they kicked them out after an hour, only an hour. Can you believe that? And then Jessica and Lydia tried to get in too, but I guess they were turned away at the door. Peter Glasburg wouldn't even let them inside Miranda's house. Did you know those two were dating? I had no idea."

She didn't stop for a breath.

"And then, you won't believe it, but Logan Kade showed up!" She sat back in a dramatic break. Her chest heaved up and down and she held onto the table. "I couldn't believe it either, but he was drunk."

"I'm going to go to the bathroom." Tanya shot out of her chair and was gone in an instant.

I twisted around, but couldn't find her. I looked at Adam. "Is she okay?"

He indicated Becky and remained quiet.

She took another deep breath. "And then Logan started making fun of Tanya."

"Wait—what?"

"Yeah. I know." Her head bounced up and down. "He was really tearing into her, calling her loose and easy and all sorts of things. Tanya started to cry, but you know what happened?"

"Adam told him to shut up?"

Becky's lips clamped shut. After a beat, she looked at him.

I did too. "What?" Neither said a word. "You didn't?"

He looked away.

Becky opened her mouth. "So no one stopped him, no one. Not even Peter and we all know Peter rules the roost at these things."

"Do we?" I had no idea.

"He does, but then *she* shows up."

"Who?"

"Her cousin." Her eyes flashed in giddiness. "And she starts yelling at Logan instead. I think Tanya texted her, but you'll never guess what else happened?"

"Probably not," I deadpanned.

"So Logan was yelling at Tanya and then that girl started yelling at Logan, who took it. He completely shut up and just let her yell at him, but then his brother shows up a half hour later."

I sat up straight and narrowed my eyes. "Mason was there?"

Her head jumped up and down again and she was panting like a thirsty dog.

I felt Adam's quietness next to me and knew he was studying me.

"And then everybody got real quiet. She shut up."

"Who shut up?"

"Tanya's cousin."

Adam offered, "Tate. Her name is Tate."

"Tate completely shut up and she looked like she was going to faint or something."

"Her face got all green." He grinned and that was when I knew that Adam didn't like Tanya's cousin at all.

"I heard that Emily thought Tate had soiled her pants or something, it was that intense. And Mason hadn't even said anything at that time."

"But he's going to, right?" I was starting to see where this was going and a sense of dread was settling in.

"Yeah. He looked like a cat who'd found his favorite mouse wounded or something. It was eerie. And he started to make fun of her, like all cruel and stuff. The things he said to her were horrible and he was only playing with her. She didn't try to defend herself. I guess Mason Kade really hates that girl, and the way he ripped into her. It was something else."

"He enjoyed it." Adam's voice was quiet.

I looked over and held his gaze. Something dark was in their depths.

He spoke again, "It was like an animal that was playing with its kill before they fully killed it. That's what he was doing with her. I've never seen anything like it before."

I held his stare and the realization that he was scared of the Kades hit me hard. I could see he was terrified of them, but Adam broke the moment when he left the table.

Becky's eyes skirted between the two of us, but she leaned forward. "And then I guess Logan finally told him to leave."

"And did he?"

She jerked a shoulder up. "I don't know. Adam never told me that, but he said there was a strange comment Logan made to him."

"To Adam?"

"No, to Mason."

"What was it?"

"He said, 'you bruised her shoulder.'" She leaned back.

I waited. Nothing. "And?"

"That was it. I guess Mason left after that."

"He bruised Tate's shoulder?"

She shook her head. "That's the thing. Adam said everyone looked at her shoulders, but there wasn't anything there. She had on some wrap-around shawl or something, but her shoulders were bare. No bruises. Nothing." And then her eyes fell to my shoulders.

I was glad for covering them up and I felt a small tingling sensation where a small bruise had formed from Mason's hand. I was tense, waiting for her to ask. But she didn't. I felt Becky's eagerness and knew she wanted to, but she held her tongue. I was grateful as I reached for my orange juice. I downed the whole thing. Champagne had been added to it and I sat back, surprised.

"What?" She held back a small grin.

"I just got served alcohol."

She giggled. "Your dad's the head coach for FC Academy and we're here with Adam's dad. Steven Quinn is powerful in this town too."

"Where did Adam go?"

She gestured to a back corner. Adam's father was close to another woman with his hand on her thigh. He leaned close to whisper something in her ear, but I looked further to the right where Adam stood and watched the exchange. When his jaw clenched, I knew he was angry, but then I sat up straight. My father had appeared out of my nowhere. Not my father. David.

And the heavily made-up woman whose hair was pulled up in a loose bun moved away from Adam's father and extended her red nails to my father. Her hand paused on his chest and she tilted her head to the side. Loose curls that fell from her bun slid over her shoulder and she seemed to be laughing when she swept them further back.

"Sam."

I ignored Becky's warning comment and stood.

CHAPTER TWENTY

"Sam." David moved back a step when I stopped near him. I felt Adam come up behind my elbow, but he remained quiet.

"Dad." And I waited. Would he correct me?

He gave me a tight smile and I knew he wouldn't. Instead he gestured towards the woman and Adam's father. "Have you met my daughter? This is Samantha."

The woman held out her arm and tried to melt me with her smile. "Hello, you're so precious, so beautiful. Penelope."

Adam's father moved away from the woman and nodded. "Steven. I think we've met once."

Adam spoke up, "No, dad. You didn't formally meet her. We left the house early that day."

"Oh yes, that's right." Then he turned to David. "David, what do you have planned for next week's game? You think we're going to pull out a win against Leers?"

David cleared his throat. "We're going to try, that's for certain."

"Dad, don't you guys have your annual football dinner tonight?"

He opened his mouth and stared at me. "Uh…"

"That's right." Penelope's laugh rang out. "I was just talking to your father about that. He said he's going to be alone tonight. Heavens, we can't have that, can we?"

"Certainly not." My jaw ached from how tight it was.

"Dad, you're going with me, right?" Adam brushed against my elbow when he moved forward. He stood close to me and I felt his tension.

"Well, this sounds perfect. Father and son." Penelope placed her hand on David's arm this time. "Father and daughter. It's almost romantic."

I tilted my head to the side and removed her hand. "And no sluts…"

There was a choked silence for a second.

And then David rasped out, "Samantha!"

Adam barked out a laugh.

His father jerked back a step.

"What?" I turned towards David with wide eyes, innocent eyes.

"Apologize."

"For what?" I eyed her up and down. "I call it how it is."

She bristled, but kept her mouth shut.

I narrowed my eyes and waited. The anger was mounting in her. Her hands clenched. Her shoulders grew tight. Her cheeks inflamed and her eyes closed till they were almost slits.

I counted down in my head. 3…2…1…and…

"What a little bitch you have, David." She leaned forward until her face was a few inches from mine.

I smirked and held steady. The Kades had taught me a few things.

She sucked in her breath and I knew her fury leapt higher. "I feel sorry for you, David, real sorry for you."

"Hey, now." He moved between us.

I sidestepped and never broke eye contact with her. "Are you bored with married men? Football coaches don't make that much money, you know."

She laughed harshly. "Private school coaches do."

"Penelope." Adam's father took hold of her elbow.

Adam's voice came out shrilly. "Hey dad, where's mom? Didn't you come with her?"

There was another brief moment of silence.

"Are you insinuating something, Adam?"

He laughed next to me and I found myself grinning along with it. "You're a smart man. What do you think?"

"Penelope."

Her head swiveled to me.

I gave her a cheeky grin. "When'd you pick up the trade?"

"The trade?"

"You know, having affairs, sleeping with married men, being a hooker?"

"That's enough, Samantha!" David clamped down on my arm and dragged me away. I twisted around and gave her a wave. "Stop it. Now."

I waited until he had taken me to the parking lot and then yanked my arm free. I rubbed where he had held onto. "That's the thanks I get from saving you from her?"

He drew upright and hissed out, "You did not save me from her. You made a fool of yourself."

"That's doubtful."

He started to pace in front of me with his hands on his hips. His tie flapped behind him as he turned and went the other way. I couldn't stop myself from smiling as I leaned against a car behind me.

He noticed and snapped, "What?"

"That's what you do when you're frustrated with the opposing team." I'd seen enough of those times when his football team wasn't playing as well as he wanted them to.

He stopped and then let out a small laugh as he reached behind his head to scratch. "I'd forgotten how smart you are."

"That woman was a filthy whore and you know it." I cooled my smile. "Just because you're lonely and had your heart broken by my mother doesn't mean you should get yourself mixed up with her."

"Samantha."

"She's bad news."

He held his arms out in surrender. "I wasn't going to get mixed up with her. I wasn't. I'm aware what kind of a woman she is, but you called her out for having an affair with Steven Quinn. He knows now that I know. She knows. His son knows. That spells trouble for a lot of people."

I shrugged. "Adam's known for a long time."

He stopped pacing. "Really?"

I nodded.

"Well, I guess that's a little better then."

"So can I still come for that dinner tonight? I know families are supposed to come."

He eyed me warily. "Does your mom know about this?"

I shrugged. "Like I care and yes, she does. She said I could go."

He opened his mouth.

I added, "And she said that in front of Mason and Logan Kade so she has to follow through with it."

His mouth closed, but I caught a flare of pride in his eyes. My chest swelled up and I looked away when a sudden burst of tears came to my eyes. I wiped them away quickly and glanced back. He'd been watching me with a sad smile. It vanished immediately.

"Are you okay?"

I was jolted at the sincerity of his voice. "What do you mean?"

"With all this, the changes, the truth coming out. Are you okay?"

"Why wouldn't I be?"

"Because you're a teenager." He said it so simply. "Because your mother can be one vicious and selfish woman. Because you got your life taken away from you." His voice gentled even more. "Remember that I know about Jeff and your friends. I know what they did to you. And because," his mouth twisted in a crooked smile, "you set my car on fire, remember?"

"Oh yeah!" I burst out in laughter and wiped more tears away. I didn't know why they were coming.

He took a small breath. "Are you okay, Samantha? Are you still running?"

I nodded.

"How long do you go for?"

I couldn't talk. My throat was so tight, it was blocked.

He sounded sad. "That long, huh?" And he took another deep breath. "I'm sorry, Sam. I really am."

I looked away. I couldn't see how haunted he sounded. Something would've broken inside of me and I was holding on tight. I was holding on so tight right now.

He continued, "If I had known what your mother wanted or what she needed, I would've tried to adopt you. I would've gone for something with the courts so that she couldn't have taken you away. I had no idea. I really didn't, but there was no way I could've been the man she wanted. I was the man she used to get her through her hard times."

"I'm sorry." My voice cracked. More tears flooded me. "I'm sorry for what she did to you."

He shook his head. "I can handle it. I have a good job. I'm still somewhat young and in shape. I'll be fine."

I took a deep breath.

"Are you going to be fine?"

I shook my head. I couldn't answer him, not then.

"I hear the gossip, you know. I heard the Kade brothers have taken you under their wing." He frowned. "I'm not sure if that's a good thing. Those boys can be cruel, but they do seem to back each other up. Are you okay with them?"

"They help…with her…"

Enough said. He nodded in understanding. "Well, I suppose I'll see you tonight then. Six o'clock. Back here."

"Okay."

He gave a small wave before he went back inside. I turned to my car, but Adam called my name and I paused and looked back. He grimaced as he approached. "Sorry about my dad and that woman."

I chuckled. "I thought I would've been the one apologizing to you."

"Nah. I liked it. You're tough."

"I didn't want her involved with David."

He nodded. "I can see that, but thanks. It's out now. My dad has to deal with it. He knows I know."

"I'm not apologizing to your dad."

He held his hands up. "Not asking you to."

I glanced back over my shoulder. "What about Becky and Tanya?"

"I'll take them both home." He gave me another tight smile and shoved his hands in his front pockets. It gave him a lean look, which emphasized his slender waist and broad shoulders.

"About Tanya…"

He shook his head. "Yes?"

"What are you doing?"

"I like her. I actually do."

"And it doesn't hurt Becky to see that…?"

"I don't know," he admitted. "I just know that I was playing a game with her before because of you. You liked Becky. I liked you. So I didn't do the right thing before, but I'm trying. I really am right now."

I nodded.

"What about you? Are you and Kade, you know?"

I shook my head. "It's about my parent's stuff and I don't want to talk about that."

"Really? No?"

"Nope."

"Oh." He ran a hand over his face. "I wouldn't have guessed that."

"Why not?" My voice cooled. "I told you that I know them, I'm not screwing them."

"No, no I know, but there was something there."

"What do you mean?"

He lifted both his shoulders up. "Does it matter?"

"Maybe. Maybe not."

He laughed again. "You're tough, Sam, tougher than I would've thought."

"Yeah…" I frowned. I was getting tired of hearing that from him. What did he think of me before? Then I rolled my eyes, like I really cared about that now. "Don't break Becky's heart, okay?"

He saluted me.

"Are you really going to start dating Tanya?"

"I think so."

I sighed. "Have fun with that, then."

He smirked. "I plan to."

And I laughed. This one was genuine, but then I waved goodbye and headed home. I had two hours before I needed to be back at the club for the football's annual dinner. I hurried through the house, but stopped short when I saw Mason in his room. Normally I would've taken the south stairs and I wouldn't have to go past his room, but I took the north stairs this time. When I breezed past, his door was open and he sat at his desk shirtless.

I braked and reversed.

He glanced up. "Hey."

"Hey." I went inside and sat on the edge of his bed.

He didn't turn around and kept his back to me as he looked at his computer's screen. "You seem in a rush?"

"I'm going to my dad's dinner tonight."

"Your dad?"

I cursed. I'd forgotten he knew, they all knew.

"My old dad's thing."

He grinned as he turned in his chair. "I understand. He's still your dad. Raised you, didn't he?"

I nodded and hugged myself. For some reason, a chill swept over me. I frowned. The windows weren't open in the room.

"Our folks are in the cities for the weekend. Again."

He didn't sound as if he cared. I frowned. "Are you pissed about that?"

Mason swung his hypnotic eyes back to me and narrowed them. I felt him searching inside of me, measuring whatever I had inside for what he might've needed. I always felt him probing me deep.

Then he said, "Does it matter? He's there. With her."

I frowned. "You say that like my mom's the other woman. Was she?" Wasn't he the other man for her?

He shrugged and stood to go in his bathroom. I waited a second, but took a deep breath and followed. As I stepped in the doorway, Mason let loose his shorts and turned on the shower.

I was struck by his nudity. He didn't care. Most guys might've done it for shock value, but he didn't care. This was Mason. Then he looked up and grinned. "Wanna join?"

I took a step inside.

His grin turned to something else.

I stepped closer and tilted my head up. He looked down and we stood close, close enough to touch. His hand brushed against my hipbone and I closed my eyes. His hand started to caress me there. A flooding filled me and a need started to throb between my legs. I held my breath and my head started to hang down. It rested against his chest.

Then I felt his lips against my forehead. He skimmed them lightly.

My hand reached up and curled onto his arm. It hung there.

When he bent forward and I felt his arm start to wrap around, I pulled back, breathless. My heart was pounding in my ears and I could only look at him, stricken. He gazed down at me and his lips moved. I knew he was saying something, but I couldn't hear over my heartbeat. I shook my head and tried to explain that to him, but I couldn't. My throat didn't work. My tongue didn't work. Nothing worked anymore except my feet. They pulled me away and I was soon hurrying to my room.

The door shut behind me, but it wasn't enough. I turned the lock and backed up three steps. I stared down and watched the handle. I waited for it to turn, but it never did. Nothing happened. He never came.

I kept backing up until I felt my bed behind my legs and sat abruptly. My arms were still wrapped around me. I sat there and waited for my heartbeat to settle, until I could hear things again. Everything was so deafening.

CHAPTER TWENTY-ONE

The football dinner was uneventful, at least for my latest standards of drama. Jill was there with Jeff and she sneered at me most of the time. Not surprising. Jessica had landed herself a date too, but I had no idea who he was. He was on the team, obviously. And while her newfound friend sneered at me, Jessica was void of emotion. She didn't ignore me like she had been till the Kade Coming Out news, but she didn't kiss my ass either. I caught her gaze a couple times and once thought she looked sad, but shrugged it off. She should be sad.

The only thing that bothered me at the dinner was the interest Malinda Decraw showed in David when she sat beside him after the second round of cocktails. She was the single mother of Mark Decraw; one of Becky's termed Academy Elite. He was co-captain and Amelia White's date that night. I knew Becky would be salivating at the gossip, but all I cared about was how many times Malinda did the hair flip.

She'd smile at David, lean close, and flip her hair. Then she would laugh, touch his arm or his shoulder (once), and flip the hair again.

When I left the dinner and spotted Mark and Amelia kissing by his car, I was tempted to corner them about Malinda's intentions. But I refrained. With my luck, that would bring more drama and as I let myself into the Kade mansion, I had enough on my hands.

Analise stood in the kitchen with a large glass of wine and two bottles beside her. Her eyes were glazed over and she swayed from side to side. Her hair was messed and looked haphazard while her white dress slipped off one shoulder. The top of her red bra was visible.

My mom was drunk.

Logan and Nate both sat on a counter with their legs dangling while Mason was propped against the doorway with his arms closed over his chest. As usual, he was unreadable while Logan had a look of delight on his face. Nate was fighting back his own laughter.

"Sam, you've been missing out!" Logan threw his arms wide. "Your mom's drunk like a sorority rush. Dad dropped her off an hour ago and she's getting drunker by the minute."

Analise rounded to me. Her body kept going, but Mason stopped her when his hand shot out and pushed her shoulder back upright.

"Thanks. You're bacb," she slurred, then took a big gulp of wine. She wiped her mouth with the back of her hand. "Housse your daddy?"

My eyes narrowed. "It was fine. Thanks."

She sniffled. "You always loved him more. Me, I'm the acdual parend. He neber wass."

"Thanks, mom. We all know that."

Her eyes got wide and her lips pursed into a sneer. "I swear, if you werend my daughter, I'd disown you."

"Really?" I arched an eyebrow.

"If you wanna him, you can hab him. Move in with him. I'm outta here." She swung her arm wide again. Her body kept going, but Nate was the one who caught her from the other side this time.

She tucked her head down. "Thanks."

He nodded.

Then she heaved a dramatic sigh and her arm dropped from her one hip. "You've god your wish, Samantha."

"What wish?"

"Me. And you. We're outta here. He kicked me out. I had a few doo many ad dinner and he kicked me out. Have to pack my stuff now. We're moving on, bucko!" Then she hung her head and a sniffle was heard. "David wond take me back now."

"Mom."

"Don't!" Her head snapped back up and her eyes were wild. "You always said it, we'd be gone. He wouldna marry me and you're righd. He won't. It's over. Finite. Finido. Finished…"

I stepped around Mason, but he moved with me. When I started to get closer to her, he moved another inch. He was blocking me. He didn't want me close to her so I stayed put. I folded my arms. "Mom, you're drunk. Everything will be better in the morning. I promise."

"You don promise. You can't promise me anything. I'm the mother. I should be promiser one, but I'm not. I cand even do that for you. I've ruined it all, Sammy."

Her head was down again and another sniffle sounded.

"Mom, it'll be okay. We can get our own place."

Analise's shoulder jerked and her hand clenched around the wine glass. When she looked back, vehemence was in her eyes. The self-pity was gone and in its place was anger. I gulped; my mother was looking at me with fury now.

"It's your fault. All of this is your fault."

"How?" I challenged.

"David never loved you. Hell, I never loved you. I should've been with your father. I loved him, but he couldn't stay. He had to go. He always had to go. I had no one. Me and a baby." She threw her head back and an ugly sounding laugh came out. "Who's going want the package deal? Well, I found David. He loved me. Not you. He tolerated you, but me he loved. I should've been with your father, your real father. But he didn't have the time for me so fine. Screw him."

"Wait, what?" I surged forward, but Mason blocked me again. He didn't put a hand up, but he stepped in front an inch. It was enough of a barrier that held me back.

"David hates your father. He loathes him. He thinks he walked out on his daughter." A hysterical laugh came out, followed by a hysterical sob. She choked up for a moment and then shook her head clear of the emotions. "Jokes on him, isn't it. Your real daddy never knew about you. Like I'd stomach that. That he'd come back for his daughter, but not me. Oh no. If he wouldn't take both of us, he didn't get either of us. Your father has no idea about you." Her eyes found me, crystal clear.

A chill went down my back and I wondered if that was evil lurking in her depths. No. It couldn't be. She was drunk, just drunk...and sad.

She sneered at me. "And you'll never know. He'll never know about you, you'll never know about him. You can't leave me, Sam. I've all you got. David won't take you back. Are you kidding me? He's probably already got another woman, maybe even a kid too. He always liked to play the doting father type. Maybe he'll pick a son this time. The daughter he had ended up being a screw-up. You always picked the worst types, Sam. Jeff. Lydia. Jessica. They're your closest and they all screwed you. Even I knew it. You're the screw up."

When she was done, no one said a word. A fly would've sent echoes through the room, but then Analise choked out a simper. "Pack your stuff, Sam. We're leaving."

Mason chuckled.

She whirled to him. "What are you laughing about—?"

Logan and Nate jumped off the counter. Neither grinned now.

She stopped whatever she'd been about to say.

And Mason stepped away from her, but towards me. He ushered me further back, at a safer distance from my mother. When he stopped chuckling, he shook his head. His voice came out bored. "Are you this crazy?"

She gasped.

Logan smirked.

"I mean, you're effing crazy if you think you can talk to her like this. This is how you talk to the one person who's stayed by you?" He rolled his eyes. "Look, this is your daughter, but if you think she's going anywhere with you when you're like this, you're delusional too. She's not leaving. You are."

Analise went pale and her body stumbled back. It looked like a sudden violent wind had whipped against her. It came out of nowhere, but there was no wind.

"Just get lost, woman," Logan snickered. He circled around her while Nate stayed in place.

Mason stepped back again and this time was effectively in front of me. He completely blocked me, even from her vision. I tried to shift to the side, but he moved back again and had me trapped against the wall. So I snuck a hand on his side and peaked around him. He didn't stop me, but he tensed at my touch.

Logan moved again and all three had encircled her. She glanced around as panic started to set in her eyes.

Mason spoke, "We've been quiet, woman. We've taken your presence in this house like calm good little boys, but we're not good little boys."

"Not at all," Logan's hyena laugh came out. His eyes flashed hatred.

"What are you—what are you do..doing?" she stammered out.

Nate spoke in a calm voice, "We're not going to hurt you."

"No." Mason shook his head."But you are drunk. You're wacko in the head and you're being semi-abusive to your daughter." Logan's laugh gentled, but the sound still sent shivers down my body. "So we could say anything to you, do anything to you, and who'd believe you? Your own fiancé sent you packing tonight and went back to his dinner."

"You guys wouldn't…" She was white as a ghost and her eyes jumped between the three of them. Then she found me and held a hand out. "Sam, he—"

Mason moved again so she couldn't see me. I heard a smacking sound and my mom cried out, "Ouch!"

I jerked behind him, but I didn't know what to do. Help her or help myself? I burrowed my head in the back of his shirt.

"How do you think this is going to end?" Mason was back in charge, so cold. It was like he'd asked about the weather.

"I..I—I—what?"

"Do you really think we're going to be bitches and let you talk to Sam like that?" Logan spoke now. "You're screwed up in the head if you think you've got the power to do that, especially in front of us."

"But—bu—you guys don't even like her!"

Nate laughed.

Mason sighed. It was a pitying sound. "Don't like her? We'd like anyone compared to you."

She gasped. "But—I didn't—your father—"

Logan snapped, "Stop choking like a little bitch. I thought you had bigger balls than that."

"Wha—huh? You guys can't talk to me like this..." But she didn't sound so certain.

Mason taunted her softly, "What he doesn't know, you're not going to tell."

"What?"

Logan came out strong, "Here's the way it's going to be. You're going to leave—"

Nate jumped in, "You're going to a hotel."

"And you're going to sleep off this drunk stupor," Mason ended.

My entire body shivered as I listened. All three of them spoke as one unit. They moved as one and they had their sights on my mother. I pressed even closer to Mason, not sure what to do, if I could at all. Did I even want to? It'd been so long since someone protected me...

"I'm not that drunk."

"You are." He said it so smooth, so soft, and so chilling. Now he left me. I fell forward a step, lost from his warmth, but contained

179

myself. He moved as a stalker, silent as a ghost. Then he motioned to Nate.

A second later, my mom whimpered out in pain. I had my hands in front of my face, but when Logan started laughing again, the sound was so delightful and so dark, I couldn't hide anymore. I took a deep breath and looked up. He'd taken hold of the back of my mother's head and tilted her head back.

Mason watched. He didn't seem affected and then he motioned for Nate with his hand again.

"No-!" My mother screamed out.

"Come on," Logan chided her and then forcibly pulled her jaw down. Her mouth snapped opened and Nate poured something down her throat. She convulsed forward, choking as liquid spewed from between her lips. Her back spasmed backwards then, but Logan didn't let her go. He clamped her mouth shut again and ran a thumb down her throat. I watched as my mom fought, but in the end she swallowed.

They did it again.

And again.

After a fourth time, after Nate had almost emptied a bottle down her, he looked up. "I think that's enough."

Mason nodded and stepped back towards me again.

Logan swept my mother up in his arms. She'd grown weak during the ordeal and the fight had left her after the second time. Her eyes rolled back as she was cradled to his chest. When he turned for the door, Nate followed.

The door closed behind them and silence filled the room again. I couldn't stop from trembling. My teeth were chattering. My arms were jerking all over and then Mason swept me against him. He cradled my head to his chest and ran soothing hands down my arm.

My hands took hold of his shirt and hung on. I couldn't let go or I'd fall. I didn't want to fall. When I thought I could speak, I choked out, "What's going to happen to her?"

His lips skimmed my forehead, so soft. "She'll go to a hotel and sleep it off."

"But…" I took a deep breath.

His lips pressed another kiss to my cheek.

I held on tighter. When his hand swept down and caught my leg, I climbed up him, grateful for the hold. I was going down otherwise. "What if she says something to your dad?" What would she do to me? I hadn't stopped it.

Mason lifted me so my legs were entwined around his waist. I hung onto him. My arms were wound around his neck. He ran a hand down my back as his other held me in place, splayed out on my bottom.

Then he kissed the side of my mouth and whispered against it, "She won't. She doesn't dare."

I sighed as he kissed the other side of my mouth. My lips moved against his. "What do you mean?"

"Your mom's a bitch and now she knows what we think of her…"

She knew what they could do to her. My body couldn't stop shaking as I realized this and pressed my forehead into his shoulder. I held on tighter, but a thought nagged me. Why had he done that? Why had all three of them done that?

Mason chuckled against my hair. "Because she'll shut up now. That's why we did it. And because she needed to know we could."

I closed my eyes and felt him moving. I had no idea where he was taking me, but I wasn't going to ask. My body had stopped shaking and a different feeling had taken hold of me, one I didn't think I could fight off. I didn't want to. Need.

CHAPTER TWENTY-TWO

Mason sat me on the couch in my room and started rummaging through my closet. The need throbbed in me, it was slowly taking over when he started to lift my arms and pull my dress off. I blinked up at him. He seemed cold, hurried. This wasn't how I thought it would be.

My arms dropped back to my lap and I stared up. Desire was thick within me, blurring my vision. Why didn't he kiss me? I wanted him to and I reached up to palm the back of his head. Something was shoved down my arm instead. He slipped it over my head too. When he lifted my other arm and pushed it through a sleeve, I realized he was dressing me.

"What are you doing?" My voice was raspy.

Mason tugged me to my feet.

"Wha—?"

He pulled up some pants and I looked down at myself. I was fully dressed, even with socks and tennis shoes.

I blinked again. When had that happened?

"You couldn't go in that."

I spread my arms wide. "Like what?"

"We're taking off." He went back to going through my closet. More of my clothes were brought out and stuffed in a bag.

"We are?"

"When your mom wakes up sober, she's going to freak out. She'll call my dad hysterical."

"What?" I sat up further to clear my head. "They broke up…"

"No, they didn't." His head was in my closet again. "My dad called me and asked if we'd handle your mom. She got drunk at his business dinner and kept going on about you and your dad. He couldn't let her stay and he had to keep the meeting so we got babysitting duty."

I watched as he kept putting things in my bag and then disappeared inside the bathroom. "What are you going to say when he calls about tonight?"

"The truth." He came back with my toiletry bag. It was bulging at the zipper. "She kept drinking. You came home. She attacked you and then she started on us so we took her to a hotel."

"What are you going to tell him why we're leaving?" Where were we going?

"Nate's parents called to invite us up. We'll be back Monday or Tuesday we took you along so your mom wouldn't start in on you again. It's a long weekend anyway."

"What if she tells him what you guys did?"

He stopped and stared at me. His gaze was piercing. "She was drunk and crazy. We didn't do anything except to help." He narrowed his eyes. "It should be four to one."

Clarity slammed into me. I heard the veiled threat and surged to my feet. "You think I'm going to rat?"

He grinned and the tense moment was gone. "I didn't think so. Check to make sure I got everything. I need to get my own stuff."

"Where are we going? I don't know what to pack."

"Nate lives in the mountains, but he's got a Jacuzzi." And he left with those parting words.

My butt plopped down on the couch and I held my bag with numb fingers. It dangled from them to the floor. All I could do was sit there. What the hell had happened? And then I realized it didn't matter. He had everything covered for me, even my clothes. All I had to do was go downstairs and go for a ride. Did I go?

An hour later as I stood in the foyer, waiting, I knew that question was irrelevant. There'd never been a question not to go.

A bag crashed next to me and I jumped back. Then a second later, another bag followed with a third beside it. Logan and Nate peered down to me from the stairway and Logan waved. "Sorry!"

I frowned up at them, but they disappeared. It wasn't long before both were downstairs and in the foyer with me.

They looked happy, not happy—radiant. Logan was bouncing in place and Nate was bent over laughing at something. The two were full of adrenalin and excitement.

I shook my head. What was happening? It was all such a daze to me.

Then Logan threw his arm around my shoulder and jerked me against him. He breathed on me. "Are you ready to par-tay?"

"Party?" My eyes got big. "I thought we were going to the mountains."

"Uh, yeah…with thirty others." Logan sighed in exasperation and then frowned before he barked out, "Hey!"

I jumped again.

"What about your friends? You want to invite some of them?"

"My friends?"

"Yeah, that nerd girl and the quarterback who wants to bang you."

"He doesn't want to bang me."

Logan squeezed me against him and tipped his head back. His hyena laugh came out. Nate started to join in.

"He doesn't."

Both kept laughing and shook their heads.

"He doesn't."

Mason appeared with two bags in one hand and a black duffel bag on his back. He rolled his eyes and pulled out his keys. "You can't even lie to yourself. The douche bag has wanted to get in your pants for a long time."

I looked around. All three gave me knowing looks. Then I threw my arms in the air. "I don't even know why I was saying that."

Logan reached out and caught my shoulders when I started to leave. He pulled me back against his chest and enfolded his arms over my chest. "Ah, our little sister, trying to be all nice and saintly."

Mason snorted and opened the door. "Saints don't set cars on fire."

We all piled out behind him and Logan chuckled. "There's that, yeah."

When we got to Mason's Escalade, my bags were picked up and thrown inside. Logan nudged me with his shoulder. "If you want to invite your friends, you better call them now. We're picking up some others and heading out."

I pulled out my phone. "What do I say?"

He shrugged. "Tell them we're going to a kickass cabin for two days, but they have to be at Joe's Gas Station in thirty minutes. A minute late and they're dust."

"Give 'em forty. We have to swing by and pick up Marissa. She's in town at her aunt's." Mason brushed past me for the driver's seat. His hand swept against my thigh.

A small tingle shot threw me, but I frowned. Marissa again.

Logan gave me a knowing smirk, but headed to his own Escalade. After Nate and I got in Mason's, they tore out of there. When I called Becky, her response was to scream. She didn't say anything else, just started screaming and threw her phone aside. I could hear banging in the background, but disconnected the call soon after that. I could only imagine what she was doing. Adam's response was more reserved. He didn't respond for a moment, and then he said in a gruff voice, "I suppose I should make sure Becky gets there. We'll take my car."

After that was done and I'd put my phone away, the guys were quiet. Nate was looking at me and Mason kept glancing at me in the rear view mirror.

"What?"

Mason snorted again and looked away.

Nate gave me a polite smile. "Nothing."

"What?" I asked again, but I knew they wouldn't respond. And they didn't. Neither said a word as we drove around town. At each house they stopped at, people would come out with bags already packed. A few got in Logan's car, but soon two others drove their cars and filled them up. No one else got in Mason's and then Logan's Escalade pulled up next to ours. Each rolled down their windows.

"Go to the gas station and deal with all that stuff. I'll pick up Marissa."

Logan nodded and craned his head to meet my gaze. "Hop on over here, little sister."

"What? Why?"

The two brothers shared a look, but Logan responded, "We need you there to meet your friends. You're going to ride with them."

"Oh. Okay." And since that made perfect sense, I climbed out and got into his backseat. Two of his friends scooted over while another two jumped in the back with the bags. We took off one way and Mason went the other way.

When we got to the gas station, the sight was almost unbelievable. Twenty different cars were parked in the back lot and people were milling around. Bags were on the ground, some were being strapped on top of other cars, and then I caught sight of Adam's car. He had parked in the far corner, away from the frenzy. When Logan parked, I hopped out, but he hollered at me, "Don't go too far."

I turned around and kept walking backwards. "You aren't actually my big brother, you know."

He flashed me blinding smile. "Not my intent, Sam, not my intent."

I frowned and opened my mouth to ask what he meant, but he was pulled away by two of his friends. The smell of booze was ripe in the air and I knew the festivities had already started. As I got to Adam's car, Becky yelled my name and I turned around. She had two plastic bags in her hands and she ran the rest of the way from the station.

When she got to me, she started to jump up and down. Her hair bounced with her. "I'm so excited for this! You can't even believe me."

I grinned at the sight.

"My giddy radar exploded at the top. I had to beg my mom to let me come. She almost didn't, but I told her I'd do dishes for the rest of the year. I'm not sure if that was a good idea, but I don't care right now." She dropped both bags on the floor and grabbed my shoulders as she started to bounce around me. "I don't care if I look stupid. I'm so excited, so excited."

Adam's car door opened and he stood up. He was watching her with wary eyes and ran a hand through his hair. "You wouldn't be able to believe the sight I found when I went to her house. I swear the entire place had been thrown around. It looked like a hundred raccoons stormed through it."

She kept giggling and her eyes got bigger. "I don't know what I'm more excited about, the cabin, that it's a Kade party, or that we got invited and not Lydia and Jessica!"

"Yeah," I had to admit. "There is that." I glanced at Adam. "Your parents let you come?"

The small smile he'd had was wiped clean. His shoulders stiffened and I saw how his jaw clenched together. "They don't have much say in me anymore."

I was about to ask what had happened, when Becky gasped and stopped bouncing.

I closed my eyes. Oh no. It'd been too good to be true. A sense of doom filled me and I turned…

Becky's mouth dropped and she pointed over my shoulder. "Look!"

I couldn't believe what I was seeing. Jessica, Lydia, Jill…and Ashley Decortts piled out of a car. Each of them had different expressions on their face, but none could hide their own excitement.

The ground fell out from beneath me. If they went, I wasn't. Bottom line.

At that moment, Mason's Escalade breezed to a halt. He parked beside Adam's car and when he got out beside me, he saw my face. "What is it?"

I nodded at them. "If they go, I'm not."

He followed my gaze and shrugged. "Consider it done." Then he nodded at Nate, whose grin couldn't be wiped off his face as he went in search for Logan. Mason stood next to me, but I couldn't look away from what was happening. Nate found Logan and the two bent their heads together for a second. Logan's head snapped up and he found me instantly. An evil grin came to his face and he snapped his fingers before he gestured to their car.

"Get 'em out," he hollered.

"No, no, no..." Jessica, Lydia, Jill and Ashley all started to shake their heads and hold their hands up in surrender. It didn't matter. They were ushered out of there in record time. One of the guys pounded on top of the car. Jill poked her head out and snarled at them, but the guys started laughing and chucking bottles at them. Garbage was thrown next. They hurried to raise their windows, but it didn't matter. Someone threw paint inside. Jessica was drenched and Lydia screamed from the back.

"Get out of here!" Jessica screeched at the top of her lungs.

Their car was soon out of there, but I couldn't look away. A tension had taken hold of me. Its grip was so tight, so powerful. I couldn't believe what had almost happened, what *had* just happened…because of me.

"Happy?" Mason asked in a quiet voice.

I jerked my head up and realized he had remained close the whole time. The rest of his car had vacated.

"Yeah." I nodded my head abruptly.

"You sure?"

He was so close. I felt his breath on me and it teased me. That same tingle started back, nagging me. It wouldn't go away… I shook my head. It had to go away. There was no other way.

"Sam?"

I choked out, "I'm fine." And I swung away. I needed to get away from him, from how he could pull me in, how I wanted him to pull me in.

Hell, I wanted to pull *him* in.

I closed my eyes, but Mason stepped back then. I took a deep breath and tried to calm my nerves. Goodness. I wanted to jump him right there and when I opened my eyes, under heavy eyelids, I saw he wanted the same thing. His eyes were dark with desire, but then he closed his eyes. As he opened them, he wore a mask once again. He was in control and he gave me a half grin. "I want your car behind mine or Logan's, okay?"

I nodded.

He nodded at Adam. "You got that?"

Adam gave him a nod from across the top of his car, with an unreadable gaze.

Mason narrowed his eyes and held his stare for a second. Neither said a word, but I knew there was some form of message shared between the two. The heated look was broken when a small girl with brown curly hair approached from around the side of Mason's car. She had bright almond eyes, a timid smile, and a white sweater that engulfed her.

"You're Sam?" Warmth oozed from her.

"Not now." Mason touched her shoulder and urged her in front of him as they walked to Logan's side of the lot.

She looked back and gave me another smile before Mason blocked her view of me.

I frowned as I realized what he was doing. He'd done the same thing with my mother. At that time, he'd been protecting me, but who was he protecting now?

"Oh." Becky panted. "My." She heaved an exaggerated breath. "Gawd."

Adam shook his head. "Can you chill the dramatics a bit?"

She looked over, still panting like a dog. "Did you see what I did? I don't even know which thing to talk about first? I can't prioritize them. This is drama overload." Her shoulders sagged heavily and she dropped her arms to her side. "It's all weighing me down. I have to get it off my chest, I just have to."

Then Adam grinned and pointed at an incoming car. "You're going to have to add a bit more to your list."

As a Bentley stopped on the other side of Adam's car, my radar went on high alert. A brand new, straight from the dealership, Porsche Cayenne wheeled in on the other side and the doors were thrown open.

The Academy Elite had arrived. And judging from their packed vehicles, they were coming on the trip.

I watched in horror as Mark Decraw went over and pumped fists with Logan.

Becky groaned next to me. "I think I'm about to collapse."

CHAPTER TWENTY-THREE

It was a three hour drive and by the time we got there, I had one thing in mind. Could I go running and if I could, how long did I have to wait before I went? The itch to get away and run free was so strong; I had to force my legs down to the floor a few times. I wanted to hurl myself out of the car each time we stopped at a stoplight in some small town.

Becky had stopped questioning me about the Kades when I went mute two minutes into the trip. Adam hadn't filled my silence either and so Becky sat back and chatted away to herself. She talked about everything: the Kades, the Academy Elite, how liberating it was to watch Jessica and Lydia get pushed out. She went on and on.

Then, after Adam got a text message, she squealed again when she snatched it from him. She twisted around in the seat and exclaimed, "Tanya's coming with her cousin!" She sang out, "So much drama!"

Adam grunted, "You need to get a life."

"I have a life." She was breathless. "Both of yours."

And then Logan's car, who'd been in the lead, slowed beside a gated driveway. We were in the middle of nowhere with trees thick on either side of the road. The last town seemed forever ago, but when the gate slowly swung open and Logan led the way through it, it was the same; a long narrow road with thick forest around it. Finally, he rounded another curve and a gigantic log mansion stood in a clearing.

It could've been on MTV cribs.

"Whoa," Adam laughed under his breath. "That's a freaking hotel. I wondered how they were going to house everyone."

Becky had fallen silent with wide eyes. Her mouth formed a silent oval and she pressed closed fists to it.

I jumped out of the car and hurried to Logan. "Where's my stuff?"

He frowned at me. "What's up with you?"

"I need to run."

"Gotcha." He glanced at my shoes. "Can you run in those? It's going to take a while to get to your bags."

I jerked my head in a nod. It'd have to do.

He gestured to a trail that started behind a garage. "It's still dark out, but it should be light soon. I'll make sure you get a good room. That trail goes up and around a lake. It'll be pretty by the time you get there. And it should be safe. Nate's parents have an electric fence that runs the perimeter so no big animals should be out there. Take your phone."

When I didn't start right away, he tapped my shoulder. "Go. It's fine."

Then I started. I walked to the back of the garage. When Becky called out and asked where I was going, Logan said something to her. I knew I was covered and as soon as I was hidden from view, I took off.

The path was covered in woodchips and it went uphill.

I pumped my knees and arms high, and even more the higher I went. When the trail veered to the right, my body leaned with it. I wasn't running. I was sprinting. I knew I should slow down. I didn't want to burn out too soon, but I couldn't. Something in me was making me go faster and faster. Sweat was soon dripping off me, but I didn't care. I barely felt it.

The mountain morning air felt cool and it fueled me for more.

The path flattened out after a steep incline. There were a few dips, all of them welcomed, but I loved the climb. My heart beat faster and it wasn't from the exertion.

It might've been an hour, I wasn't sure, but the forest opened around me and I was given a breathtaking view of a lake below. It was in a valley between two mountains. Waves rippled over it. I couldn't see through it, not from how high I was, but the water seemed to give me another burst of adrenalin.

I kicked off at a higher speed and soared past it.

The trees were a blur as I raced past them and I kept going. When my chest felt like it couldn't expand anymore and my arms had started to feel like cement, I slowed my pace. I lifted my head and breathed in the air.

I could feel the elevation in my lungs, but it only made me slow a bit more.

After what seemed like another hour, I turned and started back. When I returned to the lake, I stopped and bent over. I caught my breath, but I couldn't stop looking at the lake. Something calmed and excited me at the same time. I wanted to be a part of it and I felt crazy admitting that to myself, but I did.

And then, as I turned and headed to the mansion, I realized I wasn't scared. Maybe I ran it out of me; maybe I ran away from it enough. I wasn't sure, but a contented feeling settled over me. And then I slowed to a walk the closer I got to the mansion. I could hear bass music blaring through the woods. It might've been a mile away when I started to hear laughter.

There was a slight clearing from the hill where I was and I stopped. My feet were rooted in place.

I could see a large pool behind the mansion. It was filled with people with others streaming around it. There looked to be a hot tub and sauna as well. A few tables were kept separate behind a barrier of plants with a steel grill beside a large bar structure. I heard laughter as a few guys shoved some girls into the pool. They squealed as they were soaked.

A breeze swept around me and goose bumps covered me. I was completely drenched in sweat, but I didn't care. That had been the best run of my life. I was already anticipating my next one.

When I got back to the house and walked through the garage, there were people everywhere. I walked through, drenched in sweat, and a few girls gave me the snub. They looked me over, their lips curled up, and they turned away. I couldn't hold back a grin as this happened. I might not have wanted to buy into being protected by Mason or Logan, but I knew these girls didn't know who I was. And I sighed as I realized that. These girls were being real. They weren't being fake towards me. They weren't kissing my ass because who might've been my new stepbrothers.

More than a few guys didn't look away. My shirt and pants stuck to me like a second skin. It wasn't until I ducked into the kitchen and heard Nate's laugh when he saw me that I realized how foolish I might've looked. He saw me, his mouth opened, and he bent over in laughter.

"Shut up." I frowned at him.

He shook his head, still laughing. "Not at you, not at you…" More laughter and he clapped a hand to his knee a few times. "Look at you." He held a hand up. "You look like you went swimming and I know it's because you went running. Most girls want to look their hottest and you're…I'm sorry to say, but you go the opposite way. I like it. I really do. I admire it."

"Shut up." I frowned at him. "Where's my room?"

He pointed upstairs, still laughing, and choked out, "Fourth floor, second door on your right."

Fourth floor. I couldn't believe there was a fourth floor. And then I remembered the Kade mansion, which wasn't that small compared to this beast of a home, and decided to keep my mouth closed. When I was rounding the first set of stairs, I ran into Adam. He was going downstairs dressed in his swimming trunks and a glass of something in his hand.

He drew back and grinned. "Hey."

"Hey." I eyed the plastic cup. "What are we drinking?"

He grimaced and rolled his eyes. "Something to get me in the party mood. Where'd you go? You took off right away and Logan said you had something to do. No one questioned him, we didn't feel we could, but…where'd you go?"

I shrugged. "I went running."

He frowned. "You run?"

"Yeah."

"Oh." He skimmed me up and down.

I fidgeted under the weight of his gaze, now self-conscious. "So, anyway…you and Becky are on this floor?"

"Yeah." He drew upright. "We're in a back corner."

"And Tanya? Becky said she was coming?"

He looked away and scratched the back of his head. "Yeah…I think her and Tate will share a room in the basement. I think those are the only rooms left."

I nodded. "Does Logan know Tate is coming?"

He met my gaze for a second and just for a second the real Adam was there, the one who meant it when he promised me the world. He spoke in regret, "No…"

I shook my head. "Do you know what you're doing? Logan is going to flip when he knows she's here."

"From what I hear Logan isn't the problem." His jaw clenched and he looked away.

There it was. The unspeakable name, one of the many reasons Adam and I no longer trusted each other and as I confessed that, I wondered when that had happened—when I lost my trust in him and when he did with me? Well, I could guess when he'd lost his with me.

I took a breath and braved the front. I named the name that was between us. "Mason will know you invited her. Mason hates her."

He swung his gaze to me and I saw the pained look in them.

I fought myself from cringing in sympathy.

He wrung out, "Do you even know why he hates her so much? And what does that have to do with you?"

"Do you?"

"No." He shook his head. "But I don't have to deal with it. I care less who he likes or who he doesn't—"

"Are you kidding me?" I folded my arms over my chest and cut in. My chest was starting to rise, up and down, up and down. My heart was starting to race again. "You don't care? About me? You don't care about me? Because you know I'm connected to them. I'm connected to them in a way that few are. They're going to be my family, Adam. I can't ignore that. And I think you want me to do that, but I can't."

"Sam, she isn't your issue. She has nothing to do with you!"

"She already has!" I yelled back at him and pushed him away.

He fell back, surprised, but he quieted.

I closed my eyes and turned away. What had I said? I couldn't believe I'd let that slip.

"Don't torture yourself. You were honest just now. You were honest with me, maybe the first time." He took a breath and touched the back of my elbow. His voice was soft. "You were saying that Tate's already had something to do with you? What did you mean by that? I'd like to know. I care about you."

And then movement appeared from a back corner. I swung my gaze up, stricken. I hadn't even known a back corner existed.

Mason gave me an unreadable look, but he spoke to Adam, "What do you want here?"

Adam's head jerked up and I knew he was surprised.

I turned away. I wasn't. I'd witnessed when Mason went in for the kill. I knew it was happening now.

"What are you talking about?"

Mason laughed to himself and gestured to me. "What do you think, dickhead? What do you want? Her?"

Adam's eyes went wide.

Mason's eyes went to disdain. "Be honest. Right now, right here. You and me. Her. You want her, right? I know you do. Just say it. Put it out there, it might work."

I glanced at him. What was he doing? Mason refused to meet my gaze. His jaw was hard. Everything about him was hard in that moment. And no matter what Adam said, I knew he'd already dealt his hand.

No one won against Mason.

Then Adam broke and threw his arms out wide. "What do you want? Yes, I want her." His chest heaved up and down. "I want her, okay? I've known her all my life."

Mason grinned. "How long have you wanted her?"

"For half of that," Adam spat back at him. "Are you happy? I've wanted her since seventh grade, since the first time Sallaway noticed her."

"That's a long time."

"Stop," I snarled at Mason. He was encouraging him.

He ignored me and narrowed his eyes. Slowly, his hand reached out and grasped my elbow. He pulled me behind him and moved himself forward. It was done so slowly and so smoothly that Adam didn't notice.

I held my breath and waited for his reaction. It never came.

"You've wanted her a long time?"

"Yes," Adam cried out. "Can you blame me? You want her too. I can tell."

Mason shrugged. It was another moment like my mother's. He went in for the kill and I was pressed against his back. I pressed against him, not to hide myself, but to keep myself from saying something I'd regret. And what would I even say? I pressed the back of my hand against my mouth. I had no idea. My heart was beating so fast. It was like I was running still.

"You're right." Mason's voice was so soft, almost delicate. "I do. I'm not denying that."

"Oh god."

I flinched when I heard the disgust in Adam's voice.

Mason pressed on, almost tender still, "But I'm not going to screw another girl wishing she were Sam in my head. I'm not going to do that because you know why?"

There he was. He was going in for the kill. Adam cowered now.

It was enough. I swung away and shoved him back.

Mason glanced over.

I pushed him some more. "Go away."

"Sam."

"Now!" I pointed downstairs. "You don't have the right."

His jaw clenched. "Are you kidding me?"

"I'm not your whore. I'm not your stepsister. I'm not your anything. I thought I was your friend, but maybe not even that. You don't have a right, Mason. You'd never do this for Lo—"

He shoved his face in mine and I gasped as I fell back against the wall. "This is exactly what I did for him. You want to know what that whore did?"

I couldn't look away. My eyes were wide. My back was against the wall.

Adam ceased to exist.

"I..." I couldn't breathe. He was so close.

He pressed into me and placed both hands against the wall beside me. He trapped me, but I didn't want to go anywhere. When his knee nudged between my legs and moved up, I closed my eyes and fought back a sigh. The need throbbed inside of me again.

I was starting to think that need for him would never leave. It was so powerful, so consuming.

He nuzzled against my cheek and asked quietly, his breath a caress to me, "You want to know what she did to hurt Logan and me?"

I fell against him. I couldn't hold my head up.

I felt him smile against me, but he held me upright. He took my weight. "She screwed him. She got him to love her. For two years, Sam, she had him thinking he loved her and then she decided she wanted me."

I felt the coldness in him, even as he rested against me, and I reached out to it. I slid my hands up his arms, over his shoulders, around them, and kneaded the back of his neck. I wanted the tension gone. I was blind in it. And I was blind how he now held me in place. His hands moved to cup my bottom and my legs wrapped him. I wanted him. The need throbbed in me and I pressed against him.

I felt his reaction and grinned against his cheek.

"She came to me at home one day. I was in my room. She'd been in his and Logan was asleep. They'd screwed and she came to my room." Mason lifted me away from the wall.

I held onto him as I had the previous night. He had protected me then. He was protecting me again? Lust had confused all rational thought within me. I didn't know where we were anymore, but it didn't matter.

I slid a hand to his cheek and cupped it. I wanted him. I moved my lips so they brushed against his as he spoke.

"She wanted me. She had him and she thought I'd want her. I don't know why. I'd never given her any reason to think that, but she thought she could have two brothers instead of one. I called him. I let her try and seduce me and I let him hear the whole thing. It didn't take as long as it seemed. I saw when the call ended. Three minutes, that was all it took. Logan came around the corner with his phone to his ear. She saw it and looked at me. I held mine up and told her he'd heard the whole thing."

A tremor wracked through me.

He kissed my ear, my cheek, my neck. He whispered to me, "She tried to come between me and my brother. That's why I hate the bitch, but he still loves her. That's why he has a soft spot for her."

"Mason," I breathed out, holding on tight. I grabbed his face and held him still. I pulled back and met his gaze.

They were cloudy with desire, much like my own. Satisfaction surged through me. I affected him the same as how he affected me. It went both ways.

And then he killed the moment when he turned to the side. A ruthless emotion came through, thick and heavy, when he clipped out, "Have you been watching? This is why I'll never do what you have to do. I have her. I won't have to dream about her."

Everything stopped in me. A cold shower went over me and I was sputtering in the harsh reality.

CHAPTER TWENTY-FOUR

Adam stormed off.

We were alone.

Mason slowly lowered me so I could stand on my own and he stepped back. He watched me as if I were an animal, waiting to attack. He was ready.

He'd been hot and heavy, or so I thought, but he'd really been cold and calculating the whole time. That same unreadable mask was over him now.

"You're an asshole," I said softly.

He nodded.

"Why'd you do that?"

He didn't respond. It took another beat before he looked away and ran a hand over his head. "Don't get all girly and shit on me. That was a show. You performed well and he bought it."

My eyes bulged out of my head. I couldn't believe this was where he was taking it. "Are you kidding me?"

Something flashed in his eyes. It was gone in that next instant. He shook his head and lifted his shoulders. "What do you want from me?"

"You played me; you pulled all the right strings."

A cocksure smirk came out. "Like you said, I'm an asshole. That's what we do."

I took a deep breath. Something cold started in the pit of my stomach. It grew with each word he said and each second I was away from his touch. I hated how he affected me, the power he had and he knew it as well. He was fully aware of the power he had over me.

Chills broke out over me. I had to get away from him. I just had to. "I have to shower."

He jerked his head in a nod and started to leave.

My feet wouldn't go. My mind was yelling at me to leave, but my body wouldn't go. It didn't want to go. He had power over me… but I was pretty sure I had power over him too.

He stopped as he was about to go down the stairs. "What's wrong?"

I turned and locked eyes with him. I didn't know what he saw, but it worked. His hand clenched on the banister, his shoulders jerked upright. He sucked in a breath. I watched as his chest rose higher and higher.

I choked out, "Was that all a show?"

Desire was thick in his eyes. He narrowed them, licked his lips, and jerked his head in refusal.

Something flared throughout me and my legs moved now. I caught his hand and pulled him with me.

"This way." He pulled me a different way.

My heart was pounding as I held onto his hand. I was blind in my need. I could only focus on him. He led me through a myriad of stairs, through some doors, and finally he pulled me through the last one. I had no idea where we were, I hadn't cared to pay attention, but I knew we were far away from the party.

Mason dropped my hand and gazed at me. His room was dark. The shades were pulled so the morning light filtered through, but we were still in shadow.

He was watching me with an intensity that made my heart skip a beat. Fear froze me. I stumbled out, "I need to shower. I reek."

And then he reached forward and wrapped two arms around my waist and raised me off my feet as he walked to a bathroom. The shower was turned on and he stepped underneath. The cold water splashed down on me and I gasped. I surged forward in reaction and pressed my chest against him, but his mouth landed down on mine.

Oh god.

My hands curled into his shirt and I could only hold on.

His lips were hard on mine, a flame exploded inside of me, and I wanted more of him. I needed more. Then he started to move against me. His lips coaxed, nibbled, slid, and whispered against mine. His tongue touched the tip of my mouth and I let him in. I wasn't allowed not to. My body answered whatever demand he made. The thought of denial wasn't in me.

When my tongue touched his and his body trembled under my arms, I realized the power I had. It was addicting. It burst within me and I climbed up him. It was as before, but this time I didn't wait for him. I slipped my hand under his shirt and lifted it over his head.

Mason let it slip over and he hungrily already had mine off. My bra was stripped away in the next second and he cupped my breasts.

I gasped into his mouth when his thumb touched the tip of my nipple. He teased it and laughed against me. I nibbled at the corner of his mouth and then moved back. He caught me with a hand to my back and met my gaze.

We held each other's gaze. I couldn't look away. His eyes were dark, hungry, and they grew darker the longer we stared at the other. Then I lifted a hand and touched the side of his face. I traced the edge of him, his forehead, the corner of his eye, the side of his cheek, his lips.

He was beautiful.

His muscles shifted under me and I felt him lower me back to my feet.

I groaned in protest. I didn't want to leave him, but he bent forward and caught my lips in a hungry kiss, a long kiss. I couldn't tear away from him if I had to. Mewling, I pressed against him again and then his hands were under my bare legs. He lifted them again and as I wrapped them around his waist, he came in full contact against me.

I gasped at the feel of him. He was hard and ready.

He bent and kissed my neck, on my shoulder bone, and moved around to the other side as he walked backward and pressed me against the wall. When his hands no longer needed to hold me, he started to caress me. One slid over my stomach, up to my breasts, and he stroked them. They were hard and full. I ached for his touch. I wanted him in me, between my legs.

And then his hand moved down there. He caressed the insides of my thigh and then over my stomach, back down the other thigh. He encircled the area that throbbed for him. And then, as I gasped against his mouth, his finger slipped inside of me. His tongue swept against mine at the same time.

His other held the back of my head as his mouth consumed me, while his finger started to slip in and out. He went deeper with each thrust. I clung to him, pleading with him for more as my hips moved in rhythm. Then my hand slid down his arm, circled his slim waist, and wrapped around him.

He gasped against me this time and held still.

I grinned, intoxicated with power and need. I wanted more. I wanted him and I kissed his ear to whisper that to him.

With a guttural groan ripped from him, he pulled me from the wall and walked to the bedroom. A second finger slipped in and he curved them deep in me, deeper than before. As he lowered me to the bed, I gasped and arched my back. His fingers pushed further. He didn't need to move them anymore.

I felt it building. Spasms of pleasure joined into one long momentous ride and I rode it out. Wave after wave crashed into me. My body trembled from the climax and I lay weak in his arms. When I had settled, he grinned down at me.

I brushed back a lock of his black hair the fell forward and rasped out, "What?"

"You ready for round two?" He pulled out a condom.

I groaned and soon he joined with me.

I watched him as he bent over me. He thrust in me and when he saw me watching, he thrust harder. He pinned my arms above my head and stretched me. My breasts lifted for him and he took one in his mouth. His tongue swept around the nipple, it flicked over it, teasing it. Then his thrusts got harder, rougher. He went as far as possible. When I wanted him to go faster, he held back. He kept a slow pace. It built within me, driving me crazy. I wanted more. I screamed at him, but he only grinned back. Then his tongue dipped to my neck. He licked me and I screamed again.

My legs clamped around him and rose higher. I wanted him further inside, but then he cupped the bottom of my legs and he held them at the right spot. His penis touched the back of me and another climax ripped from me. I would've yelled, but his mouth drowned me out. He trembled along with me as we both went over the edge together.

When I was able to move again, I shivered as I remembered what we'd done.

I grew wet again and Mason lifted his head from my chest. He gave me a lazy and slow smile. "Already?"

I laughed huskily and shoved him out of me. His penis slid out. I missed it as soon as it was gone. Something was missing.

I shook my head at that yearning. "I have a feeling we'll be going again if we don't get some distance." Then I fell back again and laughed. He rose above me and cupped the side of my face. When he turned me towards him, my eyes met his.

They were narrowed and somber.

I was breathless again. My chest wanted to rise and fall, but it was frozen in place.

Then he leaned down and touched his lips to mine. It was a soft kiss, tender. As he pulled away, he pressed another to my forehead before he stood up. I sat up and watched as he strolled to the bathroom. His body was made of contour and muscles. He was sculpted as a statue. The added comfort he had with his body, which he didn't give a damn if he were naked or wore clothes, took my breath away.

I climbed out of the bed and followed him to the shower.

He opened the door, but I shook my head and climbed onto the counter. I leaned back against the mirror and watched him shower. When he realized what I was going to do, his eyes darkened and the corner of his mouth curved up, but he finished washing himself. He left the door open and as he was done, he leaned over me to reach for a towel.

His chest rubbed against my breasts.

He held himself across me. I looked over, he must've had a towel by then, but his lips caught mine. He'd been waiting for me. After a long and hungry kiss, he pulled back and strolled to the bedroom.

I tipped my head back and groaned. Everything in me was mush. My legs were jelly, but I managed to push off the counter and went into the shower. The water cooled me down. When I went back to the room, Mason was on the edge of the bed. He had pulled on a pair of jeans that rode low on his hips. As he reached for a shirt in the closet, he glanced over. "Do you have any clothes?"

"In my room." I fell back on his bed with a towel wrapped around me.

My whole body tingled with awareness. I felt alive. It was like I'd gone for another three hour run. And then his question penetrated and I jerked upright. "I don't have any clothes!"

He chuckled and sat beside me. His thigh brushed against my bare one. "That's why I asked. You want me to go and get you some?"

"How far away is my room?"

He grimaced. "Logan assigned the rooms and he put you on the opposite side of the house."

I glared at him.

He grinned. "Logan's way of a joke."

I groaned. "I can't believe this."

Mason flicked me on the shoulder and stood. As he lifted his arms above his head and stretched, he remarked, "Chill. I'll go get you some clothes."

"And if someone sees you?"

His arms dropped to his sides and he chuckled. The genuine sound of it sent another burst of tingles through me. He shrugged. "Who cares? I can always pull the sister card if I have to."

I groaned again.

He went to the door and glanced back to wink. "Not that I gave a shit about that before. I'll be back." He tapped the door twice and sent me a farewell grin before he disappeared behind it.

And I was left alone.

Alarm shot through me. What had we just done?

And then I remembered. The images of us flashed in my mind. A shiver from desire came over me and I melted into his sheets.

I wanted him again.

As more images flared through me, I rolled over and let loose a yell into his pillows. I knew that I'd want him for a long time.

What the hell was I going to do?

It wasn't long before the door opened again and he threw some clothes at me. They landed beside me and he held my gaze. My body reacted, my chest started to heave, my pulse picked up, my hands got clammy, and the need throbbed between my legs.

His eyes darkened and then he cursed as he slammed the door behind him.

I met him halfway, but he carried us back to the bed.

CHAPTER TWENTY-FIVE

When I woke later, I rolled over and looked down. Two more condoms had joined the first one on the floor and then I heard his chuckle behind me. His hand rubbed at the bottom of my back and massaged its way up to my shoulders. He sat forward, landed a kiss on my shoulder bone and scooted to the backboard. "You think I'd forget those puppies?"

I glanced back. "I did."

He grinned and stretched with a big yawn. "Those things are like putting on pants. I'd have to be drugged to forget 'em."

My shoulders sagged forward when I heard his sentiment. Some guys wouldn't agree, but I was relieved to hear his viewpoint. Then I yawned as well. "What time is it?"

He shrugged. "I could sleep the rest of the day. Good sex does that for me."

A different tingle shot through me at his words, but I frowned. I didn't want to dissect any of it and then I glanced at the clock. My eyebrows shot up. "It's six o'clock. Oh my god. I have to get out of here." I started to throw back the covers to scramble out.

"Why?" His hand caught me around the waist and pulled me backwards. His body curled behind me and he wrapped both arms around me.

Warmth and a frenzy of desire were starting to build again, but I clamped my legs shut and turned over. When he gave me a lazy grin, I smoothed a thumb over his forehead. Then I leaned close and kissed both of his closed eyelids before I whispered, "We have to get up or everyone's going to know."

He chuckled. The sound of it teased against my collarbone. "Everyone probably does."

I groaned and pushed him away. Then I did scramble out of his bed. "I hope not."

"What are you doing?" He patted the empty spot next to him. "Come back to bed."

I grimaced, though I wanted. I wanted badly, but I shook my head and threw my top over my head. "For my sake, I can't."

"Your sake?" He sat up again and frowned as he ran a hand through his hair. "What are you talking about?"

"I'm your stepsister. I'm sleeping with you. Do you realize what kind of a reputation I'm going to get?"

He crossed his arms over his chest and I averted my eyes when his chest muscles protruded out. Heavens, that boy…

"I didn't even think about that."

"Yeah, well, think about it." I gave him a short wave. "I have to go."

When I shut the door, his laughter followed behind and as I soon realized I had no idea where I was, he had reason to laugh at me. Three doors later, four hallways, and another two sets of stairs I pushed my way through a last door to find myself beside an indoor pool. Who had an indoor pool? My goodness. And then I looked up and the incredulity of the situation died down.

Logan sat on the other side with some of his friends and Mark Decraw.

My inner claws came out.

"Hey! How did you get there?" Logan waved me over.

Everyone else looked up. Most of the guys were friendly. Most of the girls' weren't, but it didn't matter. As I drew closer, I ignored the knowing smirk on Logan's face and studied Mark's reserved one instead.

"Where have you been all day?"

"Huh?" I looked down.

Logan rolled his eyes. "You've been missing in action since this morning. Most people took naps, but they didn't sleep the whole day away."

I shrugged. I couldn't peel my eyes off of Mark, whose eyes were directed anywhere but at me. "I don't even know where I slept. I never found my room."

He whistled. "Are you serious? I was sure I saw Mason showing you."

My hand clamped down on his shoulder and he winced, howling under his breath. "Remove the claws, Sam. Seriously."

I forced a laugh from me. "Ha ha…ha, Logan."

He rolled his eyes again. "Your friends are on the bottom patio outside. I know that's where you'll be the rest of the night."

I gave him a thankful grin and started forward, only to stop and look back. "How do I get there?"

Mark stood and pointed through a doorway. "You go through there, up the left stairs and the door will take you to the kitchen. The patios are out from there."

I narrowed my eyes at him. Why was he being helpful? Did he not know of his mother's intentions? I knew I should've thanked him, but I clipped out, "How's your mom?"

He frowned. "She's fine…Why?" His eyes seemed wary.

I shrugged. "No reason."

Logan's gaze had been skirting between us with a frown on his face. A look of frustration passed over him. "Where's Mason, Sam?"

I jumped. "Why would I know?"

"You saw him last?"

I looked away and cursed when my face went in flames. "I have no idea. I've been asleep the whole afternoon."

"Uh huh. Right."

When I glanced back, I was grateful to see that only Logan studied me. He gave me a tight smile and I knew that he knew. Guilt and anger coursed through me, but I frowned back at him. Then I stuck my tongue out at him before I pushed through a set of doors that led where Mark had told me to go.

When I pushed into the kitchen, so many people poured everywhere. No one looked at me and I got an extra bounce in my step from that. No one cared. That was good, very good. And I meandered through to the patios. From the top, I looked down and my eyes went wide again. When Logan said my friends were on the bottom patio, he'd declined to tell me there were six different patios. There were walkways that connected them and each patio was set beneath the other one.

When I got to the bottom, that patio was settled between a tennis court and a sand volleyball court.

Who were Nate's parents and what did they do for a living?

"Sam!" Becky saw me first and pumped her hand in the air. The fierceness of her movements sent most of her drink over the glass' edge that she held in her other hand. Amelia White scrambled up next to her and brushed frantically at her lap.

As I approached, she had snapped something at Becky, who didn't seem to care as her grin was etched from ear to ear. She pulled over an empty seat next to her and shoved it out to me. "Here. Sit here."

I sat.

Amelia scoffed and rolled her eyes as she moved a seat away on the other side of Becky. Her two other friends, Miranda and Cassandra both gave me polite smiles before they sipped their drinks. Adam was surrounded by Peter and a second guy that I didn't know. He looked like the Academy Elite, preppy and stuck-up.

"Where did you go?" Becky gushed. "I didn't know you ran. Adam said you went running. How far did you?"

I shrugged. "Far enough."

"That's so cool. You should go out for cross country. I bet you'd be awesome at it."

Adam gave me a biting smile. "Did you rest up this afternoon?"

I wanted to glare at him, but I held back and took a breath instead. "I did. You?"

Cassandra laughed shrilly and placed a hand over his. She gave me a forced smile. "Oh, you wouldn't believe how long he napped."

I frowned. "I wouldn't?"

"No." She heartedly shook her head. "Not at all, not one bit." Then she wiggled two fingers at me. "You're so secretive, Samantha. We had no idea you liked to run."

My eyebrow shot up. "Well, how could you? We've been such great friends since..." I waited a beat and gave my own forced laugh. "Oh, that's right. We're not friends."

Her smile clamped up and she glared instead. "You don't have to be mean."

I smiled back. "Why not? It's so much fun."

Becky gasped and patted her chest in an exaggerated fashion. "Could this be? Has Cassandra Uppity met her match?"

She turned her glare on her and an added coldness sparked in her depths. "Watch it, Sallaway. You're two steps from being ousted at school."

Becky seemed to purr in her smile. "Adam's been my neighbor all my life. We're good friends too."

Cassandra's eyes were sharp. "I don't see him defending you right now. Two steps, outcast, two steps and your humiliation is all mine. I like to serve my dishes best cold."

Becky lifted her hand and pretended to claw her. "Retract 'em, beeotch. We all know what they say about felines."

"What?"

She seemed to search for words. "That...they're the female version of the human species: catty, moody, and sneaky."

"You're a girl."

Becky shrugged. "I'm more a dog."

The smile on Cassandra's face was the crème of the crème and she leaned back. "You're right. You like to bound around looking like a fool most of the time when everyone knows you're just panting for any scraps from your master. You're low class, Rebecca. You used to accept it."

Becky turned green and looked away. I leaned forward, not sure what to do, but Adam remarked as he continued to lounge back in his chair, "Sullivan, chill."

She glared at him. "Why?"

He stared her down. "She's my friend."

She rolled her eyes and harrumphed before she shot from the table and stormed away.

Becky looked back up from her lap. A small smile started on her face. "Did she just leave?"

The other two Academy Elite females didn't say a word, but shared a look.

I frowned at that. What did that mean? And then we were all distracted when two new arrivals showed up. They were by the beach and paused in clear view from the mansion's top decks.

I sighed.

Tate and Tanya had arrived.

Both looked stylish, dressed in tight khakis and tank tops. Tanya's blonde hair was in curls as it lay past her shoulders and Tate's hair was swept up in some French-twist thing. I didn't know what it was, but it looked sophisticated.

Adam shot forward, but he didn't stand from the table. He raised his hand.

Tanya spotted him and gave him a bright smile and a wave in return. She started for him until Logan stepped in the middle and swept a hand around her waist. He pulled her close and seemed to whisper something in her ear. Tanya laid a hand on his shoulder and frowned, torn at some decision. When he continued to whisper and his hand started to massage her waist, she melted into him. Her head rested on his shoulder and Logan met my gaze with a brief flash of triumph before he took her hand.

Tate stood behind them with her mouth on the floor. One hand was poised on her hip.

As Logan whisked her away, no one said a word until Cassandra choked on a laugh. "Did that *just* happen?"

I did a double take. When had she come back?

Becky was quiet as she cast nervous glances at Adam. Her hands were in her lap and I watched as she kept twisting them together. When I laid a hand over them to calm her, she gave me a nervous look but pulled free. Her eyes never left Adam.

I sat back with a frown on my face.

Adam shrugged and looked away. His jaw clenched. "It doesn't matter. She was his before anyway."

"Yeah, but…" Cassandra bit out another laugh. She wiped at her mouth. "I can't believe I saw that. I love the Kade brothers. Man!"

Adam frowned at her.

She raised her hands in the air. "Did you not see that?"

"Thanks for your support." Adam shoved from the table and stalked away.

Becky went with and Cassandra snorted in disgust as she folded her arms over her chest. She stuck her chin out to glower. "Whatever. It's not my fault he's stupid enough to go after some tramp the Kades had first. You'd think he'd learn, wouldn't you? I mean, first Ashley and now Tanya…who else?"

My chest was tight. My hands were in fists, pressed on my lap. I didn't know what I was going to do, but I knew I was angry about it.

Miranda said in a soft voice, "Shut it, Cass. You're not helping."

Cass lifted a rebellious chin. "Not helping who? Or what?"

"Anyone." Her leader gave her a pointed look before she seemed to melt back in her chair.

"Look." Amelia pointed and we all turned.

Tate stood in the middle with her arms crossed over her chest. Her two bags were beside her. She stood alone, but she raised her chin and looked around. When her gaze met mine, I felt seared by it.

Her eyes narrowed and I felt that she wanted to come over and say something. And then Mason stepped out from some corner.

All eyes went to him.

Tate turned towards him.

She seemed to be waiting, but he didn't do anything. He looked at her, then looked at me, and left.

His gaze scorched me as well, but Tate turned back to me. There was a question in her depths and I gulped. I knew I wouldn't be able to hide from her for long.

CHAPTER TWENTY-SIX

Becky wrinkled up her nose and peered over her glass. "Look at them." I ducked closer and bumped heads with her. Both of us giggled, but Becky waved a hand over her face. "I'm serious. Look!"

"Oh." She was serious so I did. "Who am I looking at? There's so many."

"Adam!" She pointed again. "I can't believe him. I thought he was in love with Tanya, but look at him."

I scanned all of the packed decks and finally spotted him. He was squished at a table with the Academy Elite. When he ran his hands down the legs of...I peered across...Cassandra, I sat up straight. "When did that happen?"

She slumped next to me and crossed her arms in a huff. "They've been like that for the past hour. I can't take it anymore."

Then it clicked. "You're jealous!"

She clamped her hand over my mouth. "You don't have to screech it, but yes. Duh. You know I like him."

I waved a hand over my face. "I'm a bit drunk."

"I know. Me too."

And after we looked at each other, we convulsed together in another gigglefest. We'd been doing that a lot in the past hour. Then she pulled away and sounded out a dramatic sigh. "I'm serious, Sam. He bounced right from Tanya to her. I can't believe it. I hate that girl."

When I glanced back over there, I caught the glower Adam was sending our way and I patted Becky's hand. "I wouldn't worry too much about it. His ego's bruised. She's his band aid so he doesn't feel so wounded."

"Why couldn't I be his band aid?"

I shot her a grin. "Could you be anymore whiney about that? And besides, he values you. He couldn't use you in that way."

She sniffled. "He does?"

I rolled my eyes. "You know he does. Stop the pity party. We're supposed to be having fun."

"So says you. You don't have the Academy Snub Team breathing down their noses on you. They'd love if I curled in a ball and vanished into thin air. And Cassandra keeps throwing those snooty looks over here."

I sighed and rested against the couch we'd both procured long ago. It was set in a back corner of a side deck and gave us privacy where no one could hear us or see us, but we had a grand view of all the action around us. When the couch had emptied, Becky and I made a mad dash for it and had been drinking ever since.

She'd been sore over Adam, but as I reached for my drink, I couldn't stop from glancing at the deck above ours. Mason sat in a back corner with Marissa on one side, Nate on her other side, and Logan with Tanya over his lap across from them. There were a few others, but everyone knew that was the top tier of the social scene. When Mason grazed the top of Marissa's knees, my hand clenched around my drink and I threw it all back. It should've burned my throat, but I had ceased feeling a while ago.

It had seemed like a good idea then.

"Sam." Becky waved a hand in front of my face.

"What?" I snapped to attention.

She looked annoyed. "What are we going to do about Adam?"

What was I going to do about Mason?

"Huh?"

I caught myself. Had I said those words out loud? But I shook my head. "Why is Cassandra so mean to you?"

"I know!" She lifted her arms up and down. She pushed out her bottom lip in a pout. "I haven't done anything to her. I've always been nice to her and who am I to them anyway? Besides being good friends with Adam...and now you...and you're close with the Kades..." Her face brightened. "Do you think I'm a threat to her? Because of you and Adam, you know... No, that doesn't make sense. I'm the same boring Becky like always."

I patted her leg. I'd been doing that for the last hour. "It'll all work out. I know it. I think you and Adam will get together."

"You think so?"

I swung my arm wide in a grand gesture. Some of my drink spilled over, but neither of us cared. "Yes, I do. It might not be in high school."

Her face fell.

"But I think it'll happen. Adam's too caught up in social stuff. He can't appreciate you now because he's not mature enough."

Becky nodded. "For being drunk, we're very clear headed right now."

I nodded too. "I know and I'm talking very articulate."

"More than you usually do. You don't usually talk at all; well you do, but not really."

My face clouded. "Maybe I should shut up?"

"No." Her hand grabbed onto mine. "You need to talk more. You have very good points for me to hear. I never thought of Adam as being immature, but I can see why you think that."

She hiccupped, so did I, and we both fell back giggling again.

Then we became aware of someone who had come onto our deck. I gasped and Becky cooed.

Mason frowned down at us for a moment before he spoke. Then he tossed his phone on my lap. "Call your mom. She's going crazy. She thinks we kidnapped you."

Becky peeled her head back in laughter and I struggled to keep from joining her.

He shook his head at us. "Are you drunk?"

More laughter peeled from beside me and I nodded as I bit my lip.

"Hell, you're probably having more fun than most of us." He sank down next to me and ran a hand through his hair.

I watched the movement and wanted to do the same. A wave of need rushed over me, but I breathed out and remembered we were in public. I tried fanning myself.

When Becky had stopped giggling so much, she sat up with glazed eyes and squinted at him. "Who's your girlfriend?"

I jumped next to him.

She frowned at me.

Mason sat stiffly beside me. He didn't look at her.

"Hello!" She reached over me and waved a hand in front of his face.

He looked away and took a breath. I felt the movement when his arm brushed against mine.

She fell back and heaved a sigh. "I can't believe it. I'm your best friend, he's going to be your brother, and he ignores me too. Everyone ignores me. I'm more beneath people than I realized."

I looked at her. "You're not beneath me."

She gave me a tight smile, but spoke to Mason, "I know you can hear me and I know you're not being cruel to me because of Sam, but who's the girlfriend? I've never seen her before. She seems nice."

Mason jerked his gaze to mine. "Can you call your mom? Find me later to give me my phone."

He tore out of there and Becky shook her head as she watched him leave. "I must be really drunk because I know I shouldn't have talked to him like that, but I don't really care right now."

I shrugged and dialed my mom's number. "He's a jerk. You can talk to him however you want to."

Becky gave me a blinding smile. "Thanks, Sam."

I gave her one back. "Anytime." And then my mom's hysterical voice sounded in my ear and I cursed when I pulled it away. That was going to hurt. As I rubbed my ear, I moved away. Music, laughter, and the general shrieking sounds of a party were going to make this phone call last longer than I wanted.

When I found a semi-quiet corner, I lifted the phone again. "Hi, mom."

"Samantha!" She heaved out. "You're okay. I've been so worried. You have no idea. I thought about calling the cops."

"Why would you do that?"

"Because of what they did to me. I can't believe you didn't help me, but then I thought maybe you couldn't. Maybe you were too scared of them."

Alarms went off in my head and I sat back on my heels. "Are you kidding me right now?"

She got quiet. "Samantha, you were there. You saw what they did to me."

I sighed into the phone. "Mom, are you drunk again?"

A shadow moved over me and I spun around, my heart stopped for a second, but my shoulders dropped when I recognized Mason. He grinned and moved forward to curve a hand around my waist. As he bent close to listen in, he brushed against me and his breath caressed my cheek.

"Sam, are you there?"

I choked out, my throat full with desire, "I can't deal with this, mom. I'm fine. We went away to Nate's cabin. I told you about it last night, but you were so crazy and drunk. I suppose I'm not surprised you didn't remember." I waited a beat.

Mason's hand started to rub circles on my hip.

I bit out, my voice rushed, "You haven't been saying any of this crazy stuff to anybody else?"

There was silence on the other end.

"I can't believe you, mom. What have you done this time?"

"Sam, stop lying to me."

"Okay." I remembered when I had walked into my old house and saw her with tears in her eyes and two empty bottles of wine beside her. It was when she had told me we were leaving. "That's what I'm doing. I'm lying. I'm always lying to you. I'm the crazy one in this family. I'm the one who was married to David and left him for James. Yes, I'm the one lying right now."

"You don't have to be so mean to me."

"Oh, mom. Stop drinking. I don't want to hear what else you've cooked up. I'm fine. We're all fine. Stop saying crazy stories like that, unless you're trying to do something. Are you trying to do something?"

"Why would I make that up?"

"I don't know. Why do you ever do anything? For more money? I have no idea." And I ended the call.

Mason stood still next to me and then he swept me up in his arms. "That was great."

I tried to stop myself from smiling against his neck. "Why?"

"You knew my dad was listening?"

When he set me back on my feet, I gave him a small grin. "I didn't, but it'd be something she would've done."

He laughed again and slid his phone in his pocket.

I took a deep breath. "Why'd you ignore my friend before?"

His jaw tightened and he pressed his lips together before he looked away.

I added in a quiet voice, "And who is the girlfriend with you?"

He swung his gaze back and gave me a hard look. "Are you kidding me? You know that's Marissa."

"I don't. You've never introduced her."

"What are you doing right now?"

"Nothing." I started to move away, but he caught my arm and pulled me back.

"Come on, Sam. Don't be all jealous and insecure. Marissa is a good friend of mine. I'm protective of her."

He used to be protective of me too. I swallowed back that pain. "You're right. I'm sorry about that."

"Sorry about what?" He studied me intently. "What are we talking about?"

"We had a good time. It's not anything more than that. Just, please don't admit anything to Logan. I think he already knows and if he knows for sure, can you imagine all the teasing I'm going to get from him?"

Mason gave me a disgusted look. "Are you serious? I'm protective of Marissa because I'm the reason she had to switch schools a couple years ago."

I fell silent, but I didn't pull my arm away.

"She's a nice person, she's genuine. Some girls didn't like that we were friends and they tore her to pieces. Catty stuff always happens to her whenever she's around me. She doesn't have any female friends. That's why I didn't want to introduce her to you or anyone else. You have friends, Sam. She doesn't. If she met you, you would've introduced her to your friends, and that's when that crap usually happens. I nipped it from the beginning."

I remembered Tate's words. "Was it Tate that tore her to pieces?"

"She was the ring leader, yeah. And she'd do it again. If Marissa isn't with me, she's with Nate. It's that bad. Tate blames her for why I hate *her* so much."

I nodded. "Okay."

"Okay…what?" He seemed to be measuring me. I felt him trying to get inside me. "Are you okay now? I'm not going to apologize for your friend. She freaks me out. I'm not going to lie. I don't like her, but I'll tolerate her for you."

A chuckle escaped me. He felt the tension leave me and pulled me against him. "Yeah, I can see that."

He pressed a kiss to my forehead. "Are you going to get wasted tonight?"

"Seems like." I gave him a sloppy grin and he pressed a kiss to it. I sighed as his lips left mine. "It seems like it's my night with Becky tonight, she's down in the dumps because of Adam."

"The quarterback who wants to bang you?"

I shook my head. He knew exactly who Adam was. "Yes, she likes him."

He grimaced. "She could have better taste in men."

"You want her to go after you instead?"

His eyes got wide. "You should encourage those two to date."

I laughed and pressed against him some more. His hands dropped down and started to caress the inside of my thigh. He cupped the side of my face and started to bend down when someone burst through the foliage that had granted us our privacy.

We whirled around and froze.

Logan stared at us with his mouth hanging open. Then he snapped his fingers and threw his arms around in the air. "I knew it! I knew it! Oh hell yeah! I knew it!"

Mason tackled him and hissed, "Shut up about it!"

Logan pushed him off, laughing. "I won't say anything, but man—I knew it."

Mason shoved him back. "What are you doing here?"

He gestured to me. "The mom thing. I knew she was going to call her. Did you?"

I nodded.

"She covered us and made it seem like her mom made the whole thing up."

"Really?" Logan glanced at me with wide eyes.

I shrugged. "If your dad really loves her, he'll forgive her."

He choked out a laugh. "And if he doesn't and you guys are sent packing?"

I knew my eyes had a chill in them when both moved back a step. "I'm pretty sure I can move back in with David until college."

"And your mom?"

Ice went down my veins. "And I'm sure she'll find some other guy to mooch from."

"Man, you really loathe your mom, huh?" Logan whistled under his breath. "I'm just happy that we got dad off our backs."

Mason gave him a sharp look. "He send you something?"

"Yeah, an apology text."

He rolled his eyes and took Logan's phone. "Guess that's supposed to make up for the other ones, huh?"

"Whatever. We're covered. And I've got my own piece to pound tonight." Logan gave us a salute. "See you later, siblings. Have fun with your incest relations."

Mason punched him, but Logan dodged it and ducked from our hidden spot.

I grinned at him when Mason turned back. "Becky's going to come looking for me."

He grinned back and touched my shoulder. "Have fun getting drunk again. Don't screw the quarterback."

"Ha ha!" I flipped him the middle finger as he left, but couldn't wipe the grin off my face when I heard his laughter.

CHAPTER TWENTY-SEVEN

When I woke up, I rolled over and found myself in a large bed with Becky half scrawled on me. As I pushed up, pain flared through me and I touched the side of my face. "Ouch!" I hissed and hurried to a mirror. A large bruise had formed on the side of my jaw. It was swollen and had already started to turn color. I groaned and rested my forehead against the mirror.

How had that happened? It was fresh so I'd have the bruise for a few weeks. Great.

"Hh...whassis?" Becky blinked at me rapidly as she struggled to keep her mouth from hanging open. She wiped at her eyes and sat further up. "What happened? Where am I?"

I chuckled, surprised at the hoarseness of my voice. "My guess is that we're hungover." I grimaced as I sat down on a couch. My rear was sore so I moved even slower because of it. "What happened to my face?"

Becky choked out a gasp and covered her face as she fell back against the bed.

I winced against the pain. My whole face was now throbbing. "Tell me I didn't make a fool out of myself."

She groaned as she stopped whimpering. "It hurts to laugh."

"Tell me about it. It hurts to breathe."

She raised her hand to brush back some of her hair, but it dropped to her lap with a thump. "Everything's so hard right now. This sucks."

"Becky." I cleared my throat. "My face. What happened?"

"Oh, that."

"Yes, that."

She tried to hide a yawn, but it won in the end. After she finished, she started to yawn again. "I don't really know what happened, but you had to go to the bathroom so we snuck off somewhere. You kept saying you knew about a private bathroom. I don't know."

I groaned on the inside. I'd probably been trying to find Mason's room.

She added with a sour look on her face, "Anyway, we finally found a room and we snuck in. We didn't know whose it was, but then that girl who was attached to Mason's hip was in there and that girl, Tanya's cousin, was in there too."

I sat up straighter, or I would've. Pain seemed to slice through me with each movement I made.

"What was her name again?"

"Tate," I rasped out.

"Oh yeah!" She started to smile, but it died right away. "Tate was in there and she was being really mean to that girl, who for being Mason's girlfriend, doesn't have any fight at all. The girl just took it and she was standing there crying. She kept saying something about where Nate was, but I couldn't make it out. We were both so wasted."

I closed my eyes. I couldn't imagine what I had done.

"And then you clobbered Tate."

"I did what?"

"Yeah." She nodded with her eyes wide, semi wide for being hung-over. "You just swung your hand out and punched her. Then you started to say something about being a bully and she was the disloyal bitch and that was it. She went back at you. That girl kept crying so I started screaming for help. You got way more wallops in than she did. You're pretty spry. I had no idea." She started to laugh, but hissed from the movement. "She kept trying to hit you and you'd just run around her. Then you'd hit her from behind or something. You're hilarious when you're drunk."

"Oh no." I groaned into my hands. Had I really gotten into a fight? "Anyway, some guys ran in and separated you too. I didn't see you for a while because they carried you to where Mason was. He took you into some back room and then Logan rushed in there from somewhere else. He was only wearing jeans, which weren't buttoned or zipped up so everyone knew what he'd been doing." She wiggled her eyebrows. "If you know what I'm saying."

So I'd interrupted one of his many romps with the pep girl. Something in me didn't care at all.

"And then they kicked Tate out."

"What?" I looked back up.

"Yeah." She gave me a lazy grin. "Mason came out and shoved her outside. Someone had her bags packed and they threw them out. She must've had her keys in them because I heard that she drove away in the middle of the night. Nobody really cared, but I guess she had a few friends here. They were saying that wasn't fair to her, but then Mason and Logan's friend, that one that's always around said they could go as well. Everybody shut up after that."

"Mason and Logan didn't say anything?"

"Nah." She shook her head as another yawn came over it. "They'd already gone back to you by then. Oh, and we could hear that girl crying through the door. She should've shut up by then, I mean, you punched someone out for her. She could've been more appreciative."

I shook my head. I had no recollection of any of it. "So how'd we get here?"

"This is your room. You were in there for about thirty minutes and then somehow you snuck out."

"I said that?" I grinned slightly.

She nodded her head with a wide smile as well. "You said something about not needing their protection and you snuck out. I guess Mason and Logan got into some tiff. That's what you told me."

"I said that too?"

"Uh huh." She chuckled. "And then you and I went to the indoor pool. I had no idea it was even there, but you did. No one else was in there. We stayed down there the rest of the night until…that's where my black out starts. I have no idea. I remember drinking and swimming and you lecturing me how we weren't being smart, but we were being fun."

I groaned with my head in my hands. "I don't want to deal with anyone today. What time is it?"

Becky shrugged, still curled up among the bedcovers. "I'm sure it's time to start packing. Everyone was going to leave after breakfast today."

I swung my heavy head to the side and saw both my bags in the corner. I grunted. "Looks like I'm packed."

Becky snorted before she rolled off the bed. "I gotta find my room. See you in a bit."

"See you." I waved as she stumbled out the door.

She hadn't been gone long before someone else knocked. I tried to yell for them to come in, but it sounded like a frog's croak so I heaved myself up and opened the door wide. I expected Mason or even Logan, but instead I was in for a surprise.

Miranda Stewart, Fallen Academy's elite queen bee stood at my door.

She gave me a timid smile and brushed a strand of her auburn hair back. I didn't know why, it looked perfect pulled high in a clip with small braids decorating her head. A few wisps were allowed out and it gave her a softer look. Maybe that's what she was going for.

Her emerald eyes sparked in warmth and she folded her hands in front of her. "Hi, Samantha."

The sound of my full name kicked me in gear. It sounded so formal and it should've. We weren't friends.

"Miranda."

She glanced over my shoulder. "Can I come in or do you have company?"

I chuckled. "Becky just left."

"Oh." She glanced down at her hands. Then she laughed softly. "I realized how that sounded. I didn't mean to imply anything."

I narrowed my eyes. The Miranda Stewart I knew wasn't this self-conscious shy girl. She was tough and smart enough to control the rest of the Academy Elite. She was the brains behind so many operations. I didn't know what I'd done to warrant her attention.

"Well." She took a deep breath. "I'm sure you're wondering why I'm here."

My mouth stayed closed, but I gestured for her to come in. As she perched on the coach, I leaned against my dresser. The bed looked tempting, but I didn't trust myself to stay out of it the rest of the day.

"I came to apologize for Cassandra. She tends to react before she thinks sometimes."

"Why are you saying this to me?" I was surprised at my blunt tone. Maybe it was Mason's boldness or how the truth seemed to always fall off Becky's tongue, but one of them had rubbed off on me.

From the slight widening of her eyes, Miranda must've shared in my sentiments. She sighed. "Because I don't want an enemy from you."

"Why?"

"The truth?"

I lifted a shoulder. "What else?"

She took another deep breath and smoothed her hands down her jeans. "Because you're really powerful right now and I don't want a war at school."

I was stunned once again. "Why would there be a war?"

"Because Cassandra is jealous of you." Her eyes darkened and she looked at her lap.

Ah ha. I nodded in understanding. "So you're saying that she's not going to stop with her jabs?"

There seemed to be genuine regret in her eyes. "Yes, but you have to understand where it's coming from. Adam's always liked you and he's always championed for you. He wanted you to come into the group, and not as his girlfriend. When you turned him down, it seemed to hurt him even more and he'd already been hurt by Ashley too. Cassandra is very protective of him."

"And she wants to date him."

"I can't say anything about that, but I know she wasn't nice to you or Rebecca last night."

"So what do you want from me?"

She stood and gave me that same sad smile. "Cassandra is one of my best friends and I love her to death, but know that she doesn't have our support if she's mean to you. She doesn't have my support. I like you, Samantha. I always agreed with Adam. I thought you would've been a great addition to the group."

When she glanced at her watch and then the door, I knew her visit had ended. She said what she wanted so I followed her to the door and held it open for her. "I guess I should say thanks for your warning then?"

She laughed again, the sound was so delicate. No wonder she'd been made the Queen. I wanted to give her a crown myself and stand guard before her.

"I guess. Thanks for being... understanding?" She gave me a small wave before she left. "See you at school today."

After I closed the door, I stood in the middle of my room for a while. The whole thing was odd to me. She thought I would've been a great addition to the group; that meant I was out. Then I shrugged. That sounded like too much drama anyway.

As another yawn came over me, I tried to hurry into the bathroom and not think about Miranda's odd visit. What would've taken me twenty minutes took an hour. I wasn't moving at a fast pace, nor was I thinking at a fast one. When I heaved my two bags to the bottom of the stairs, my arms felt like lead and Logan's hyena laugh scraped against my ears.

I covered them and groaned when I saw him come around a corner. "Stop, please."

He laughed even louder and scooped me up in the air. I was bundled against his chest and he twirled me around. "What's wrong, sister? Too much activity for you last night? You aren't sore or anything, are you?"

I burrowed into his chest. "Stop. Please. I beg you."

"Your new nickname is Slugger. One wallop and that's how you handle business." He was gleeful in his amusement.

It was sickening.

He started to bounce me in his arms. "My Slugger Sister. I'm going to make you a tee shirt with that slogan. Slugger Sister. Everyone will call you that!"

Tanya came around the corner in a tight white tee shirt, low cut v neck, and slinky jeans. She wrapped her arms around his waist and pressed against his back. "She's not my sister. I can't call her that."

Logan held still as she continued to press against him, then he smirked at me. "Sorry, sis. Someone else is needing my attention."

After he deposited me back on my feet, I smoothed out my clothes. "Somehow I think I'll get over it. Thank you, Tanya."

She gave me a blinding smile as Logan swept her up instead. "No problem, Sam. See you." She started giggling as he skipped out the door with her.

"Hey." Mason came around the corner with a duffel bag over his shoulder. He bent and picked up my two. "You're riding with me. Your quarterback took off this morning."

"You have room?"

He flashed me a grin as he held open the door with his shoulder. I ducked around him and tried to ignore the flare of warmth that sizzled through me. "Nate's headed back home today and he's taking Marissa with him."

"Really?"

I wasn't sure if I was disappointed.

"Yeah." He threw all of the bags in the back of his Escalade and slammed it shut again. I wasn't surprised to see it was full with other bags. "And your buddy can come too, but I don't want her talking to me. She can talk to you, that's fine, but no questions to me."

I gave him a salute.

"Very funny."

"I thought so." I couldn't hold back a small grin before I went and told Becky the news. And as I expected, when I found her with a plate full of pancakes and muffins, she dropped all of it and started screaming.

"Three hours in the same car as Mason Kade!" She grabbed my arms and started jumping up and down.

"Ugh. Stop." Pain seared through me. I backed away and tried to hold down whatever last meal I'd had. "I am never ever going to get in another fight again."

"You better not drink like that then."

"That too."

Becky giggled behind her hands. "I'm sorry, Sam. It's so exciting."

I shook my head. "You can't talk to him, you know."

She nodded. Her smile couldn't be wiped off.

"You're a bit strange in the head."

"You already told me that once," Becky informed me as she followed me out to the car. It was as if she'd never been hung-over. The Becky I woke up beside had transformed at the news of our car ride. Energy flowed out of her and I sighed. It was going to be a long drive.

I needed coffee.

CHAPTER TWENTY-EIGHT

Mason dropped us off at school. My bag stayed in his backseat, but Becky tugged hers out. When he asked what time to pick me up, she started giggling. We glanced over and she saluted us with her hand. "I'll find my own ride home. Thanks." Then she pivoted on her feet, clapped her heels together, and marched off.

He gave me an unreadable look and I sighed. "She's tired and… snarky…"

He shook his head. "I don't care. What time do you want me here?"

I scratched the back of my head. "Uh…quarter after three?"

"Done. See you." And he zoomed away.

As I turned and headed after Becky, I caught a lot of stares from those who lingered in the parking lot. Then when I entered the hallway, I got even more. I groaned as I glanced at my phone. It was a little after noon—lunch hour. No wonder there'd been so many around their cars.

Becky was nowhere in sight so I targeted my locker instead. As I got there, Miranda Stewart greeted me. She seemed to appear from nowhere. She gave me one of those serene smiles that hovered on her lips. Her hair hung loose in shining curls this time and she readjusted the books in her hands. Warmth oozed from her. "You got here!"

I frowned as I opened my locker. "You seem happy about that?"

She glanced over her shoulders and then gave me another smile, this one seemed secretive. "Everyone knows about the Kade Trip."

I fought the urge to hang my head. Of course everyone would know.

She stepped closer and lowered her voice. "I spoke to the rest of the group on the way back and they want to return the favor to Mason and Logan."

"What are you talking about?"

Her eyes seemed to dance. They were sparkling. "Come on, like you don't know."

"I don't. What are you talking about?"

"Logan's friends with Mark, but they're not that great of friends. I assumed we were invited because of you."

"You weren't."

"Oh." Her back straightened and her shoulders stiffened. Then she let out a soft laugh. "Regardless, I'm throwing an intimate dinner. I've extended invitations to Mason and Logan, but I wanted to invite you in person."

"An intimate dinner?"

"I throw them all the time, but it's usually only for our close friends."

"The Academy Elite," I mused and tried to remember what book I needed for the next class. It was fifth period… My hung-over brain was still going slow.

She laughed again. "That's right. I'd forgotten you knew about that name. That's what your friend calls us, right?"

"And Adam's."

"Hmmm?"

I looked up and held her gaze. "She's Adam's friend too. He's got a soft spot for her."

"Oh, I know. I know." The corners of her mouth turned downwards, but they flipped up a second later. "So I would love if all three of you guys would come to my dinner tonight."

I sighed and turned to her. "Look, don't do this."

"Do what?"

"Mason and Logan won't come to your dinner."

"But you haven't even talked to them about it yet."

"Have they ever come before?"

"I've never invited them…" A small frown had come back to her as she started to look around. A small audience had appeared around us. They weren't close, but they were within hearing distance.

Here we go again…

"They won't come. I know them. They don't care about anyone except themselves. Trust me."

She looked down at her feet. "They seem to care about you…"

I lifted a shoulder. "If they do, they do, but don't invite them. They won't come and it'll make you look bad. You told me this morning you didn't want a war, but that's what you're starting. It won't work with Mason and Logan. Everyone knows they're jerks because they don't care about anything or anyone."

When she looked back up, she was transformed. A fierce determination shone through her emerald eyes and pinned me down, but she edged closer and lowered her voice to a whisper, "You're right. You're completely right. Thank you. I know this came from a good spot with you so I'm not going to invite them. I never was."

"I thought you said—"

She gave me a tight smile. "I didn't. I was testing you. I wanted to know what you would do and you proved me right. You proved some others wrong."

"What are you talking about?" I shook my head. Was she mad? "There's no dinner?"

"There's a dinner, but do you really think I'm crazy enough to invite the Kade brothers? Everyone knows they don't care and we all know that we weren't really invited on that trip. You invited Adam, he invited us, and no one else cared if we went or not. That's how we went on the trip. You're completely right. Mason and Logan don't care about us, though I think they should. Everyone knows they should've gone to this school. They should be our friends, but they're not. They made their choice."

I eyed her up and down and noted how her hands were in small fists, how her jaw was stiff, and how her shoulders were bunched together. A massive knot was going to form between them.

I spoke softly, "You're a bit pissed with them, huh?"

"What?" She looked taken aback.

"Nothing." I grabbed my fifth period book. "So no dinner tonight?"

"Oh no. I'm having a dinner and you're invited. You don't have to come; no offense will be taken if you don't. We all know you're probably tired." She lingered on my bruise. "But if you do, Adam will pick you up."

I grinned now. "He's not picking up Cassandra?"

Miranda grimaced. "Between you and me, I hope those two don't do more than their flirting. He doesn't care enough about her, and she deserves someone who's going to be there for her. Adam cares like that about you."

Oh no…

She laughed and waved at me. "Don't worry. I'm not going to play matchmaker. Everyone can tell that Sallaway did a number on you, but I do hope you'll come to dinner tonight."

"Can Becky come?"

Her eyes held mine steady. She didn't blink. "No."

So that's how it was going to be. I should've known.

Miranda looked over my shoulder and she chuckled to herself. "Look at that, I did you another favor."

Another one? I looked over and saw Jessica, Jill, Lydia, and Ashley at some lockers. All four of them stared at us with different emotions. Jessica was livid, as was Jill. Lydia was trying to fight off a smile at me and Ashley surprised me when she grinned.

Miranda added, "They wanted to confront you about why you wouldn't let them come on the trip, but now that I've deemed you one of my friends," she laid a hand on my shoulder. "They wouldn't dare." Her laugh was confident, it bordered on the verge of being cocky. "Welcome to the Elite, Samantha. I hope to see you at dinner tonight."

As she strolled down the hallway and linked elbows with Emily Connsway, the only female in their group who hadn't gone on the trip, Miranda stopped and lifted her head for a kiss from Peter Glasburg. He hadn't gone on the trip either. When both of them looked over and gave me a grin, I was jolted enough to jerk my hand up in a wave.

"What'd she want?"

I turned around. Becky was frowning at them with something else in her eyes. I narrowed mine, was she hurt that I had talked to her?

"She was giving me a heads up that Jessica and Jill wanted to confront me about the trip."

Becky's eyes narrowed and I knew there was suspicion in them, but then she yawned suddenly and her shoulders sagged down. "I'm so tired. I can't handle any more fights."

"You can't?" I touched the side of my face. It was still tender and the pain started to throb again. "I don't remember you helping out from your version of the story."

She grinned and linked her hands together in front of her. It was a self-conscious movement. "I would've, but you were so funny to watch. And you kept telling me she could handle it. You were taunting her, actually."

"Was I?" An old comfort settled between my shoulders. That sounded like something I'd do. "Did it piss her off?"

"Oh yeah. She started to swing at you more and more. She got sloppier after that and you kept dodging her, then you'd give her an uppercut from nowhere."

I gave her a sloppy grin. That had made me happy. "Want to go for burgers tonight? I think I need some protein."

"Can we do pizza instead? There's an air hockey table at Gino's." As we passed a group of football players, she looked up, but quickly looked back down.

Adam was in the center of the group. He leaned against the lockers with his feet crossed beneath him. Cassandra Sullivan was pressed against him, as close as she could be without his arm around her. She had a hand splayed over his chest and was smiling up at him. When he met my gaze, his grew cold and he straightened.

A few of the guys looked over and said hello to me.

My feet tripped over themselves, but I stumbled down the hallway with a frown. When did football players say hello to me? Even when I had dated Jeff, and some of them were his friends, they'd never spoken to me.

Then I looked up as Becky and I were about to head into the classroom. Miranda met my gaze down the hallway. Her eyes seemed to be laughing at me, but I had an odd sense that she knew exactly what happened and she knew why it happened. Then she pretended to tip an imaginary hat to me.

Was that her first favor?

Welcome to the Elite, Samantha.

Her words came back to haunt me. Had I joined their ranks without realizing it? And if I had, what did that mean?

And then something else happened that took my breath away.

Jessica and Jill sat at a table behind Becky and me. I was tense, ready for whatever they were going to say to me, but they each gave me a bright smile. "Hi, Sam! How was the party?"

My mouth dropped.

Hell froze over.

Becky's head dropped to her lap and she couldn't silence her giggles. Her shoulders shook.

"What?" I said to them.

Jill's smile widened and Jessica's stayed, but the ends of her mouth seemed strained. Lydia plopped between them and clasped my hands. She nearly smacked her forehead against mine. "I didn't know you were friends with Miranda Stewart! That's awesome, Sam. Why didn't you tell me?"

The teacher started roll call, but I couldn't shake a chill when I turned back around. That had been the favor Miranda had referenced. She cast me as her friend, no one would touch me now… except the Academy Elite.

I clasped my eyes shut.

I didn't want to deal with them. They were on a whole other league.

The rest of the day followed the same pattern. Amelia White asked me to sit with her in sixth period. She offered her notes from the morning classes I missed and Emily Connsway saved a seat beside her in our last period. Mark Decraw gave me a few wary looks, but he extended his fingers in a wave once. And then Miranda passed me in the hallway after school. She called out, "See you later, Samantha!" before she bent her head and laughed at something Emily said to her.

I shook my head as I pulled out the two books I would need for homework and turned around. I bumped back against my locker when I saw Jeff behind me. His dark hair was gelled up in a haphazard nest and his eyes were fierce. He frowned at me. "What are you doing?"

My hung-over cloud of confusion cleared suddenly and I snapped back to reality. I shoved him back. "What are you doing? Whatever you have to say, you have no right to say it. Get out of my face, Jeff."

He rolled his eyes and stepped closer. He lowered his voice to a grumble. "Jess is crapping her pants. Now you're suddenly all powerful and popular. What'd you do? How'd that happen? And what are you going to do to her?"

I reared back and took a long look at him. I thought he was angry, but I saw concern in his eyes now and something akin to fear?

I lowered my voice as well. "Why are you worried about Jessica? Shouldn't you be concerned about Jill, your girlfriend?"

"You weren't betrayed by Jill. You weren't friends with her. Jessica's the one that stabbed you in the back."

"Exactly!" I said in a sharp tone.

Heads turned our way.

I rolled my eyes, but quieted my voice. "I was the one stabbed in the back. Jessica could probably stop worrying if she'd apologize to me."

"What are you talking about? She has—"

"She hasn't said a thing to me."

He held my gaze for a minute and then edged back. "Are you serious? I thought she apologized a long time ago. I thought you were being stuck up and not accepting it."

I was amazed at his stupidity. "For one, I don't automatically have to accept an apology and two; you're the only one who's seemed sorry for what you did. Lydia's a beach ball. She keeps blowing from one side to the other. She's never apologized either and Jessica hasn't said a thing. She ignored me and then said hi once to me. I'm not going to sweep it under the rug."

He ran his hands through his hair, pulled his hair into a spiky Mohawk, and messed it up again. "I know they're both real sorry. It's got Jill paranoid. She thinks they're going to dump her for you and now all this crap." He swept his hand up and down the hallway. "You're in with the popular clique. How did that happen? You've never cared about any of that crap."

"Jeff," I sighed. "You and me are okay. I think you should leave it alone. Don't try to protect or apologize for Jessica and Lydia. That's for them to do, not you."

"Yeah, I know." He let out a ragged breath. "I'm just so pissed for messing our group up. I tore us apart. I should've said no to Jessica, but she kept asking. She made it seem so exciting…"

When my phone vibrated, I saw it was Mason. He sent a text: **Here.**

"Look, I have to go. My ride's waiting."

He nodded his head and pulled the ends of his shirt together. The movement emphasized how thin his frame was. I'd forgotten how skinny Jeff had always been, but he pulled the look off. Trendy baggy jeans and a polo that was supposed to look vintage gave him a preppy look with an edge.

I chuckled and punched his shoulder lightly. "You look good, Sallaway. Jill must be good for you."

The side of his mouth curved up. "Hey, thanks, Strattan. That means a lot coming from you."

I shook my head, still chuckling, and headed to the parking lot. I figured Mason would have football practice to get back to so I didn't want to make him late. When I cleared the school and saw him parked front and center, I was aware of the attention he was warranting.

His window was rolled down and he flashed me a grin. He tapped the side of his car twice. "Come on. Coach is making us do two practices tonight."

I picked up my pace and got inside. As Mason wheeled his Escalade through the parking lot, he drove past Adam. He held my gaze as we passed him and I watched as his mouth tightened. Cassandra was beside him. Her expression mirrored his.

Mason chuckled, "Your quarterback's pissed."

I took a deep breath and tried to relax in his seat. "Yeah, well, I have a feeling a lot of people are going to be pissed at me."

He glanced at me. "What are you talking about?"

I shook my head. "I'm going to make some people very angry in the next week."

CHAPTER TWENTY-NINE

Mason dropped me at home and took off for his practice right away. As I lugged my bags through the mansion and up to my room, I found a note on the kitchen table.

Hi, honey! James and I are in the cities, gone to the Bangor for dinner. We'll be back tonight! Love you! XOXO

I dropped it back on the table and fought the urge to tear it up.

Since I knew I'd do my homework later, I pulled out my running shoes and laced them up. Then I hit the pavement hard. I ran for two hours, three would've winded me too much, my body was wheezing too much when I rounded the last curve to the mansion. Panting, with sweat streaking down my body, I went back to my room and as I got into my shower, I was tempted to lock my door.

No one was home yet, but I didn't want to deal with Analise when they did return.

An hour later my phone vibrated and I answered, "Hey, Becky."

She groaned on the other side. "I can't go out for dinner."

"Really?" I tried to hold back the disappointment.

"Yeah, my mom is all furious at me. She said I could go as long as I didn't miss school, but she found out that I missed half the day today. I didn't do it on purpose and she found out that it'd been a Kade party we went to. I had no idea how she found that out. I told her I was going with you and your family to a cabin. She likes you, but now she knows all about your parents' divorce and everything. I could murder whoever told her that stuff."

I crawled onto my bed and rolled on my back. "Gossip's pretty rampant. I'm sure it got out somehow about the party."

"Not to mention that your mom's hooked up with James Kade. My mom seemed pretty bent about that one for some reason."

I frowned into the phone. "Does your mom know mine?"

"Your mom used to be in some committee at the country club with her, but I think my mom's more mad because of your dad. You know everyone loves Coach Strattan."

"Yeah, there is that…"

"Anyways, so I was just calling because she won't let me go out to Gino's with you."

From the way her voice quieted, I felt a kick in my gut. I knew something else was going on and I sat up. "She won't let you go to Gino's or she doesn't want you to go with me?"

"Both."

I could imagine the glower on her face.

Becky added, "Oh gawd, I'm so sorry. My mom doesn't want me to be friends with you anymore. I guess she called a bunch of other moms and they were told by their kids that you're tight with the Kade brothers. My mom's scared of them, everyone's moms are. My dad was ecstatic. He wants to meet them; he wants to talk football with Mason. Yeah right, like that's going to happen."

I drew my knees against my chest and hugged them tight. "So we can't talk at school?"

She snorted. "Forget that. I'm still going to be friends with you. My mom can't tell me what to do with that, but she won't let me go to Gino's tonight. I'm sorry, Sam. I know you wanted to go so you didn't have to go to that Elite dinner thing."

"You knew about that?" I grinned into the phone. Of course, she knew

"Of course I knew. Who do you think I am? It's not my first day on the gossip pages. Everyone knows that Miranda invited you to the Elite dinner tonight. Only I knew that you weren't going to go." She paused for a beat. "Are you going to go now?"

"Uh…"

I was about to say that I wasn't sure, but Mason threw open my door. "Logan's going crazy on your mom." And he was gone in a flash.

I said in a rush, "I have to go."

"What? What's going on—"

I pressed the disconnect button and threw it on the bed as I hurried down to the kitchen.

"Are you kidding me?!" Logan cursed as he stood in the foyer. His chest was rising up and down at a rapid pace and his hands were balled into fists, pressed tight against his legs. His eyes were wild in anger and his jaw kept clenching and unclenching.

Analise looked annoyed dressed in a white lace dress. She still held onto her white clutch. A string of white pearls were nestled between in her cleavage. James stood between them, dressed in a black formal suit. Whatever Bangor was, it must've been for the formal and expensive.

I snorted to myself. Of course it would've been.

Mason stopped in the doorframe and held onto the post above his head. He was quiet and my mother glanced back at him every now and then.

Logan spat out, "Are you seriously trying to tell me what I can't do?" His eyes were narrowed at an alarming level.

My mom patted her chest in a dainty fashion. "I am voicing my opinion. It's eight at night. I don't think it's appropriate for you to go out this late. You should be studying, staying in."

Logan snorted out a laugh as he shook his head. His hands were still in fists. He opened them and closed them back up. He kept doing it. "I can't believe you. Who the hell are you, woman?"

Analise glanced back at Mason and then she saw me behind him. Her shoulders lifted a bit and she stood a tiny bit straighter on her feet. "Since everyone is here, I'd like to make an announcement."

"Not another one," Logan muttered under his breath, still glaring at my mother.

She cleared her throat and took James' hand in hers. "I have gone room to room and emptied out all of the liquor that was in this household."

Mason didn't react, but a nerve in his shoulder jumped. Other than that, not a muscle moved. Logan shook his head and cursed some more. Both of his hands rose in the air like he wanted to put them around her neck. "Dad, control your whore."

James was in his face in the next second. "You will watch your mouth, son."

Logan's mouth clamped shut, but he heaved a deep breath and continued to shake his head. "I can't believe you. You're going to let her tell us what we can drink or not drink?"

His father's voice was quiet. "All three children in this home are underage. And since all three of you claimed Analise was in a drunken fit the other night, both of us deemed it a responsible choice to be rid of all alcohol."

Logan's smile was dangerous. "You think we're the problem?"

His father stepped back once. "No, I don't. I saw her that evening as well. She *had* been drinking too much." He glanced at me. "She was under a lot of emotional anxiety that night, but this is an answer that can help multiple levels for a problem I'm sure that's yet to be unearthed."

Mason bit out a laugh. His hands clenched around the post above and his muscles grew tighter at the movement.

Everyone looked at him and quieted.

"She doesn't want you to go out?" he spoke to Logan.

He gave a short nod. "She thinks I'm being irresponsible."

Mason turned his gaze towards his father, but spoke to Analise, "You might be her mother." He gestured towards me, over his shoulder. "But you're not ours. We have a mother." Then his eyes met his father's again for a brief second. It was a meaningful one.

James turned on his heel and left the room.

My mother's mouth dropped open and her hand jerked after him. "Wha—uh? What are you doing? James!"

Logan grinned in victory and shared a meaningful look with his brother.

Mason dropped his arms abruptly. "Our mom's got custody of us. We can go back to her anytime we want. You might want to remember that."

Tight fists flung against her legs and she stomped her feet. "I cannot believe you two! You are the two most horrible children I have ever met—"

"We're not children." Logan got in her face. "And we're not yours. If you dare try to tell us what to do, you'll regret it. I promise that."

She looked around and I saw how frantic she was. When she found me in the corner, she spewed, out, "I don't know what you have done to her, but I will make it my mission to destroy you two."

I jerked forward in surprise.

Logan's hyena laugh sounded out, but Mason tilted his head to the side, just a slight movement.

Analise sputtered to a halt. Her hands were forcibly pressed against her as her knees trembled.

"You really need to stop threatening us. It makes it worse." Mason turned with a hard smirk on his face. He touched my shoulder and glanced back at her. "You should think about that."

She gasped and choked on it. Her cheeks filled up and her hands fluttered around her in a helpless pace. Tears filled her face and she brushed furiously at them. "You don't—you don't—you don't threaten me, *boy*!"

His chuckle was a soft one, but it hit her hard. My mother started waving her fists around in the air.

Logan rolled his eyes and pulled out his keys. When he turned for the door, she screeched at him, "Where are you going?!"

He ignored her and the door shut on his heels.

Mason had already disappeared back upstairs when my mother turned back around. She bent over and took deep breaths, all while she was patting her chest at the same time. Then she looked up with fresh tears in her eyes. She tried to wipe them away.

"How do you do it?"

I frowned. "What do you mean?"

"They like you. How did you do it?"

I shrugged. "They're never going to respect you."

She looked away. I watched as she wiped more tears away. Then she turned back. "What do I do?"

I gave her a sad smile. It was almost heartbreaking to see her like this, almost. "You'll never win against them. All you can do is exist beside them. That's it."

"That's it?"

"Like he said, you're not their mother." When she opened her mouth, I cut her off. "And you're not mine anymore, not really."

She was jolted back.

I narrowed my eyes. "I don't like you. I don't know if I ever did. I love you, but I don't respect you either. And I doubt I ever will again. You're lucky to still have me here. You haven't done anything to help me, nothing at all. You only hurt me, mom."

She pressed the back of her hand to her mouth. More tears streaked down her face. "I'm sorry, Samantha. I really am."

My eyes held hers. I didn't know what I was looking for, maybe a weakening within her or something I could grasp onto. I had no idea. I saw emptiness instead. And I felt it within me. It rose up as I watched my mother break before my eyes.

I took a deep breath and spoke in a quiet voice, "Look at you. This is what they've done to you already and they haven't even tried. They could destroy you, mom. It's not the other way around. You could never touch them. You're an annoying gnat to them. They've put up with your presence because James loves you. I can see that too. He does." It hurt to say what I was going to say next. "Focus on him. Focus on your relationship with him. Ours is gone, but maybe it could come back someday. Not today. Or next year, but sometime in the future. Just…focus on your future husband, mom. That's all you can do right now."

I turned away and started for my room, but I paused when I heard her whisper. "I'm sorry, honey. I'm so sorry."

Then I gripped the rail and went back to my room.

It was 8:30 when I checked my phone again and I had three text messages from Miranda, along with a voice message from her. Dinner had come and gone. They wanted to know where I was, if I was going. I had finished listening to her message when Mason knocked on my door.

I frowned and motioned for him to come in.

He studied my face. "What's wrong?"

I shook my head. "Nothing I can't handle."

My phone vibrated again. It was another text from Miranda—they'd all gone to some bar. I glanced up at Mason and asked, "You don't want to go somewhere with me, do you?"

He grinned back at me. "What? This late? What would your mother say?"

I couldn't stop my laugh. "I don't think she'll be saying much after what I said to her."

He stopped grinning. "What did you say?"

"Nothing, that she was lucky I was still here and we didn't really have a relationship anymore."

His eyes studied me. I felt his intensity and wanted to curl up against it. He asked me, "Did you mean that?"

I jerked my head in a nod. "I did." My eyes found his. "I'm close to asking David if I can live with him. He raised me all my life. If my mom knows who my real dad is or not doesn't matter to me. David raised me. He's my dad and she knows I'll push that if we'd ever go to court. The fact that I'm here, it's by a hairs' width."

He came inside and perched on the arm of one of my couches. "So where did you want to go?"

"Some bar. Some people at school invited me to their dinner. I didn't go and now they're out. I feel a little bad that I ditched on them."

Mason shook his head. "Let me guess, these aren't the people that are used to being ditched?"

I shook my head too.

"Do you know what you're doing?"

I wrapped my arms around my knees. "No."

His eyes held mine.

And I grinned. "But I don't really care either."

He mirrored my grin. "What bar are they at?"

I texted Miranda the question and she gave me an answer a second later. I held the phone up. "The Ryder."

Mason bit back a laugh and pulled out his phone. "I'm sure Logan's had his piece by now. Maybe he'd meet us there."

I stood and ran sweaty hands down my pants. I frowned at them. Why were they so sweaty? Then Mason looked back up when he was done. He grabbed my hand and pulled me between his legs. I held my breath as he leaned in close and pressed a kiss to the crook of my neck. He inhaled and held me close. I felt him fit between my legs and almost closed my eyes. I wanted to tell him to forget it and pull him to my bed.

When his phone vibrated, he lifted it for me to see.

We're there!

He chuckled against my neck and kissed it lightly. His hand curved around my waist and held me tighter. "Looks like its game on. Your quarterback's going to be there?"

I wrapped my arms around him and tilted my neck at an angle. His mouth started to explore it. Then I sighed against him. I didn't know if I'd ever get enough of him.

Mason moved back and whispered as his lips teased my skin, "You're going to ride me long and hard tonight."

I grinned against his neck. It was what every girl wanted to hear.

CHAPTER THIRTY

When we got to The Ryder, I saw it was a bar attached to a hotel. As soon as we entered, I remembered that Amelia's dad owned the place. It explained why they could drink at the bar and when we got there, they had congregated in a back corner, away from the other customers. It was a ritzy hotel and the neon red and black lighting set an intimate tone to the bar.

Miranda saw me first and waved us over by a pool table. She stood in a tight black dress with a red belt around her midriff. The rest of the girls were dressed in similar dresses, all tight and in different colors. I wondered if they planned it. They looked cliquey and expensive. Each of them wore dangling diamond earrings that matched their dress color.

"Hi, guys!" Miranda gave me a big hug. "I'm so glad you could come. The rest were disappointed you didn't come to the dinner."

Mason gave her one of his unreadable looks and she shifted on her feet. Her hand twitched for a second. It was the only movement I caught that made me wonder if she was uncomfortable. I would be.

"Mason, thanks for coming." She was so formal and gracious.

He shoved his hands in his pockets and went to the bar.

As he did, she laughed and touched the base of her neck. "I'm not going to take that personal. I shouldn't, right?"

I shrugged. "I told you. They're assholes."

"He certainly must like you. Mason Kade has never come to one of my get-togethers."

"I thought he showed up at the one last weekend?"

She peeled out another burst of laughter. It was high pitched enough to make me pause. Was she being fake or was she drunk? Something wasn't fitting with her. She giggled into her hand. "That wasn't him coming as a guest. We all thought he had come for his brother, but instead he came to lay into that girl." Her eyes lingered on my bruise again. "You remember—the one I heard you got into a fight with."

Miranda seemed to be waiting for me to say something, but I wasn't sure what it was. When I started to ask something stupid, I was picked up and thrown over someone's shoulders. Logan's hyena laugh sounded as he twirled me around, bent over with my rear on display. I felt him patting it and he whistled under his breath. "You've got a tight ass, Sam. No wonder your quarterback wants to bang you so hard."

Someone gasped and someone else choked on their drink.

"Put me down, Logan." I tried to be fierce.

He laughed some more, but lowered me down. As he sat me on my feet, he lifted back up, but was close enough to brush against my body. When his eyes met mine, I saw a dark humor in them. I tensed and got ready.

I didn't want to be friends with these guys, but I wasn't sure what to do about it. Mason asked in the ride over if I wanted to piss them off now or wait for the perfect moment. I didn't have an answer and I still didn't. Still, whatever Logan was doing I knew he wanted to piss someone off.

As I caught a jerking movement from the corner of my eye, I wondered if he'd come for Adam. I watched as my former friend had a scowl on his face and he downed the rest of his drink in a savage motion. Cassandra was beside him with his arm around her waist. She wore a frown as she watched him. I thought I saw some concern in her depths as well.

Miranda gutted out a laugh and stepped forward again. "Logan, you've come as well."

He curved an arm around my waist and raised an eyebrow. "Weren't we invited?" His tone was too confident, too smooth.

She visibly swallowed and looked around. "Uh, of course you guys were invited. I assumed Samantha told you. You're both here."

Logan shot Adam a look. "I thought about bringing Tanya, but she thought it would be awkward. Plus, she needed an hour to get ready..."

Adam's scowl grew darker, but he didn't respond. Peter Glasburg and Mark Decraw stood between the two. They tried to look casual as they stood with their pool-sticks, but each couldn't contain their frowns. They threw Mason looks as he remained at the bar. He had a drink in hand and looked relaxed.

"Uh...she could've come if you liked?" Miranda's nervous laugh rang out high pitched. She cleared her throat and sounded more normal as she said, "All of you could've brought dates with you. That option is always open to the group."

Emily snorted out, "Of course, most of us are already paired up."

Miranda stared hard at her. "What are you talking about, Emily?"

The brunette smirked at her and sipped from her martini glass. "Come on, Miranda. You're with Peter. Cass is with Adam now. Amelia and Mark suck face most of the time."

Logan's grin grew as she continued.

"You should've brought in a guy next, not Samantha Strattan." She lifted her martini glass to me. "No offense, Sam, but everyone can tell you don't care about social things. Everyone knew Jessica Larsen slept with your boyfriend for two years. That would humiliate most people, but you acted like you didn't care and I don't think that was an act. I think you really *didn't* care." She scoffed at Miranda again. "You just wanted to bring her in because you hoped Mason and Logan would come with her. You never cared about her until you heard she was close to them."

"You're drunk, Emily." Miranda glared at her. "You should go sleep this off. You don't want to be rude."

She snorted again and tipped her head back to finish the rest of her martini. Her thin legs wavered underneath her, but she kept her balance when she raised her empty glass. "Another, bartender!"

Logan chuckled as she went to the bar. "I like her."

"You do?" Miranda had grown pale.

"She tells the truth." He sent her a smirk. "That's all we can ask for...right?"

"The truth?" Adam barked out as he straightened from the wall in a sudden movement. Peter and Mark jumped back in reaction. "What's the truth, Logan? Huh?" He started to stalk forward, but Cassandra tried to slow him down. She was in front with a hand on his chest.

Logan slipped his arm from my waist and maneuvered me behind him. In the blink of an eye, Mason was in front of me too. Miranda gasped and looked around wide eyed. She kept glancing from the Kades to Adam.

Everyone watched him.

His angry scowl intensified and he bit out, "Why'd you take Tanya? You didn't care about her before."

Logan's shoulders jostled in silent laughter. "Are you kidding me?"

"No!"

His shoulders stopped and stretched out instead. "Are you pissed because you never got there?"

"I think...um...I think..." Miranda stepped between them. Her arms were shaking.

Peter moved her aside and puffed out his chest. "Guys, let's be civil here."

"No!" Adam tried to shove him aside, but Mark shot between them instead. Cassandra was pulled out of the way by Miranda.

Logan sounded calm, too calm, as he chuckled. "Let him through. He's got something on his chest. Let's help him get it off. This is the trust tree, right? Here we go, therapy group for everyone."

"You think you're so awesome, don't you?" Adam growled. He had a glass of beer in his hand now. He waved it back and forth in the air now.

"I prefer badass."

The growl grew. "'You're so rich', 'you're so hot', 'everybody wants you.' I am so sick of you two—"

"Both of us?" Mason's voice was low, eerily low.

Everyone snapped their attention to him.

Logan laughed. "Wait your turn, Mase. My fun first."

Mason shot him a dry look, but Logan ignored it. His grin grew wider and he beamed at Adam. "Come on, tell me more. I'd love to hear what else you hate about me." He tsked him with a finger in the air. "Just me, though. You hear that? We'll move onto my big brother in the next session."

Rage leapt to Adam's eyes. I stepped back from instinct. I'd never seen so much rage within him before. My heart started to pound. It grew in speed as Adam bent his head. His mouth had curved in a hateful scowl.

"You laugh at me? Are you kidding me right now? Do you know who you're messing with?"

Logan's laugh sounded genuine. "Do you think I care? You're the guy who gets the leftovers. That's what I know about you."

Adam grew silent. My heart was pounding so loudly. It was deafening to my ears.

"I had Ashley before you, and during you." Logan's smirk grew. "I had Tanya before you and *again* before you. Who else is there?" He made a show as he turned around. He tapped his finger to his chin and he paused when his gaze rested on me. "Who else is there?"

"Logan." It was a quiet warning from Mason.

Logan twisted back around; the delight on his face was unsettling. "There's got to be others. Tina Schnieder? She told me you wanted to date her too, but no one knows about that one. She goes to public. She's beneath you, right? Isn't that you thought about Tanya? You

TIJAN

thought for sure you had her in the bag, she goes to public. All those girls are beneath you, isn't that what you think?"

Adam's face was set in stone. The hand that clenched his glass was white around the knuckles. A quiet crack was heard. The group had grown silent and everyone heard it. Another crack sounded.

Logan's voice was so quiet now, going in for the kill. He bent his head forward and his eyes were narrowed. "What about your friend Casssandra there?"

She whipped her head around. Fear was evident as she started to shake. "What are you talking about..." She stammered out, "I..id... Idnever..." She bent forward and took some shuddering breaths. Miranda scurried away from her with a look of terror on her own face. Peter held her hand in his now and he lifted it to his chest.

Adam was white around the corner of his mouth. He turned his head slowly, so slowly. My heart pounded in my ears. My hands started to tremble and I knew my knees were quaking against each other.

He asked in a soft voice, "Is it true?"

Cassandra's mouth hung open. Her eyes bulged out as she looked from Logan's confident smirk to Adam's tightly controlled face. "I...I..."

"Is it true?" Adam asked again.

The tenderness in his voice sent chills down my back. I hugged myself and tried to ward off the promise of violence in the air.

"I can't believe you." He seemed so calm, but his eyes were too dark. "You know how much I hate them."

Logan and Mason glanced at each other and both wore a small grin.

Cassandra's voice was hoarse. "I didn't—it was stupid of me, but... Oh gawd. I'm so sorry, Adam."

Emily started laughing by the bar. She saluted her martini glass in the air. "Way to go, Cassie. Way to start the New Year by being honest."

Cassandra hissed at her, "Shut up, Emily. Like you haven't done the same thing. Logan's probably slept with all of us, Miranda included."

Miranda's eyes got wide and Peter jolted away from her like he'd been burned. She turned to him and pressed her hands to her mouth. "I haven't, baby. I haven't. I swear."

He studied her with narrowed eyes. "You've always wanted Logan to be in the group. You've talked about it for years."

Her hand shot out and she pointed at them. Her foot stomped down. "Only because they should've been in our group. They were supposed to pick our school. We have the better school. Just because they have a better football team, that's the only reason they picked public. They were supposed to be in our group, but instead everyone wants to go to the public parties. Everyone thinks Fallen Crest Public High is so great, all because of them! They were supposed to be at our school. Fallen Crest Academy is the better school. That other school is beneath us, it should be beneath us. They should be kissing our feet. That's the only reason why I've talked about them. I swear, baby!"

Logan bent over laughing. He slapped a hand on his leg. "Man, you guys are so easy. It's been, what? Ten minutes?" He continued laughing as he shook his head. "My job here is done. Have a great night, ya'll."

Adam frowned. "What are you saying? You didn't sleep with Cassandra?"

"Oh no. I did, at the party actually. I was just with Tanya later. Emily was one time and I think," He frowned at Amelia who stood beside Mark. "...Halloween last year?"

She gaped at him, but jerked her head in a nod.

"He's joking," Mark burst out, but he turned sharply on her.

She closed her mouth and slowly turned her head from side to side.

"Amelia!"

Her shoulders lifted up and she held her palms outward. "You didn't want exclusivity, Mark. What do you expect? He's hot."

"You're a slut."

Everyone turned to Miranda who was glaring at Logan. Her hands held her glass tightly. Her arms were still shaking, but not from fear this time. She repeated, "You're a slut."

Logan smirked and glanced at Peter. "I don't hide it."

Her eyes went wide again and she whirled to her boyfriend, who looked away at the same time.

Emily exclaimed, "This was a great idea, Miranda. We should invite Strattan every time."

At this, all eyes went to me. I realized that it looked like I was cowering behind Mason and Logan so I shouldered past them and straightened my back. My chin rose and I stared Miranda down. "You sent me text after text tonight and you called me. You were begging me to come. So I came. If you want to blame me for this, fine. I told you to stay away from Mason and Logan, but you didn't."

"I didn't invite them."

I rolled my eyes. "We all know you wanted them here so here they are. You got what you wanted. I bet you don't want it anymore. You can't control them and you can't control me."

Her eyes narrowed. "Who said I wanted to control you?"

"You've been trying since you warned me Cassandra was jealous of me."

Cassandra gasped. "Miranda!"

Miranda moved back against Peter, who raised a hand to her shoulder. He started to rub up and down her arm in a soothing motion. She sent me a withering look. "You can leave, Samantha. Good luck at school tomorrow."

"Sam," Adam spoke up.

I met his gaze and saw the loathing there. "Don't bother, Adam." I tugged on Logan's arm. "Let's go." And both of us started for the door, but when we realized Mason wasn't following, we turned back.

He watched us with lidded eyes.

Logan frowned. "What are you doing?"

Mason gave him a tight grin. It didn't reach to his eyes. "We have a problem now." He turned towards the group. "She's one of ours and you declared open season on her."

"I didn't." Miranda seemed to melt back into Peter's arms.

He gave her a hard look. "You did."

Logan went to his side. His mouth curved upwards, mocking them. "I did this for sport tonight. You really want me to go after you, pissed if you've done something to Sam?"

Mason shot him a look. "Because it's all you, right?"

Logan grinned at him. "I told you. My fun first."

He rolled his eyes and walked to me. As he drew abreast, he took my arm, and tugged me behind him. "Logan, they got the message."

"I hope they do." Logan's eyes held a much deeper message as he scanned the group.

My legs were shaking so much. As we drew closer to Mason's Escalade, he swept me in his arms and I hung on. I wouldn't have made it otherwise. He deposited me in the seat and went to his own. Logan paused in his open door. He frowned over at me. "Are you okay?"

"I'll be fine, just shaken up."

All amusement had vanished. Both of them watched me with grave eyes. Then Logan sighed. "What do we do?"

Mason continued to watch me as he spoke to him, "We wait and see what happens."

"And if they do something to her? We can't be there during school hours. This is why we didn't go to their school. We didn't want to deal with them."

"I know."

I swallowed as my eyes held Mason's. A promise passed through him to me and my body warmed to it. I wanted it, even now, I wanted him.

"Mason, hell. I think I opened a bigger can of worms than I thought." Logan slapped his hand on the Escalade's door. "I'm sorry, Samantha."

I tried to shrug against the seat. My shoulder lifted halfway. "I've dealt with worse."

"They're vengeful bitches. And they don't forget."

My eyes held onto Mason's. "I told you I was going to piss off some people this week."

He grinned back at me. His hand touched my knee and I clasped onto it.

CHAPTER THIRTY-ONE

I rolled out from underneath Mason's arm that he had thrown over me. One of his hands cupped my breast and I fought back a snort. Of course he'd fallen asleep cupping a feel. After I snuck to my room and got ready for school, I headed downstairs. Moustefff always had a lunch bag ready for me, but I was surprised to see my mom behind the table. The lunch bag was plopped in front of her and she had a steaming cup of coffee beside it.

"You're drinking coffee again?"

She snorted and picked it up. "I hate tea. I tried it, but I hate it." She took a big whiff of the coffee. "And this stuff, it's so addicting."

I eyed her up and down. "Are you feeling okay?"

She gave me a polite look and pulled the ends of her robe tight. "I went to your room earlier, but you weren't there. I guess you went for a run, huh? Anyway, I owe you an apology. Hell, I owe you a lot of apologies."

"Mom?" I glanced around. "What's going on?"

"I was completely wrong about everything." And she brought out a manila folder.

"What's that?"

"It's a tentative deal with David." She took a deep breath. "It says that he has rights to you as a father and you can live with him, if you'd like…or you can visit him…whatever's your choice. I can't keep you from him anymore."

"Anymore?" I picked up the folder, but hesitated to open it. "What are you talking about?"

"He got a lawyer, honey, and that lawyer said he had rights to you. Plus, with everything you've said to me and how I seem to be the worst mother in the world, I didn't fight it. It's the right thing to do. He raised you. He's your father, not some hotshot lawyer out in Boston."

"My real dad's a hotshot lawyer in Boston?"

She shrugged. "It doesn't matter now. I contacted him last night and told him about you. So you might be having two fathers to deal with."

"And the change of heart came because...?"

"Because I was wrong." She looked up. My heart skipped a beat. She seemed so earnest. "I do love you and I haven't been the best mother to you. I've put myself first. I've continued to do so, but you were right last night. I saw that I lost you. Losing your respect, when it's spoken to you from a seventeen year old who's looking at you like they're thirty-that said a lot to me." Her laugh sounded hollow. "It said a whole hell of a lot."

I fingered the edge of the packet and glanced up. "You told my dad about me?" I was breathless, though I didn't know why I should've been.

She took a big sip of coffee. "I wouldn't get your hopes up, hon. He's a big arse."

"No, I know, but...um..." I looked at the manila folder in my hands. "So I could live with David if I really wanted to?"

She took another deep breath and nodded. Her head moved so slowly. "You sure could...you could be there tonight even."

"Really?"

"He's been fighting for you since day one."

"He has?"

"Yep, he has." She looked away and wiped something away from her eyes. When she looked back, she gave me another bright smile. Her lip trembled. "I wanted to keep you all to myself. I didn't want to share you or lose you, but I can't control that. I see that now.

You told me that last night. But, honey, I love you so much." She lurched forward and grabbed my arm. "You know that, right?"

"I know, mom."

It felt right to call her that. She'd been Analise so much, but she was my mom at that moment. I gave her another smile. "I'm not going to leave, mom. I'd like to see David, but you're my mom. This has become my home."

I glanced up and saw Mason. He hesitated on the stairwell.

When I gave him a small smile, he came into the kitchen. His eyes fell on the folder in my hands. "You want a ride to school?"

"Sure." I tried to say it brightly, but my life had just been spun around. Two dads... I couldn't get that through my head. What did that mean?

Mason grabbed something from the kitchen and started for the door. I turned to follow and my mom shot up from the table. "Honey, are you okay with this?"

"Yeah." I beamed back at her, or I tried to. "I'll be fine, mom."

"Are you sure? I could call in for you. You don't have to go to school today. I'm sure it's a lot to take in..." She seemed timid as she stood beside the table. Her steaming coffee cup was forgotten behind her.

I waved as I went through the front door. I heard Mason get into his Escalade. "I'll be fine, mom. Promise. Have a good day."

"You too, honey..."

He pulled out of the driveway and waited until we'd gone a block. "So what was that about?"

I still held the manila folder in my lap. "She gave rights to David. I can see him if I want to and she called my real dad last night. I guess he's some hotshot lawyer in Boston."

After a few blocks, Mason wheeled into a fast food drive-through. "You want anything?"

I shook my head. I couldn't believe this was happening. He ordered me a coffee anyway.

He handed it over. "So are you going to stay with him now? That's what you wanted, right?"

I shot him a look and sipped my coffee. I hissed when I felt how scalding it was. "Yeah, but there's…" I glanced at him warily. "That's not in the cards."

He grinned from the side of his mouth and eased his Escalade into my school's parking lot. "You snuck out of bed this morning. I was hoping for a morning ride."

I grinned as memories from last night sent a surge of heat through my body. Need started to throb between my legs again and I clamped them together. I couldn't go to school hot and bothered, and aching all over…again. Last night had passed from one sensual moment to another. Mason had taken me on an insatiable journey and every time I thought I was done, he slid back in and started it all over again.

We'd slept for two hours, tops.

As he parked front and center, I spotted Adam at his car. He was with Mark Decraw and Peter Glasburg. Everything sexual left me and I tightened my hold on my coffee. "Yeah, well, we'll have to do it another time."

He nodded in their direction. "You want me to stay for a while?"

"No." I did. "You have to get to your own school."

"Alright. I can't run you home after school."

"Why not?"

He grimaced as he stretched back in his seat. "I'll have enough time to come get you and head back for my practice. Can you hang out there for a while? I think Logan would love it. He can show off his throwing arm for you."

"Sure. See you." As I reached for the door, the first warning bell went off and everyone started to head inside. Our eyes met and held as I walked around the front to the door. As I neared it, I expected to hear him zoom off. It never happened and I turned around.

A blast of cold air hit me. It drenched me.

Mason was out of his car and he was face to face with Adam. Peter and Mark were behind him. All three of them had fierce expressions on their faces and firm jaws, but Mason looked relaxed as he eyed each of them up and down.

My stomach dropped. This was not good.

"Hey, hey, hey!" I ran back and shoved between them. Not good. Not good. That kept going through my head.

"Where's your little bitch boy now?" Adam tried to reach around me.

Mason smirked. He looked calm. The other three were shifting on their feet, but he never moved, not an inch. He drawled out, "Bitch boy? That was a bitch move. You waited until a girl stepped between us?"

Adam flushed, but snarled. "One swing, Kade. One swing. Isn't that what they say about you?" His lip curled up. "It only takes one punch for Mason Kade."

"Stop!"

"Usually." He shrugged and as he lifted a hand to scratch his chin, all three jerked in reaction. Mason's smirk grew wider at that.

"I mean it!" I turned around and around.

"Is that right?" Adam tried to push at him again. Mark and Peter both grabbed him as they got in front.

I surged forward and tried to help, but I was bumped backwards. I skidded from the movement, but Mason caught me. He slid an arm around my waist and lifted me to the side. "Trying to hurt a girl?"

Adam growled and lunged again. "Let me go. I can take him."

"Come on, man. Think about this."

"Adam, please. Don't do this." I started forward again. Mason caught me and held me in place. His hand stayed on my hip. "Just stop, Adam. This won't do anything."

Adam choked out a hoarse laugh. "Are you kidding me, Sam? Someone needs to knock 'em down a step, him and his bitch boy. They think they're gods around here. I don't think so. I don't think so!" He spat on the ground. "He's got nerve to show up on my territory. This is mine, Kade!"

Mason lifted an eyebrow. "She yours too?"

"Mason!"

His eyes went wider and he choked back his retort to lunge forward again. His friends grunted and strained to hold him back. Peter snapped at him, "This is what he wants. You're playing into his hands."

Mark was whispering something to Adam while Peter kept a wary eye on Mason.

"I don't care," Adam ripped out. "I don't care one bit. I want this done. This has to be done. Someone's gotta do it. Everyone else is too scared so I'll do it. Let me do it!"

Mason's soft chuckle enraged him further.

A knot of dread and fear expanded from my stomach. It was crawling all over me. My legs started to shake, but then I caught movement around us. People were starting to congregate towards us. I cringed when I heard someone yell 'fight' and then a bevy of lockers slammed shut from inside.

"Your sidekick's not here. What are you going to do, man?" Both of Adam's arms were lifted up and pushed backwards by Peter and Mark. They continued to hold him back as they leaned all of their weight on him.

"I don't fight with words." The corner of Mason's lip was curled up. "I'm quite capable of handling Quinn all on my own. Let him go. Come on. That's what he wants."

"Shut up!" Mark glared at him.

The last bell rang and I glanced around. No one was in class. The crowd doubled in size and a loose circle had started to form around us. Becky dodged around a group of guys and started to come to my side. I shot my hand out and shook my head so she braked a few yards from me, but edged in closer. When she mouthed if I was okay, I shook my head.

No, I wasn't okay. Mason was severely outnumbered.

Suddenly, Adam shoved Mark aside and his elbow caught me in the face.

"Hey!" Mason barked as he caught me and pulled me behind him. "If you want to fight, fight me, not your buddies. Sam just got clipped."

Mark cried out as he caught one of Adam's arms, "I'm sorry, man. Sorry, Sam—" He was about to say more, but Adam cursed and lunged once again. "You're a piece of crap, Kade!" He continued to bite out curses.

Mason sighed and motioned for him to come forward. "Just let him go. This will get done a lot faster. I have school too."

Peter lifted his head and yelled, "If you'd shut up, man. You're not helping."

I felt Mason's impatience. The one hand he kept on me was tense, so tense I wondered if he realized he was going to leave a bruise. Then I stopped wondering. He looked like he was amused by the whole thing, but a nerve jerked under his shirt. I saw it through the opening of his shirt. It was his only tell; everything else about him was silent. He was completely still.

I knew he was ready for an opening.

And then something happened. He jerked forward, hooked an arm around Peter's neck and threw him to the aside. Adam swung, but Mason dodged and instead tackled Mark to the left. They both fell to the ground, but he scrambled back up in the blink of an eye. He turned around and it was now him and Adam, no one else.

Adam took a step forward and opened his mouth—

Crack!

Mason punched him between the cheek and mouth, one time, and then he stepped back.

It looked like it happened in slow motion.

Adam's eyes rolled to the back of his head and he fell with a loud thud to the ground. His head smacked against the cement twice and his limbs bounced back up before they settled down.

There was silence in the crowd.

"Oh my god!" a girl screamed. Another started to sob.

I rushed to Adam's side and patted his cheek. "Adam? Adam…"

"What's going on here?" a teacher cried out.

"Holy, man…" "Did you see that?" "Shiite." Another guy whooped in laughter and others started to yell back and forth. People were starting to push and shove against each other.

Becky's mouth had dropped open. She was frozen in place.

More teachers were starting to push their way in and then I heard my dad's voice in the background. "What's going on? Let us through."

"Oh no—" I hurried up and started to push Mason into the crowd. "You have to go."

When we got to his Escalade, he smirked down at me. "Why? They'll say it was me. I knocked him out cold, Sam."

"You can leave. You might not get in trouble."

He rolled his eyes. "Are you serious? I'm not going anywhere. I'll face the firing squad here."

I sighed. "Do you know what you did?"

He turned back to the crowd, but shrugged. "I don't care."

"You attacked a student on school grounds. They could get you expelled from your school."

"Maybe." His jaw stiffened.

"Samantha!" my dad hollered.

I jerked around, but he hadn't spotted us yet. "Go, Mason. I mean it."

He shook his head. "I'm not going anywhere."

"Samantha!" David's voice was closer now. And then he broke through the crowd to us.

I turned to face my father, but I hissed behind me, "He could have you arrested."

David stopped in front of us and he placed both hands on his hips. He stared at me for a moment and then Mason before he took off his coach's hat and rubbed at his head. "Do you know what you've done, son?"

"Yes, sir."

My eyebrows went up when I didn't see a smirk on his face and heard respect in his tone.

"Basey," David hollered behind him.

One of his assistant coaches popped up. "He'll be fine, sir. He'll come around. We just gotta get him inside."

My dad took a deep breath. "Alright, well, you heard him. Let's all head inside." He pointed at Mason. "You, go to the principal's office."

He nodded. "Sure…where's that at?"

"Sam?"

"Yeah, dad?"

"Take him to the principal's office."

"Sure thing."

"And do me another favor?"

I halted at the frustration in my dad's voice. "Yeah…?"

"Call your mother and his father." He turned around, but I heard him mutter, "This should be fun."

CHAPTER THIRTY-TWO

Mason and I were in an empty classroom. His head was bent down, cushioned by his arms and I was starting to wonder if he'd fallen asleep. He couldn't have. And then someone sped past the door, screeched to a halt, and backtracked to stand in the doorway. Logan greeted us with his arms spread wide and a bright smile on his face.

"One punch, Mase?" Logan laughed and launched himself on our table. "Next time I think you should get him to knock himself out."

"Logan, dude." Another guy followed him in, looking irritable. I recognized him from one of their parties. "You just took off. This place is bitch heaven, at least grace me with some bread crumbs."

"Ethan, chill. They're easy."

He grimaced. "I'm not talking about those; I'm talking about the dudes. They're all over. Their pants are pressed so tight I keep expecting to smell aromatherapy or whatever my mom sells with her scentsy stuff. They fart daisies. I know it."

Logan laughed and hit him in the backside of his head. Ethan shot away and glared again. His eyebrows rose at an alarming height.

Mason sighed and leaned back in his chair. "We've been cooped up here for four hours. Dad showed up after an hour and we were hauled back here."

Logan smirked. "Was he dressed to impress?"

"You know it. Remind 'em who brings the money in." He glanced at me. "Her mom had some lacey bridal dress on."

I glanced down and folded my arms. A stab of pain went through my gut when I remembered how Analise had pranced through my school's doorway. It'd been her second time to visit. The first time had been an event for David.

Both brothers shared a grin. "You're totally going to get off for this."

Ethan shared in their dark humor and grinned. "Isn't one punch considered assault or something? My cousin knocked a guy out cold. That dude had been harassing him and his girlfriend and my cousin got the rap for it."

Mason shrugged and stood. He started to pace. Even with his muscular physique, the gracefulness of his walk reminded me of a lean panther trapped in a cage. He kept glancing at the open door. The bell had rung again and students passed by. I had stopped watching after a while. Not one person went by that didn't look in. They all wanted to get a glimpse. We were on display at a human zoo.

I asked Logan, "Aren't you guys supposed to be in school? It's one in the afternoon."

"Yeah, right. I'm not going to be there when my brother's over here. Besides, coach sent me over." He nodded at Mason. "We have twofers for the rest of the week. He said you have to make them all, tonight too, if you're going to play."

Irritation flared over his face and he scowled. "Against Roussou? Of course I'm going to play. It's our second chance to beat them. I hate their quarterback."

"More than the Academy's?" Ethan joked.

Logan tipped his head back to cackle while Mason flexed his knuckles. "Whatever. I'm sick of this. I'm starting to wish I hadn't finished him."

Logan looked taken aback and thrust his hand out towards me. "Whatever. The guy's going to back down. He knows you can beat his—"

Ethan interjected, "One punch, mofo."

"—and now he might calm down. His panties are all twisted because of Sam anyway—"

"Hey!"

Ethan frowned at me.

"—but now he'll go away and lick his balls a bit. I think we should do it again to make sure he's down for the count and knows who is boss. What do you say? Hunt him down after we kill Roussou Friday night?"

Mason stopped and glared at him. He looked ready to bark something, but changed his mind and pointed to the door. "Ethan, leave."

He jerked his head up. "What?"

"Leave. Five minutes." Mason gestured to the door again.

Logan tossed his car keys at him. "Go get some sandwiches, I'm hungry."

"Are you kidding me?"

I lifted a hand. "Can you get me a latte?"

His mouth fell.

"See you. Thanks." Logan chuckled and waved his fingers at him. "Family meeting, mofo."

He growled and then stomped out the door. As soon as he was gone, Logan folded his arms and stuck his chin out. "You've got the floor, Mason. Go ahead."

Mason threw him a dark look before he swiftly pivoted on his heel and pulled the door shut. As soon as it clicked in place, he was in Logan's face. "Are you kidding me? You want another go at this kid?"

"Yeah. I want to be there this time."

"Logan, this kid isn't some public student. He's Academy. His dad does business with ours. We can't keep fighting these pricks."

"Why not? He's a loser?"

"Because dad could suffer for what we're doing."

Logan rolled his eyes. "Oh, come on. Dad owns this town. He's running half the state. He's got businesses all over the world. I don't think we need to worry about this kid." He gestured to me again. "Besides, you really like how he keeps sniffing around Sam? You know he's rallying to come back around with her again. I bet you anything he was going to try last night, but she shot him down."

"This isn't about Sam."

"Yeah, it is."

Mason stood in front of him and faced him squarely. "You're going to be selling that crap?"

Logan lifted his chest up. "Why wouldn't I? It's the truth."

"Then you're on his level. You want to see who has the biggest balls. Congratulations, Logan. I do. I punched him out."

Logan narrowed his eyes. "You're putting me on his level?"

Mason shoved his face against his. "I'll punch you out too."

Logan shoved him back and jumped off the desk. I braced myself, ready for round two, but Mason shook his head and backed away. "Grow up, Logan. It's fun and all, but dad's involved. You think this is good for him where he has to throw his weight around so I don't go to jail and you want to do it again? Pricks like this guy don't get bullied down."

The corner of Logan's mouth twitched. And then he exuded a deep breath and jumped to the floor. He shook his hands in front of him and seemed to be shaking something off. "Whatever. Fine. You're right."

Mason growled and crossed his arms over his chest. "Damn right I am. *If* I get out of this, we stay away from these guys for a while, alright?" He tapped Logan's chest with a finger. "Okay?"

Logan shoved his finger away, but the corner of his mouth curved up. "Fine. You're usually right about these things, but man—I wanted to punch that kid. You don't know how hard it was to get that text that you knocked him out and I wasn't there."

"Take it out on Roussou Friday. Those guys are a better fight."

"Yeah, maybe."

They both fell into a shared silence and I held my breath. I was unsure what to say or if I wanted to break whatever camaraderie they'd fallen into. My hands were shaking and I tucked them under my legs, but I tried to quell my voice. "I don't really understand what just happened with you guys, but am I the only one worried about Mason here?"

Logan cracked a grin and he was back to his usual cocksure way. "He'll be fine. Dad will get him off. We need to worry more about your situation."

I shivered as I remembered the few times I had glimpsed when Miranda or any member of the Elite had walked past our doorway. If looks could kill…

"We can't do much about that." Mason shot me a brief look and I saw the apology in his eyes. "Mom's coming."

Logan shot up straight. "How do you know?"

"I texted her."

"Why? Dad can handle this."

"Yeah, but what if he can't. She's got better connections."

Logan expelled another breath and shook his head. "Oh man, you're playing with fire. Dad, Analise, and mom in the same room."

I lifted a hand. "And David…with my real dad maybe coming someday?"

"What are you talking about?" Logan shot Mason a look. "What is she talking about?"

He lifted a shoulder. "Her mom called her real dad. He might be coming."

"What? No. She's with us." Logan looked at me. "You're with us. You can't leave."

One of my eyebrows went up. "Uh…I wasn't planning on leaving. I don't even know who he is."

His shoulders relaxed. "Oh, good. I like having a sister that's banging my brother."

"And shut it with those references." Mason reached out and pushed him back a step. "I'm getting sick of it."

Logan's smile slipped and he shoved his hands in his pockets. "Yeah, sure. No problem."

No sooner had he uttered those words when the door opened again. We expected Ethan, but I sat up straight when David walked in. James and Analise came in behind him, but they rounded to the other side of the room while my dad stopped inside of the door.

James shared a look with Mason, but Analise kept fidgeting with her hands in front of her. She'd glance up every now and then and I followed her gaze the last time and my own widened as I sat up. Malinda Decraw had come inside and stood beside David. She touched his hand for a brief moment before he took a breath and stepped towards us. She remained behind him, but I couldn't get that touch out of my head. It was a sensual caress, one for comfort? Why was it so sensual? Why was she here?

David cleared his throat and tugged his shirt out an inch. "I—uh—a decision's been made." His eyes found Mason's and they hardened.

Mason lifted his chin, but that was his only reaction.

David narrowed his. "When Adam woke up, he wouldn't tell us what the fight was about." His eyes skirted to me with a dark question in them. "But he admitted that he was the initial aggressor. He said you were trying to leave, but he wouldn't let you. Then when you got out of your vehicle, he harassed you and threatened you. Fallen Crest Academy does not take Adam's actions lightly, but since you charged him and knocked him out, we've decided on a punishment. Adam's parents do not wish to pursue criminal charges against you. Instead, they have agreed with the following discipline in three parts."

Mason's mouth hardened, but he was stone face otherwise.

David glanced at me again. An unreadable emotion flashed in them, but he slipped back into his professional mode. "Since you are not a student at Fallen Crest Academy, they are unable to seek expulsion or suspension in any form. However, we've already sent word to your school's officials and we highly recommend that you be suspended from them—"

Logan surged forward. "No way, he'd be out of the game on Friday. We need him against Roussou."

"Son." James clasped a hand on his shoulder. "Let Coach Strattan finish."

Logan quieted, but glared at my dad.

David continued, "As I was saying, we are seeking a suspension for you, but it will be up to your school if they follow through with that recommendation. Now, after four hours of deliberations we've decided that you will volunteer at our school's alumni festival this Saturday."

"What does that mean?" Mason had leaned back against the table where I sat, but he stood now. His arm brushed against my leg.

I glanced down at the contact. A shiver went through me, but my heart pounded. He had said three parts, those were only two…

"You will help with the set up, you will do whatever I tell you to do throughout the day to help out, and you will help with the clean up. There is a dinner that night for the volunteer and staff. I will determine if you will be invited to that or not."

"Oh." Mason leaned back beside me again. His arm was loose again. "That's fair."

David frowned at him.

"You said three parts," I spoke up. David turned towards me and pinned me with his gaze. He was trying to search inside of me. His eyes narrowed and they glanced back and forth from Mason and me.

"Sam," my mom hissed.

David held a hand up. "No, that's fine, Analise. I did say three parts and the third part's already been taken care of. Your father has made a generous donation to the school."

Logan snorted. "Dad, you bought his way out—"

James turned on him. "You will keep your mouth shut, Logan."

His eyes widened and his mouth jerked in reaction, but Logan shrunk against the counter he sat on. His eyes took on an angry leer.

James' eyes were lidded, but he turned towards my father and jerked his head down in a nod. "As you were saying, David…"

My dad cleared his throat once more.

Malinda moved forward a step and touched the small of his back.

My heart snapped and I jumped to my feet. "What are you doing in here?"

"Samantha!"

I ignored my dad and walked to her. "You're Mark's mother. You have no connection to anyone in here. Why are you here?"

Her mouth formed a small oval, but she looked to David.

He stepped between us and spoke in a quiet voice, "She is here for me. She's become a good friend to me, Samantha."

I fell back, reeling, and looked at my mother. She had grown pale with a hand pressed against her chest. Her other hand clung to one of James'. It was hidden from eyesight, but I still saw it. When she realized that I saw it, she gasped and retracted her hand to her side.

Why was she pale? And why did she need comfort from James… then I understood. My heart sank and my stomach had dropped to the floor. It was really over with them. My mom had moved on with James, David was starting to move on as well… My head fell forward and I hugged myself.

A hand touched my side gently. Mason tugged me back by the belt loop on my jeans. He tucked me behind him and moved forward a step. "I heard that festival is for two days?"

David was still looking between us. "Uh—yes—yes, it is." He frowned. "Why?"

"I could volunteer both days."

"You could?"

"Man," Logan hissed softly.

Mason nodded. He held his gaze steadily. "It's the least I could do."

David gave him a sad smile. "Your school won't suspend you. We both know that, they need you for their football game."

The corner of Mason's mouth twitched. "What time should I be here on Saturday?"

"Seven sharp. Come to my office."

Mason's head jerked in a nod. "Will do."

David looked at me. "Would you come to my office later today?"

I stared at Malinda behind him. "No."

"Sam."

He waved a hand in the air. "It's fine, Analise. I can talk to her next week."

My mom trembled, but she nodded at him and tried to muster a smile.

For a moment, David looked around the room and then he gave out a soft sigh. "I guess I'll be in touch then…"

James strode forward and held out a hand. "Thank you, David."

They clasped their hands in a firm handshake and studied each other for a beat. Then David nodded again and turned for the door. He held it open as Malinda swept out before him. Pain sliced through me when I saw his hand touch the small of her back and remain there, even after they went in the hallway.

When the door closed, I was barely aware of Mason. He stood and I heard his voice at a distance, "Mom's coming to town. We'd like to stay with her at the hotel."

"I think that'd be for the best this week…"

"Fine."

"Fine."

And then there was silence. David and Analise were actually done… The realization settled on my chest and a wave of tears threatened me. I rushed from the room and shoved through the hallway. When I found an empty backroom, I locked the door, kept the lights off, and slid to the ground. My forehead touched my knees and I sobbed.

CHAPTER THIRTY-THREE

I went to my last two classes, though I didn't learn a thing. My body had gone numb again. I missed that feeling and I was itching for another three hour run. My body ached for it.

Becky chatted to me after school. I had no idea what she said, but I nodded my head at random moments and she kept chatting away. When I looked for my keys in my bag, I cursed and hit my head against my locker.

"What?"

I mumbled, "Mason drove me today."

"He did?" She straightened from a locker. "Oh, right. That makes sense, why he was here…wait…is he coming back to give you a ride home?"

Then my phone beeped and I pulled it out. He had sent me four text messages and the last one read: **Two practices tonight, then with mom and Logan. Can you get a ride home? Need me to send someone?**

I cursed again. "Can I get a ride home with you?"

Becky's eyes got wide and her lips clamped together. A strange gurgle escaped her lips.

"What does that mean?"

She whispered, "Adam gave me a ride." She jumped back and pressed a hand to her mouth. "I'm sorry."

"No, that's fine. I'll think of something."

She edged closer a step. "He can't come and get you?"

I shook my head. My throat was so closed up, had been all day. "No, they have two practices tonight and their mom's in town."

And that meant I wouldn't see either of them all week…probably… I swallowed over a lump.

"Hey, I bet Adam would give you a ride!" Her head bounced up and down. "Yeah, yeah. I bet he would. I think he feels real bad. He called me last night and said that he wanted to make things better with you. He wanted all three of us to be friends again."

"He did?"

"Uh, yeah. I mean, why would he make that up if he didn't mean it?" Her grin turned sloppy and a glaze drifted over her eyes.

Oh boy. I recognized that look.

She sighed dreamily, "Wouldn't it be wonderful if all three of us hung out again? And then maybe he'd realize he needed me in his life?"

I gave her a blank stare. "What do you mean? You are in his life; he gave you a ride to school."

"Yeah, I know." Her eyes drifted downwards and she bit the corner of her lip. "I was just meaning that if us three were better friends. It felt like we were going to be before, but then he got all weird and mad at you. It changed when he found out about the Kades, now that I think about it."

"Becky."

She turned to me. Her eyes clicked into focus. "Uh?"

"What's going on with you?"

Her eyeballs went from side to side. "What do you mean?"

"You're weird, weirder than normal." Then it clicked in place. "What have people been saying about me?"

As soon as I said that, she sucked in her breath dramatically and scooted away from me.

"Becky." I clamped onto her arm so she couldn't go any further. "What's going on?"

She patted her chest and it rose higher and higher. It looked like she was hyperventilating or having a panic attack. I hoped not, I needed answers.

"Becky!"

"Okay, okay." She dragged me down the hallway and into the empty theatre. It was dark where we were, but the lights were bright on the stage where a group of people stood in a small circle. I didn't care what they were doing up there.

"Spill. Now."

She looked in pain as she rushed out, "MirandaStewarthatesyouandnow everyoneelsedoestoo." She took a deep breath. "And everyone thinks Adam and Mason fought over you. Everybody knows something happened at the Elite dinner Miranda had and that you guys went there, but no one will say what happened...so...people are figuring out their own guesses."

"People think Mason and Adam fought over me?" A blast of cold air rocked me again. My stomach dropped out again and a surreal feeling of terror started to settle in. Was I ready for this? The knot had doubled in size. I forcibly swallowed one more time. I knew what would happen if people found out...

"No, yes, I mean—I don't know. We don't really know. Some people think it's about Logan. I'm not sure why, because of Tanya or something. I have no idea. Everyone knows Logan took Tanya away from Adam and we all saw that Cassandra and Adam were flirting. Now they don't even talk to each other. Something happened."

"Oh." Relief washed over me. Adam's fight with Logan over Tanya made more sense, didn't it? "Yeah, I mean, Logan wasn't nice at the dinner. He rubbed it in Adam's face."

"Rubbed it in?" A hollow laugh came from behind me. Jessica gripped her books tight and glared at me. "We heard he was practically having sex with Tanya at the dinner. No wonder Adam popped his cherry and went after Mason today." She eyed me up and down and curled her lip in a sneer. "We also heard that Emily Connsway laughed in your face. Way to go, Sam."

The theatre door was open and a small group had congregated behind us.

"Give it a rest, Jess." Lydia sidled up beside her and leveled her with a piercing look. "Stop making up lies, stop being a bitch, and apologize to Sam for what you did."

Jessica's back straightened. "Me? Apologize? What did *I* do to her? She stood there and let Logan Kade humiliate me. He used to like me and she ruined that. You ruined my life, Sam. Thanks a lot."

Jill pushed forward to stand beside them and chewed on her lip. Then she burst out, "I'm sorry for being a bitch, Sam. I was threatened because of Jeff." She waved towards Jessica and Lydia. "And I didn't want them to do to me what they did to you so I tried to be friends with them. You know, get closer with your enemies and all…that…" She hung her head and trailed off.

Jessica whirled towards her. "You're such a whore, Jill. Sam's not going to be your friend. She hates you and me. She hates Lydia too."

Lydia gasped. "I don't think she hates me. I'm trying to be her friend." She looked at me with pleading eyes. "I'm really sorry. I really am. And I don't care if Jessica hates me after this. I should never have covered for her and Jeff and lied to you. I should've apologized to you right away too." She edged closer and shoved Jessica back a few steps in the process. "I really miss you and I'll do anything to be your friend again."

"Lydia!"

She ignored Jessica and gave me a shaky smile. "I don't care if the Elite don't like you. I'll support you and stand by you the whole time. They don't scare me."

Jill sighed. "Yes, they do. They scare everybody…well, except for maybe Sam, but still."

"Hey…?" Jeff stood at the back of the crowd, and they opened for him. His face was twisted in confusion. "What's…what's going on here…? Do I even want to know?"

Jessica turned her glare off and went to his side. She gave him a seductive smile as her hand traveled up his arm. "Hi, Jeff."

"Hey!" Jill removed her hand from his arm. "I'm not going to let you sleep with him."

Jessica's eyes didn't blink. "Can you give me a ride home, Jeff? My car's in the shop for an oil change."

He blinked at her. "Uh...sure...yeah, okay."

"Jeff!" Jill seethed.

He met my gaze for a second, but shrugged at his girlfriend. "It's just a ride home. I'm not going to sleep with her or anything." Then he motioned for Jessica to follow and the two left.

Becky's mouth hung open. "I—" She blinked. "I can't believe that happened."

"Lydia, do you think they're going to...?" Jill blinked back some tears. Her voice hitched on a sob.

"Yes." Lydia didn't waste a second. "They are. I'd dump him in a heartbeat if I were you."

My eyebrow rose. This was a different side to Lydia that I'd never seen before. When she gave me a small smile, I almost gave her one back. Almost.

Jill's mouth fell open and tears started to fall down her cheeks. She wiped them away, but turned and darted down the hallway.

Lydia shook her head. "I don't feel bad for her. She knew what they did to you."

I shrugged. "I don't care anymore." I never had. "So you and Jessica aren't friends anymore? She's going to think you betrayed her for me."

"I know."

"She's not going to let that go."

"I know." Lydia gave me a sad look. "I miss being your friend. I'd like to earn that back and that's what I'm going to do from now on."

"Hey!" Becky grabbed my arm. A smile spread from ear to ear. "She can give you a ride home."

"You need a ride home?"

"Uh, no. I'm okay." Nightmares flashed in my head. I wasn't sure who knew that I was staying at the Kade mansion and I wasn't going to let Lydia be the first one to know for certain. "I'll find—or call—someone else."

"Are you sure? I can give you a ride home. It's on my way, you know."

"I'm okay. Really." Every cell inside of me relaxed. She still thought I was at David's.

"Wait. Are you still at your dad's house or…?"

I gave her a bright smile. "Speaking of my dad, he wanted me to talk to him so I'll see you guys later." I pushed through the crowd and hurried away before either of them formed more questions. People would figure it out, if they hadn't already, but I wasn't going to help it.

As I got to my locker, I grabbed my bag and phone. When I went to the parking lot, I started to call my mom, and I couldn't believe she was my last resort, but stopped abruptly. I blinked a few times, but then I put my phone away. My mom was already there. She was waiting in her convertible.

"Hi, honey." She waved her fingers at me. "I got you a coffee."

"Mom," I started as I got inside. "I really can't handle much right now so if you've got any more bombs to lay on me, can you leave them for another day?"

Her smile slipped a bit. "Are you okay, honey?"

I stared at her. Had she not been there when I stormed out of the classroom? "I'm perfect."

She laughed. "Well, I don't know about that, but you're pretty good."

My mouth wanted to fall to the ground. Where had the mom from this morning gone? She professed she wanted to change and now I got the Barbie fake mom again.

At a stoplight, she let out a deep breath. Her voice dropped to a normal tone. "Well, I'm sorry about those bombs, but I do have one to drop on you." She paused for a beat. "Your father's in town."

I closed my eyes.

"And he wants to meet you."

"Oh no."

"Tonight."

I wanted that run. I needed that run right now.

I looked at her. "How long is he in town?" My voice came out breathless.

"It depends on you." She held my gaze until the light turned green. As we started forward again, she gripped the steering wheel with clenched knuckles. "I don't like that he's here, but he is. David's going to flip about this."

My heart was pounding again. It was a horse track. "Mom, I can't..."

Her hand clasped onto mine and she squeezed it. "I'm sorry, honey. I really am, but your father's a jerk. If I tell him you don't want to see him, he won't believe me. He'll show up anyway and I'd like to avoid that, if possible."

"Mom." My voice was a whisper now. "I can't. I really can't."

She kept driving and we were almost home when she murmured, "Okay, honey. I'll tell him you're not ready."

Everything sagged forward at that. As soon as we got home, I unbuckled and bolted for the door. I was back on the pavement within ten minutes with my running shoes on and my headphones in my ears.

Three hours later when I turned into the driveway, my stomach had stopped rumbling. Everything was numb in me, it was the way I liked it, and I was blind to the three cars I passed as I let myself inside. I trailed through the house and eyed the droplets of sweat that slipped from me. I doubted my mom would care, not that I ever did, but the small grin that formed on my face was wiped away when I went past the dining room.

A man sat at the table with my mother and James. He had striking blue eyes and broad shoulders. He looked in his forties with a strong jaw and a lean physique. Confidence and authority exhumed from him. As he turned towards me, he never blinked. I felt pinned under his gaze and steeled myself. He was trying to read into me, as only Mason tended to do sometimes.

"Sam, honey." Analise jumped up. "You're back from your run."

I couldn't answer her. I couldn't look away from this man.

She laughed nervously. "This is your father...Garrett Brickshire."

"You're the hotshot lawyer from Boston?"

The corner of his lip twitched. "You're the pain in the ass daughter I never knew about?"

"My mom said you were a jerk." I paused. "That was an understatement."

"She said the same thing to me." He stood and my eyes widened. He kept standing up. And he towered above my mom and James.

"How tall are you?"

"I'm six four. How far did you run?"

I would've shrugged, but my body couldn't respond to me anymore. "I have no idea."

"You're not training for a marathon?"

"I run to run."

We were locked in some form of battle. Neither of us could look away, neither of us could back down.

His mouth twitched now to a mocking grin. "You should keep track of what you do. Your achievements define you."

My lip curled upwards. "Then I'm not worth your time. I don't have any achievements. You can go back to Boston and your hotshot lawyer life."

He blinked.

He broke. I won.

Then he laughed in a smooth baritone voice. "Yeah, you're my kid alright." He turned to Analise. "I still want the test done, but I'm 99% sure she's mine."

She huffed out, "Like I'd lie to you after seventeen years, Garrett."

He chuckled. "I think you lie so much you don't know when

you're not." His eyes met James. "No offense to your future bride. I'm sure she loves you well enough."

A look twitched in James' eyes. "You've seen her for yourself. Now you can return to your hotel to wait until Samantha is ready. I believe she should determine when and if she's ready to meet with you again."

The cockiness vanished in Garrett's eyes and he drew himself to an impressive height. He reached for James' hand. As they shook, he said, "I've heard of a James Kade. Though the circumstances are strained, I'm glad to have met you."

"You as well, Mr. Brickshire."

They studied each other for a moment. It reminded me of the exchange between David and James earlier, but this one was different. There was an edge to it that I hadn't felt in the classroom with David.

Then the moment was broken as Garrett passed by me. "I'll see you later, kid!" He thumped me on the shoulder before the door shut behind him.

I needed another run.

CHAPTER THIRTY-FOUR

The rest of the week was quiet. I knew Garrett was at some ritzy hotel. Analise told me he offered to pay for my own suite so we could get to know one another, but that was the one and only time she mentioned him. I was content to let him sit and wait.

School was also quiet. Lydia never left my side, which was refreshing. Becky was right beside her and the two seemed like long-lost kindred souls. She insisted that Adam wanted to make things right again, but he never approached me. I caught a few looks from him, but that was the extent of it. The Elite had fallen quiet as well. Miranda and Amelia glared every now and then, but as the week progressed their glares faded. Cassandra rolled her eyes whenever she saw me and she would whisper to whatever friend was nearby, but I never let it bother me. It hadn't before, why would I start now?

Of the four Elite girls, Emily was the one who hadn't changed with me. She never talked to me before and she didn't now. There were no glares or eye rolls either. One time she bumped into me, but kept going. From the distracted look on her face, I was inclined she didn't know who she had bumped into. And judging from how she hurried away, I didn't think she cared.

The only Elite member who did talk to me was Mark, and both of us felt awkward about the exchange.

He stopped at my locker one day and looked above my head.

I turned around to see who was behind me, but there was no one. "Can I help you?"

He cleared his throat and looked in pain as he did it.

"Mark? Hello?"

I spotted Lydia and Becky down the hallway. They were giggling about something, but both stopped in their tracks when they saw who was in front of me. Hands flew over their mouths and their heads bumped together. They scurried into a nearby bathroom and I knew they wouldn't save me either.

He continued to stare over my head and his mouth kept twitching. I grew tired of waiting and snapped my fingers in front of him. "Hey, I'm down here. Look at me if you're going to talk to me."

His eyes widened a fraction. "Oh yeah…"

Oh goodness. Here we go again.

"Um…okay, this is really *weird* to say, but…uh… My mom wanted me to invite you to our house tomorrow night."

"Why?"

"For dinner." He looked down now and almost jumped back a foot. He frowned, twisted at his shirt's collar, and looked away. "This is so uncomfortable."

"And perplexing." I grabbed his shirt and hauled his face down so he was eye level with me. "Why does your mom want me over for dinner?"

"Because of Coach."

"Explain."

"Oh, uh, they're dating." He reared back. "You didn't know?"

My heart shrunk. "I had hoped to forget it. Thanks for reminding me."

His mouth twitched up now. "Hey, no problem. Okay, so she wants you to come over around six. Can you bring a bottle of wine?"

"I'm underage."

He shrugged. "Get one from your mom; tell her it's for the dinner."

"And is it?"

He grinned again. "Nah, man. We can drink it later. I figure you can come to dinner and then we can take off for the party afterwards.

It'd look cool to show up with a bottle of wine, you know. It's like we're mature and grown up."

"What the hell are you talking about?"

"The Kade party." He frowned at me. "You didn't know?"

I glared at him. "Well I do now, don't I?"

"Yeah, it's going to be awesome. They're throwing it in some huge suite at a hotel. My dad's stayed there a few times. It's supposed to be out of this world."

So they had time to spread the word about a party, but not invite me? I folded my arms over my chest and leaned back against my locker when Mark bounced away. He slapped hands with another guy as he did so and they started laughing. I watched his lips and knew he was talking about the Kade party, the one I hadn't been informed about. Then again, I shouldn't have been surprised. Mason and Logan disappeared after Tuesday. They were with their mother the whole week. James went to their hotel one night, but Analise and I hadn't been asked to go along.

I never heard from them the rest of the week. A part of me tried to be reasonable. They were busy. They had lots of practices and I knew both were intent on demolishing Roussou, tonight's game.

It made sense why I had slipped their minds.

I groaned and let my head fall back with a thump against my locker. It made no sense. They should've called me, or texted.

"Hey." A soft voice spoke and I opened my eyes. Adam stood in front of me with a grim look on his face.

"Hey."

He looked around. "Do you think we could talk somewhere?"

I gestured for him to lead. I had no idea where to go.

He gave me a small grin before he started off and looked back every now and then to make sure I was following behind. As we passed the bathroom, Lydia and Becky popped back out. Their eyes went wide again and there was a repeat performance from before. They scurried back in with hands over their mouths and heads together.

I rolled my eyes and saw a mirrored reaction on Adam's face.

When he pushed open a door, I saw we were in some room with televisions, keyboards, and computer screens loitering around. Cords were everywhere. "What is this?"

"It's where the media geeks hang out."

"Won't they need this room?"

"I don't care. They won't come in until we're done."

And with those words, an awkward silence fell over us. I looked at him, he looked at me. Neither of us spoke. So I slumped down on some couch. When did the media geeks get a couch for their room? Then I stopped caring as Adam cleared his throat and fiddled with his thumbs.

"Just say what you need to say, Adam. We can leave as soon as you're done."

He expelled a deep breath. "That's the thing; it's harder to do this than I thought it would be."

"To do what?"

His eyes found mine and pierced me. "To apologize. I've been trying to do it all week, since Tuesday, but I couldn't muster the courage."

"You need courage to be nice to me?"

He laughed. "I need courage to humiliate myself for you again."

I frowned. Humiliate?

He ran a hand through his hair and rubbed at his jaw. "Look, I'm real sorry about everything that's happened. I've been a huge ass and I know that doesn't even cover how I've been towards you."

I looked away. Did I want to hear this? Then I sighed. It didn't matter. Here it went...

He continued, "You know that I liked you, I still do if I'm being honest. When I found out that you were tight with the Kade brothers, I went crazy. I was jealous and I was a prick and you have every right to never talk to me again. I was acting like a spoiled douche bag that didn't get his prize."

I looked down. "I think that's putting it mildly."

He chuckled. "Yeah, probably. Look, Mason had every right to knock me out. I said something horrible about you to him."

My head jerked up. "What'd you say?"

He choked on his next words. "What? He didn't tell you?"

"No, he didn't so you tell me. What'd you say?"

He grimaced. "I'd rather not."

"Adam."

"You're going to hate me even more now. I thought you knew."

I couldn't ignore how he kept looking at the door. "Adam. Speak now."

He groaned and messed up his hair. "Oh—fine. I might've mentioned something about if he was dropping off his whore…or something like that. I'm not sure what word exactly I used, but it wasn't a nice one."

I swallowed a lump of coal down my throat. "And what'd he say in return?"

"Besides the punch? He might've said something like I looked pathetic, I'm not sure. That whole day was jumbled up to me. I was stupid that day, real stupid. I deserved what happened to me."

"You deserve to get hit again, if you ask me."

He grimaced. "I know and I'm sorry. I'm really sorry. My dad asked me what I said to piss off Mason Kade. When I told him, he said the same thing. He said I was being stupid and then my mom told me I was acting like a spoiled brat."

"Why were you? I never told you I was going to date you."

"See, that's the thing." He sat on another couch and cursed when a bunch of cords obstructed his way. He shoved them aside. "I thought maybe you didn't want to date me because you weren't over Sallaway. I thought you needed time and I was going to try and give that to you. I wanted to give that to you, but then I saw how Kade handled you. Literally handled you at their party and I went crazy. I couldn't believe that ass—" He stopped as he saw my face.

"I'm just real sorry. I am, Sam. And I'd really like for you and me to be okay. I know Becky's been hammering at my ass since day one with you. She won't let it go."

"So are you here for me or for her?"

"Both," he groaned. A grin slipped past his lips. "Miranda is livid with me. She wanted to upstage you, but the whole thing between me and Mason made it impossible for her to do what she wanted. I kept telling her it wouldn't work. You wouldn't care."

"What was she going to do?"

"I'm not sure what it was, but she was sure you were going to get mad."

"How would you know I wouldn't care?"

He threw me a look. "Because you don't care about anything. It's your M.O. You don't give a damn and no one can touch you because of it."

I folded my arms over my chest. "Really?"

"Yeah. I think that's why you go on those long runs, so you don't feel anything."

My foot twitched as he said that. Since Mark told me about the party, I was planning on going for a run as soon as I got home after school. Being numb got me through every day. Why mess up a good thing?

"So…are you still pissed at me?"

I started laughing and once I started, I found that I couldn't stop. I bent over and continued to laugh into my knees. My shoulders were shaking so much. Then sobs started to come and I couldn't stop them either.

"Sam?"

I couldn't respond. Tears flowed freely down my face, but I kept laughing. They started to blend in a form of hiccups that my body kept bursting out with.

"I'm really confused. Are you okay?" He sat beside me and I felt his hand touch my back. He jerked it up right away, and then touched between my shoulder blades again. "Are you okay?"

I wasn't. My word, I wasn't.

The laughter subsided and I kept crying. I couldn't stop the tears. Each sob wracked its way through my body and then Adam turned me into him. I couldn't help it. I knew I shouldn't have, but I burrowed into him and more and more sobs kept wreaking havoc over me. He patted my shoulder and then held me against him. He lowered his head so his chin rested on my shoulder and he murmured against my neck, "Let it all go. Let it out. It's the only way. Let it all out, Sam." His hand started to rub circles on my back.

"Oh my god. I'm sorry." I pulled away and wiped at my cheeks. I couldn't believe I'd done this. "I've been a mess lately."

He frowned and his lip twitched. I knew he had something to say, but he held it back. Whatever it was, I didn't want to hear it. I couldn't handle it so I stood and backed away.

"Sam, you can cry, you know. I'm here for you. Anytime. Call me and I'll come get you. I promise."

He seemed so sincere. Something dark filled me and I shook my head. "And when you see me with Mason again? What are you going to do then?"

His hands pressed against his side and his shoulders straightened. He kept his voice neutral. "Nothing. I promise. I won't do a thing anymore." Each word seemed to bring him pain. "If you want to be with him, then so be it. I wish you…happiness…"

He looked away and his jaw clenched.

It wasn't over. "You might mean your apology now, but nothing's really changed. You hate that I'm with him—"

"If you're with him then why are you crying on my shoulder?" he bit out. "He's not here for you. Have you ever cried on his shoulder?"

"This was good timing for you."

"Like hell it was! You broke down in front of me. I rather doubt there are a lot of people that you've broken down in front of. You're always so in control of your emotions, but not now. You let me in.

That's what happened here. You trust me, even if you don't know it, you trust me. I know you do."

"Stop." The word slipped from me. My voice was shaky.

"Sam, think about that." He held a hand out to me and I couldn't bear the sight of his pleading.

I shouldered away his hand and slipped from the room. As soon as I had collected my bag, I bolted from school. The week had started with a bang and it ended with one. As soon as I got home, I went on a run and three and a half hours later I limped my way home.

I'd been running too much. It was starting to become unhealthy, but it did its job. I collapsed in my bed as soon as I left the shower. When I woke it was dark out and I grimaced in confusion. My phone peeled through the cool night air and it lit up my desk.

I groaned, but pulled myself up and stumbled to it.

Logan's name flashed across the screen.

I snapped it open, not sure if I was ready for this. I mumbled out, "Ello?"

"You didn't come to the game?"

"Huh?" I squinted at the clock. It was after nine? I should still be in bed. "Logan," I groaned. "I was sleeping."

"Our biggest game this season and you weren't here!"

"Oh god." I pressed a hand to my head. "You're not going away, are you?"

"No, look, I'm pissed. You should've been here tonight."

My insides started to stir awake. "Are you kidding me? How was I supposed to know? I haven't talked to either of you all week."

There was silence for a second. "You haven't?"

"No," I snapped out. "I had to hear from Mark Decraw that you guys are having a party tomorrow night."

"Oh…I'm sorry, Sam. I really am. I thought we told you about that."

"How would you? You'd have to communicate with me to do that."

"No, I thought, oh man, I thought Mason must've been talking to you since the two of you are…"

"Stop right there. We're not dating. We're not anything. For me to know what we are there'd have to be a conversation about it and I haven't heard a word from him so there's definitely been no conversation about that." My chest was heaving up and down. I patted at it. I needed to calm down.

My phone beeped in my ear and I cursed as I pulled it away. Mason had sent me a text: **Want to eat? I'm hungry.**

I groaned into the phone. "Is he there with you?"

"Who?"

"You know who."

"No," he sighed. "I was calling to chew you out, but that didn't turn out how I thought it would—"

"Where's Mason?"

"I don't know. I'm being honest. Some of the guys are headed out for pizza and then there's a party. I was going to see if you wanted to come with, but now I'm scared to ask you. Why? Did he call you now?"

"Yeah."

"Call him back. I'll see you tonight." His voice got cheery and the dial tone blared in my ear next.

I cursed as I glared at the phone. It beeped again and it was another text from Mason: **Are you home?**

Then I heard his voice in the hallway. "Sam?"

It wasn't long before my door was pushed open and he flicked my light on. I was blinded for a moment.

"Hey, did you get my texts?"

I snapped my phone shut and drew my robe tighter around me. "Yes."

He grinned and ran a hand through his wet hair. He looked like he'd showered. "You pissed at me because I haven't called all week?"

"Nope. Not at all. I cried on Adam's shoulder today."

His eyes narrowed and lingered on my face. "Did you?"

"Yep. I did."

"Okay. I don't know what to do with that. You want to get some food with me? There's a party tonight."

"Is there?" I cringed at the jealousy in my voice. It wasn't like me. "I'm sorry. I'm acting stupid."

His eyes took on a darker look and he shut the door behind him. He turned the light off and it wasn't long before his hand was on my knee. He murmured against my skin as he tenderly nudged me back down on the bed. "I'm sorry I haven't called this week. I am."

My neck arched when his lips found it. His hand swept from my cheek, down my arm, to my waist, and swept back up to cup my breast. I groaned when I felt his hand work its way past my robe and his thumb grazed over my nipple. His mouth replaced his thumb and I felt his tongue sweeping around it next.

He whispered against my breast, "It won't mean much, but I thought about you. All week. I wanted to do this and I knew if I called you, I'd come over and do this."

"Just…" I braided my hands through his hair and pulled his head up. "Shut up."

He chuckled before his mouth slammed onto mine.

CHAPTER THIRTY-FIVE

He thrust in me a last time. My legs were wrapped around his waist and one of his hands held them up as the other braced himself on the bed above my head. My entire body lifted off the bed as my climax ripped through me. Waves of pleasure rode through me and I trembled as he held me in his arms. He trembled with me and then tucked me in front of him to curl around me. He tucked his chin into the crook of my neck.

When he yawned, his whole body yawned with him.

Something fluttered in my stomach at the feel of that and I laced my fingers through his. "No party for us tonight?"

He chuckled and his breath caressed my skin. "It's three in the morning. It's a bit late for that."

As he tightened his hold on my waist, my eyelids started to close, but my whole body felt renewed and invigorated. "Are you going to stay the night?"

He cursed and reached over me. "I need to set the alarm."

When he was done, I turned and slid one of my legs through his, the other was on top of his and I snuggled against him. He pressed a kiss to my forehead and my body tingled as he brushed back some of my hair.

"Your mom's not expecting you?"

"Nah. She knows we're out. She's not stupid. Logan probably won't go to the hotel either." He chuckled and skimmed a hand down my side. "He dropped that girl. Did you hear about that?"

"Tanya, the one Adam liked?"

He smirked. "The *other* one he liked, yeah. He dropped her after the game and went off with some other girl."

"He called me after your game. He was pissed I wasn't there."

He smoothed back some of my hair and ran a thumb over my cheek to my lips. "I wasn't sure if you'd come. I figured if you came, I'd want to bend you over." He grinned. "No offense, but you get in my head."

"Do I?" I grinned as I caressed up his arms. His muscles twitched under my touch.

He groaned and wrapped his arms around me to hold me tighter. He rolled to his back and pulled me on top. I laughed huskily as he ran his hands over my body. When he hardened between my legs, I closed my eyes to enjoy it. The heat was gathering again. As he smoothed circles on my back, I laid my head on his chest.

I was intoxicated with him and I murmured against his skin, "When do you have to get up?"

"In three hours."

His hands started to explore some more and when he dipped a finger inside of me, I was helpless. Desire coursed through me and I was soon throbbing again. It wasn't long before I had enough and sunk onto him. He responded quickly, but after he had thrust deep, he gasped and shoved me off.

"What?" The need for him was making me blind. I only wanted him.

"Condom," he rasped out. He rolled over and reached for one. As soon as I heard that wrapper, I reached for him again. When it was slid on, I raised my hips and sunk down again. I pushed him deep and he fell back with a groan. Then I rolled my hips and started a rhythm. His hands grasped onto my thighs and he pushed and pulled me until we were both gasping for breath. As my climax was nearing, I dipped my head and touched his lips with mine. His tongue swept against mine and took control of the kiss. A primal emotion took root. I was helpless against it. Our hips slammed against each other and we hurdled over the edge together. Waves exploded in me and I trembled as each rushed through me.

"Sam." It was a whispered caress from his lips before he placed a gentle kiss on my lips again. Then he held me against him as his own body trembled with mine. After our breathing had steadied, he murmured, "I only need two hours of sleep anyway."

I bit back a laugh and raised my head. "So now we sleep?"

His eyes were on my lips as his hand cupped the side of my face. And then he cursed. "I can't get enough of you."

"You *have* been gone all week."

"Yeah." His hand started to trace up and down my back now. "I think my mom's going to stick around for the month. She's got some friends that she wanted to visit. Dad's going to love that."

"I met my dad." I flushed as I said it. I hadn't meant to, but as soon the words left me, something lifted off my chest.

He met my gaze through the darkness. "You did?"

I nodded before I pressed my forehead to his chest. "He was here Tuesday night when I got back from a run. We didn't talk much."

"What'd you talk about?"

"He asked if I kept track of my achievements and I told him he could go home, I wasn't worth his time."

He chuckled, but then his hands skimmed down to my waist and he lifted me higher on him. He started to nuzzle underneath my chin and as the same need started to stir inside of me, I closed my eyes and surrendered. We both knew he wouldn't get any sleep.

And when his alarm went off, neither of us slept a wink. With a huge yawn, he rolled over and shut the alarm off before he slowly turned and sat on the edge of the bed.

I sat up and scooted against my headboard with the sheet gathered around me. "Are you going to be okay today?"

He shook his head and then shrugged. "Shower. Then I'll tell you."

When he stood from the bed, he checked his phone, cursed, and yawned again. I watched as he tried to shake the yawn away, but it didn't go anywhere. Then I realized I had one also. I was still yawning when he came back from the shower.

He came to the bed and bent down to press a kiss to my forehead. "I'm going to get some clothes from my room and take off." He swept a hand down the side of my face and lifted my chin. I gazed at him through sleep deprived eyeballs. They should've been sucking the moisture out of the air, but I didn't feel an inch of my exhaustion.

"Okay."

"I'll see you tonight?"

I nodded and my eyelids were already starting to droop as I nestled under the covers. I was faintly aware of my door opening, but my bed was so comfortable. I was asleep before it closed.

When I walked into the festival, I wasn't sure what to expect. I had never been one for school events so the sight of streamers, balloons, blown-up slides and fun houses wasn't what I had in mind. Booths were spread out everywhere within the school. They started in the parking lot with one for coffee and cappuccino and one was even snuggled in a back janitor's closet for Fallen Crest Academy flags.

Little kids darted around my feet. I saw more than enough of my classmates and our teachers positioned everywhere. When I passed the football booth that had footballs with Fallen Crest Academy's name on it and made with our colors, I saw David chatting with some parents. Then I realized they had old varsity jackets on and knew these were the alumni.

I wandered through the entire school, even up to the third floor, before I found Mason. He had been tucked near the art room behind a table of white lacey doilies. He was lounging back in his chair, his arms crossed over his chest, his legs crossed underneath the table, and his cap pulled low enough to cover his eyes. As his chest rose up and down at a steady rhythm, I enjoyed the sight for a moment before I kicked his feet.

He jerked back, startled, and threw back his cap. A snarl lit over his face, but he relaxed when he saw me. "I didn't know you were coming today."

"What if I'd been my dad?" I shrugged. "Why not come, it's my school."

He grunted. "What does he expect? He stuck me up here selling some church ladies' handkerchief things. No one wants these." He eyed the coffee in my hand. "You got another one of those?"

I grinned and pulled out an energy drink.

"Thanks." Then he nudged the other chair out. "Want a seat? Keep me company?"

"So you can sleep and I'll sell the doilies?" I was aware of his hungry gaze as I sat beside him. Every nerve in my body was awake and kicking because of it. Who needed coffee when I had him?

"No one wants to buy from me. I look angry when I'm tired."

As he yawned again and tried to cover it with his hand, I thought he looked adorable. His eyes were softer from the fatigue and his eyelids drooped a bit. His lips were a little swollen from our kisses and his skin looked bright with color. When I caught sight of the hickey I'd left under his shirt's collar, I reached over to tug his shirt to the side.

He grinned when he realized what I was doing. "Yeah, I keep moving my shirt too, but it always goes back. I'm sure people have already seen it."

"I hope not." What if David had seen it?

"Who cares if they do?" He studied me as he said that.

"What? I'm supposed to say something or...what?" Was he testing me?

He cracked a grin and squeezed my knee. "I'm messing with you, but I don't care if they see it or not."

I'm not sure how to react so I grew quiet and sat back. After a few minutes, I knew he'd fallen back asleep, but it was a relief. His presence affected me so much. I had a hard time making clear decisions, especially when it came to him or us. After an hour and after I had sold three doilies, I nudged his foot. His eyes opened and he was awake, just like that. There was no sudden movement, no snort. Sometimes he reminded me of a machine.

"I'm going to wander around."

He groaned. "Please stay. You make this somewhat bearable."

I grinned at him. "Could you be more dramatic?"

"Yes."

Something bolted inside of me when I saw he spoke the truth. He was unreadable again and my finger itched to reach out and touch his lips. Those delicious and earth-shattering lips that could do wonders on me... I shook my head to clear the lustful thoughts.

His eyes had darkened as he watched me. "You want to go to my car? I have a lunch break coming up."

"Your car? Now that's romantic."

"It's the best I can do. I don't know this place and I'm pretty sure every hidden nook and cranny is being used."

I arched an eyebrow, but I saw the teasing light in his eyes. Oh how those eyes could unravel my wardrobe in a heartbeat. "I'm going to get some more coffee."

"Get me some?"

I nodded and moved past him. He leaned forward and his hand grazed the back of my thighs as I went.

A jolt of lust coursed through me, but I readied against it. It was a feeling that I was starting to grow accustomed to, but as I pushed into the bathroom, I wasn't ready for the sight I saw in the mirror. The girl who looked back had sex-crazed written all over her. Her lips curved up in a seductive tease with a blush to her cheeks. And the lust in her eyes had darkened them so they wore an unrecognizable gleam. My skin glowed and I touched it in wonder.

Who was this stranger?

The door shoved open behind me and I turned away, but I was too late.

Cassandra laughed abruptly as she stood beside me and washed her hands. She eyed me in the mirror. "Who've you been banging, Strattan? You look good."

I flushed under her gaze and watched with helpless horror as my skin seemed to glow even more. "Maybe I should be asking you that. How are things with Adam?"

She snorted and reached for a paper towel. "I think you'd know more about that than me. He told me you two made up yesterday."

I looked down at my hands. Had we? Maybe…

She continued as she patted her hair, "I'm not stupid. I know he wants you, he's always wanted you, but you don't want him." She snorted again. "And he doesn't have a chance against the Kades. I'm just waiting until he realizes that and gives up."

I looked back up. She was so cold.

She shrugged and smiled brightly. "What do I care? It's not like I really need a serious boyfriend now anyway." She laughed to herself. "And I heard Logan's back on the market. He was at Fischer's again with some other chick."

Every cell in my body had snapped to attention when she came in. I spoke through stiff lips now. "Maybe Adam will want Tanya back?"

She tossed her hair over her shoulder and her laugh seemed genuine. "Yeah, right. Adam didn't even like her that much. No way he'll take her back after Logan had her twice over him. Hell, he did it to rub it in Adam's face that he could get any girl he wanted." She eyed me up and down in the mirror. "You haven't been with Logan, have you? That'd be…surprising…"

My eyes grew wide at her suggestion and my chest was suddenly so heavy. There was no way she could guess the truth; she was so close to it… My heart started to pound in my ears again.

"Have you?" She blinked at me. She seemed more earnest now.

"No." The disgust was evident in my voice as I spat out that word.

She relaxed and laughed again. "Oh, for a minute I thought…

Nah. You don't have the stones to do that. I mean, your dad would freak for one."

My heart continued to pound.

Then she finished with a taunt, "And you'd never live down your new rap as a whore. Everyone would call you a whore." She smirked to herself in the mirror and finished patting her hair. "On second thought, get to it. Maybe Adam will finally let you go. I could use the break."

As she swooshed from the bathroom, I was barely aware of her departure. I kept hearing her words. *Everyone would call you a whore.*

I gulped and looked down. My hands had started to tremble again. My knees quaked against each other and I clung to the sink to steady myself.

Everyone would call you a whore.

What was I doing?

CHAPTER THIRTY-SIX

When I left the bathroom and headed for the coffee cart, I wasn't sure what I was feeling. Was I worried about everyone finding out about Mason and me—yes. Was it enough to paralyze me with fear—no. With that decision made, I was more annoyed than normal when I snapped my order to the girl behind the coffee counter.

"Whoa, what's wrong?"

I stopped in my tracks at the sight of Adam. And then I tried to force myself to relax. "Hey, how are you?"

"You okay?" His eyebrows were arched high with his own cup of coffee in hand.

I rolled my shoulders back. "Yeah, I'm fine or I will be."

"Huh?"

"Nothing, just an annoying run-in with Cassandra in the bathroom."

"Ah." He nodded his head. "Gotcha. She does that to me too."

"I think she's decided to try her luck with Logan again."

"Yeah, she told me the same thing." Something sad flashed in his eyes. "It won't work, will it?"

I shook my head. "Nope and if it does, I'll tie him down and do a drug test on him."

He grinned. "Yeah, you seem pretty tight with both of them."

"I guess…" I eyed him warily. We were treading into forbidden land, could he handle that reality? He couldn't before.

He spread his hand wide. "Hey, I'm okay with this. Really. I've given up on that, but I won't for your friendship. I'm going to do whatever it takes to keep your friendship."

An arm was thrown around my shoulders and Logan's body fell hard against my side. He smirked. "Really?"

Adam drew to his fullest height and the gentleness in his eyes vanished. A hard look entered instead when he clipped out, "Really."

Logan's body shook in silent laughter. "You just want to keep her friendship, huh?"

"You got a problem with that?"

"Yeah, I do. She's going to be my sister, man. You think I want a parasite hanging around her because that's what you are. You're one of those guys who sit back and wait for the guy to screw up. When she's hurting or lonely, you guys swoop in. Hell, I should tip my hat to you guys. I couldn't do it. I couldn't wait around and watch the woman I wanted be with another guy, waiting until there's a break with them, until she's vulnerable." He mocked him. "Yeah, it must take a special kind of guy to do that."

Adam's eyes had narrowed to a dangerous level. His hand was clenched into a fist, but he kept it down and pressed against his side.

Logan continued, "Or maybe that's what makes creepers. I've got a different viewpoint on stalkers now…"

Adam's lip curled up as he tried to mask a sneer. "You're calling me the creeper? What are you doing?" His eyes pointedly slid to me and it took Logan a second before he launched himself forward. His arm was thrown back, his fist ready, and look of hatred came to his eyes.

Adam's eyes went wide as he saw it in slow motion, but before Logan's fist connected, Mason tucked an arm around his chest and threw him backwards.

He cursed as he tried to twist away from his hold. "Let me at him, Mase. Come on."

Shaken, Adam puffed out his chest and smoothed his hands down the front of his pants. "Hey, man. If it weren't true…"

Mason glanced over his shoulder. The look of warning made Adam shut his lips. "Shut up or we'll do round two, somewhere private."

Logan threw over his brother's shoulders, "Where there won't be teachers or some girl to save you."

Mason glanced at me and I narrowed my eyes. There was a searching look in him. I lifted my chin. What was he looking for? Then I tried to search inside of him. What was he thinking?

He blinked and the look was gone. The normal unreadable wall was back in place. He threw Logan in front of him and neither seemed to care about the crowd that had formed or who Logan ran into.

Adam seemed frozen in place.

Cassandra's voice came from behind me. I gritted my teeth as I heard her coo, "Logan, are you okay? Did he hurt you?"

Logan barked out an ugly-sounding laugh and shoved her to the side. "Back off. You've got no chance."

I tried to suppress a smile at that, but couldn't so I looked down.

"Oh shut up," she cried out in anger. "You do not laugh at me, whore."

My head came up and my eyes widened. Her fury was directed at me. She approached with two steps and a hand in the air. "You dare to laugh at me? Do you know who I am? Or what I could do to you? I would demolish you, slut. I would run your name through the mud so much you'd beg me to let you out of your misery. You'd be—"

Something snapped inside of me and I marched up to her. I knew my eyes were dead when they met hers and she shrunk away, a little bit. "You think you scare me? Nothing scares me. Nothing, Sullivan."

"Whatever..." she tried to laugh it off and turn away.

My hand clasped onto her arm and I whirled her back around. I was in her face and all the hatred I had boiled to the top. "You want all the dirt on me. Here you go. I hope you take notes. My mom's a cheater. She left my dad for another guy and took me with. I was living with two guys who hated me because of that. Then I found out my boyfriend was screwing my best friend and my other best friend knew about it, for two years. Next bombshell—my dad's not my dad. Think it could get worse? It did. I had no one. No friends, no nothing. The guy who raised me all my life couldn't talk to me because of stupid legalities. Now my real dad's in town, my mom's hit me a couple times, and I'm screwing my future stepbrother. You think I'm scared of you?" A hollow laugh broke out of me. "I can handle anything you've got up your sleeve."

There was silence around me and then she belted out a hysterical laugh. "I knew you were sleeping with Logan. Of all—"

I slapped her.

Then I stood there and waited for her reaction. She gasped and reeled back with a hand pressed to her cheek. Her eyes bulged out and she was seething. "You just—"

My face was calm, devoid of emotion. I didn't feel a thing. "I did. What are you going to do about it?"

She watched me, torn for some reason.

My eyebrow lifted. "Are you going to hit back or are you going to tattle on me?"

The tension was thick in the air. I felt it swirl around inside of me and knew she could see the storm inside of me. I wanted her to hit me. I wanted to hit her again…I wanted a reason to unleash my hell on someone…

Her shoulders slumped forward and she looked down as she stepped back.

I clipped out, "Are you backing away from me?"

She looked up. I caught the scared look in them. Then she turned and was swallowed up in the crowd.

I stared after her and started to look around. Miranda Stewart stood there, so did the rest of the Elite. I met all of their gazes unflinching. One by one they looked away. When I got to the last one, I was surprised to see pity in Adam's gaze.

"What are you looking at?"

His chest lifted up and down. "I told you. We're friends. I may hate your stepbrothers, but not you. Never you."

Logan bit out a curse. "Is he serious?"

Mason turned on him. "Shut up." He strode forward until he blocked me from Adam's gaze. His back was to me, like so many other times. "Message received, Quinn. You're not going anywhere, but neither are we."

Adam flinched, but a resolved look came over him.

Then Mason reached behind him and grasped my arm. He turned and led through the crowd, dragging me behind. Logan followed, but threw a few dirty looks behind him. He muttered under his breath, "Gonna bust your face open."

We hadn't gotten to Mason's car before David's voice hollered through the parking lot, "You can't leave, Mason. You agreed for the whole day and tomorrow."

Mason let go of my arm and cursed as he turned back around. Empty cars were parked all around us and a slight chill breezed around us after a soft rain. The cars were wet and small puddles had formed on the pavement. David approached us with a forceful stride. His jaw was clenched tight and his shoulders were thrown back.

He raked his gaze over me, but spoke to Mason, "You can't leave. That's part of your discipline."

Mason cursed at him. "Forget your little agreement. I'm not staying in there where my brother and your daughter get attacked. You've got a bunch of angry pussies on your team. They don't know when to shut up and leave things alone."

David's mouth turned into a frown. I felt his gaze over me again as he asked softly, "You were attacked, Samantha?"

I jerked away.

Mason stepped in front of me again. "Quinn's obsessed with her. That doesn't bode well with the rest of the girls in your school. She should switch to public school. We could protect her there."

David stepped around him and reached for my arm. "Sam, is this true?"

I hissed as I swung my arm away, but I sent Mason a searching look. What was he doing?

"Sam."

"What?" I wheeled to the only father I knew. "What do you want? The guys in there hate Mason and Logan. You were stupid to think this would work out and Mason could last the whole weekend."

David looked down. "I tried to steer him clear from them."

"It didn't work. Think of another plan, but surrounding him with those guys won't work, especially if he's alone. Logan and I were there to support him."

David's jaw clenched. "Who were they, Sam? Who targeted him?"

I wanted to throw my hands up in frustration. He wasn't hearing me. He didn't get it. "No one, but they don't mix. Mason, Logan, and me—we don't mix with this school."

"You've gone here all your life."

"I don't mix anymore."

"You don't want to go to school here anymore?"

Logan stepped forward and brushed me back with his arm. "She's not saying that, sir. Fallen Academy is a good school. Sam will be fine, but she's saying that you can't ask us to get along with your football team. It won't work, sir."

David looked between the three of us. He breathed in and out and then murmured, "So it's like that, huh?"

I closed my eyes. His hurt was evident.

He added in a quiet voice, "You're one of them, aren't you? I tried to tell you—"

My eyelids came back up. "Are you kidding me? Is this really about Mason and Logan or is this about you and mom? Why'd you want Mason to volunteer at the festival? Was it really because you needed the help or is it because you wanted one of James Kade's sons under your thumb, for even a little bit?"

"Sam." Mason touched my arm.

I whirled to him. "Back off."

He moved a step away, but there was no judgment in his eyes, only understanding. My heart jerked at the sight of that. I didn't want him to understand me. No one could. They'd only pity me instead.

He blinked and it was gone. His hand moved away from my arm.

David looked between the two us, but sighed. "Samantha, your mother said I could have joint custody of you—"

"My real dad's in town."

He had his mouth open and a sound choked out of him before he shut his mouth.

I glanced down. "She's lying to you, whatever's going on between you two about me, it's all a lie. She called my dad a week ago and he's in town. He wants to get to know me." I looked back up and tears had formed at the corners. "I'm eighteen in four months, David. None of this will matter anyway. I don't know why you're even going along with it."

"Because I care about you." He touched my arm instead. "You're my daughter, Sam. I raised you. It's never going to matter who your real dad is or what your mom says. I've been there since you were born. You're my family too."

The dam broke in me and I turned as I covered my face. David hugged me to him and I cried into his chest.

We stood like that for a while until Logan cleared his throat. "This is touching and all, but…I'm uncomfortable right now."

I could sense the disapproval from David as I lifted my gaze. A smile touched the corner of my lips instead. "Get in touch with your emotions, Kade. It might do you some good."

He looked in pain. "Yeah…"

Mason cleared his throat. "Can we go? The touchy-feeling scene is done."

David shook his head. "What my daughter sees in the two of you—"

"She's not really your daughter." Mason didn't blink as he leveled him with a look. "She comes from someone else and you were the one who swooped in to raise her, but like she said—she's going to be 18 and it's not going to make a difference. It'll be her choice." He stepped forward and his chest touched my back. An arm curved around my waist and he pulled me against him before he kissed my shoulder where my shirt had been pulled to the side. His breath fanned against my skin. "And she's made her choice, a couple times now…with me."

David's face had turned to stone.

My stomach twisted into a knot and I felt it drop to my feet. I didn't know how to undo what he'd done.

Logan covered up a laugh behind us, but I knew he wasn't hiding back his smirk.

Then David bit out, "Why did you want me to know that?"

Mason fell silent.

My dad jerked forward a step. His eyes gleamed with some emotion I couldn't place. His jaw was so rigid. "You made a grand show here, Mason, and you wanted me to know that my daughter is sleeping with you. Congratulations. I figured it out long ago, but your delivery was in poor sportsmanship. Why'd you do it?"

"Do what?"

"Deliver your triumph how you did." David's eyes were unyielding. "You wanted to hurt me. You wanted me to know that she's sleeping with you. Why? Are you threatened by me? Do you think she'll listen to me if I tell her to dump you?"

Mason's arm stiffened around my waist, but he remained quiet.

David went on, "I don't like you. I don't like either of you, but I respect you as football players. I don't think you've ever been coached by someone that you respect and I don't think you've ever respected another man, even your father. I've watched the two of you on the field. Everyone has in this state and you are both ruthless. You're the best and you make damn sure everyone knows it on the field, but the one thing that always strikes me isn't how good you both are, it's your level of respect. You don't respect anyone else on the field, but you respect the game. Every time I watch you, I think to myself what kind of men are you two? What motivates you?"

"You think you're the coach that we're going to respect? Did you raise Samantha with Disney movies too?" Mason's tone was mocking and it sent chills down my back. His arm wasn't moving around my waist.

David moved back a step and he sounded sorry when he spoke. "I think of the men you could've been under my watch. You would've been twice the men you are now."

Logan had grown quiet, but Mason let go of my waist and moved me behind him. He was face to face with my father now and his tone had gentled. "You think we're two kids who grew up with bad parenting, but you're wrong. I might not respect my dad, but I love him and I respect my mother. You've never met her. You don't know a damn thing about Logan and me, but you're reaching for straws. I don't like you, but you're a great coach. I've watched you too and I know you're a great coach, but your players don't respect you, sir. They listen to you because you motivate them, but don't misunderstand that. They don't respect you. If they did, Quinn would never treat Samantha how he does. She's a prize to him. You want to paint us as the bastards that grew up with no competition. You want to paint our dad as someone less than you, but you couldn't be farther from the truth. We grew up knowing who we're going to have to deal with during our lives and guys like you, guys like Quinn are a dime a dozen. They're around every bend in the road. Logan and I aren't stupid enough to buy the crap most adults try to sell."

He turned and met my gaze. I flinched under his stare, but held it. He was looking for something inside of me and I knew I couldn't look away. I couldn't quake or tremble so I settled my nerves, stood upright, and lifted my jaw. My eyes were hard as I stared back at him.

Mason turned back to my father. "I respect you as a coach, but I don't respect you as a man. You should've never let Sam go."

The fallen look on my dad would haunt me forever. That knowledge trembled inside of me and I turned away to press into Mason's arms. He swept me up and pressed a kiss against my forehead. As he deposited me in his vehicle, I didn't hear anything. Logan should've been laughing. My dad should've been yelling. I should've been crying, but there was nothing. Just silence.

It echoed throughout my body.

CHAPTER THIRTY-SEVEN

We went to their hotel. It was some ritzy place. I didn't care and I trudged behind them as we rode the elevator to their top floor. Of course they'd be staying in the top suite, it only made sense, but as we got there Mason pressed a different button. Logan got off and gave us a salute with a cocky smirk. "See you later." The elevators slid to a close on his words and we rode the elevator down two floors. It stopped on the one between and as it opened, I stepped back into Mason's side.

Garrett stood there, waiting for the elevator. His shocked gaze swept over me and then Mason. He murmured in a fake Southern drawl, "A bee's bit my asscheeks to be seeing you here. How are you?"

I pressed my forehead into Mason's side and his hand swept around me. He answered for me. "Who are you?"

"Her dad."

I flinched at his tone.

I heard the smile in Mason's voice. "Really?"

"Aren't you Helen's kid?"

"What about her?"

I jumped at the sudden intensity in Mason's voice, but his hand swept up and down my back. He held me against him.

"Nothing. I like your mother. She's quite a woman."

"I think so."

"So how do you know my daughter?"

Mason chuckled. "That's something you can ask her when she's ready for questions."

There was a heavy silence after that. I knew both of them were waiting for me, but

I shuddered and melted against Mason. His hand held me close and I felt a soft kiss on my shoulder.

I needed it. I needed all the support I could get at that point. Everything was out. It wouldn't take a genius to figure out that I never meant Logan, but Mason. I knew my whole school would be buzzing about my relationship and my father—David—what could I say about him? He was gone. I felt it in my bones. And now we saw my other dad...what did I even think about him?

He knew Mason and Logan's mom.

That was weird.

Garrett chuckled as the elevator opened on our floor. "You and your men, little girl. They're all waiting for when you're ready."

Mason hit the emergency stop and turned to face him. I had started to step off, but waited with a pounding headache and a tight chest. What was going to happen now? I wasn't sure how much more I could handle...

"What are you talking about?"

Garrett wiggled his eyebrows up and down and skimmed a hand over his face. "I figured it out, took me a second, but I forgot Helen was married to James Kade. It all makes sense now. So what are the two of you doing here? I'm guessing Analise doesn't know about this relationship...*is* it a relationship or you two kids bumping uglies to piss the folks off?"

Mason's smile was a veiled threat. "And it's your business because...?"

Garrett narrowed his eyes and studied Mason for a moment. My heart pounded in my ears as I waited. It seemed to stretch out into strained silence as the two stared at each other and then Garrett broke with a curve of his lips. He shook his head and stepped forward to unlock the emergency brake. "You got balls, kid. Helen would be proud."

As the doors started to slide close, Mason's hand stopped them. They retreated back and he narrowed his eyes this time. "You're the guy bumping uglies with my mom?"

Garrett's eyes widened a fraction. "How do you figure that?"

"She came to town for me, but she's staying because a friend of hers showed up. The timeline makes sense. You've got the floor below us."

"That's a leap, kid."

"Not a kid and it's not a leap if it's true." Mason's face was chiseled in stone. His eyes didn't twitch. "You're the guy, aren't you?"

The amused smirk vanished from Garrett and he pushed up from his leaning stance. He stretched to his highest height and moved a step closer. As he looked down his nose at Mason, a warning look came over him. "You could be breaking a few hearts if you start spreading that around."

Mason smirked and stepped back. His hand fell to his side. "She told me he was married."

My mouth fell down, but no sound came out. My heart was deafening now.

Garrett's eyes slid to mine. As the doors started to close again, he drawled, "Ya gotta keeper there, girlie."

When the doors had closed and the elevator moved down, Mason swept a hand around my back and propelled me towards one of the two doors on the floor. He slid his card in and opened it as I entered first.

I didn't look around before I whirled back to him. "My biological dad is cheating on his wife with your mom?"

Mason grinned as he started to shred his clothes, but it didn't reach his eyes. "I guess."

"Your mom is a cheater."

He toed off his shoes and grabbed my hand before he pulled me towards a king size bed in a corner of the room. As he sat down, he tugged me between his legs and looked up. "My mom's a bit hard when it comes to men, especially after what my dad did to her."

"She's the other woman." I slid my fingers through his hair and took hold. As he started to rest his forehead against my stomach, I raised his face to look up.

His eyes were bleak. "She wasn't before and it's complicated."

"It's always complicated."

"Your mom was the other woman too. My dad was the other man."

My heart started to pound again. When I heard a slight condemnation in his tone, I was breathless as I asked, "Is that what you think is normal?"

Would he cheat like they all did?

"Cheating?" A dark loathing flared over his face and I stepped back in reaction. It was intense. It rattled me for a second. "Cheaters are weak. They're selfish and they're cowards. No, I'm not a cheater and I never intend to be." He focused on me. "Why? Are you?"

A laugh ripped out of me. My hand reached for him again and I closed a fist over his hair. "After my mother, now my biological dad, and what Jeff did to me? Are you kidding me?"

His eyes softened and he slid a hand underneath my shirt. "People don't know what they're made of until they're tested. You need to pull yourself out of a situation and think of the collateral damages, if it's worth it."

"You speak from experience?"

He grinned and leaned forward to kiss my stomach. My shirt was lifted higher and he started to tug me down onto him. Both of his hands went around my back and up to my shoulders as he pressed me down. I sunk down and felt him harden between my legs. He kissed his way around my neck to my lips and whispered against them, "I had a girlfriend once."

I wound both arms around him and held him against me, tighter than I knew I could. "Oh yeah?"

"She cheated on me." He leaned back and waited for my reaction. "What?"

He laughed and nipped at the corner of my mouth. His lips nibbled their way around my lips before he opened against them. His tongue touched the corner of my lips and I opened for him. He swept inside and his hand gripped the back of my head to hold me still. The ache started to throb inside of me and I squirmed against his lap. I needed to get closer, I had to.

Then he pulled back and fell against the bed. He gazed at me with lust in his eyes. They darkened as he nudged me higher on his waist. "My friend, Marissa. She cheated on me."

"Are you joking?" I frowned at him.

He laughed and lifted my shirt over my head. "Yeah, I am about her. I didn't date Marissa. I had a few other girlfriends and most of them cheated, but I wasn't surprised. I wasn't dating them for their caliber, if you know what I mean?"

"You didn't cheat on them?" His hand slid to my back and he tipped me down to him. I was breathless as my head landed on his shoulder where I turned and licked. My body stretched as his hands slid to my bottom. He cupped my cheeks and grinded me against him.

"I've never cheated. Being faithful was one thing I valued as I grew up. I made my mind long ago that I'd never be like my dad. I'd never do that to a woman I respected, even to someone I didn't respect. I won't lower myself to those standards."

I whispered against the side of his mouth, "Logan cheats."

He caught my mouth with his and whispered back, his lips brushed against mine, "Not if he loves the girl and I don't give a damn what he does." Then his mouth took command of mine and I was lost after that.

I tipped my head back, but I was blind with lust. As his hand slid to my pants and he slipped two fingers inside of me, my throat was full. I couldn't talk anymore and I groaned when he rolled me underneath him.

Thirty minutes later, after Mason arched over me for his last thrust, my body collapsed onto the bed and I waited as the waves rode over me. He groaned and fell onto me. I welcomed his weight. He entrapped me, but I felt sheltered. Safe. My legs felt heavy with exhaustion and slid down the length of his to fall onto the bed.

It wasn't long after that when he propped himself on an elbow beside me. My throat was still thick with desire and I gazed at him. My fingers twitched to touch the side of his face, to feel how soft his eyelashes were, the slight stubble on his chin, the dip in his shoulders where his muscles attached together…I wanted to touch all of him again.

I struggled to clear my throat and asked in a hoarse voice, "Is it always like this?"

He shook his head in a slow motion. "No. It's not." His eyes darkened again and he bent down to me.

I tipped my head back and met his lips with mine. It was a soft kiss, but it didn't deepen into more because a soft beep sounded before the door swung open. Mason cursed and jumped to block me from whoever entered.

"You better put some clothes on because if you think that sheet's going to keep me from having a word with your new girlfriend, then you're not the son I thought you were."

Mason cringed. "Mother, leave."

"I want to talk to her—"

He spoke over her, "We will come upstairs to have this conversation."

She laughed and the sound gave me chills. There was an intelligent shrewd tone in her voice, but the anger sat me up in attention. "With Logan to interject with his snide comments, I think not. This conversation will happen without your brother's snarky attitude. You think I'm a fool so the three of you can team up against me? I'm no fool, Mason James. Logan likes your litty bitty. He's told me that he supports the two of you." She drew in an angry breath. "I'm not having it."

"Fine, mom." Mason had been holding a sheet in front of him and let it drop. "We'll have it out like this."

"Put something on," she hissed. "I'm not some high school cheerleader you can intimidate or make me squirm by showing your penis. I've seen it before. I was the one who changed your diapers."

He bit out a laugh and sat down instead. He gathered the sheet around his lap again, but kept his back to me.

"Oh for the love of your grandfather, she's going to have to face me at some point. Get some clothes, Mason. I've been waiting all week to meet Analise's daughter. It might as well be now," her tone gentled.

Mason's shoulders stiffened. "It's not going to happen like this, mom. Go upstairs. We'll be up in a few minutes."

There was a silence that filled the air with more tension.

Then she sighed. "You're not going to budge, are you?"

"And you're not going to come over and move me."

"You're as stubborn as me." She bit out a laugh that resembled Mason's. "I don't know if I should curse your genetics or mine. Fine. Be upstairs in five minutes, not a minute late or I'm coming back down."

When the door shut, he looked back and grimaced. "She's been after us all week to call you. She's the real reason we didn't call."

I drew my knees against my chest and hugged them tight. "Why does she want to meet me so much?"

"Now it's because of this, but it was about revenge against your mom before."

"Revenge?"

He ran a hand over his face and looked exhausted. His shoulders slumped and he let out a deep sigh. "My mom's not dumb. She's known about Analise since she was poking around dad. And knowing that the guy she's been seeing is your biological dad, I'm not too surprised. My mom can be calculating, Sam."

I swallowed over a painful knot. "Why did she want to see me before so much?"

He stood and started to pull some clothes on. As he poked his head inside of his shirt and tugged it down, he remarked, "I think she wanted you to like her more than your mom. Logan and I haven't been quiet. She knew you weren't happy with Analise any more than we were. But now…" He trailed off as he looked towards the door.

"But now," I prompted.

He shook his head and bent to grab my clothes. He handed them over as he sat beside me again. "I have no idea."

As I fitted my bra on and reached back to clasp it, I muttered, "I bet she thinks I'm like my mom now."

He didn't respond.

I looked up and saw the pity in his eyes.

"Don't," I hissed at him. "You don't feel sorry for me, not now after all the crap that's happened to me."

The corner of his mouth curved up. "You don't know my mom."

"I know you respect her." I held his gaze for a long drawn out moment. "I know you love her and you want to protect her."

"I did." He leaned forward and kissed me. "But that was before I realized something."

"What's that?"

He stood and waited until I pulled on my underwear and jeans to tug me beside him. Then he drew me in his arms for a tight hug and spoke against my shoulder, "I'm pretty sure my mom went after your bio dad to get back at your mom."

I lifted my arms and hugged him back. "Why do you think that?"

"Because in my mom's thinking, Garrett's the only guy your mom couldn't get."

"Why do you think that?" I leaned back and looked up.

He ran a finger down the side of my face in a gentle caress. "It's something I might do, if I was pissed off enough."

"If that's true, then…" A stone dropped to the pit of my stomach and a cold feeling started to sweep through my body. "Then you're right. I should be scared of your mom."

He grinned down and lifted me so I wrapped my legs around his waist. Our eyes met and held as his hand spread out over the bottom of my back. He leaned forward and nipped at my lips. I grinned and caught him in a deep kiss when he did it again.

When he started to walk out of the room and to the elevator, he sighed against my lips, "I won't let her do anything, Logan too." He breathed against me again. "I think that's why she's so mad. We won't let her hurt you."

When the elevator rose to their floor, he set me on my feet. The door opened and he took my hand in his. "You ready for this?"

I gave his hand a squeeze.

CHAPTER THIRTY-EIGHT

When we entered the top suite, I drew in a deep breath and let go of Mason's hand. He glanced back, but I shook my head. I needed to do this on my own, somewhat. Logan sat on a couch in the corner. He had two bags of chips on the table in front of him, a small television in his corner, and a cooler beside him. His smile couldn't be wider on his face and when he saw our entrance, his hand slid into the cooler. It came back up with a beer and he started to chug half of it down.

"Are they here?"

I flinched at the tone of their mother. When no one answered, she came around the corner. Her hand was raised to fix an earring in place. When her eyes lit on me, her hand fell down in slow motion. She straightened and crossed her arms over her chest as she lifted her head high and her shoulders were squared.

For a moment, I was speechless. She was beautiful. She had a model's body, tall and lean with long legs. She wore a white business skirt with a pale pink cashmere sweater over it. A necklace of white diamonds rested above her cleavage. They matched the diamonds in her ears and I caught a flash from her wrist. My eyes couldn't get any bigger at the sight of the diamond bracelet there. Even her pale pink high heels shimmered from the diamonds on their straps.

She had golden blonde hair, which looked streaked from sunlight and that rested high in a loose bun. Tendrils fell to the nape of her neck and with her clear blue eyes; she looked the image of a goddess. But her lips had formed into a sneer as she took her time to study me in turn.

Her wrist flicked at me with irritation. "This is Analise's daughter?"

Logan choked out a laugh, but guzzled some more of his beer.

Mason and their mother threw him a glare. He sank back against the couch and raised a hand across his lips. They were zipped.

Mason frowned at him, but sighed. "Yes, mother. This is Samantha."

Someone buzzed on the door and Logan jumped to his feet. He scurried around the room to open the door. Garrett Brickshire straightened as he viewed the room dressed in a navy blue suit. He'd been leaning with an arm near the top of the door.

"What's he doing here?" Mason rounded to his mother.

Logan's eyes widened. His smile grew and he hurried back to his seat. He picked up a bag of chips this time and started to munch on them.

Their mother grimaced, but swept past us. She rested a hand to Garrett's chest as his lips skimmed a kiss to her cheek. She gave Mason a small smile. "I figured it's appropriate. He is her real father after all, and you know about the two of us. We can deal with two birds with one stone tonight. Mmmm? Don't you agree?"

Mason glanced at Logan. "You okay with this?"

He made a show of showing his zipped lips again and shrugged.

"Thanks." Mason didn't hold back a wry tone to his voice.

Logan bobbed his head up and down as he reached for another beer.

And then there was another buzz at the door. Helen frowned as she walked to it and peered through the peephole. "Who could that be—oh my god." She turned back with a panicked look on her face. Her chest started to rise and fall at a rapid pace and she seethed at Mason, "Were you behind this?"

"What—no..."

Garrett rubbed a hand over his jaw and shook his head. A low baritone chuckle escaped him. "Now, darling, it only seemed appropriate for me to call her. She is my daughter's real mother after all."

"Garrett," she snapped and cursed at him. "Now's not the time to be charming."

He lifted a shoulder and arched an eyebrow before he perched on a couch's end. "Answer it, darling. They're going to find out anyway and it might as well be now. They can't be angry at us later for withholding information. I know Analise would throw that at me."

"Mom, what's going on…" The words died in Mason's throat as she opened the door and his father walked in, followed by my mother. Both of them wore reserved expressions, but when Analise saw Garrett, she sucked in her breath. Her face stretched at every angle over her skull. She looked in pain and then her eyes swung towards Helen. A confused look replaced the horrified one.

Logan groaned behind us. Something that sounded like a mix of laughter and curses slipped out. He snorted next and pressed his head into a couch cushion as his shoulders shook.

"Honey, what are you doing here?" Analise asked me. She was cold and formal.

"Helen? Why are we here?"

All eyes turned towards James, who was frowning at Mason.

Garrett stood from his perch and stretched to his fullest height. "She didn't call you. I did."

Analise jerked forward with fists clenched to her sides. "Why?"

He swung his head towards us. "Ask them. I was doing my fatherly duty." His lip curled up in a mocking manner.

"Sam?"

"Mason?"

"Garrett, what are you doing here? Sam, did you call him?"

I choked on my own vomit. "Are you kidding me?"

He drawled out again, "Nah, the girl doesn't want anything to do with me, Lise. You did a good job. She hates the sight of me."

I ducked my head and wished I could disappear. This was not somewhere I wanted to be.

"Why? What did you do to her?"

"Honey," James tone was soothing. "We were called here for a reason. Helen, you weren't behind this?"

She choked out an angry snort. "Are you kidding me? I'd like to handle our sons without your interference."

"And why would you have to handle them?" His tone cooled. "Mason? What is your mother referring to?"

Analise's look was filled with loathing as she glared towards Garrett. "Why in the world are you here?"

Helen's laughter peeled out this time. "I can take credit for that one, Analise." Her lip curled up in disdain. "You're going to find out anyway. Everything's going to come out now."

"What are you talking about, Helen?"

"Helen, let's spare some of the sordid details."

She threw a seductive grin towards Garrett. "I think I'm going to have to. Your ex doesn't look like she can handle all the details, not just yet anyway."

My mother paled and she jerked forward a step. "What are you talking about? Garrett, what is she talking about?"

He threw his head back and rolled back his shoulders. A cocky smirk came out. "I'm leaving my wife, Lise. I fell in love with someone else." And he threw a pointed look towards the middle of the room.

Analise seared everyone with a glare. "And why do I get the feeling you're not talking about your daughter?"

Helen smirked and poised with a hand to her hip. "He's talking about me, *Lise*. We were going to wait until his divorce was final, but we're engaged." And with that, she flipped a ring around on her finger. The diamond was double the size of my mother's. It sparkled as she wiggled her fingers around. "You like it? It matches the rest of my accessories. Only another woman can appreciate my outfit."

Mason groaned next to me and sat on the couch beside Logan. He passed the chips and the two munched away.

Analise gasped as the information sunk in and James cursed under his breath. He pulled his fiancé back with a hand tucked around her arm. "Are you kidding me, Helen? And how did the two of you meet? I'm supposed to believe it was by chance?"

"Oh no." Helen oozed with arrogance. "You see, when you started to run around behind my back with her, I hired a private investigator. And I learned all sorts of things, including the biological father of Samantha Jacquelyn Strattan. From there, all the pieces fell into place. It wasn't even hard to get the man Analise never could. Garrett and I had instant chemistry—"

He grunted. "We did. Screwed on the first date." He shrugged then. "Of course, it helped that my wife had already cheated on me and I learned about it that day."

"Oh my goodness." Analise bent over as she started to pant. "Honey, I can't breathe."

There was a look of enjoyment in Helen's eyes that had me snarling. I shot to my feet. "They called you here because of me. I'm screwing Mason."

And then someone else buzzed at the door.

James bit out a curse as he wrenched it open. He stopped in shock as David stood there, with Malinda behind him.

David scanned the inside and turned back. It wasn't long before Malinda left and he stepped inside.

"Great." Analise was livid. "This is great. Where'd your girlfriend go this time? She's not here to support you?"

David frowned, but his eyes rested on me. A tinge of concern had seeped into them. "I can see this is a family-only matter. Malinda came with me for support if I should need it. Her son came as well. I believe he's attending a party in this suite later on."

Logan choked on some beer and struggled to keep it in. Mason belted him on the back.

"Who called you?"

David glanced around, but Garrett lifted another finger in the air. The look of amusement was evident as he couldn't hold back a grin. "I did. Again, I thought it was only appropriate."

"Garrett," Helen hissed. "Stop interfering."

He extended a hand towards me. "She's my daughter. I called her mother and the man who's her real father. He raised her all her life." Then he strode forward and shook hands with David. "I'm the sperm donor. Nice to meet you."

"You too." The two sized each other up and after a moment stepped back.

Analise rolled her eyes. "You two are okay with each other?"

Garrett gave her a polite smile. "We've both had to deal with you."

David added, "It's a bonding experience."

Logan choked back another laugh. When everyone turned to glare, he displayed his zipped lips again and stuffed a handful of chips in his mouth.

"You let them drink in the open?"

Helen turned, at a loss. "Excuse me?"

"They're underage, Helen. They aren't allowed to drink." He gestured towards his sons, who both had a beer in hand. "And they're throwing a party here tonight?"

"Well," she glanced towards Garrett. "I had no idea. I had dinner plans for the evening."

My mother cleared her throat. "Can we get back to the part where my daughter said she was screwing her future stepbrother?" She glared at me. "I'd love to hear how this came about and why no one else seemed surprised."

No one spoke a word.

Her head started to swivel around. As her eyes found James, he gave her an apologetic look. "I had my suspicions."

She gasped.

Garrett lifted another finger. "I knew too. I caught 'em in the elevator."

"You did not." My hands found my hips. "We were standing in there and you got on. End of story."

"He had his arm around you and he kissed your shoulder. It was pretty evident, sweetie."

I snarled at him, "I'm not your sweetie."

David cleared his throat. "I knew as well, Analise. I was going to tell you, but I had hoped for a family dinner of my own this evening first." His eyes held mine. I felt my stomach drop at the sorrow in them. "That didn't occur as I had planned."

I looked away, burning. What did it matter? What did he matter anymore? He let me go… A small voice in my head told me that he didn't, though. He had fought for me since the beginning. I swung back to him and he gave me a small smile for encouragement.

"Who else knew about them?"

Helen gave her a polite, but lethal. "I walked in on them. They'd just had sex."

"You're screwed, brother," Logan whispered out of the corner of his mouth. Mason shot him a look, but stood beside me. He regarded the group with a grave look on his face. "What do you all care about? I screw girls. You know this."

"Not your stepsister!" my mother cried out.

He bore her down with a look that silenced her. Shivers went down my back, but I didn't dare glance up. I didn't want to remember that from him. Then he taunted her in a soft voice. "You should be happy, Analise. My father isn't a mechanic and my mother's not a cashier at the local grocery store. Your daughter did well for finding a bedmate."

Logan hooted out in laughter now.

She flushed as she remembered her own words. "This is not right. The two of you should not be—"

Garrett rolled to his feet again. "You can't do a thing to stop her, Lise."

She whirled to him. "Shut up, Garrett. You've had nothing to do with her all your life. You have no right to start now—"

With two steps he was in her face. "I have every right. I had a daughter that I didn't know about. You kept her from me! You had no right to do that. Maybe it's my turn now. Maybe I should be her parent now."

She paled even further. "No!"

David stepped forward. "I wouldn't be averse to that. I've been in talks with Analise about sharing responsibility of Samantha. I've offered to pay for her college already."

"You have?"

"I have." His eyes gentled as he turned to me. "I wanted to talk with you about some of those plans I've made with your mother at dinner tonight."

"You did?"

"Well, that's just dandy! You all knew my daughter was boning her stepbrother and no one had the decency to call me?"

"Watch it, Analise. Your age is showing." Garrett smirked at her. "And I did call you."

David stiffened as he turned. "Why would I call you when you haven't had the decency to consult me in any matter? You wanted to take her from me completely. You wanted to wipe her from my life."

"She's a bitch, isn't she?" Garrett threw an arm around David's shoulder.

"She is." Then his lip turned downwards. "Samantha, as the man who has raised you all your life..." He glanced upwards.

Garrett gave him an approving nod and patted his shoulder.

David continued, "I have to ask if this is a cry for help? Are you with Mason because you wanted all of our attention?"

Helen snorted and crossed her arms again. "Well, she got it."

I glared at her, but gentled as I looked at my father. "It's not a cry for help, David. It's—"

"They're hot as hell for each other!" Logan shot to his feet. "I can't keep quiet anymore. You all are stupid idiots if you think that. Don't you know her? Don't you know Mason? My god, I'm embarrassed to call you *ass*-dults!"

"Logan," his mother hissed. "Shut up. You promised."

He flipped up his middle finger. "I don't care. I can't handle this. My game is talk. You tried to take that away." He shot an arm towards Mason. "He fights. I talk. That's the magic of our twosome fearsome. Sam's one of us, man. She's got the guts to do the dirty deeds if we don't. She watches out for us too. Ya'll are stupid if you didn't see this coming." He thrust his arms out wide. "The three of us are a magical team. No way are you screwing this up."

James asked him with a dry voice, "Really?"

Logan puffed up his chest before he downed the rest of his beer. "You don't know what it's like being a Kade. Sam does. She's conquered and proved her loyalty runs deep." He flinched. "Real deep if I'm guessing at how far Mason goes in her—"

"Logan, shut the hell up!" Mason smacked him in the back of his head.

He came back up with a brighter smile. "And I'm proven right, again! You guys should hire me for this talent I have. Mom, I bet you have a better sex life with that Garrett dude than you did with dad."

"Logan!"

He turned towards James. "And dad, I bet your sex life is pretty good with Analise. She strikes me as the slutty type."

"Logan!"

He grinned broadly. "And David…I don't know you that well, but you strike me as conservative. You're only going to be with a conservative woman, maybe one that looks exotic though. I can tell you have control issues. You don't like anyone who is wilder than you, probably why you had problems with your ex, huh? As for the current one, she's hot under the covers, but I don't know if you want her to be." He shook his head in sympathy. "You might want to take care of that."

David frowned as he looked away.

"And Garrett," Logan tsked tsked him in approval. "You're a wild one, I can tell. That's why I know Mason's got a good one. You and Analise both are hot ones in bed. I can tell. It's why my mom and dad like the both of you. Both of them are vanilla in bed, I bet. I'm sorry about that. I bet the two of you had wild sex together." He shook his head in wonderment. "Two of the same types rarely work out, too much drama. A wild one and a vanilla one always go the distance. They balance each other out."

Garrett chewed the inside of his cheek for a moment as he regarded the sudden outburst. Then he nodded in approval. "I like you. You speak the truth. Inappropriate, but the truth."

Logan puffed out his chest. Then the smirk dropped from his face and he clipped out, "Good. Then leave Sam and Mason the fuck alone. You've screwed up our lives enough."

Mason slid him a look. "I was going to get to that. I was waiting for the right time."

Logan looked annoyed. "Whatever. I had enough being quiet."

I slid my eyes towards him and he saluted me before he dropped back on the couch. "Continue on as you were…" He pretended to bow to them as he opened another beer, and passed one to Mason.

I caught mine as I sat on the couch with him.

Mason slid down beside me and Logan curled an arm around my shoulder. He drawled against my cheek, "It'll throw them off. Their visionary senses will tell them we're screwing and they'll get confused." His hand slid down towards my breast.

Mason warned, "Don't even try it, Logan. I'm the fighter, remember?"

His hand slid back up to my shoulder. He gave me a pat. "Threesome fearsome. No one stands a chance."

I grinned at him. "What about Nate?"

He tapped his beer with mine. "When he's around, it's the foursome fearsome. You can add any 'some to that name. Thank goodness, huh?" Then he groaned. "I really need to get laid tonight."

Mason tipped his head back. I felt the tension in his body and reached for his hand.

Logan leaned forward. "We might be having that party in your suite." Then we looked at the room as their voices were raised at each other. "Something's telling me the adults aren't going anywhere tonight."

My mom chose that moment to lift her hands in the air. "I don't care what you think I've done wrong in my parenting. I've been the one there for her all her life."

I closed my eyes. It was going to be a long night. I already knew it.

CHAPTER THIRTY-NINE

The adults remained in the top suite so the party was moved down two floors when Logan paid for the other suite on Mason's floor. Text messages were sent out and soon the elevator had started to ring its arrival. The two doors were left open and it wasn't long before a swarm of people filled the floor. I had been with Mason and Logan for a while until their public friends started to show. After Ethan sent me a few frowns and narrowed glances, I took my exit and it wasn't long before I heard Becky's excited voice.

She squealed somewhere, "I can't believe this! This is awesome!"

When I stepped on a chair, I saw them inside the doorway and sent a text that I was near the kitchen. It wasn't long before Becky and Lydia pushed their way to me and landed with flushed faces.

"Hey, guys." I narrowed my eyes.

Lydia let out a silent burp and tugged her skirt down to flaunt her hipbones.

"You guys are drunk."

Becky flung herself at me for a hug. As she fell against me, she gurgled out, "Am not. Spoilshoret."

"We're not drunk." Lydia pulled her back and linked their elbows together. She puffed up her chest and flipped her hair over her shoulder.

"You are. I know what you look like when you're drunk and I can smell the booze on Becky's breath."

"So what if we're drunk?! It's Friday night. We're allowed." Becky seemed sure of herself. "And besides we're celebrating your awesomeness. Oh yeah. You're awesome. You're the queen of being awesome. You are a god-dess, you are." Her head bounced up and down with each word and her smile grew at each nod. "And you're my friend. I'm so glad you're my friend."

"Mine too." Lydia beamed.

"Oh boy." I sipped the beer Logan made me take. "How are you getting home?"

Becky pointed a finger at me. "How are you getting home, missy? Or are you sleeping here...with your boyfriend?!"

"Yeah. Your boyfriend." Lydia giggled at Becky, who bumped heads with her.

"Don't worry," Adam's voice came from behind me. "I promised Becky's parents that I'd watch out for her. They weren't keen on letting her attend a Kade party, but I persuaded them. Plus, I think Lydia's staying at Becky's tonight anyway." He gave me a small smile, but I caught the apprehension in his depths.

"Thanks," I said lightly.

Lydia had been watching us and cooed, "You guys will make a great couple."

Becky nudged her.

"I mean, someday...maybe...not." She hung her head, but snapped back up with a bright smile. "I forgot to tell you. Jessica's hating you right now. She's so jealous of you. You got Logan Kade. Can you believe it? Well...I guess you can, but still—you're dating Logan Kade."

An arm was thrown around my shoulder and I closed my eyes. *Speak of the devil...*

I didn't need to look to know a very smug smirk was on Logan's face as he drew me against him. "When did this phenomenon happen?"

Becky's eyes went wide, but Lydia edged closer with a secretive smile. "Maybe about the time you realized you couldn't ignore her phone calls. I mean, she lives with you, right?"

Logan drew back with a frown. His arm tightened around my shoulders. "You're saying that I'm stuck with her?" He threw me a look. "Your friends suck."

Lydia flushed and moved back again.

Becky's mouth dropped open before she got red in the face. "Hey, I'm sick of people saying that Sam doesn't have good friends. I'm her friend. I'm her best friend, even if she doesn't know it, but I know I am."

Adam added, "She is. I've seen her in action."

Her finger jerked back up. "And you better treat her right, not like her last boyfriend. He sucks." She pounded her chest with a beer in hand. "I know. I'm his cousin. I can say that. And he cheated on her. He was a fool. You better not cheat on her, Logan Kade."

A look of admiration took root in his eyes, but he deadpanned, "And if I do?"

"I'm going to come for you."

He chuckled. "Really?"

She stepped forward and bumped her chest to his. The movement wasn't smooth and she would've tripped if Adam hadn't caught her elbow.

"You're right. You have ninja moves," he encouraged her.

"Stop," I said under my breath to him.

Then, with a different sounding laugh, he squeezed me against him again and kissed the side of my head. "No worries. I'll be your boyfriend for as long as you want me to be." He glanced at Becky. "I hope I won't meet you in a dark alley, little girl."

Her eyes rounded. "Really?"

"I've got moves too, little red." Logan shook his head and laughed under his breath before he tapped my arm once and left.

Lydia swooned, swaying on her feet. "I need dry panties."

"Lydia!"

Becky frowned at her.

Adam cringed behind them, but gave me a wry look. "Are you going to tell them?"

I shrugged.

"Tell us what?"

"Yeah, what?" They looked back and forth.

"Hey, dude!" Mark Decraw pushed his way through the crowd and slapped a hand on Adam's shoulder. "I've been waiting for you for an hour, man."

Adam grimaced. "Yeah, it took longer than I thought it would. Sorry about the wait."

"No worries. I scored some free drinks at the pool downstairs." Then his gaze swung wide and he took the rest of us in. His eyes widened a fraction when he saw me. "Hey, Sam. I heard upstairs got intense."

My eyes cooled. "Yeah…"

"You think everything's going to work out? You know, with you and M—"

"I don't want to talk about it." I folded my arms over my chest and waited. My heart started to pound. What right did he have to talk about my family struggles? He wasn't family. He didn't know a thing about it.

"Oh. Okay." He looked towards Adam and shifted to the back of his heels.

Adam looked around the room.

So did Lydia while Becky's eyes were glued to me as she mouthed, *What upstairs?*

Then someone laughed as they passed by. "Awkward!"

Lydia and Becky made eye contact and bent over giggling. Adam frowned more and he started to scratch his head.

I wasn't sure what I was supposed to do. Did I join in? Did I pretend I didn't know what Mark was talking about? Did I pretend I was friends with Adam again? I had no idea, but I did know that I was separate from the group now. My relationship with the Kades had shifted me higher than my friends, but if they were like this with the assumption that I was sleeping with Logan, what'd they be like when they learned it was Mason?

I closed my eyes as I felt the urge to find the treadmill in the hotel's gym. It was already closed, but I was sure the Kade name had some pull.

"Oh hey," Mark tried to sound normal. He failed. "There's Pete and the crew. I'll see you guys later. Sam…"

I jerked my head in a stiff nod, but I couldn't keep the scowl from my face. Who did he think he was now because he was privy to information about my family?

Becky and Lydia's heads squashed together, but Adam tugged me backwards, away from them. He spoke in my ear, "Calm down. Mark didn't mean anything by it."

I hissed out, "He doesn't know me. He doesn't know anything and now he's talking to me about my life? Who the hell does he think he is?"

He gave me a pained smile. "He's my friend and he wants to get to know you."

"What?" I stared up at him. "Why?"

"Because he wants to break the news that he thinks his mom and Coach are going to get hitched, but he doesn't know how to."

"What?!" Everything in me sunk at that moment.

"Yeah." Adam raised a hand down the backside of his head and rubbed at his neck. "He thinks you should know, but I guess it's supposed to be a spontaneous thing. He's going to be family, Sam. And he's stepping out from Miranda's wrath."

I closed my eyes. I couldn't do anything else. And I stood there.

Adam reached for my shoulders to pull me close. I shrugged him off. And I could hear the bitterness in his voice. "Look, Stewart doesn't want any of us to be friends with you, much less talk to you. I told her to go to hell and so did Mark. He's doing this for his mom and for Coach and, in some weird way, for you too. He feels bad about your situation."

I spoke through gritted teeth, "I don't care about being in the Elite."

"I know. We all know that and I think that pisses Miranda off the most, but it doesn't change the fact. You've got another year at the Academy, much less the rest of this year. Look, the girls won't go against Miranda. They might not all agree with her, but they won't go against her. If you—"

A hand wrapped my waist and pulled me backwards. I closed my eyes because I didn't need to look. Heat and lust washed over me when Mason urged me to turn around with a hand on my hip. I met his gaze once and when I saw the smoldering depths there, I knew the game was up. I was swept against his chest and burrowed there as he started to rub my back while the other one cradled my head to him. He spoke over me, "You're starting to piss me off, Quinn."

Adam's hostility was evident. "I'm friends with her friends. What do you expect of me, Kade?"

Mason's arm tightened on my back. He swept down and started to massage the side of my hip, grinding me against him in the same motion. My heart pounded and the need started to throb again. I gasped against his chest and started to move with him.

"Isn't that…convenient." Acid dripped from Mason's voice.

"What's going on?"

Some of the tension left Mason at the sound of his brother's voice.

"Mase, why you holding my girlfriend?" He sounded bright, cheery. Then he turned serious. "Ah, got it. Truth time, huh? Quinn, why are you always around Sam? You must have a boner every time you talk to her, or think about her, smell her… Do you use your mom's lotion? The pretty smelling stuff when you jerk it?"

"Um…" Becky was hushed immediately. "No, I won't shut up. What's going on? Sam?"

My eyes snapped open, but I knew I couldn't turn around. It was all over my face. I'd been in his arms for a minute and I wanted to drag him to a bedroom. My face was heated and I could imagine what the rest of me looked like. They'd call me a whore after this and it would stick. I knew it.

When I started to turn, Mason kept me in place. His voice was rough as he clipped out, "Stay away from her Quinn. If you keep trying to get in her pants, we're going to have a problem."

Logan sidled up next to us. I felt his presence beside Mason. "And stop playing the dumbass game. You know what we're talking about."

There was silence for a heartbeat and then Adam's laugh grated out. "Are you two serious? You don't think I know what you're doing with her? You're just having fun with her. You're using her to piss off your parents. Mark's told me a little bit. I thought Sam had daddy issues, but the two of you—"

I was transferred to Logan's arms in a flash, but I whirled in time to see Mason lunge for Adam. He knocked him backwards and then took hold of his shirt and slammed him against the wall. Adam didn't fight back, but the two glared at each other as Mason bent close. His mouth moved and Adam's face went white. He lost more and more coloring as Mason continued to speak in his ear. Then, after Mason stopped and held his gaze for a long tension-filled second, he stepped back and delivered one last punch to the side of Adam's face.

He went down, but he wasn't knocked unconscious. As he lay on the ground, he stared at Mason with fear starting to take root in his eyes. No one went to his side, but Becky broke through the crowd and dropped to her knees beside him. She touched the side of his face, but glared at Mason. "What's your problem? He's a good guy."

Mason's eyes cooled, but he glanced at me before he turned back.

My gut twitched as I realized he was in control. He'd been in control the whole time. He hadn't lost it when he went for Adam. Then Logan murmured in my ear, "Quinn's not the hero your friend thinks he is. It's time it came out."

But I was riveted by the scene unfolding before me when Mason placed his hands on his hips and gave my friend a look of regret. I shoved out of Logan's hold and scrambled to his side as he spoke to her, "You think he's a good guy? He used you to get to her."

Becky's eyes were scorching. "Did he tell you this?"

Mason shook his head. "I'm a guy. He didn't have to say a goddamn word. He's been sniffing around Sam since she was done with that other guy."

I touched his arm and was surprised. He wasn't tense. As he looked at me, he swept me against his side and pressed a kiss to my forehead.

"Sam? None of this makes sense."

My heart broke. She was a little girl in that moment. I closed my eyes as a sense of déjà vu hurled through me. She sounded how I felt when I walked into my home and was told we were leaving my dad.

Shattered.

"Sam." Adam spoke this time. He sat up with a hand still cradling the side of his face. "Just tell her. Tell her everything."

My tongue was thick as I struggled out, "Adam told me that he was using you to get to me. He admitted it to me, Becky. You were the only one I talked with after I found out about Jeff's cheating. And he's known about me and Mason—"

"You and Mason?" Lydia's were narrowed as she stood behind them. "I thought, but then…"

Logan whooped out, "You guys are so stupid! The two are together. They're hitched at the hip, literally right now. I'm starting to get pissed. Why's it so easy to think she's with me, but not my brother?"

"Because you're you…" Miranda spoke up. The Elite had joined the crowd around us. "And he's…"

"What?" Logan puffed out his chest and narrowed his eyes at her. "I'm what?"

"Nothing." She clamped her mouth shut and her cheeks grew pink. She didn't look away when he stepped closer to her.

"I'm what?" he asked again, softer this time.

"You're...no one can get Mason. No one's gotten him before."

Mason growled next to me. "This is starting to get stupid. That's enough." He stepped in front of Logan and pushed him back. "What are you doing? You're making this worse."

"Am I?" The corner of his lip curled up, but his tone was hostile. "You can't handle hearing how everyone thinks you're better than me?"

Mason yanked him close and whispered in his ear. As he spoke, Logan's chest started to heave up and down. His mouth tightened and his eyes went flat, and then he shoved him back in a violent push.

"Logan."

"Stop," he snarled at him and pushed through the crowd. As he was swallowed up, Mason stood there and stared after him. Something changed then. He turned towards Miranda and a deadly aura came over him.

But then someone else stepped towards him. "Mason."

I gasped in relief at the sight of Nate. He flashed me a small grin, but urged his best friend away from the crowd. I hurried to follow and found them in a private corner to hear the last words, "I'll take care of him."

Mason shook his head. "You sure? That bitch—"

Nate stopped him. "I'll take care of it, okay?" As I stepped closer, he smiled and pulled me in for a hug. "It's good to see you. I'm happy to hear about you and Mason. He'll treat you good. I promise."

Mason tugged me back and lifted me so I wrapped my legs around him. He held me in place, but spoke over my shoulder, "You'll make sure he's okay? This is important, Nate."

"I know. Chill. I'm not an idiot. I know what I'm doing."

"I don't want problems between me and my brother—"

"Would you stop acting like this is my first job? We've been doing this crap for years. It's not like I don't know how to handle Logan, you know. I *am* friends with him."

Mason's hand started to rub against my bottom and he kissed my shoulder. Then he added, "I know. I'm worried because of—"

"He's over Tate. He knew you were being a good brother." Nate shook his head. "For my sake, take her in the back and get happy. Both of you. Everything will be sorted out. Logan will be his normal self tomorrow."

I twisted around. "How are you going to do that?"

Nate gave me a smug look and a chill went over me. A flash of memories washed over me then.

"When Nate and Mason team up, they always do something."

"He's bad news, like really bad news. I heard him and Kade are not a good team together."

My own mother's voice on the phone, *'I'm sure he's not that bad of a boy. Mason seems very sure of himself.'*

I never asked, but I was sure she'd been talking about Nate and now I started to wonder what they meant. Nate had been kind to me, but I saw a different side of him as he answered me. "I'll get him to bang the queen of your school. He already started the groundwork and she bit, she bit hard."

"Miranda Stewart?" A sick feeling started in my stomach. "She's dating Peter Glasburg."

Nate's eyebrows furrowed together. "Because that always means she won't cheat, huh?"

I flushed and buried my head in Mason's neck. His hand rubbed up and down my back. "Fix it, Nate."

"I will."

I felt Mason nodding. "Thanks. And thanks for coming."

Nate laughed on a carefree note. "Yeah, it took me longer than I thought. Never knew I'd be thankful for some pirate movie they're shooting in Brazil."

"Your parents are strict."

"Yeah, well, we gave them reason to be."

Mason's body shook in laughter. "Yeah, we did." He nodded once again and then took me to a back bedroom.

As he sat me down, he flipped the lights on and locked the door. A king size bed was in a corner with a couch and kitchen area on the other side. A small bathroom was attached and I spotted a Jacuzzi inside. A fleeting thought passed through me, I would've thought people would've found this room before now.

"I had a key card to it. No one could get in here."

"Oh." I hadn't realized I'd spoken out loud.

Mason regarded me for a heartbeat before he sat on the edge of the bed. He bent forward and raked his hands through his hair. His elbows rested on his knees and he stayed like that as I crossed the room to sit beside him. I took one of his hands in mine and he looked up. There was a haunted look in him and I gasped. I knew it'd haunt me now as well. I lifted a hand to smooth out the lines in his forehead and asked, quietly, "Why am I a little scared of you right now?"

He closed his eyes and rested his forehead against mine. He breathed out, "Because I'm a jerk."

I swallowed painfully as my heart was pounding. My breathing picked up and it became erratic. "Why do I feel sorry for Logan right now?"

"Because I'm hurting him."

A piece of bark formed in my throat. "How are you doing that?"

He whispered against my lips, "Because you're the second girl that he's wanted and I got."

My heart picked up its pace. A herd of elephants were stampeding in my ear, but I asked the question I never considered it until now, but I had to ask it. "Does he love me?"

With our foreheads against each other, he looked up and met my gaze. His eyelashes touched mine and I felt his breath against my lips. "I don't think he does, not in that way."

My heart was beating so fast now. It was a continuous beat. I was breathless as I opened my mouth. "Do you love me?"

His hand encircled the back of my neck and he lifted my face as he adjusted on the bed. He peered into my depths. And then he moved so he was below me and I straddled him. His hands slid to my back and he ground me against him. I gasped as I pressed down harder. I couldn't get closer. I needed to get closer. I was starting to become blind with the need.

As he touched his lips to mine, I heard him whisper, "Yes." And then he rolled me underneath him and I was lost. Again.

CHAPTER FORTY

I wasn't sure what time it was the next morning when I woke. I had knocked the clock off the nightstand at some point and a jolt of warmth rushed through me at the memory of it. Mason was sprawled out on the other side of the bed. I blinked at the sight of his tight butt. The sheets had slipped down to his thigh and I was tempted to run a finger up the backside of his leg and over his cheeks. They were tanned, muscular, and itching for my touch.

"Don't even think it," he mumbled out of the corner of his mouth. One of his eyes opened enough to see me with his face pressed into his pillow. A half smile spread over him and then he tugged the sheet across my lap. It was wrapped around my legs and I was soon pulled into his arms.

He nuzzled my neck and pulled me over so I was across his chest.

When he started tickling under my arm, I pulled away, breathless. "Stop it!"

He chuckled and gave me a quick kiss. "You have morning breath."

"So do you." I kissed him back and soon he rolled us to our side. Our legs and arms were wrapped around each other and it wasn't long before I felt him harden against my stomach. "How long do you have the suite?"

He ran a finger down my arm and grinned as goose bumps poked up. "For as long my mom's around. Logan and I didn't want to stay with her so we got this one. He'll probably keep that other suite for the day until everybody's been kicked out."

I shivered when he started to plant soft kisses under my jaw. "Will he be okay? You know…about me and stuff?"

His mouth lingered at the corner of my mouth before he pulled back and settled on his side. He propped himself up on his elbow. "Yeah, he'll be fine. Logan's not an idiot. He doesn't really want you, but that bitch pushed his button."

"And that is?"

He groaned and fell to his back. "Ever since Tate, Logan's never forgotten that she wanted me. He loved her, but she wanted me and worked her way through him to get to me."

"They were together for two years."

"Yeah." He gave me a rueful look. "I'm not exactly welcoming to girls."

"But I saw you with that girl at the house when I caught Jeff."

He shrugged. "She'd been on me for a while and I never pushed her away. I had an itch to scratch, but she was too drunk. We didn't do anything."

"You said that you had some girlfriends before?"

"A while ago, when I was young and stupid. I haven't had to work at getting sex for a long time. If I want it, I can pick the girl. Basically."

"And me?" I grinned down at him and he gave me a knowing smirk.

"What do you think?"

"Am I just for sex? I *am* convenient."

He tugged me down so I was sprawled over him again and lifted his hips against mine. "Does that feel convenient to you?" His voice was breathless as he cupped my head and turned my lips to his. He brushed against them. "You've been on my mind ever since that damn gas station. I couldn't shake you and then when you moved in, it's been torture. I get hard the second you walk in a room."

"So you're saying…" I opened my mouth and his tongue swept in. He took control of the kiss and I tasted his desperation. I pulled back as I realized it was for me. The hunger in him was insatiable.

"What?" He reached for me again.

I scrambled up as a different emotion raced through me. My teeth started to rattle against each other and my arms started to shake. My knees buckled when I tried to get up so I scooted to the farthest side of the bed.

"Sam? What's wrong?" Concern was thick in his voice.

"I..." I closed my mouth and stared in horror. He held my gaze, but there was no fear. There was no self-consciousness or doubt. That's when I realized that he never questioned himself. He was so strong, on the inside and out. For the first time I was intimidated by Mason Kade and I had no idea what to do about it. So I stumbled out the truth, "I love you."

"I know."

"You know?" I didn't even know.

"Sam, I'm not stupid. You've been on lockdown since you moved in. That's why you go running. Any time you start to feel something, you numb yourself. I get it. Trust me, I do. But I know you wouldn't be with me or done half the stuff with me that you have if you didn't love me."

"But..." I hadn't known. Why hadn't I? A cold feeling took root in my gut.

"Hey," he said in a soft voice and moved so he was close again. He moved on his side and tugged me so I faced him. His forehead rested against mine again. "Everything will be okay. I promise."

I sucked in a tortured breath. And then I surrendered. "I'm scared."

"I know."

"After everything's that happened..." I didn't know I was trembling until he wrapped an arm around me and pulled me tight. The shaking stopped and a sense of safety started to seep in. This time it wasn't a temporary feeling, it wasn't going to leave after he left the bed.

"I'm tired, Mason."

"I know."

We both knew I wasn't referring to sleep.

And then nothing mattered. His lips touched mine and it was tender. He didn't roll me underneath him this time, but lifted so I was on top and then he let me set the pace. After I climaxed and collapsed on top of him, I blinked back tears. It was different. The tears were different. Our love making had been different and the way he held me was different. Or maybe I was the different one?

"Stop thinking." Mason brushed a kiss against my shoulder and laughed. "We'll have plenty of time for that later. Right now, we need to shower. I'm hungry too." And he picked me up, bed sheets and all, and started for the bathroom.

I shrieked, laughing, as I hit his shoulder. "Put me down." I was gasping as he did and danced out of his reach when he pretended to lunge for me again. I felt drunk. I wanted to giggle and smile, and never stop doing both of them. As we showered together, a delicious tingle raced up and down my spine. My heart never stopped pounding and I was lightheaded by the end. Afterwards, he slid on some jeans and started to tug me towards the door. I laughed and dug my feet in. "Let me put some clothes on first."

The corner of his mouth curved up, but his eyes darkened as he watched me.

I sighed. "You should too."

He smirked at me and dropped his jeans to pull some boxers on. He left the shirt and socks behind as he caught my hand. I dressed in a hurry and finished tugging my shirt down when he dragged me behind him and out the door.

As soon as we stepped outside, his demeanor dropped. The standoffish Mason was back in place, but his hand continued to hold mine. A buzzing sensation spread through me when I realized I was grateful for the touch. I missed the feel of his body against mine and knew I was addicted. Then I admitted to myself that I didn't want to kick this addiction. It was threatening to take control of my life and I was okay with that.

Nate smirked at us as we approached the kitchenette and gestured from the coffee maker. "I called in the works. Bagels, omelets, bacon, pancakes." He held out a cup for me. "And coffee."

I inhaled the aroma and groaned. "I just cheated on Mason."

There was a moment of silence before Nate burst out laughing. "Sorry, bud. I think I'm going for your girl."

Mason flashed him a cocky smile and popped some bacon in his mouth. "No worries. I had her primed before we came out."

I shot them both a look and sank down in a chair with my coffee. And then I started to take in the scene around us. A few girls sat at the table with their hair pulled up in haphazard ponytails. They were sprawled in chairs with bags under their eyes. One of the girls narrowed her eyes at me, but stopped halfway. She lifted a hand and let it drop down with a loud smack. "Hi. I'm too tired right now. I'm Natalie."

I nodded and sipped my coffee.

She jerked a thumb beside her. "This is Kate and Parker. We go to school with these dickwads."

Nate laughed as he lifted one of the girls and took the seat beneath her. He held her on his lap, but she never resisted. The movement had been done with an ease that spoke of its history. He'd done this many times with that girl. She nestled back in his chest and gave me a droopy smile. Her eyes shot over my shoulder. "Logan's missing in action, Mason. We're not sure where he is."

He had taken a cup of coffee for himself and lounged against the farthest counter. He lowered it from his mouth now. A scowl took form. "Nate?"

"Relax," Nate hissed at him and pointedly looked at the girls. "It's done."

Mason visibly relaxed. His coffee was lifted again.

And then the door to the suite was thrown open. Logan entered with his arms spread wide and an arrogant smirk on his face. "The deal has been done."

Natalie lifted haughty eyes. "What's done, Logan?"

He winked at her, but crossed the room and pressed a kiss to my forehead. He whispered to me, "Last night was a show. Did Mason fill you in?"

"A show?" I turned hard eyes towards the kitchenette. "Mason."

He held my gaze for a minute and looked past my shoulders in a pointed fashion. A sick feeling took root before I turned. Everything seemed in slow motion and I froze at the sight of Miranda Stewart in the doorway. She wore nothing except for a long white buttoned-down shirt that grazed beneath her bottom. Black lacy panties could be seen and she looked back with wide eyes. I gulped as I saw fear in them. That look doubled when she surveyed the room and I turned as well. All three girls had disdain on their faces and each of them didn't contain a smug look.

Miranda's throat jerked up and down as she met my gaze.

A normal girl would've had sympathy for her. Everything went flat inside of me and I stood to stand beside Mason. He lifted his arms over my chest and leaned forward to rest his head on my shoulder. We watched together as Logan motioned for her to come in. As she did, her throat moved up and down again and she dashed for his lap. As soon as she was there, she curled in his arms and turned her back to the table.

Natalie spoke, "Oh. My. Gawd."

Another started laughing. "Are you serious, Logan?"

The third girl in Nate's arms laughed with her friends, but pressed her face against his arm.

I asked underneath my breath, "What is going on?"

"Logan's got a new girlfriend. That's what's going on." Mason sounded amused.

I twisted my pinkie to curl around his and leaned all my weight back on him. "Was that his idea or yours?"

"Mine."

"Does Logan know that?"

His chest moved up and down. There was no response.

"Mason," I prompted. My heart was pounding again. I wasn't sure if I wanted to hear his response.

"No."

I sighed, "At least you don't sound proud for that fact. You manipulated him and you got Nate to do the dirty work. He thinks he's dating Miranda to protect me, doesn't he. And he's not. He's doing it because you got mad at her because she pushed the one button you're worried about. That Logan will go away someday because Tate wanted you and you got me too."

"Don't tell him. Please."

I turned around in his arms and looked up. He gazed down and the wall fell aside. It was the guy who was with me in the bedroom, the one who told me he loved me. And my heart broke. I couldn't look away. I couldn't move away. I couldn't tell his secret and when I turned back around to the group I knew everything changed in that moment.

Mason and I were linked together with that one plea. And as a shiver of dark excitement wound through my body, I didn't want to be anywhere else except at his side, no matter where it would take us.

My fingers slid through his and clasped on. Hard.

http://www.tijansbooks.com

CPSIA information can be obtained
at www.ICGtesting.com
Printed in the USA
BVHW091530020119
536873BV00033B/1849/P

9 781682 304778